BLOODTHIRSTY

INTERNATIONAL BESTSELLING AUTHOR
CASSANDRA FEATHERSTONE

AMAZON VERSION ONLY

Original Ebook/Print Cover: Pretty in Ink Creations
Editing, Proofing, backgrounds, & Formatting: Dirty Sexy Words/ Storm shield
Editing/Little Tailfeather Publishing
Cassandra's logos: Pretty in Ink Creations/Artlogo
ARC Team(s): Cassandra's Claws
Sensitivity Readers: Brit Mason, Gail Jericho
Translation Consultant: Mo Jacobs
Legal Services: Joshua Farley, esq.
Images/Fonts: Depositphotos, Shutterstock, Canva, & Photoshop

No GenAI was used within this book. All errors and greatness are by an ADHD muppet.

CONTENT WARNINGS

This is a *whychoose contemporary romance with poly elements*—our FMC, Remy, will not have to choose between love interests.

There are many situations included that are intended for <u>mature audiences (18+).</u>

In this book, there may be instances/references that could trigger some individuals such as:

- *HACKING*
- *SMUGGLING*
- *DECAPITATION*
- *DECOMPOSITION*
- PAST TRAUMA (PHYSICAL & EMOTIONAL)
- VIOLENCE
- EMOTIONAL ABUSE
- ALCOHOL ABUSE
- PTSD
- BLOOD
- DOMESTIC VIOLENCE
- FOUL LANGUAGE- LOTS OF IT.

- GRAPHIC VIOLENCE
- UNHEALTHY COPING MECHANISMS
- DEATH
- BODY MODIFICATIONS
- FANCY PIERCINGS
- EXPLICIT TORTURE / RENDITION METHODS (BRIEF, BUT THERE)
- ELECTROCUTION
- WATERBOARDING
- DENTAL EXTRACTION
- CUTTING
- BEATINGS
- STARVATION
- SOUND TORTURE
- SLEEP DEPRIVATION
- SENSORY DEPRIVATION- NON SEXUAL
- RESTRAINTS
- GUN VIOLENCE
- KNIFE VIOLENCE
- DANGEROUS FEATS THAT SHOULD NOT BE ATTEMPTED AT HOME
- RAW SEX
- A SHADOW DOUCHE
- WIRE PLAY
- INAPPROPRIATE USE OF GUITAR STRINGS
- LOTS AND LOTS OF SNARK
- POP CULTURE REFERENCES
- EASTER EGG APPEARANCES OF CHARACTERS FROM OTHER SERIES IN THIS UNIVERSE
- *THEFT*
- *ASSASSINATIONS*
- *HEISTS*
- *EMOTIONAL MANIPULATION*
- *SEXUAL COERCION (USED AS A WEAPON BY MCs BUT NO CHEATING)*
- *BAD DECISIONS MADE BY ALL AT TIMES*
- ROUGH SEX
- PUBLIC SEX

- BDSM
- BODY PARTS USED AS A MESSAGE
- HUMAN TRAFFICKING (MC)
- KIDNAPPING (SOME MCS, SOME OUTSIDE MAIN GROUP)
- THREATS OF SEXUAL ABUSE — BUT DOES NOT HAPPEN ON OR OFF PAGE
- DRUG USE
- DRUG SALES
- POOR TREATMENT OF SUBORDINATES
- FORCED VOYEURISM (NOT NON-CON)
- EXPLOSIONS

No sexual practices in this book should be taken as safe or appropriate for real life application.

Content warnings are important and I don't ever want to harm a reader.

AUTHOR RAMBLINGS

When I bought a set of contemporary covers last year, I had a fleeting thought that I would 'give it a try'.

Little did I know that by the time the first book in the series came out, the covers would be useless due to a disappearing designer and I'd be months behind on my writing schedule due to unforeseen interpersonal issues. Even so, I figured bringing Remy and her men to life would be as easy as it has with Jolene, Jack, Rogue, and the others in my PNR worlds.

I was wrong; I was so wrong.

Though *Bloodthirsty* lives inside of my *Legends of the Ouroboros* universe, the creation of a contemporary series within that framework was both challenging and frustrating at the same time. I'm a perfectionist and I *know* I can't achieve that, but I strive for accuracy in every possible way.

In PNR, I can magically zap people places or use power/attributes to explain why or how things happen. Contemporary worlds don't have that luxury, so my NSA agent, Melvin, has had a *hell* of time watching me research things that I'm surprised didn't land an FBI agent on my doorstep once a week.

That, too, made the crafting of the world take longer and I'm actually glad for it.

Why?

Because I took my time with Remy and the others—I really learned their voices and their personalities. In fact, by the end of the book, I was frustrated that it was time to stop!

Bloodthirsty taught me a lesson about remembering not to compare myself or my process to others. The way I write will always be mine, whether it's in the real world or a fantasy one. I will always weave intricate tales with characters who are more than a trope or a re-imagining of what's come before—and that's okay. Changing my sub-genre doesn't change the care with which I build my worlds and relationships; it only changes the scenery and set pieces.

I hope you love Remy and her men as much as me and don't send angry beavers after me once you get to the end.

Blood and guts,

Cass

NOTES FOR READERS

A few things you should know…

Because Remy travels the world to kill people, there is foreign dialogue. I have made the *translations clickable end of chapter notes* to help.

This is a multi-book series, so *everything will not be revealed in the first book.* I promise it will all tie up with a HEA; don't worry!

There are some words that are slang, jargon, or foreign that may seem to be spelled wrong—*please use my form at the beginning of the book rather than report to the retailer* if you think something is wrong. It may not be and I want to make sure it doesn't get taken down so everyone can read!

Fictional people/organizations who are part of the *Legends of the Ouroboros* universe (but not this series) are mentioned. *If you haven't read their books, it won't keep you from enjoying this one.*

If you see this book *anywhere besides Amazon KU (in ebook format),* please reach out to me via social media. Pirating kills my ability to write full time and I am so grateful for your help.

A NOTE TO MY LOVING FAMILY MEMBERS AND FRIENDS...

THANK YOU FOR SUPPORTING ME BY BUYING MY WORK, BUT EVEN THOUGH YOU WON'T FIND MAGICAL FAE PORN, I SUGGEST YOU PUT THE BOOK DOWN.

THIS IS BOOK ONE TO A BLOODY, MURDERY, SPICY SERIES THAT WILL HAVE LOTS OF KINKY SHIT EVENTUALLY. EVEN IF YOU DO ENJOY IT, I'M NOT READY TO HEAR ABOUT THAT.

RUN AWAY! I PROMISE YOU DON'T WANT TO GOOGLE SOME OF THE TERMS.

CAVEAT: IF YOU CHOOSE TO KEEP READING, KNOW THAT AT NO TIME WILL I EXPLAIN TERMS, POSITIONS, THEMES, TROPES, OR ANY OTHER PART OF THIS NOVEL AT FAMILY EVENTS, IN GROUP CHATS, OR ON SOCIAL MEDIA.

DON'T ASK.

BLOODTHIRSTY PLAYLISTS

CHAPTER TITLE SONGS

THE GUILLOTINE'S FOCUS PLAYLIST

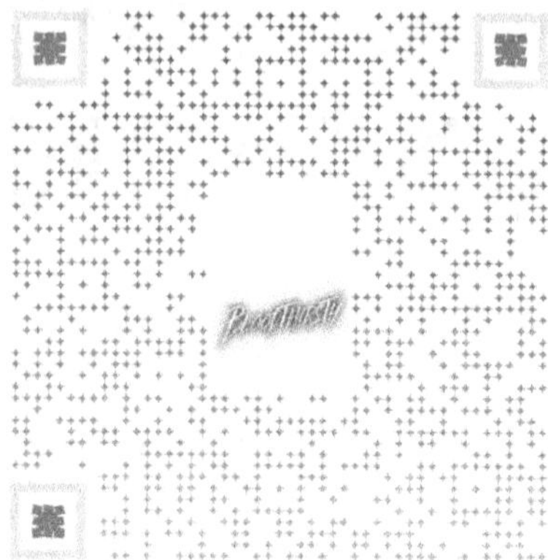

DEDICATION

To all the women who have survived their trauma and no longer give a fuck whose fragile ego they trample on when setting their boundaries...

While Murder is not always a viable solution, an elbow to the face makes your point nicely.

WHAT IF I BREAK YOUR TRUST SOMEDAY?
~SPONGEBOB

TRUSTING YOU IS MY DECISION, PROVING ME WRONG IS YOUR CHOICE.
~PATRICK

Forever

WAIT!

A FINAL REMINDER BEFORE YOU READ...

My series typically have prequels, gap novellas/novels, and bonus material that are integral to your having a satisfying reading experience.

If you have not read the other pieces in this series, you may feel as though you have missed critical details, developments, plot points, and other information. This will cause the book to appear to have continuity gaps that it does not have.

If you have not read the bonus material for this series, it is available online here, in audio versions (if applicable), and in print special editions (if applicable).

I highly recommend consulting the bonus page prior to reading this new title so you're up to speed on all the things going on in this world.

Happy reading!

Forever

QUEEN BEE

THEY DIM THE LIGHTS IN THE CLUB, AND THE SPOTS CLICK ON AS THE curtain slides open.

It's a full house tonight in the little burlesque club off the Rue Pierre Montaine.

Chez Arc En Ciel is not well known compared to the *Moulin Rouge* or *Le Lido*, but the wealthy from both sides of the Seine gather here for shows four nights a week. If you pass the various layers of security checks to even be permitted to book a reservation, you also have to be able to afford the two thousand Euro per guest cover charge. If you don't eat or drink anything, that's all it will cost; however, that would get you blacklisted.

Intro music pumps through the speakers and I stand on my mark in the opening position. My cane is resting on the wooden boards of the stage by my front foot as I pretend to lean on it. Roars of applause echo through the room as our troupe of dancers catch the lights, sequins sparkling like diamonds when the stage lights rise. We're dressed in pinstriped black pant suits and fedoras to match the big band style opening to the song. As soon as the horn-filled intro finishes, the dance begins.

I follow the routine with precision, snapping and popping my hips to the beat as we spread out across the stage. You wouldn't know by the fake smile on my face that I'm scanning the crowd. Two fan kicks later, I've rotated past the proscenium, and I think I've found my mark. Twirling, I stop in the place I need to be for the bridge, singing along as if my life depends on it. It might, to be honest, because I need to sell my cover tonight, so no one notices me.

The Guillotine moves in the shadows, but tonight, she's in the spotlight.

My ass shakes as I dance my way through the song, swinging the prop cane I'd replaced with one of my design. You wouldn't know by looking at it, but it's not the painted balsa the other dancers have for a very specific reason. I need it to complete the mission that forced me to spend two months in Paris working my way into this job at *Chez Arc En Ciel*. If I can't strike tonight, the surveillance, counterintelligence, and time spent building this cover are wasted because my mark is leaving for Asia tomorrow.

Tonight, the Cobra dies for his sins.

The break of the song slows the music and the dancers pour into the crowd to wiggle around the rich assholes. It's choreographed, but it's also to advertise each girl for private dances in the lounges upstairs. We're not strippers—not that there's a damned thing wrong with a woman using her body to support herself—but we do bare more skin in the closed rooms. The *laissez-faire* attitude of the owners means as long as we kick them thirty percent of the fees for those dances, they don't care what any of the girls do in the rooms. I'd find it sleazy, but the girls who work here are highly skilled performers who choose to make thousands of dollars a night rather than peanuts in some ballet troupe or chorus line.

By the time I've flirted my way to the VIP tables, the Cobra is staring intently at all of us. Spotlights pin each one of us on the floor at the bass hits, and I swivel my hips as my free hand slides down to the secret spot on my jacket. In unison, we tear the jackets off to reveal rhinestone studded bras with straps crisscrossing our waists like shibari ropes. A lift of the fedora and pop of my hip, along with the beat, draws the fierce-looking brawler's eyes directly to me. I pout prettily and stalk towards his table with the swagger of a tiny dicked asshole that owns a monster truck.

His thin lips pull back over the famed curving fangs he had implanted. Dark, glittering eyes follow every move I make as I approach, and I pretend to whip my hair from side to side as I check for his guards. They're here somewhere, but I need them to be far away so I can beat my escape before they notice. When I get within inches, I tap his leg with my cane and spin around to shake my ass in his face. The grunt of approval makes me want to heave, but I turn, holding onto the prop with both hands. My feet click on the floor in a soft shoe step as I make 'fuck me' eyes at the dirty bastard. He leans back, his pants tented as he gestures towards his lap.

Fucking gross.

I don't care about his weapons trade or what happens when people get the shit he moves. I have no clue why I have to take him out. The reason they have sentenced him to death isn't part of my contract, and I'm nothing if not a dispassionate observer of the darkest parts of human desires. Twelve years at *l'Academie* ensured I care very little about anything that isn't directly related to my ability to complete my jobs.

Sighing, I dance closer and drop onto his rather unimpressive erection and wiggle. There's plenty of cloth between us to prevent him from doing anything I'd make a scene over, so I focus on the task at hand. I slip the cane behind his head, resting the wood against his neck as I tug him forward. The move reads as playfully bringing his face to my breasts, but at the last second, I click the release built into the custom weapon. One end slides open to reveal the razor sharp garotte and before he can say a word, I yank it through.

Faint gurgling is the only noise besides the end of the song, and I carefully slide the sides of the cane together. Climbing off the nasty fucker, I put my hands on his cheeks so I can pretend to flirt with him while I arrange the head so it looks as if he's leaning back in the booth. It needs to look realistic to allow me to return to the stage with the others. When I have it settled, I back away from the booth, blowing fake kisses as I walk backwards through the crowd. I almost collide with a dark-haired guy with his collar pulled high as I head for the stage, and I roll my eyes. Whatever celeb that is trying to keep their face away from the paps is doing a shitty job of it.

The entire troupe takes a few bows and shuffles off of stage left to the wings. I exhale a sigh of relief when the next group enters on the opposite side. I haven't heard shouting yet, so I don't think the Cobra's men realize he's down. Now I take this emetic pill, have a vomiting episode, and I'll get sent home.

That's when Arabella Montaigne, the burlesque dancer, will cease to exist, and Remy Arsine Benoit will re-emerge.

I smile to myself as I chew on the tablet that will have me retching my guts out in a few moments. This is a more complex extermination than I usually prefer, and I can't leave my normal calling card behind. The Cobra's head had to remain in the booth rather than get delivered to his home in a basket.

Such a shame, that. I quite enjoy the reactions my little gifts engender when they're discovered.

Walking into the dressing room, I carefully strip my costume off, putting all the pieces in my bag. Every item in the locker room that belongs to me gets placed in the duffel carefully as I wait for the effects to hit me. It won't do to leave loose ends, even if my prints have never touched a single surface in this place. My gut roils and I turn, facing one of the other dancers as the vomit finally comes. Gracelia screams like she's being skinned when I hurl on her and it's everything I can do *not* to smirk through the chunks.

"C'est la merde!" she shouts, running for the showers as if she's on fire.

It takes less than a minute for the owner to send me home for the night. I walk out the back door of the building with everything just as the sirens scream.

Perfect timing, as always.

I jump into the first cab I can hail, directing him to the *Hôtel de Crillon*. Their suites are the ritziest in Paris, and it's my go-to hideout when I'm here. I used to only stay in the Bernstein Suite, but some rich fuckwad purchased it six months ago. If I could track them down and beat the hell out of them, I would, but I booked my schedule until late 2025. Assassins with my skill set and accuracy are getting harder to find. They forced the old guard into retirement because they refuse to adapt to the digital age. Too many cameras, crime labs, and hackers running about to do everything Cold War style.

The future of murder for hire is millennial, people. We're old enough to be stable, but young enough to be agile with new technology. Plus, most of them are broke AF from crooked ass student loans.

It's not an issue I have, but I've been in the business since I hit double digits. You don't survive *l'Academie des Invisibles* if you haven't killed someone before the end of primary school. It's unheard of.

I was eight the first time I used the weapon that would become my signature.

Shivering, I tap on the window of the cab and bitch the driver out. He's taking a longer route than necessary to raise my fare, and I'll have his guts for garters if he doesn't knock it the fuck off. A string of curses in French erupt from him when I voice the accusation, and I slam my palm on the window with enough force to crack the plexiglass barrier. He almost drives into another car, but when he regains control, he makes the requested adjustments to our route.

We arrived at the front entrance after a few more arguments and a traffic jam around the *Champs*. I throw the euros at him in disgust, memorizing the medallion number for later. He's not worth my time, but I have quite a few contacts who might be interested in black-mailing a cabbie in town. Getaway cars are cliche in the crime world now. Most ne'er-do-wells like myself find greater comfort in anonymous taxis or ride-share accounts hacked through the deep web accessed on burner phones. If your ride doesn't know you're a villain, there's no one to flip if law enforcement comes looking.

I never look the same for any job—ever.

I will not *use* Arabella Montaigne as a cover in the future, and once I move to the location of my next job, I'll ensure that she meets with a terrible fate. It's a lot more work to slowly kill off my alters once I've used them, but it's also why I've never even come close to being caught. The dancer with long wavy red hair, freckles, and big green eyes will never grace the streets of Paris again after I hop a plane. She will, however, get a minor story in the paper and an obituary when I decide how she tragically dies.

The Guillotine will rise from her ashes and be reborn.

Forever

RAISE HELL

ONCE I DITCH THE RED WIG, I STUFF IT IN THE BAG WITH THE REST OF Arabella. I'll drop this in a random dumpster across town, and the first step towards her demise will be over. I drop onto the bed, sprawling out on my back. This job took more time than I like to devote to one termination, but I enjoyed learning the routines. Since I escaped from *l'Academie* twelve years ago, I've been a ghost, and ghosts don't make friends. The girls at the dance hall reminded me of friends, and there's a pang in my heart now that I have to leave.

C'est la vie, Remy, I tell myself.

I was born into this life and though I'm no longer controlled by the whims of a shadowy criminal organization, I can't imagine doing anything else. Can you imagine someone like me trying to fit into a suburb or working at a bank? It's a ridiculous proposition. The only people I've ever been close to got trained to lie, cheat, steal, maim, kill, or con their way through life. I don't know how to be human; I put on the skin of a normal person and play the role.

Pushing up on my elbows, I blow my hair out of my face. I need to blow off some steam. My after-assignment stress relief is find an anonymous hottie and spend the rest of the night with alcohol and orgasms. It's my treat to myself, and afterward, I pack up and head for the next locale. Since I'm behaving like a teenage girl, I should definitely go out and raise some hell to get this morose bullshit out of my system.

It's Paris. I'll find a sexy guy or girl—hell, maybe both—and work through my little post-job funk. That's all I need: distraction.

The vanity in the bathroom has options in case my cover gets blown, so I'll be able to go out without fear of someone remembering me. I never travel without the kit for at least four identities; I learned that lesson in the early years. You can research until your face turns blue, but sometimes, fate throws a curveball—you have to be prepared to pivot. I barely escaped that hit with my hide intact and I've carried the lesson about being a morally gray Girl Scout with me ever since.

I force myself off the bed and walk in to look at the three other wigs on their stands. I'm fond of the periwinkle blue bob, but I don't think I have it in me to go clubbing tonight. The voluminous blonde wig with its fat waves is so trite; however, pretending to be a clueless American is easy as hell in any country. Everyone expects them to be about as worldly as Cheez Whiz and you can giggle your way to damn near anything if you throw in a Southern accent. Blonde it is, then.

Before I pull it on over the wig cap I'm still sporting, I check the tag dangling from inside: *Naomi Sue Blanchard of Pilot Point, Texas.* Looks like I'm going to a tourist bar tonight—if I'm lucky, I'll be able to Google a real country fried nightmare without resorting to something awful like the *Hard Rock.* Picking up the wig head, I carry it over to the sink as I augment the smokey eyed look I'm sporting at the moment. A few tweaks here and there allow me to move from 'silent film ingenue' to 'college girl who watches makeup TikToks.'

"Hi, y'all! I'm Naomi Sue Blanchard. Nice makin' your acquaintance," I mutter to myself as I pull on the short jean skirt and pale pink cami. A fitted kelly green zip up emblazoned with the Greek Letters for Alpha Kappa Alpha and a pair of matching pink cowboy boots are next, followed by the wig. When I look in the mirror, I find the picture of a Texas sorority girl and I grin in satisfaction.

Whoops.

My grin is a little too feral for Naomi, so I stay by the mirror, practicing softer expressions so I don't scare away my potential party companions. Wouldn't want to get all dressed up and have no one to fuck.

I gather all the bits and bobs associated with this identity, filling the future burn bag before I go. I prefilled the clutch with everything Naomi needs to go out so I check myself one more time in the mirror. Yep, I'm good. I wink at my reflection as I pull my phone out to search for the best bar to seek relaxation in tonight.

Yippee ki-yi-yay, motherfuckers.

WALKING DOWN THE BUSTLING STREETS, I HEAD TOWARDS THE M12. My maps app says I'm about five minutes away from the station, and I'll take it to the Pigalle stop to get to this tourist-y bar on Rue Frochot. The *Reverse Cowgirl* was the first thing that came up when I searched for a bar. A country western themed bar in the middle of Paris is nothing if not meant to draw in clueless Americans who are longing for a taste of home. It's probably filled with expats and college tour kids. I'm a wee bit older than them at thirty, but I've passed for as young as sixteen when necessary.

It's amazing how fast the aging process reverses when you aren't surviving torture that poses as training at an elite academy for criminals.

I have Airpods in my ears to keep nosy old biddies or creepers from approaching me, but my experience over the years has taught me to never deprive one of my senses in a public place. That's why I don't have music playing in them; instead, I make use of the amplifying effect they have when paired with my phone as a headset. It's a nifty little feature most people don't realize they have, and I make use of it frequently. Tonight, it's preventing me from having to beat the shit out of any asshole who tries to grope poor, sweet Naomi while I ride the Metro.

Five stinky stops after I hitch my ride, we stop at the station I need, and I pat myself on the back for not needing to break anyone's arm. Even the Guillotine can behave when she chooses, and since this is my reward for a job well executed, I didn't want to flee a crime scene instead of getting trashed and fucked. I emerge at street level, keeping my head down as I make my way through the crowds. They flood Paris with people in the early spring, and it's a Friday night. Even at almost midnight, people are winding their way around town from club to club or bar to bar.

It's a perfect way to stay lost, and I'm glad I picked Naomi for my identity tonight.

The Reverse Cowgirl is innocuous on the outside. I'm a little surprised it's not spackled with signs and obnoxious lights that would surely draw in the college kids, but that's okay. I open the heavy double doors, striding inside with my Naomi mask on—all smiles, wide eyes, and pink lip gloss. Quite a few heads turn, but the attention stays on the bull riding ring in back or the TVs set to ESPN at the bar.

Huh. Interesting joint.

Sliding onto a barstool, I bat my lashes at the blue-eyed bartender. He's dressed in a wife-beater and low slung jeans with a strong, all American jawline. Definitely an ex-pat, so I'll need to be careful what I say to him other than my drink order. I don't want to give myself away if he is familiar with a piece of my Naomi legend. I'd be horrified and shamed in my profession for such an idiotic mis-step.

"Evenin'. Y'all have Ranch Water?" I give him a blinding smile as I lean forward on the hardwood of the bar. I'm hoping it also gives him a good boob shot, which should distract him enough to keep the detailed questions at bay.

I'm not American—at least, I don't think I am. No one from *l'Academie* knows exactly where they're from originally. We're taken from orphanages and foster systems all over as children, carted off to the island, and re-educated. The intake staff sanitize, medically evaluate, and prepare the 'recruits' for the first few weeks, and after that, classes begin. They erased all traces of our pasts through technology and rigid training until we graduate at eighteen.

That's when we become full-fledged members of the most powerful crime syndicate in the world—if we survive the process.

Ol' Blue Eyes looks at me critically, then gives me a curt nod and moves down the bar to grab a glass. I must have passed his inspection because he mixes the mineral water, lime juice, and tequila quickly. When he returns, I slip a few extra euros across the wood with Naomi's card.

"Start a tab for me, handsome." I lift the drink, sipping it through the straw as I wait for him to bring it back. I tuck it in my small bag and push off the bar to head to a table on the wall. My back will be to the wall and I'll be able to see the entire bar —which is my preference. I sit on one of the high stools, scanning the crowd for a suitable hook-up. There are hot guys and girls in tight jeans and boots all over, so it won't be hard to find one.

"Yeehaw, Darla! He's in town for the concert tomorrow!"

The high-pitched squeal piques my attention and I turn to where a group of girls are staring at the TV screen like horny zombies. My eyes widen when I see his face—he's a little older, a lot hotter, and more famous than Jesus.

And he's here in Paris as of this morning.

Dark kohl rimmed emerald eyes, a stubbly beard, cropped raven hair, and the mother of all attitudes—that's world famous bad boy country music star Coda Ramone. His emo rocker appearance paired with the cowboy duds and his raspy vocals have made him one of the biggest stars in the sky for the past decade.

Underneath the flashy Grammy winner is his true skill set—the one he learned on a remote island many years ago. Coda Ramone is an immaculately packaged member of the syndicate that operates in the open. He's what they call a 'fixer'. His wealth and fame allow him to move in both legitimate and illegitimate circles—everyone loves a star.

One of his current hits starts playing in the news' background report and suddenly, it hits me like a ton of bricks. The eyes… I've seen his eyes recently and not on the TV. Those sparkling green orbs looked at me this evening over a pulled up collar as he made his way past the stage and towards the restrooms. When I thought it was a celebrity hiding, I was correct.

Coda's rep wouldn't get harmed a whit by being photographed in an elite burlesque bar. He dressed in muted tones and hiding his famous smirk because he was on assignment. Somewhere in that club, he was sealing a deal for The Five. A source was accepting payment for orchestrating a solution or a client was providing information on a problem.

Godfuckingdamnit.

Did he recognize me? He couldn't have. Not only am I older, but I don't look like the miserable teen from twelve years ago. I've gained enough weight to look normal, and I was trussed up as Arabella, who looks *nothing* like Remy. Between the disguise and time, there's no way Coda saw the real me.

When I escaped, I left my life at *l'Academie* behind, including Coda Ramone and the band of bad boys he ran with. They were my salvation, but I needed to get away from there. I couldn't be owned by the *Les Invisibles*—or anyone—for the rest of my life. I watched too many recruits die trying to live up to their insane standards.

I longed to be free.

Once I stopped running, I thought about contacting them. I could have used an encrypted phone or Tor network, but it seemed like a clean break was best for everyone. I didn't want to put them in the crosshairs of the Commandant if we got caught. Conversely, I couldn't bear to think that they might have forgotten me. Or worse, they might have disapproved of my actions so much they turned me in to their handlers.

That would have broken my heart into a million pieces.

Gulping the last of my drink down, I catch the bartender's eyes and hold up two fingers. He nods, lips curving up as he starts my refill plus one. My night's becoming less a celebration of my perfect execution and instead, a more morose trip down memory lane.

I need to get laid.

Wiggling off the stool, I sashay over to grab my drinks, trying to slip back into Naomi again.

That's when the door to the bar opens and all hell breaks loose.

REBEL YELL

THIS IS THE TYPE OF BAR I FUCKING HATE.

If I didn't have to maintain my cover every second of every day, I'd never set foot in one of these groupie-filled nightmares again. My agent Charice picks them out strategically—just popular enough to make certain I'm 'seen' out being rowdy with the locals before my concerts. There's always booze and drugs and enough girls to solidify the bad boy image without putting myself at risk by haunting the bigger clubs and bars.

And cameras, of course. She tips off the rags after a while. It creates buzz, and it gives me an excuse to peace the fuck outta there without disappointing fans.

It's the price of being *Coda Ramone*, and I know it, but it's not as if I have a choice.

The door to the *Reverse Cowgirl* swings open. Once a few chicks figure out who I am, the chaos begins. I steel myself mentally for the fawning, grasping hands and coos of my legions. I'm not saying I haven't enjoyed the company of a groupie or a thousand, nor am I saying I'm better than the people who shell out hard earned cash for my records or concert tickets. Country rocking bad boy is my side hustle, and I look at all of it from a business perspective. We made every public appearance or statement in service to keeping Coda Ramone in the spotlight for as long as I can. My notoriety allows me to complete my jobs for *Les Invisibles* with relative ease.

Who doesn't want to please a billionaire music god?

Thus, I'm able to manipulate and make deals others cannot—doors open for Coda Ramone that don't open for mere mortals. Invitations come by the pound, and I'm able to choose acceptance to those that either furthers my legend or services my true profession: fixer extra-ordinaire.

Fixer is a simplistic term, of course. I use my fame to gain access, and my access to gain trust. Once I do that, I can identify weak points and leverage whatever I need to accomplish my goal. If you can afford *Les Invisibles'* prices or trade them something they want, your problem—whatever it may be—will get solved quickly and quietly.

Fairly ironic, given that your issue gets resolved by a world renown celebrity, but the world is full of contradictions.

"Oh, Coda, I *love* your music," the blonde that's attached herself to my side while my thoughts ran off with me coos.

The redhead bobs her head like a seal. "*Me, too.*"

I flash them the billion dollar smirk despite being bored as fuck after being here five goddamned minutes. They can't help being needy girls desperate for validation anymore than I can help being in a shitty mood. After all, I *don't* want to be here and the HVT from earlier got iced before I could receive his intel.

Iced by the fucking *Guillotine* in the middle of the fucking club, of all things.

My fury knows no bounds. I only flew into Paris for this last-minute booking, so I could milk the Cobra for everything he knew, but he got himself assassinated. Not only did I *fail* my mission—and I *never* fail—but I somehow missed the goddamned Guillotine running amuck in my presence. The national debt of five small countries could get paid off by the bounty on that assho*le*. Imagine what *LI* could make auctioning the world's most sought after assassin?

I'd never have to work again—even if I technically don't now.

"Did I say something wrong?" Red asks.

The girls pout at me, and I sigh. Bloody hell, it's time for the act. If not, I'll get accused of abusing the sheep again. "No, darlin', of course not. Sometimes, the *mood* just strikes me and I get a little melancholy. That's usually when I end up writin' a song or two."

Simpering follows, and I lead the entire crowd following me to the bar. The clearly gay bartender does his own pitch and I gracefully flirt while I order. Wouldn't do to offend him and have my drink filled with spit. I'm well known for not being choosy about partners —men, women, groups… I've done it all.

Hell, there's a nasty rumor about a trip to Mexico that Charice is *still* trying to quash. Turns out it's much harder to control the internet when you're not working for a global crime organization. My handlers offered to have their people deal with it, but I figure infamy is just another type of fame, right?

Besides, I didn't *actually* fuck a goat and anyone who thinks I did is a fucking moron. Why would I go for farm animals when I have my pick of any dude or chick I run into daily? It's blasphemy to even consider.

My absinthe arrives, and I smile for real this time. Even in Paris, a bullshit place like this serves it exactly how it should be. It's one of my favorite vices, and the girls coo as I drink it. Charice, my manager, always includes it in my rider, so it's become part of my persona—my signature, if you will.

"I wish I could drink that like you, Coda, but I've never liked it. I'm just too much of a *lightweight* to drink something so *strong*," Blonde says as she clutches my arm against her breasts.

Arching a brow, I pretend to consider that before giving her a smirk. If I wanted to, I could have her bent over the pool table in ten seconds. Unfortunately for Blonde and Red, neither of them interest me in the slightest. "It's best if you stick with your White Claw, sugar. I wouldn't want anything untoward to happen to you."

She looks at her friend, and they exchange a pout. I'm sure they just saw their chances of bagging a music idol fly out the window and they're trying to figure out how to recoup. Instead of waiting for their next scheme, I push off the bar and tip my hat at them. They're calling my name as I saunter back to the action at the pool table, checking out the talent to see if it's worth a go.

There are a couple of decent players, one shark pretending to be an amateur, and girls hanging off the tall tables as they watch the money change hands. I could probably find some sport here, and that'll help me pass the time until they alert the paps to my location.

I check my Apple Watch and frown. How has it only been twenty minutes? Christ, I'm never getting through this night. If I hadn't had a piss poor result earlier—missions that don't go as planned put me in a foul mood—I might not be annoyed. Rotten luck it happened *before* my famous guy duties, but when it rains, it pours.

"Yo, guitar boy. You want in on a game?"

My eyes narrow as I study the mouthy frat douche. I could squash him like a grape with my biceps alone, but that's not Coda Ramone. I give him a lazy grin and tip my hat, nodding. "I'd be much obliged, sir. What's the buy-in?"

"For a scrawny rich boy? Two hundred," the popped collar fool replies.

Oh, I'd love to break this little shit's neck.

Killing isn't my specialty—info is my game—but we all train for every specialty until we're assigned a class at *l'Academie*. I'm as lethal as any of their assassins. It's just not how I typically solve my problems. So I pull the roll out of my pocket, peeling off two

Benjamins and slapping them on the rail of the table. "I'm in, jockstrap."

His friends snicker like a pack of hyenas, and it takes everything in me not to snarl at them. I watch him rack the balls, then turn my head, whistling sharply at the bartender. He catches my eyes and I give him a nod, indicating I want a refill. If I am going to get through this bullshit, I need quite a few.

"Break, music man. I'll give you a handicap," the dick says as he laughs.

I sigh. This moron has done less actual work in his life than my rock god alter ego has, and he wants to smirk at me. Sipping my absinthe, I scope the table, watching for slant in the slate and other imperfections that might make this game tilt. Once I have the lay of the land, I walk over to the wall and pick a stick.

"C'mon, man! I fucked your mom faster than this." The buffoon chuckles and his friends join him as they gather in their little circle jerk.

"Excuse me, friend. I don't believe I heard you correctly," I reply as I chalk the end of the stick, my eyes darting from the table to the stupid fuck briefly. I'm trying to hold my temper in check; It took weeks to spin the PR after my last bar brawl.

The crowd of dumbasses guffaw again, and the dipshit responds, "Your mom, dude. I said I fucked her faster than you're breaking."

That's two. I never give them more than two.

A loud crack echoes as I break the stick over my knee and advance on him with a menacing look. "Don't tell them I didn't give you a second chance."

"Oh, the whiny eyeliner wearing homo thinks he can take me! Bring it on, sissy!" Douchey Chad—I assume, I didn't ask this shitstain's name—gestures to his friend, and I roll my eyes.

Charice is going to kill me, and the guys will lose their minds.

I use the sticks in my hands to hit two of them in the nose as I leap over the table. Once they're stunned, I pivot to the two-collared moron and ram my knee into his junk. He doubles over and I grin, watching the larger crowd form. I know there are phones recording, so I wink as I jump onto the pool table and fling my hat off to the side. This has to be a show now.

"Who's next, eh? Any other dickless homophobes want to make jokes about the poor orphan billionaire? Have at me, assholes!" I add a pretend slur to my twang, making it seem like I'm drunker than I am. Drunken fights are nothing new for Coda Ramone, and it won't be a blip on my 'official' mission reports.

The jackasses I hit are on their feet now and the rest of the frat assholes in the bar have joined them. Someone yanks me backwards off the table and as I tumble, I push the button on my watch to let the guys know I've done it again. They need to know that I will be in the news for a couple days.

As the growing crowd closes in when I hit the floor, it occurs to me I *may* have bitten off more than I can chew this time. There's at least thirty dudes in this circle kicking like they're trying to win the World Cup, and I haven't worked out my escape route yet.

Suddenly, a hole opens up in the rings of dumb fucks. All I see is a blonde chick dressed in the pink and green colors you see all over the South. I can't see her face, but the move she uses to get the two guys off me is *definitely* Brazilian jujitsu. She growls something at the crowd that makes them back off slightly, and before I pass out, I feel her yanking me off the floor and dragging me towards what I assume is the door.

Holy Hank Williams, I think I might love this chick.

Forever

I FORGOT THAT YOU EXISTED

WHY? WHY DID I SAVE THIS IDIOT? NO ONE CAME TO MY RESCUE WHEN I escaped the island — not him or any of his posse.

Because you've always been better than them, Remy, and wearing a blonde wig doesn't actually change who you are.

Fucking logic. I hate my brain.

Also, letting Coda Ramone get his shit stomped in the same city I took out a mark he had a meeting with will draw more attention than I prefer. *Les Invisibles* will dispatch agents to find out if it was a direct attack on their asset and that alone might lead to someone connecting the dots to me. If they connect that with the signature I left on the Cobra, it might blow my entire persona.

*Only **a man** could show up, destroy years of hard work, and need to be rescued from their own ego.*

Sighing, I drag the blacked out, bulky asshole to the nearest outdoor cafe and prop him up in a chair. I eluded the paparazzi at the front by using the dingy back alley, but I have no idea if anyone else is following us. The weight of the emo cowboy was enough to keep me focused forward rather than behind—a mistake that could get us both killed.

Good thing I stopped in one of the connecting alleyways to ditch the Naomi wig and the AKA jacket. I stole Coda's leather and fluffed my hair up, making me look more like an old lady than a Texas college girl. The dark red lipstick in my clutch helped—never leave home without a few emergency makeup change products tucked in your bag—and by the time I hit the bustling streets, I turned into Remy.

Not that I'm remotely used to being Remy in a public place. It's too dangerous with all the CCTV cams all over cities. One good face rec program and the *Les Invisibles* will have retrieval units dispatched. I've avoided that for over a decade, but technology is improving every day. That's why I've become such a master of disguise.

Now I'm risking everything to protect the fuckwit who abandoned me.

Nice decision making, Remy—real adult. He's covered in tatts and muscles, so you let your lady bits do the thinking. *You're smarter than this*, I chide myself as I arrange him in the chair. A quick check of his watch tells me there's *Les Invisibles* tech, so people will be here for him soon.

Biting my lip, I think about whether he'll be safe in the interim if I leave. Even if I never wanted to see him, I don't want him to get assaulted by some crazy ass *Fatal Attraction* girl. Pulling one of my comfort weapons out of the right jean skirt pocket, I slide it open and closed as I wait, watching the wire glisten in the starlight.

Schink, schink, schink…

The sound is soothing, and it calms my frayed nerves. Killing always does. Even if I'm not taking a target out, imagining that I am is good enough. My eyes drift over to the man passed out in the bistro chair. He's easily as hot as a grownup as I thought he'd be when we were kids.

Who am I kidding?

Coda is eleventy billion times hotter than I ever could have dreamed —leather, ink, streaked hair, piercings, and fuck only knows what else the music god is hiding. He groans and I narrow my eyes, ready to bolt before he gets a good look at me without my costume. I can't have people from my past find out who I've become if I want to stay free. That's why I choked his ass out in the alley, by the way.

Don't give me that look, moral compass.

First, his little Fender stood at attention, so I don't think he *hated* it. Second, I'm well versed in choking someone in both the safe *and* dangerous way, so I knew I wouldn't cause him damage. Regardless, I had to do it. I was going to ditch the Naomi cover as quickly as possible to keep us from being followed. Last, but definitely not least, he's at least 250 plus pounds of solid muscle, and I needed to keep him from struggling while I hefted him.

After all, I'm *much* more experienced at heaving dead weight around —live people are another story altogether.

My eyes catch a faint glint on a roof a block away, and I curse under my breath. Stupid mental detour made me careless, and that is most definitely a *Les Invisibles* sniper setting up a nest. Time for me to yeet myself into oblivion once more. I look down at the prone musician with a sigh of regret for the future that never was. Leaning over on instinct, I press a kiss to the scar on his right eyebrow like I used to when we were young. Sentimentality floods me, and I shake my head, backing away from him as if he'll infect me.

No time for feelings, Remy. The Guillotine cares for no one. People are merely a means to an end.

With that firm coaching echoing in my head, I pull the jacket collar up, turning on my heel and heading towards the nearest Metro. I'm already punching up routes as I round the closest corner, and I can barely hear the crowd as the team finds their missing operative in the cafe. They certainly don't see me peeking at them as I lean on the corner of a building while I toggle things on my phone like any other person on the street. When I'm sure the *Les Invisibles* have their boy safe, I push off and continue my journey back to the fancy hotel.

I need to gather my shit and visit my storage unit for a restock on identities. I've burned two today, so I need the third one for another city. I don't like recycling within the same calendar year, so the raven haired pixie will get slated for a job next year. I'll need at least five spares for the job I have lined up in Prague, and I have to get packing.

The trains leave early, and I have to catch the next one to Berlin.

"P*ROCHAINE ÉTAPE, L'A*LSACE-L*ORRAINE*[1]," THE CONDUCTOR CALLS AS he walks the aisle.

I poke my head out of my cabin, pondering food as my stomach rumbles its agreement. Food hasn't been a consideration since before my performance in Paris, and I've consumed enough tequila to flood the Yucatan. It's probably time to hydrate and fill up my tank. Even if I have the entire sleeper to myself by design, I need to review documents to prepare for the next target. Staying drunk until I reach Berlin is tempting, but not practical and not *at all* like the Remy who slips on the mask of The Guillotine.

That's more like the Remy who had friends even while she survived some of the worst training known to humankind—but she's dead.

Seeing Coda in person has thrown my entire life into a tailspin and if I could, I'd go back in time and just kill the asshole. At least then I wouldn't be lolling in the past and thinking about the 'could haves'. It was all naïve, childish dreaming, and it's better that they put a stop to it before we all got killed. That's what I decided when I got off that damned island, and I'm not changing my mind because Coda grew up to be the bad boy wet dream of every woman with eyeballs.

So you admit you lust after him…

For fuck's sake, brain. I shake my head and step out of the car. I'm wearing a short, mousy brown wig that belongs to Hannah, the librarian from Brooklyn. My round black glasses, eco-wear, Doc Martens, and Manhatten Portage messenger bag filled with my shit complete the look. I'm so incredibly hip that I'm sure people wouldn't be surprised if I pulled my jar of artisanal pickles out of my bag to eat with my lunch.

The dining car is mostly empty—there's a woman with a tiny human at the other end, an older gentleman with his wife in the middle, and a lone businessman in an overcoat and fancy suit at the table closest to the bar. The old folks are playing a card game—likely gin—and the kid is making obnoxious amounts of noise for someone who is being fed. Mr. Suit Guy keeps giving them annoyed looks before flicking his paper and diving back into what can only be the financial section.

Never fails. Dudes gonna dude no matter where they are.

I walk over to the bar, adopting the accent I need as I order a sandwich, a water, and a soda. I'd prefer a fucking *drink*, but I'm not indulging that vice again until I've completed all the work I stuffed in this bag. It's concealed on a small tablet that will keep nosy people from prying over my shoulder as they walk by, and I have plenty of leaflets and papers about local festivals and co-ops to scatter around the table while I eat. I'm beyond thorough when I create my legends, and my work is so detailed that even the best forgers in the world would have trouble discerning what's real and what's fake.

I should know; I was taught to do it by the best forger ever.

Shaking off yet another memory—this one of Professor Arnaud—I plop down in the booth with the best vantage point and wait for the server to bring my sustenance. While I wait, I meticulously shuffle papers and fliers around, drop pens and a pad, and make the space look like I'm a hipster planning my monthly rally calendar. After the food arrives, I make space for it and to settle the tablet at my waist so I can read as I eat.

The crawl of the video on my screen is slow at first, giving me time to memorize coordinates, dates, and times. After that, pictures flash by quickly, and then maps. At the end, there's a vocal clip I'll need my AirPods for. Cursing under my breath, I dig in my bag for them.

Of course, that stupid little fuck would include sound; it's not part of the standard package for most jobs. Something about it is important enough to risk being called out for poor form. Sound is the easiest method of getting caught—too many mics in phones, vents, and Judas knows where else anymore. Including that media in this package is a risk that had better be worth it.

"The enclosed audio is essential to identifying this target. Appearance will change at will, and they will arm him with the most secure tech available. He hasn't been seen in a decade, preferring to operate from behind a screen. This clip of his voice is the most identifiable piece of intel we can give outside of the bits of his code we have gathered over the past year. That is included for your reference in an accompanying video. We will pay your most elite rate, Guillotine, to have this bothersome gnat wiped from the face of the planet. Usual methods. We will monitor drops in cities of your choosing. Send requirements via the first available one in Berlin."

I frown. This is *not* how this works. I don't take jobs on spec, and I sure as fuck don't use someone else's dead drops to communicate. That's how assassins get caught by the fucking *Feds* or whatever the hell the country you're in has. My irritation with my bad evening—and now this bullshit—is riding high when I click the icon for the voice recording. I'm ready to rant when the rasp of the voice makes me gasp and drop the tablet. It clatters to the loud with a thump, drawing the eyes of all the passengers. I duck my head as if hiding a blush, and pick up the tablet, hastily cleaning up the mess I made.

The business bro glares at me over a pair of tinted lenses and I roll my eyes at him. If I weren't in my 'shy Hannah' guise, I'd flip the asshole off, but that's just bad tradecraft. I make a sheepish face at him then make quick work of the food I no longer feel hungry for. I can't let the people here notice me more than they already have, and not finishing my plate would give them another reason to recall me.

But the voice…

I sip the soda, definitely wishing it was spiked now. Yet another ghost from my past has reared its ugly head, and I have absolutely no idea if it's a coincidence or if I'm being played.

Otherwise, why in hell's name is the voice of Raz Miranda being sent to me for an execution?

---

1. Next stop, Alsace-Lorraine.

Forever

ABCDFU

AFTER I MADE CERTAIN TO FINISH UP MY FOOD, I TOTTERED BACK TO MY cabin to go through the files sent by my client. I'm rarely aware of the true identity of those who hire me, and this is no exception. The people who can afford my services are meticulous and ruthless— they know leaving a loose end could put them on the wrong end of someone else's target list. Occasionally, there's a minor slip in the materials they provide and if I'm inclined, I tug the thread until it pulls free.

But not knowing who they are protects me as much as it does them, so I'm quite judicious about exercising that curiosity. It's much easier to eliminate your assignment when you assume the person has done a misdeed in their past or present that brought me to their door rather than speculate about motives.

The simple truth is: innocent people die in the name of greed and vice all the time. Assassins can't work if they weigh worthiness or guilt—we are the tools of the trade as much as guns or bombs. The decision to use our skills is on those who pay, not us. 'Why' is not a question we have the luxury of asking if we want to remain successful.

I'm not a 'good person' in the common moral sense, and I don't pretend to be—no one who survives *l'Académie* does so with any kind of normal human code intact.

However, this job has my teeth on edge. What are the chances I'd have to save Coda Ramone on a random booty hunt one night and receive a termination request for Raz Miranda the next morning? Something isn't right in Mudville—I'll be damned if I let old sentiment lure me into a trap.

The information in the files should *never* have been given to a CEO or monster. His bio isn't accurate—it's probably one of a hundred false identities he's cultivated over the years. Raz has spent the better part of a decade being as much of a ghost as I am. If he hadn't, he wouldn't be the most highly paid hacker on the planet. I'm not surprised the client doesn't have a name or a face to put on their data. Raz is as skilled at disguise as any graduate and he has the edge on erasing footage that could have glimpsed him.

But what minute act of carelessness led to him being marked for death? He has never been on the radar.

Every incident in the news or whispered on the streets attributed to *La Araña* [1]has remained unconfirmed. No one can ever prove whether the infamous hacker was involved—and he never takes credit publicly. Raz learned at a very young age that getting credit for your genius leads to making enemies and, in our line of work, that leads to death. Watching several of his classmates face the consequences of their egos during our training drilled that into his mind before he even hit puberty.

How did he attract the attention of such a dangerous person?

Movies and TV glamorize criminals like us—they show flashy tropes and mediocre characters who have zero sense of how the underworld works. Assassins who meet with clients or hackers who sign their work, even grifters who let their true faces be seen everywhere they go. In the real world, the professionals are far less concerned with notoriety; in fact, the names we choose are mere whispers of our abilities.

Ben Franklin had it right when he said, 'two can keep a secret if one of them is dead.' *L'Academie* and its 'recruits' have remained in the shadows for centuries simply because no one who dares speak of them out loud may live. Its operatives are both everywhere and nowhere at the same time. We are weaponized by the age where most people are still squabbling at recess.

Invisibilia sunt, umbrae tantum relictae.[2]

Recruits learn their motto as early as we learn to read and write, and by the time you enter grade school, they select your name. When you successfully complete your first assignment, you receive the honor of being marked as one of their own. The ceremony is long and screams of cult brainwashing, but every single student attends. Chanting staff and students line the chamber as you walk up to the Commandant, waiting eagerly for the medical staff to strap you down and choose the spot where your loyalty will get branded for life.

I remember the screams of others vividly, but not my own. I was told I did not move or make a noise. For my dedication and bravery, they added another mark to their brand of ownership: the symbol of the Six.

The addition of that UV tattoo ink placed me on the path to an elite team of operatives within my class and sealed my fate with the *Les Invisibles*. Only the future members of the High Legion receive it—my path in *L'Academie* was set the second the needle touched my skin.

Too bad I made other plans...

The memory pinches as I recall making those plans with people who eventually betrayed me. I could blame it on youth or naïveté, but in the end, I learned my most valuable lesson at the hands of students, not staff. The mantra I adopted once I escaped has served me well in the interim years, so I suppose I should thank them for helping me thrive on my own.

The only person you can trust in this world is you, Remy. No one will ever save you; you must depend on yourself.

These files are bringing the past out of its cage, and I don't like it. Perhaps old sentiment got the best of me in Paris when I saved Coda from his own bullshit, but I can't let it affect my reputation. He and Raz didn't let their emotions affect their judgement, and I should do the same.

Raz Miranda has no one to blame for his predicament but himself.

Whatever sin he's committed, he dies by sundown on Friday.

THE TRAIN LURCHES TO A STOP AT BERLIN HBF AND I STAND, stretching as I gather my things. I got work done before the interchange in Cologne, and once I hopped on the line for the second leg of my trip, I didn't have the privacy to continue. I popped my AirPods in and pretended to nap, though I was acutely aware of every single person in the car. Situational awareness is paramount when trapped in a speeding box of metal, and though I feel certain I attracted no more attention than a normal woman traveling alone, I don't have the luxury of letting my guard down.

It's early morning in the capital city, and the crowds are bustling as I disembark. I prefer this kind of backdrop, if I'm honest. Moving through the shadows can be beneficial, being a random face in a mass of commuting workers is better. It's harder to be seen on CCTV, and the hurried automatons are more concerned with arriving on time than chatting with those around them.

Anonymity is an assassin's best friend.

It's a short walk to Fritz-Schloß Park. I'm a day early for the requested drop, and I want to scout the location. However, I have other needs before I'm ready to risk being seen in the area. I flag a cab, loading my minimal luggage in the back with me as I direct the driver to my destination. *"Fahren Sie zum Hotel Rossi.[3]"*

"Sind Sie zum ersten Mal in Berlin[4]?" he asks as he pulls away from the curb.

Of course not, you moron. I just spoke to you in German.

Growing up on a remote island full of orphans and retired criminals left me with very little patience for the inanities of regular social interactions. I can do what I need to complete a mission, but chatting with a garrulous cabbie isn't part of my plans for today. The more you connect with people, the more likely they are to remember you later. Being rude will cement my image in his mind as a nasty American and nothing more.

"Ich fahre lieber schweigend.[5]"

The huff from the front seat is one of total affront, and I smile to myself. This guy will tell his friends about the shitty fare he had within minutes of dropping me off and I'll be nothing more than an irritating memory. His driving gets more erratic as he mutters to himself, and I go back to scrolling through my phone. Now that I'm able to relax, I want to see if the media has anything to say about Coda's bar fight.

Bad Boy Rocker hat schlechte Nacht[6]

Not the most clever headline, but in the age of twenty-four-hour media, copy isn't what it used to be. The German versions of all the major news outlets are reporting a similar tale—country rock star Coda Ramone disappeared during a drunken bar fight in Paris. He reappeared the next morning, rumpled and laughing as the paparazzi snapped his walk of shame into the Ritz Carlton with his manager Charice.

They're calling his shiner 'rebel sexy'. Fucking spare me.

I guess no good deed goes unpunished, though, because that fuck-whistle got quoted as saying a 'sexy Southern blonde' saved his life when a minor disagreement turned into a brawl. The article says he would like the woman to reach out to his team so he can invite her to a show personally so he can thank her backstage. He even suggested she hit him up on the 'Gram so he can make sure she gets in.

That will make Charice's life a misery for the next twelve hours. He knows every blonde in the city will ping that account in desperate hopes of meeting their idol.

The moron created his own little Cinderella story, and he did it to promote his dumbass concert. If I wasn't furious, I'd have to admire the skill he was so meticulously trained to wield to keep his cover intact. Instead, I'm rearranging my schedule to push sleep back until I scan the web for any photos of either of us in the bar or on the street.

Men. There's a reason I don't bother with them outside of sex or death— they're nothing but fucking trouble.

"Wir sind i'm Hotel Rossi angekommen, gnädige Frau.[1]"

I roll my eyes at the now grumpy ass driver, forking over the euros flashing on the meter. He doesn't move to help me with my bags, and I have to count backwards in my head to keep my temper from getting the best of me. I tipped him despite his shitty attitude, and now I'm left to haul my shit to the lobby on my own. I slam the car door when I get my things out and the profanity that follows makes my lips curve as I walk to the doors of the hotel.

He probably discovered the crude drawing I sliced into the seat while I was studying the internet. It isn't very flattering, especially to his manhood.

The Guillotine may not get her vengeance on this rude motherfucker, but at least he'll think twice about muttering nasty comments about women under his breath while he drives.

---

1. The Spider

2. They are invisible, leaving only shadows.
3. Drive me to the Hotel Rossi.
4. Is this your first time in Berlin?
5. I love to drive in silence.
6. Bad Boy Rocker Has Bad Night
7. We have arrived at Hotel Rossi, Madame.

Forever

SABOTAGE

Despite being exhausted, I combed the feeds and the web for images of the mysterious blonde the idiot rocker mentioned in his interviews. Once I was satisfied I hadn't gotten caught on camera anywhere that I could find easily, I set a scanning protocol for multiple web layers. No, it's not a typical skill taught to my brethren, but I've always made it my business to learn everything I can to keep myself breathing. I knew the scan would take a few hours before it even nicked the bottom of the Tor networks. To pass the time, I showered and flopped down for a few hours of hard sleep.

My alarm went off a few minutes ago. However, I'm still lying here staring at the ceiling as if it holds answers to some great riddle. I have a vaguely unsettled feeling about everything that's happened the past two days, and I don't know why. Perhaps it's too many 'coincidences' or maybe it's just the deep gut feelings I get that tell me when it's time to run as fast I can. I don't ignore my gut—not since the island. It's reliable and more accurate than anything else I have in my tool kit. So the sensation niggling at the corner of my mind is worrisome.

Maybe it's leftover sentiment about the job you're here to accept.

I suppose that's possible. Assuming I'd never run afoul of the other five members of the Six in my profession was definitely naïve. *L'Academie*'s finest lieutenants have probably crossed my path before, but I rarely pay attention to things not in my immediate viewfinder. Obviously if they'd been noticeably present during one of my operations—like I now realize Coda was—I would have made a note. I didn't think that one of them would end up in my crosshairs.

It's ironic that Raz is the one who taught you how to code the scanning program you're using and you're here to kill him.

No fucking shit, it is. Everything I know about tech and programming is because Raz spent months teaching me the most useful parts of his designation. It was a fair trade, though, because I repaid the favor by instructing him on the best ways to eliminate a target while making it look natural or like an accident. Hackers are most often nowhere near their intended marks, but occasionally, things have to be done in physical locations. He needed enough knowledge to get in and out of places without arousing suspicion—the skills necessary for that were split between me, Dwyn, and Jinx.

Rolling to my side, I squint at the clock on the bedside table. My hand flies to my chest as my thoughts drift to the other three members of The Six. I let out a long, shuddering breath as I remember. I do *not* have time to take this ugly trip to the past. It's been done for many years, and getting upset now won't change the outcome. The future I envisioned as a teen is nothing but a dream unfulfilled, and I'm better off not indulging in wistful thinking.

I stretch and hop off the bed, heading for the bathroom to pin my hair to prepare for whichever persona I'm going to adopt. Once I finish the basic hygiene shit, I toss my roller bag on the rack and start unpacking the three identities I selected for the German leg of the trip. It sounds like paranoia, but I'll switch to a new set once I arrive in Prague.

Over the years, I've set up full service storage units in nearly every major city I've taken jobs in. I have hundreds of units in dozens of countries stocked to the brim with identities, weapons, tools, and items for disappearing. There are separate locations where supplies get sent, all under yet another layer of shelf corporations and untraceable accounts. I simply use what I need when I'm in town, and circle back months later to replenish. Nothing is done linearly—that's how good criminals get nabbed.

The Guillotine survives by leaving nothing to chance.

I chose a razored raven wolf cut with a tag reading '*Harley Mannheim of Chicago, Illinois*', a strawberry blonde bob labeled '*Lizabet Hurst of Frankfurt, Germany*', and a long, wavy pink wig with the name '*Kate Archer of Brisbane, Australia*'. The accompanying clothes, accessories, and identities get enclosed in each vacuum sealed bag, so I open them one at a time. Christ, I *was* tired when I packed this kit. Usually I don't pick multiple identities requiring accent work, but I've got a full house with this set. I got some rack time, or I would be hard pressed to get dressed.

After I see the full effect, I decide to go with Kate. I won't wear the same disguise to the meet, and her fairly natural makeup look and athletic wear are the least time-consuming option. I pull on the black jogging pants, sports bra, and zip up hoodie quickly, then settle the wig just so. The entire look is familiar, but I shrug it off as I toe on the tennis shoes. Hotel Rossi is only three minutes from the park, and I'll look like I've gone out for an evening run.

I tuck my phone in the armband, headphones in my ears, and strap the hidden belt around my waist. It has ID, some euros, and a lipstick size version of my favorite weapon—just in case I run into trouble.

Now I'm ready to rock.

Heading to the lobby, I note they don't have security cameras in the stairwells. I used the elevator to get my bags up, without drawing attention to myself. That's a point in favor of staying fit, though, because anywhere I can avoid prying eyes is where I'll inevitably stay. The door at the bottom opens onto the street. I look at people bustling by briefly, like I'm deciding which way I want to go. Finally,

I turn and head down the block, jogging to the end of the block at a medium pace.

By the time I've circled the entire park, I'm pretty sure there aren't any long range operatives perched on the surrounding rooftops. I didn't notice repeat foot traffic in my loop, so it's unlikely there are trained folks watching the entrances and exits. I enter from the west side, making my way down the trails past the closed swimming pool. The drop is supposed to occur at one of my regular drop points along the track in the Poststadion. That area is saturated with athletes and families, so I can disappear into the woods behind it once I've claimed my drive.

It's not as populated as I'd prefer right now, but I pretend to stop at the distance marker and look at the smartwatch on my wrist. I stretch, bending this way and that as I scout the area surrounding the outside. They held the Olympics here in the thirties, and the park is part of some green corridor area. At least, that's what the sign I have my foot propped on says. I enjoy learning tidbits about the places I go, and I tuck that away for later. Who knows when I'll need a random fact to impress a mark with?

I jog to the stadium after I do a thorough visual sweep. Hopping a short fence, I cross the pitch to the stands. Ten rows up and seven over, I put a foot on the bleacher and pretend to stretch my hamstring. While I'm bent over, I feel underneath the bench for my prize. It only takes a moment to locate the thin plastic pouch taped there, and I tuck it in my palm as I run my hand up my leg. I straighten, slipping the drive into the pocket of my sweats quickly.

Turning to leave, it occurs to me that what I just found shouldn't have been there—I'm four hours early. A rush of fear trickles down my spine, and I put my hand up to my eyes as I look across the field. The press box *might* have someone in it, but the glare on the glass makes it impossible to know. I can't tell if the vague shadow is a person or a damned coat rack.

Just fucking perfect, Remy. You've spent thirteen years being the shadow that goes bump in the night, and in the past two days, you've been nothing but amateur hour. It's going to get you killed.

Shaking my hair over my shoulders, I take the stairs on the bleachers and step out onto the track. If I run a few laps before I leave, I'll be able to keep my eye on the booth to see if anyone slips out. And if there is someone there, it will seem a lot less suspicious if I'm just a chick doing laps at the stadium.

That's what you hope, at least, Remy.

AFTER I RETURNED, I STASHED THE DRIVE IN A SAFE PLACE FAR FROM MY room. I didn't bring my signal detector for the scouting trip, and now that I'm getting a bad feeling about the meet, I refuse to keep it in my room until I've scanned it. Five flights and a long ass walk across the entire building gets me to my room and I breathe a sigh of relief that either no one is following me, or they aren't bold enough to approach yet. I strip Kate Archer from my body, scrubbing my face clean as I pace the bedroom.

Do I sneak down to my hidey-hole sans disguise and scan the drive, or do I leave it until tonight?

The spot is pretty secure for an 'on-the-fly' drop. I'd prefer to eat, get ready, and find a good place to store my things so I can hit the bricks for Prague as soon as I'm done. I don't *have* to go back now, but on the off chance, the person in the booth *wasn't* associated with the hit on Raz, it tells me I have an additional asshole—or assholes—tracking me. Going back for the 'real' drop might flush my stalkers out and allow me to dispatch my problems all in one go. I'm all for efficiency; I haven't survived on my own without being able to handle a crowd if need be.

That's what I need to do—get rid of this bullshit before Prague. After that job, I'll lie low for a while. Tahiti is nice this time of year—I hear it's a wonderful place. Maybe I'll head to the South Pacific for a couple months and work on my tan.

Can you imagine me lying on the sand trying to become a honey baked ham? I'd go insane on day one.

I wasn't raised to lie around. My work is my joy in life and without it, I don't have a fucking clue who I am. As far back as grade school, I've been an assassin and the only other thing I wanted was freedom. I have both now, and I'll be damned if I let some penny ante cock-waffles try to auction me off to the highest bidder. This shit ends tonight.

I head to the sitting room to call for room service. I can start stretching and getting my muscles warm while I wait for the food. I'll need a fuckton of protein and carbs to have the energy necessary to flee or fuck someone up—whichever is the most prudent.

No one crosses the Guillotine and lives to tell the tale.

Heads will roll.

Forever

BAD IDEA

FUCKING CODA.

That dipshit has gotten us into more jams than I can count, yet here I am in Germany cleaning up one of his messes. Despite putting the public call out for his mysterious blonde, he knows she's not in Paris. After his retrieval, Jax and Dwyn flew in to run our own investigation—given our profession, we can't be too cautious about unknown saviors who drag one of us out of a dangerous situation. Humans do nothing out of the goodness of their hearts, and whoever this chick is, she's no different. They inspected every inch of him for surreptitious trackers or evidence of who this sorority bimbette was.

I mean, honestly, how many bubbly coeds can deadlift 250 lbs and carry it to another location? That's suspicious on its own, but that she was nowhere to be found when one of the world's most famous rockers woke up is telling. She didn't do it to fangirl and since Coda got bruised but not harmed, she also wasn't there to take him out. The question is: *why* would this oddly strong stranger get him out of there and abandon him *right* before *Les Invisibles'* team arrived? I think the whole thing stinks of a competing organization, and everyone but him needs to lie low for a couple months to throw them off of our trails.

Coda is determined to find and investigate the supposed good samaritan. He's driven by his frustration at failing to complete his assignment earlier in the evening, and when Coda Ramone gets emotional, the entire world has to suffer. That includes the rest of The Five, so here I am in Berlin, following a lead based on the single fingerprint we found on the screen of his Apple watch.

We almost didn't have it because the idiot stripped when he got back to his hotel and couldn't remember every single thing he'd worn in his red haze of rage.

Of course, if a group of drunk frat boys had taken me out—no matter how large—I'd be embarrassed, too.

L'Academie trained us better than that and he'll be hearing from the Commandant once we check in. His little performance in the press saved his ass, but the attention it drew to his presence in Paris outside of his cover was unacceptable. I wouldn't want to hear that lecture.

Best I don't tease him mercilessly about it then, right?

Wrong.

No way am I letting that dick get away with getting his ass beat in some college bar. His flashy persona overrides his brain sometimes and now all of us are paying for his carelessness. Dwyn had to drop his surveillance, Jinx had to smooth over an absence, and I'm not in my cave where I belong. Mo flat out refused to come unless it was absolutely necessary and none of us could guarantee that. The fingerprint belonged to a Texas college girl—Naomi Sue Blanchard—but I haven't completed all the layers of my search parameters yet.

If she's a fraud, I'll find out.

Since the cursory search of Paris hotels and hostels didn't turn up anyone by that name with a room on the books, I broadened my approach. Coda had a vague recollection of height, weight, and age, so I ran a script on the CCTV and security camera networks around the place he was found. Another few lines of code helped me set parameters for recognition and I discovered three women who *might* fit the bill, though none were a sorority chick with curly blonde hair. All we needed to do was figure out which woman matched the fingerprint of 'Naomi Sue Blanchard' from Texas.

While Coda flashed his pearlies at the press, Jinx, Dwyn, and I traced the movements of our respective suspects. Dwyn's target headed for Berlin, and Jinx's stayed in the city. Mine ended up in Italy, but I cleared her quickly. My chick was definitely a tourist, so I headed to Berlin to join our resident thief. He had a feeling his girl was the right one, and since his instincts were almost never wrong, I humored him.

I'm convinced Naomi Sue is an alias, but if it is, it's pretty fucking good. That doesn't bode well, and I told the rest of the guys as much. If she has false documents and records good enough to pass even my initial checks, she's got serious backing. *L'Academie* trains its recruits to be some of the best forgers in the world and, clearly, this random chick isn't one of ours. The Five know every operative by name and skill set—it's part of our job.

Where the shit did she come from and why did she save Coda?

I returned to the screens in front of me in the van. I've been parked here for hours, waiting for the mousy-looking girl from the train security feed to emerge. She took a taxi here this morning and, contrary to her shy appearance; she left the driver in a snit when she got out. I didn't want to risk exposure by getting out to grill him, but I sent Dwyn to find him. I don't have the slightest why it's taking so long for that asshole to get back. Unless he got distracted by something shiny he wanted to knick along the way.

It wouldn't be the first time and it won't be the last. His brain rarely focuses on anything as intensely as taking what doesn't belong to him, and he'll stop everything to swipe something if he thinks he can get away with it. Dwyn lives for the challenge of doing shit like that on the fly; if he has time to plan, nothing is out of his reach. Most of the shit he's stolen for clients is listed as top priority recovery among law enforcement agencies worldwide. The rest of his heists are for everything from information to black market crap that no one will admit to owning, much less losing, so he's wanted by the good guys *and* the bad ones.

Too bad they're more likely to locate D. B. Cooper than Dwyn O' Shanahan.

Like most of The Five, he's a ghost. Coda and Jinx are the only two of us who have public covers, and that's because it aids their skill set; otherwise, they'd be phantoms like Dwyn, Mo, and I.

Rubbing my hand over my face, I sigh. I can't leave the screens, but I need to piss and eat soon. If Dwyn doesn't come back from his trip to find the cabbie, I'm going to strangle his happy-go-lucky ass. He's been gone at least three hours, and this is ridiculous. It's like working with a fucking squirrel sometimes.

I'm near losing my temper when suddenly the back of the van opens, and the grinning psycho pokes his head in.

"Miss me, Razzie?"

Jesus fucking Christ, no.

I hurry back from my necessary break. Dwyn promised to watch the monitors, but if he's not scoping out a heist, his attention span is like a toddler. I can't dawdle and expect surveillance to be maintained. As it is, I'll probably have to rewind the feed and make sure he didn't miss the nondescript girl leaving because he saw a shiny bit of tin.

There's a reason *l'Academie* puts us in our specialty tracks so young —people are better suited to some things than others and it often manifests in childhood. The students were told that all the time. I've never seen proof they were wrong, so I assume it's true. It definitely is with my four brothers. Mo has always been physical and the 'hitter' track was perfect for him. The spotlight loves Coda, and smooth talking comes easily to Jinx. Tech speaks to me, and Dwyn is crazy enough to execute the most daring of thefts without once considering what would happen if they caught him.

Death was her art.

Frowning, I shake my head. If I can help it, I'll never think about that topic again. The Five was once The Six, and we never talk about the day that changed. Each of us deals with the choice we had to make that day differently: Coda parties, Mo climbs in the ring, I hide, Jinx never takes off the mask, and Dwyn takes risks to feel alive. Losing her damaged us so irreparably that we rarely travel as a team anymore; over the past decade, we've drifted apart without our anchor.

Remy is dead, Raz. The girl never could have survived that explosion. Even if she did, she'd never forgive any of you for your betrayal.

Determined to stop my moping, I cross the street and head towards the van when something catches my eye. A pink haired woman in athletic gear passed by before I went into the restroom and now she's back again. The park would make a far better jogging area. I can't fathom why she looped around the block again. I slip behind a large crowd of teenagers, watching the cotton candy color as it heads towards the next entrance to the park. It's almost like she's trying to make certain no one is following her.

Which definitely means I should follow her.

It could simply be an extremely cautious woman avoiding being cornered by a creep, but something about the way she moves and how casually she scopes her surroundings trips my wires. It feels... purposeful. So I trail behind her, keeping to the edges of her vision so it doesn't appear like I'm stalking her—which I am—and cause her to veer off course. I'm forced to walk past her, pretending to talk on my phone loudly when she stops to stretch her hammies, and I use the fake call to stop and shout in angry German at the device.

I pretend not to notice her turning toward the Poststadion, continuing my loud one-way conversation with my imaginary call. Pinky jogs around the edge, disappearing from my view. I head over to see if I can jimmy my way into the press box. Wherever she's going is on the back side, so if I can spy across the pitch, I might see her. She could be the frumpy librarian from this morning. The transformation would be pretty drastic, but I know a few people that could fool their own mothers with disguises. It's possible that she could be the blonde from Paris.

The lock is a tragedy, really, considering the history of this building. I can open it in less than a minute and head up the stairs to the booth. Pinky's there, her foot up on the bleachers like she's stretching again, and if I weren't used to spotting minute details on security feeds, I would miss her snatching an object from under the metal. She palms it masterfully, and again, if they hadn't trained me as well as they did, I wouldn't have even noticed. The sun filters through a cloud, and I step back, momentarily blinded by the light.

When the brightness fades, the woman is jogging around the track like a pro. I missed something, and I'll be damned if I know what. There are no cameras I can see, but I won't be able to see this area from the van.

Fucked over by the sun—it's not my goddamned day.

I slip down the stairs and run back to the park. Dwyn will be waiting, and I get the feeling we're going to be stuck together watching that stupid hotel entrance. After all, Pinky has to come home sometime, and I'm determined to either rule her out or identify her as a threat.

Either way, this ends tonight.

Forever

BANG BANG YOU'RE DEAD

I LOOK IN THE MIRROR ONE LAST TIME, CHECKING MY NEW PERSONA FOR any flaws. Kate Archer, like her predecessor Hannah, died in the hotel incinerator hours ago, but Harley Mannheim is alive and well.

The trendy razor cut black hair of my guise is paired with thick black eyeliner, matching lips, and an assortment of chains and locks that scream emo girl. I'm wearing a tattered MCR tee, pleated schoolgirl skirt, fishnets on my arms and legs, and thick ass knee-high shit kickers with lifts in them complete the outfit. I tucked everything I need for this meeting in a ratty black messenger bag with band patches safety pinned in strategic places.

I look ready for the Warped tour for sure.

After I ate and went down to scan the drive for bugs, I slunk out the back entrance of the hotel as Kate to catch a cab to my storage unit in Berlin. I used the equipment there to cross the burned IDs off my master list, leave notes on what needs to be replaced where, and packed my kit for Prague. All of that is now waiting in an anonymous locker at the train station, along with my ticket and a change of disguise.

All I have to do is clean up the mess and I'm off.

Of course, I have multiple plans for what happens if someone forces me to alter my course, but for the moment, I believe everything is in place. I can dispatch my would-be stalker, verify the drop was legit, and whisk myself to the next stop in my winding path to completing the mission.

For now, I've wiped all traces of my true self from this room and the hotel, all the way down to leaving the fake Kate fingerprints all over the room and hallway to create a trail that will only dead end. My crumbs lead everyone astray and it's why no one has ever realized the Guillotine is a woman.

Humming under my breath, I pop my AirPods in and head down in the lift purposefully so cameras catch an entirely different person exiting the building. Using confirmation blindness to my advantage has always been one of my tricks—people don't see what they aren't looking for, so a non-pink haired woman dressed in direct opposition to either of my previous guises will benefit me.

This time, I loop the park in a different direction, stopping to browse at store windows full of everything from books to BDSM gear, so I seem to move in a random pattern. I duck into allies and through back exits to avoid the main drag as I work my way back to one of the park entrances under the twinkling stars. When I finally reach the Poststadion, I'm walking through the dense woods behind it to make certain I have a view of the box before I set foot anywhere near the pitch.

Meandering like a tourist is the best way to throw off a potential tail; they expect marks to move directly towards their intended goal without pause, so they ignore you.

The lights in the arena are off, so I pull the fancy night vision equipped glasses out to scan the bleachers from the edge of the forest. The glowing green highlights a rabbit hopping along the edge of the fence, but nothing human sized yet. Flicking the setting to full thermal imaging, I adjust my position so I can sweep the area for signatures belonging to weapons or electronics. The glow lights what looks like a lost cell phone, but nothing else untoward.

I creep forward, keeping the special glasses on so I can continue monitoring the scenery as I approach. Something about this job, this drop, and all the events of the last few days has me on edge. I don't believe in coincidences and I sure as hell don't believe in butterflies flapping their wings, causing chaos. Everything happens for a reason, and it's usually bad.

When I get to the fence, I check my watch. It's nine on the nose, and by the time I get to the pickup location, I'll be a minute or two late. Not usually my style, but my gut is screaming for an overabundance of caution, so I'll have to let go of my OCD for this one. I lift my leg to climb over the metal when I spy a small object flying across the field. It's a drone, but it's got something hanging from it and I squint as it glides to the bleachers, dropping the object.

Before I can blink, there's a small explosion, then a cloud of metallic dust that immediately catches on fire and forms a fireball. The blast wave knocks me backwards and I feel like they have slammed me into a brick wall as I fly through the air. Struggling to pull oxygen into my lungs as I lay flat on my back and watch the cloud of fire spread outward after several more explosions, I realize my predictably punctual professionalism almost got me killed.

By a fucking homemade, drone-activated thermobaric bomb, no less!

Who does *that shit?!!*

My mind races as I consider the possibilities outside of some political megalomaniac, but I can't even figure out who would be that desperate to kill me. I've always kept my identity secret and my whereabouts unknown—the drive I picked up in Berlin is also hidden in several other places in the city so the employer doesn't know which drop I'll visit to collect the information.

Unless they set off five other bombs tonight, the fuckers who did this knew I'd be here specifically.

Rolling to my side, I slowly make my way to my feet, trying to triage my injuries as I do so. Possible concussion—check. Probable dislocated shoulder—check. Cuts, scrapes, bruises—check. Ears ringing like the bells of Notre Dame—double check. I look down, feeling the world spin slightly, but I know I have to move before they get the cops in the woods.

I put one foot in front of the other, forcing myself to focus on getting out of the woods and onto the crowded streets. Once I do, I stumble into the first *die Apotheke*[1] I find and pretend to be zonked out on club drugs.

The guy behind the counter barely acknowledges my presence before going back to watching a football match on his small TV. His nonchalance makes me breathe a sigh of relief, and I gather up the items I'll need to clean myself up once I get to the train station.

The sling, bandages, antiseptic, and stitch kit doesn't even make Mr. FC Union Berlin blink, thankfully. I scoop the bag up with my good arm, use the card registered to Harley to pay, and give him a hazy goodbye. I'm hoping all he remembers is a drugged up club hopper with some injuries and nothing else if anyone comes by to question him.

Watching the crowd as I hustle towards one of the back allies I used earlier, I hear the sirens as fire trucks race towards the park, followed by the *Landespolizei*[2] cars with lights flashing. The nearest alley is next to the burlesque bar, and I chuckle at the juxtaposition of starting this idiotic quest for one and ending it at another thousands of miles away.

Irony is a stone cold bitch.

I stopped because I have to put my shoulder back into place before I get to the train station. Injured women draw far too much attention in those types of places, and I need my arms to carry my bags. Ducking into the shadows, I put the bag on the ground and swallow hard. I have to brace myself because I know how badly this is going to hurt; it's not my first rodeo.

My palm is flat against the brick and I close my eyes, pushing backward with my hand to pop the joint back in with the FARES method. A scream nearly rips from my throat and I muffle it with my good hand to keep quiet. The pain is agonizing, but I know it will fade once I can get settled on the train with a bottle of tequila or two. Easing my arm into the sling, I wince until it's settled in place.

With a deep breath, I wipe the tears off my face, grab the bag of supplies off the ground, and get lost in the crowd again.

I have to get out of this city before it kills me.

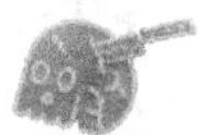

THE STATION IS MODERATELY FULL WHEN I ARRIVE, GIVING ME THE opportunity to get lost in the crowd as I wander aimlessly to divert attention from my true path. I lost my fucking glasses in my tumble, so I have to be careful of camera angles that would benefit biometric facial rec scanning as I dodge the tourists and locals catching their trains. Luckily, I'm able to keep my head down, looking at the boots that change my height by a few inches while I move from one area to the next in a winding line to my locker.

When I arrive at the correct bank, I pause in front of a few others, touching them with the latex print tips that lead to Harley's ID to throw a potential crime scene tech off the trail. I ball my hands at my sides as I approach the actual storage for my bags, nails scraping the tips off until I'm left with only my own skin. I'm not worried about leaving identifiable marks of my own—thanks to the initiation ceremony.

L'Academie burns your fingerprints off with acid to prevent clumsy agents from leaving their mark on accident. They also pull all your teeth and replace them with caps, alter your DNA, and shave your head. You spend the first few weeks of your acceptance into the fold in the infirmary as you heal from the painful body modifications and plastic surgery they require before active duty.

Membership in Les Invisibles is not *for the weak—body or soul.*

Despite all the secrecy and torture, they are painfully aware of law enforcement techniques, even the most innovative spy technology. They taught us to create prints for our IDs, as lack of evidence is as suspicious as actual evidence at crime scenes. They made wigs from human hair with tags embedded by special artisans. On high profile assignments, DNA is created in labs to leave behind to throw off the scent or point the finger at particular people or organizations—nothing gets left to chance.

The Commandant accepts nothing less than perfection. Anyone who fails him is subject to discipline that may or may not include a complete reprogramming of their body and mind. The only exceptions are The Six—Five now—who are given leeway to correct their occasional missteps by recalibrating their missions to achieve the goal while in the field.

Through any means necessary.

Shaking my head at the vile memories of my silent ascension to their elite, I open the locker and yank out the waiting luggage. The smallest bag has a new identity to assume once I find an appropriate place to duck into, and the rest is for the next stop in Prague. With the events of tonight, I may need to redirect the client to a different location for the next drop—or more than one.

Assassins can never be too careful, especially when plans start going wrong one after another. It screams trouble and I have to listen to the voice in my head telling me not to let my guard down.

I strap the bag on and roll the suitcases away from the bank of lockers at a leisurely pace. There should be a hallway at the end of this platform that leads to offices. If I can duck into one of them, I can switch my persona and ditch Harley in one of the trash bins. Once I'm clean, I'll grab some food at a cafe and plug the drive into my tablet to go through the intel on it.

"Fehlschlagen! Fehlschlagen! Bist du verloren?[3]"

Oh fuck. I've caught the eye of some overzealous steward.

"Ich... ich bin so verloren. Ich bin ein amerikanischer Kunststudent und bin gerade hierher gezogen. Können Sie mir helfen?[4]" I stumble over the words with a thick accent, as if I'm struggling to remember how to communicate.

The man's scowl melts away, and he's all smiles once he hears I'm a tourist. No surprise—as much as locals say they hate tourists, it's a huge part of their economy. *"Ich helfe Ihnen gerne weiter. Wohin gehen Sie?[5]"*

Fluttering my lashes, I tilt my head. "Paris. I want to tour the Louvre before my internship begins."

He switches to English once I do, chattering on about where the platform for those trains is and how beautiful Paris is. Of course, the steward can't help tossing in a few barbs about the French or suggestions for better art in Berlin. After I let him go on for a reasonable amount of time, I disengage, heading in the direction he indicated until I feel his gaze leave my back.

I'll have to find another place to switch from Harley to the new look—I've spent far too long under these cameras as it is.

---

1. Drug store
2. Police
3. Miss! Miss! Are you lost?
4. I... I am so lost. I am an American art student and I just moved here... can you help me?
5. I'd be delighted to assist you. Where are you headed?

DEAL WITH THE DEVIL

FUCKING CODA!

Until his drunk ass got into a fight and subsequently rescued by a mystery sorority girl built like the chick from *Encanto,* I was having a fantastic time knicking my way through museums in Spain. I'm sure Razzie was getting his rocks off hacking bullshit white hat stuff while he waited for his job to begin—he's the epitome of a bleeding heart criminal—and Jinx was working his way into the knickers of a HVT married to an important Russian attaché in London.

Every one of us was doing what we love during an intelligence gathering period for our larger missions, but he *had* to go off-book *again.* That moron has been out of control with his legend for over a decade and I'd lay a fat Benjamin that it's because he was drunk, stoned, or some combination of the two.

None of us have ever been able to soothe his demons like her.

I shake my head to clear it of the past—fuck nostalgia. *She* made her choice; *she* left *us.* We had a plan, a good one, and Remy fucked it in oblivion by going rogue. Coda may still mope over it, but I'm way past her betrayal. She forced our hand and got herself killed—we didn't have an option.

However, his decade of self-loathing needs to end. Every time anything goes wrong on a job, he sinks into a pit of despair and uses the rock star persona to cover for his flagellation. I'm tired of putting our goals aside to save his ass time after time.

Hell, Mo flat out refused this time, so he's tired of it, too.

Raz and Jinx are softer than us, though, and they'll always come running. That's why I was stuck in a fucking van for two days, and it's why I'm ducking cops now—ridiculous sentimentality.

I click the button on the left side of my watch, connecting it to the secure line Raz hacked the OS to add. "Status report: everything is *fucked*, man. If this is the chick that you followed from Paris, she's changed looks *again*, and someone is definitely trying to take her out."

"That's the glut of emergency personnel flying to the park?"

"Dude, you gotta look up from your screens occasionally. Did you *not* see the *column of fire* explode from the location?" Raz squawks a bunch of shit in my ear and I roll my eyes, waiting for him to click his way through the news feeds to confirm. "A goddamned drone flew across the field, dropped a charge, and activated a thermobaric bomb. The whole place is damn near leveled."

The hacker goes silent for a moment and I'm sure he's calculating the math on how to assemble and deploy that kind of explosive. His secondary skill set is munitions, and this is probably making him geek out, though he won't admit to it. *La Araña* can't even let his friends see what a nerd he is when he's working.

"Dwyn, that's serious shit. I mean, the timing alone has to be perfect, not to mention the mixture and the transport…"

Duh. It's practically a miniature weapon of mass destruction.

"I know, man. If I hadn't been spying from the other side of the pitch, I'd be Jell-O. I'm not sure she survived." My lips turn down and I ponder why I'm disappointed. I've been pissed since I boarded the train in Alsace-Lorraîne because I had to cut my thieving spree short, but now I'm a little blue.

I love the chase; that's probably it.

Raz barks something, and when I don't answer, he growls. "Pay attention, numb nuts. Your ADHD is going to get you killed some-day. I *said* if she's eluded us through two countries and three plus identities, it's likely she's a pro. It's also possible she got out alive and injured."

"She was pretty close to the blast, Razzie. She's definitely fucked up if she got out." My respect for this unknown chick ratchets up as I consider the amount of wounds she has to be sporting from shrapnel alone. "She'd be bleeding, for certain—maybe even need stitches. But the blast wave knocked me off my feet, and I was at least a hundred thirty-five meters away, give or take. The girl was less than forty-five."

I hear rapid-fire clicking and I know he's hacking local hospitals. "A pro wouldn't hit an ER unless they had no choice, but it's worth a spider to watch. While it scans, I'll get into CCTV feeds in a ten-mile radius of the blast and dip into merchant services to check card purchases of first aid crap bought in between your arrival and now. That might give us a clue."

"What about figuring out what kind of psycho would set off a ther-mobaric bomb in the middle of a Berlin park? That seems relevant," Jinx patches into the convo, sounding annoyed as hell. "By the way, thanks for checking on me, fuckers."

Chuckling, I head towards the closest taxi stand, deciding I'm better served looking for escape routes than urgent care options. "At least we didn't call Mo."

"Think again, asswad." The dark rumble of our pseudo-alpha echoes on the line and I roll my eyes.

Mauricio is *not* in charge of us; we don't have a leader. But if you asked him, he'd swear he's the king of the castle. It's true—his strength and skills are the most aggressive and action packed, but if anyone has tried to fill the shoes of our missing leader, it's Jinx. Grifting requires a three-hundred-sixty degree look at every problem, and his unflappable patience makes him the least likely to start a civil war over every decision.

Yet here's Mo booming his thundercloud over the line like Zeus.

"You couldn't be bothered to drag your ass to the Motherland with us. Don't act like you're running the show, douchebag," I growl, irritated with his imperious bullshit. I know he's working for multiple crime families and organizations at all times, but when he gives a fuck, he always makes time.

It's been a while since he's given a fuck for anything but a job.

"Gentleman," Jinx sighs. "This isn't helping our situation. We have to regroup."

There's a pause on the line as everyone metaphorically tucks them back in their pants. When my cab stops by the closest train station, I hand the cabbie euros, not worrying about change as I wait for someone to speak. No one does and I feel the urge to go steal things to take the edge off. Instead, I break the silence. "Where the hell is the dipshit who got us all into this?"

Mo's laugh is dark. "Between Charice and the Commandant, he'll be feeling that spanking for at least a few more days. Once he's done licking his wounds, he'll join us."

"Us?" Raz mutters and the keys click even faster than before. "I thought you said this was a waste of your precious *time*."

"That was before someone set off a WMD near three members of The Five, Miranda. All the High Legion are demanding blood. I'll be there within two hours."

Fuck me. I'm not sure that's going to make a difference.

His statement starts another round of squabbling on our secure line, and I tune it out as I slip through the crowds. I know Razzie is looking for a trail, but I have a *feeling*. Listening to my gut always works out when I'm on missions, and I will not stop because fucking Mo thinks he's the head dick in charge. Pausing at the map, I memorize the station quickly—that's one of my more rare gifts. If I see a floor plan once, I can memorize it within seconds and create a 3D replica in my mind. The tutors called it something like 'hyper-spatial-topographical synesthesia', but I call it a genetic lottery ticket.

I turn away from the map, looking out into the atrium of the station as the plains and curves of the map fill my vision. The guys are *still* arguing about what the plan will be when Mo gets here, but I'm busy figuring out where I'd go if I was a mystery woman with our skill set and I needed to hide. The offices on the second floor would be a good place to clean up—nosey lookie-loos that will squeal on you often invade bathrooms. Picking up my pace, I hit the escalator and slide down the rail until my feet hit the tile of the second floor.

"Dwyn, are you listening?!"

Clicking the button on the earpiece, I disconnect the call. I don't have time for their petty power plays. Coda may have been the first of us to notice this shadow, but now I'm intrigued. If she survived and dragged herself here without getting caught, this chick might be interesting enough to fuck. Obviously, it wouldn't be anything more because of my lifestyle, but I live for a challenge. Life has become frightfully boring in the past decade, and I'm always chasing one dangerous high or another. A rival organization with a talented chick feels like a high-stakes game I could get invested in for a while.

I duck my head, marveling at how little note regular people take of their surroundings. I've picked the pockets of seven rich idiots by the time I get to the section of the second floor where I saw lockers. It's not like I *need* the money—I need the excitement. My brain races like it's on speed every second I'm awake, and I have to pacify it by constantly staying in motion, constantly challenging it. Lifting wallets while I sneak through crowds is a game more than a vocation, though I make a fair amount of cheese off of it. I never steal from anyone who doesn't look like they can spare when I'm playing around—my inability to sit still shouldn't keep someone's kids from eating.

That might be the only shred of conscience I have, to be honest.

I pull the eyeglasses out of my inner jacket pocket, settling them on the bridge of my nose as I study the lockers. A few clicks switch the lenses to the forensic setting and I walk through the rows until one lights up with more than smudges and smears. They touched this unit with *intention* and there's no way it's the one I want, but it tells me the mystery operative was here. Purposefully leaving a false trail smacks of training as thorough as my own, and though I'd like to stay to find which place she ditched her gear, I need to continue my game of cat and mouse.

Making my way out of the storage area, I walk towards the hallway where I spied the offices earlier. There are two employees chatting near the entrance and I pause, pretending to check my phone as I listen to their grouchy German. They bitch about shifts and bosses for a few minutes, but they don't move—a sure sign my girl isn't here. These guys aren't guards, but they're witnesses, and even if eyewitnesses are unreliable, it's a chance I wouldn't take.

My mind replays the topography of the station, looking for another place she could hide while she changes her appearance. Since the restrooms and offices are out, the next best place would be the employee areas. Places this big are always hiring new people and most of the staff would be used to new faces cropping up without notice. If she can pop into wherever they store their shit for shifts, she could pop open a locker, ditch the emo girl get-up, and put on a new face quickly.

The injuries will be all they'll remember and if she's smart, she'll come up with a story they won't want to share.

I finally hit payday dirt when I recall a room marked 'Nur Angestellte'[1] on the other side of the tracks. That's where she headed;

I can feel it in my bones. Pocketing the glasses, I walk over to the tracks, glancing at the boards near the stairs for train schedules. Jumping across would draw a shit ton of eyes—though I could parkour it—and I don't want to outrun the station police.

The next train comes in twenty minutes, and the schedule for the sleeper car destinations is hours from departure. I should be able to wait and watch without missing her.

Settling in on a bench facing the other side of the station, I open the line to Raz. They're all still bickering and I snicker to myself. All talk and no action makes The Five dull boys.

"I think I have a lead, dickheads. Going dark to monitor Berlin Hbf. Don't do anything I wouldn't."

They don't have time to reply before I cut them off again, amused with my advice.

Let's face it—that's a pretty short list.

---

1. Employees only

Forever

NO

I CONSIDERED USING THE EMPLOYEE AREA TO SHED MY SKIN, BUT IN THE end, I didn't think I'd be quick enough to avoid a bunch of nosy questions because of the sling. Instead, I found a janitor's closet nearby and picked the lock. It's small, dark, and stinks like chemicals, but I'm able to hide the Harley wig and some of her accessories behind boxes of supplies. I'll toss the rest in various garbage cans as I head for the coffee shop upstairs.

Stripping is a gamble—an actual maintenance staff member could come in at any moment—but I can't wriggle out of things with this damn shoulder.

Unzipping the suitcase, I pull out 'Melanie Hannibal of London, England.' She's got shiny auburn tresses streaked with golden highlights, a smart black pantsuit, Louboutins, and tasteful accessories. A pair of small wire-rimmed glasses complete the look, and I use a makeup wipe to remove all the heavy makeup from Harley. It's too dark in here to apply the replacement makeup, so I'll have to make a quick stop in the restroom, but this will do.

"Okay, Remy. It hurts like a bitch, but if you can leave the sling in the bag until the train, you'll be stealthier," I murmur to myself.

As if that settles it, I shove it in my briefcase and sling it over my good arm. There's a plastic bag on one of the shelves, so I put the rest of the Harley disguise in it and tuck that under my arm before I open the door. I have to tug the rolling suitcase with my bad arm, but it's not too heavy so hopefully I'll make it to the cafe without incident. Opening the door slowly, I slink out of the closet and make my way down the platform, keeping my head up so I look busy and impatient.

Melanie has little time for tomfoolery and less for peons—I like her.

Walking through the crowds is easy when you're wearing an RBF—men leer, but they give me a wide berth. I stop occasionally to pull out my phone and pretend to check emails or messages so I can drop small bags of Harley's get-up in them. Something about the station doesn't feel right, but I haven't caught any eyes lingering on me longer than normal. I'll have a better vantage point when I get to the shop because I can position myself at the angle that lets me scan the passers-by easily.

My paranoia is high because of the bomb and seeing Coda; I know it's unlikely that I've been made. My former team member looked directly at me in my disguise and didn't even pause, so it's doubtful anyone else has a clue who I am now or who I was before. The explosive was meant for The Guillotine as an internationally known assassin, not for the woman behind the icon. I just can't shake the feeling that the hit placed on Raz is too conveniently timed, though.

Could someone be looking to take out The Five and simply targeting me as a secondary coup?

I shake my head at that thought. *L'Academie* is far too entrenched in both legitimate and illegitimate circles to come at head on and taking out their elite team would certainly be a declaration of war. War is something they are well prepared for—they have thousands of members in hundreds of countries placed everywhere from the underworld to government. Mobilizing their assets would take little time and almost no effort, so a net of operatives would hunt the person challenging them from both sides of the law.

When I reach the cafe, I locate the best view at the station-side tables and sit with my back against a wall. My bag is within reach and I placed my suitcase where one swift kick would trip an approaching enemy. The waiter appears, jotting down my request for a massive amount of food and coffee, his eyes wide when he leaves with a large tip before I even get my order. His blindness is what I'm paying for and the story I fed him will keep his mouth shut out of sympathy.

I wait quietly, working to log myself into the new tablet and phone I had stowed in the messenger bag. I stored everything in servers locked with better than military grade encryption in several off-shore tech vaults, so I can switch devices as much as I feel necessary. I rarely keep the same tech for longer than an identity; it's another way to put yourself on radars you don't want to show up on.

The Internet is abuzz with Coda's 'good Samaritan', but no one seems to have a clear picture of her, nor have they named Naomi. That story has pushed the random murder of a prominent businessman in a burlesque club further into the shadows, and I smile. Maybe saving his stupid ass wasn't such a dangerous plan, after all. It made a pleasant distraction from The Cobra's timely demise, and once I get out of Germany, I can focus on the Raz job.

My bank account shows the transfer for the slimy asswipe's elimination—a hefty sum that only adds to my vast personal fortune. I don't live like a billionaire, of course, but I have the resources I need to disappear forever if I decide to retire. I have no intention of doing so soon, but it's comforting to have the option to escape the bounties on my head if I choose.

Once my fuel arrives, I pop my AirPods in again, watching the travelers and business people as I eat. The stubborn sensation that I'm being observed won't go away, but nothing out of the ordinary catches my gaze. There are no familiar faces, no nosy onlookers, not even a grinning lech or snotty kid looking at me.

Perhaps surviving a blast with minimal injuries is making me edgier than usual.

What I need is a week of sleep, a gallon of tequila, and some serious fucking—not in that order. I need to relax or I won't be able to focus on figuring out why I almost got my ass blown to bits. Taking a huge gulp of the black coffee, I check my watch. I have an hour before my train leaves and I cannot wait to lie flat, even in one of those stupid cars.

If I get lucky, I won't be anywhere near other humans while I regroup and recover.

THE SLEEPER CAR TO PRAGUE HAS MORE PEOPLE THAN I'M COMFORTABLE with, but I didn't have the option to buy it out or switch modes of transpo so late in the game. Air is faster, but *much* riskier and I avoid sea travel at all costs unless it's a short distance. Being locked in a cargo hold for days reminds me of my escape and it adds so much time to a journey that it's only a nuclear option.

Besides, I would have had to change my entire route to get to a port city and then swap IDs several more times before I got to my final destination. That's as bad as driving and I refuse to burn that many resources if I can simply hide in my room for most of the trip. The cabin isn't huge, but it's comfortable enough to make do.

If I can find the tequila I was considering earlier, that would perk this shit up considerably.

Stopping at the small vanity mirror, I pull Melanie's tresses into a sleek ponytail and shed the suit jacket. I'm left in a black satin blouse and boot cut dress pants, so I perch her glasses on my nose. I should look standoffish enough to scare away any unwanted attention. Grabbing the small wallet with her money and cards out of the briefcase, I exit the room and double check the locks before I walk brusquely towards the dining car.

I pass the usual odd assortment of people taking an overnight train: business people, student tourists, parents taking kids to visit relatives, and a few who may be ne'er-do-wells. The mini-garrotte in my pocket and the knife tucked at the small of my back keep me from worrying about the last category; if one of them were to make trouble, I'd take them out before they laid a hand on me. Small time thugs are *not* one of my many, many concerns at this point.

There's a full house at the counter when I roll up to it, and I groan under my breath. Given that it's ass-crack o'clock, there shouldn't be this many people milling about, but that's my luck lately. I pick a spot near the least populated end, rifling through the menu on the counter with my 'fuck off' face firmly in place. I want to buy a fifth of tequila and some limes before I scurry back to my private compartment to nurse my irritation.

"Pardonnez-moi, mademoiselle[1]?"

A tap on my shoulder *almost* has me reaching for the blade in the small of my back, but I hold off. My posture stiffens as I turn around to look at the hot, sandy-haired guy in black. He's about my age, sporting a leather jacket and a tight tee stretched around what looks to be a lithe frame. I squint at him through Melanie's glasses, pinching my face into a look of annoyance.

"May I help you?" I ask haughtily. I can answer in French, but why give this smirking fool the satisfaction?

His grin widens, revealing sparkling white teeth against his lush lips. "Perfect! You're English."

I mean, for the moment I am, Mr. I Can't Take A Hint.

"Stunning observation." I purse my lips and arch a brow. "Am I blocking your way?"

"Ouch. Are you that eager to get rid of me? You don't even know me." Hot guy pouts and I roll my eyes at him. "I can help you get the bartender's attention."

I snort, raising my hand and crooking a finger at the dude behind the counter. He nods and finishes what he's doing, heading towards us quickly. "Looks like you've outlived your usefulness."

His laugh reminds me of someone, but I can't quite pinpoint it. The baritone is musical and the playful expression he keeps giving me is undoubtedly attractive. I'm no stranger to random sexual gratification and he's definitely flirting—perhaps this is the Universe finally swinging the pendulum my way. I could use some mindless orgasms to clear my head before I have to plot this job.

Plus, isn't 'I almost died' sex supposed to be amazing? I've never come close enough to partake before.

The server makes his way to us and I order two bottles of tequila, two glasses, limes, and a salt shaker. Mystery dude's eyes widen and I shrug. "What's your name, slick? If we're going to drink together, I'll need something to call you."

"Let's go with Slick for now." His dimples deepen as he watches me remove my glasses and tuck them in a pocket. "Just to be fair, and all that jazz, tell me yours."

"I'll go with Jazz," I grin at him, enjoying the banter. He's obviously not going to be a Stage Four clinger if we're not giving real names. I know he's not married—I checked for telltale signs of a removed ring well before I called the waiter over—so I'm not concerned I'll have another mess to clean up.

"Okay, Jazz," he replies, taking the tray when it arrives. He pays quickly and I nod my thanks, waiting for the other shoe to drop. "Shall we find somewhere less crowded to enjoy our drink?"

Fuck yes, we should.

"I have a private cabin; we can go there."

Turning on my heel, I make him follow me as I head towards the sleeper cars. He doesn't know I have a second room next door I purchased specifically in case Melanie had to disappear. The eyes from the terminal made me nervous enough to book it under a different alias for my friend, and it allowed me to feel like I had an escape route if need be.

Little did I know how much escaping I'd get to do there...

1. Pardon me, miss?

TRUTH OR DARE

Aren't I the luckiest thief in town?

I hopped this tin can hoping to find our secret girl, but I haven't seen the emo chick since I boarded. Boredom led me to check out the dining car, and here I am, following an uptight businesswoman from London who's *bound* to be a hellcat in the sack. If I can get laid *and* track the exploding girl, I'll win the pot this month for sure.

Don't be judgy.

The rest of The Five have no interest in anything serious, and we're a bunch of genius level assholes who have a monthly pool for sexscapades. It's very American frat boy, but we don't give anyone the wrong idea about our encounters and we're always safe. Nothing happens without express consent—unlike some of our nastier brethren in *Les Invisibles*—and we obviously don't publicly out the women or men who take part.

We're just not meant for genuine relationships because of our jobs and the wreckage left by the night she died. Jinx and Coda usually have the most points simply because of their specific skill sets, but I'm always centimeters from winning. I make up for quantity with quality because I'm bent like a paperclip. Plus, those assholes work together a lot, and they don't invite the rest of us, which doesn't bother Raz or Mo, but it pisses me off.

I'm a big fan of group projects.

This woman, however, called to me from the second I spotted her from the doorway of the car. Something about the way she carried herself screamed 'freak in the sheets' and I'm definitely *here for it.* Tight-laced women like her are used to being in control, and they practically salivate when you pull out the Dom growl.

I'll have her on her knees before we run out of limes.

The high ponytail bounces behind her as her curvy ass sways with her brisk gait. I'm fairly certain it's extensions or a wig, but that's so common nowadays that I don't give a fuck. If they did not train me in subterfuge, I'd never know—it's a high-quality beauty modification and it had to have cost a fortune. I hope it doesn't slide off while I'm fucking the living shit out of her from behind because that's a buzzkill.

I'm a hair puller and she's got a nice, long leash to tug while I spank that round ass.

"Are you coming in, Slick?"

Her voice pulls me out of my reverie and I nod, flashing my teeth at her. I'm not judgy about body mods because I've had damn near everything done at least once since my initial rebirth at the ceremony on the island. Keeping my visage and frame fresh helps me fade into the background so I can do my job more easily. It's never anything major—just enough to keep from getting on any watch lists. *Les Invisibles* employ the most cutting edge, well-trained surgeons in the world to care for their operatives and I make use of them whenever I see fit—all the members in my skill set do.

"Wild horses couldn't drag me away," I reply as I follow her into a cabin that's palatial compared to mine. Looking around, I take in the luxurious wood paneling, small sitting area, and double bed. I could certainly afford a room like this, but I don't see the point—travel is for getting from one point to another. This kind of spread is more up Jinx's or Mo's alley.

Jazz looks at me with an amused expression as she stows her things in a drawer. "Are you gonna put the tray down and join me on the couch or gawp at the furniture longer?"

Rolling my eyes, I sit the tray on the small table in front of the couch tucked against the wall. "It's not like I haven't seen a joint like this before; I just don't book them myself. Feels wasteful—or it did until now."

The smirk she gives me as she kicks off the pointed heels is wicked, and the groan that escapes her afterward is sinful. "Fuck, I'm glad to be shod of those things. They look good, but they're murder on the toes."

I sit next to her, angling myself into the corner and lift her legs into my lap. No one is more shocked than me when I massage her reddened feet gently. It's not my style to be this intimate with a one-nighter, but something about her…

"Holy shit, that feels good," she mutters as her eyes close. The tension in her frame lightens and after a few minutes, she damn near purrs with satisfaction while I wring her toes between my fingers.

Thieves have strong, nimble fingers from years of learning to pick locks, pockets, and lift items off unsuspecting marks.

When she's literally melting into the cushions, I let go. A strange sense of satisfaction creeps over me and I try to shrug it off by grabbing the first bottle of tequila to pop it open. Her big blue eyes open to watch me with a drowsy expression reminiscent of a cat as I pour us each a shot.

"That was both unexpected and appreciated," she murmurs in a husky voice. "Did I find the last gentleman in Germany somehow?"

"Hardly." I chuckle as I hold my glass out for her to clink. "Cheers."

After she downs the first round, Jazz scoots closer and drapes her legs over mine as she reaches for the salt and bowl of limes. "This time, we'll do it right."

"As you wish." Her lips quirk at the reference and she leans in to lick a spot on my forearm, sprinkling salt on it. I do the same to her, then pour the shots. Within seconds, we toss the alcohol back and our eyes meet as we exchange arms. Jazz holds up a single lime, and I bite it, catching her fingertip purposefully as I do so.

I never move this fucking slowly, but this feels like a high-stakes game of chicken, and it's making my cock twitch.

"Don't bogart the lime, Slick." The enigmatic woman darts forward and places her lips against mine, stealing the fruit from my mouth and leaving a hint of honey behind.

Watching her suck on the fruit, a thousand dirty things flitter through my brain: pounding into her from behind as she holds the back of the couch, splaying her out on the bed tied with ropes on the curtains, sharing the tequila as she rides my cock with her ponytail bouncing… Instead I pour the next shot, ignoring the pressure in my pants that she has to notice. This is too intriguing to ruin by shooting my load early.

Literally.

"How does it taste?" It's a fair question, given the flavor she left in my mouth, that's still teasing my senses.

Wine colored lips curve over canines that are a little sharper than most, and her eyes dance with merriment. "Like tequila and *un paon*."

An unexpected bark of laughter leaves me and I pull her face back to mine to kiss her hungrily. Everything about this woman excites me in a way I haven't felt in a long time. Our lips clash, biting and suckling at first, then our tongues dance as I tilt her head. Jazz wiggles until her thighs are on either side of mine, pressing against me as she kneels on my lap. I can feel the heat of her pussy through those thin slacks and my hips lift to grind into her hard.

Her fingers slide down my shoulder to my shirt, working buttons as the battle of mouths continues, and I groan when she rakes the tips of her nails over my skin. Once she parts the sides, she pulls back to look at the tattoos and scars covering my hard muscles, her brow quirking. "I didn't take you for an ink man, Slick. I'm pleasantly surprised. Where are the scars from?"

"Grew up in a rough neighborhood," I lie effortlessly. It's not entirely untrue, but I sure as fuck can't tell her I was raised by an academy for criminals and they tortured us as training, now can I?

"Mmm," she murmurs, reaching up to push my jacket off my shoulders. I wriggle under her, drawing breathy gasps as my dick hits her while I get my arms out of it and then my shirt. Her eyes roam over my shoulders and biceps, one hand squeezing the muscle. "I like it. Makes you seem… dangerous."

You have no idea, Jazzy.

I don't answer that; instead, I lean forward and bite her lower lip, sucking on it as I work the buttons on her blouse. When I pull back, I push it off of her shoulder and my eyes widen. Her shoulders, torso, and arms are covered in raised UV ink I can feel, but can't identify the exact pattern of in this light. The skin is a Braille map of some intricate artwork that you wouldn't know she had unless you were right up against her, and she's wearing a racy balconette bra with a million little straps. Hard nipples decorated with small knife shaped bars with ruby blood on the tips greet my eyes, and I raise my head to gape at her. I sure as fuck was right about 'tight-laced on the street but a freak in the sheets' and I'm going to come in my pants if she's hiding more beneath those conservative pants.

"Something wrong? You seem… speechless," Jazz purrs, her eyes dark with mirth. "I didn't grow up in an English rose garden, either."

Chuckling, I dart forward and tug on one of the hottest pieces of body jewelry I've ever seen with my teeth. She makes a sound that grabs me by the balls and I raise my hand to tweak and tug at the other side as I continue working her breast with my lips and teeth. Her hips rock over my cock, our bodies imitating what is definitely going to be some ache inducing sex.

Jazz throws her head back, the ponytail hanging down to brush my legs, and that does it. I'm done playing; if I don't get naked with this woman soon, I'm going to blow my load like a fucking middle schooler with a Playboy. I lift my head and grin as I gather her up, dropping everything to the floor as I carry her to the bed and toss her onto it. She bounces briefly, then props herself up on her elbows as she grins wickedly at me. I growl under my breath, stripping my pants, belt, socks, and shoes as quickly as I can. The smile on her lips spreads as the rest of my ink and steel is revealed makes me preen, and when she sees the magic cross, she licks her lips hungrily.

My turn.

I crawl onto the bed, unbuttoning her slacks and tossing them aside. My eyes blink as I take in the matching garter belt, sheer stockings, and ink that covers her form to her feet. Her entire body is one large piece and I wish like hell I had a light to see what she's sporting. Alas, I don't, so I duck my head and tug the lacy thong down with my teeth. A shiver runs over her, and I look up, winking.

"You didn't think to mention this sexy shit of yours, huh?"

Her shoulder rises and falls carelessly as dark eyes look down at me between her thighs. "I'm fond of surprises, Slick. You've been a nice one so far, but your mouth has better uses than all the questions."

Indeed it does.

Shoving her thighs further apart, I lean in to inhale her scent. The scent of jasmine and dragon's blood catches my nostrils, and I let out a slow breath. It makes her squirm in front of my face, so I push away the memories that triggered to focus on the pretty pink pussy in front of me. She's not bare, but close enough—someone carefully waxed a small heart shape on her mound, with the point ending right at her apex. It's another cheeky surprise, and I shock myself by placing a light kiss right there before I spread her lips.

Holy Dismas, I think I'm in love.

Jazz is decorated with a matching bejeweled dagger over her clit and a few tiny silver rings on either side of her labia. They dressed her cunt up like a fashion model, and that level of dedication makes me rub my cock on the bedspread. I want to fuck her into this mattress right now, but something tells me I'll enjoy continuing to draw this out even more. She digs her fingers into my hair, arching her hips up greedily as I nip at her clit. I slip one hand between her lips, tracing her opening with a fingertip as I suckle and tug on her sensitive nub and the piercings. Every motion brings another flood of wetness to my fingertip and when I slide it inside of her, she moans darkly.

Chicks who aren't afraid to scream are my favorite.

"Sweet hell, Slick, keep doing that… right there…"

Her raspy muttering is hot as hell and I follow her lead, slipping one more finger, then another as she writhes under my mouth. I can feel the trickle of her juices running down my hand as she rocks into me, and I grin. Jazz has her fingers tugging at my head hard enough to sting; I fucking *love it.* Coating my last finger and thumb in the ample lubrication she's providing, I slide one more finger inside of her, then push my thumb into the tight hole behind.

A scream rips from her throat, and I bite her clit lightly. Her body goes rigid, and she wails again before bucking wildly. Come squirts out of her like a damn bursting and I continue thrusting my fingers until the shudders stop. Her body goes slack for a moment, only harsh pants breaking the silence of the room as I clean every drop from her shiny, sparkling pussy with my tongue. By the time I lift my head, she's smirking down at me with a red face.

"That better not be all, Slick."

Hell the fuck no, it's not.

I roll up to my knees, face shining with her juices as I grasp her hips and flip her quickly. The girl of my dreams gets the picture quickly, pushing onto her hands and knees before looking over her shoulder with a wink. Yanking her hips to mine, I drive my cock into her as deep as I can go, savoring the throaty moan of pleasure she lets out. I can tell she's ready for it to get rough and so am I—more than ready.

Slamming my hips into her over and over, I lift a hand and smack her ass. Jazz whips her ponytail over her back, her eyes meeting mine over her shoulder as she pushes into my thrusts and the weight of my palm eagerly. I deliver a few more rough slaps to her pale skin, and she takes each one with enthusiasm as her pussy drips over my dick.

Fucking perfect.

My pace picks up and I grin, holding her red ass cheek for purchase as I lift my other hand. I reach down and wind the long ponytail around my wrist to yank hard as I hammer into her harder and faster. Her groans turn to loud screeches and she rocks on her hands to meet every twist of my hips.

I rub my hand over the hot skin I spanked, savoring the animalistic feel of our fucking. Jazz is giving as good as she gets and I won't last much longer. I stop for a moment, pulling her up so her back is against my chest and I'm holding her neck taut with her hair. My hips snap faster, and when my balls tighten, I slide my head up to grasp her throat.

That does it.

Her walls flutter and grip my cock like she's trying to milk it dry, the orgasm crashing into both of us hard enough to make me see stars. Once the world comes back into focus, I let go of the ponytail, breathing hard against the back of her neck. My come is dripping over her thighs when I pull out, but she flops forward onto the bed with a satisfied sigh.

"Rest first, round two in a few."

Yes, ma'am.

Forever

REBEL

Luckily for me, Slick is a heavy sleeper.

I sneaked out before the sun came up and hide myself away in my room next door while I cleaned up and got my shit together for arrival. More's the pity, but the train to Prague isn't *that* long, and though my itch was thoroughly scratched, I still have this odd sensation of being watched. Copious sex and alcohol didn't dim my hyper-alert senses for very long, so I'm taking it seriously as I stuff the remnants of Melanie into a few tied off trash bags. She was *a lot* of fun in the end, but I can't risk my tryst seeing me again as we arrive.

The announcement startles me as it blares over the speakers, and I look at the mirror one last time. Now I'm Starla Jaansen, an intrepid investigative reporter with a short purple pixie cut, freckles, and a nose ring. I look five years younger with the light makeup and pink glossy lips paired with a long-sleeved halter, overalls, and Doc Martens. I stowed the briefcase in the suitcase and I'm wearing a rainbow Ita bag with various pins inside the clear display pouch. The remains of Melanie's ID are shredded and flushed down the toilet, including her tickets and passport.

I spend as much on making fake IDs as I do disguises, but it's how I've stayed alive in the shadows as long as I have.

Peeking at the video feed from next door on my phone, I wait for Slick to leave, frowning at the look of disappointment on his handsome features. Despite not seeming like he'd get attached, he looks perturbed at my absence, so I'll need to watch him leave before I exit my compartment. My new persona is rock solid, but my arms are exposed and I'm not sure how much he could see in the dim lighting last night. The massive full body art I had done after my escape from the island is not immediately noticeable in normal lighting, but since it was used to cover scars and brands, some of it draws attention if you know what to look for.

Turning my trauma into art was part of my self-prescribed therapy.

When my one night wonder finally exits the train—sans baggage, I notice—I step out of my room and roll my way to the doors. I just barely make it off the train before they call the new departure, and I have to duck and weave around busy travelers. *Praha Hlavni Nadrazi* is crowded with early morning commuters and tourists—the perfect escape into anonymity. Once I'm above ground, I hail a cab, giving the driver the name of my hotel.

This time, the driver doesn't chatter and I'm able to dive into information about my various drop sites around Prague. I'm not eager to choose one out of the public eye again, though I have no idea if my current employer is the one who tried to blow my ass up or not. Theoretically, the contractor who devised and implemented that device isn't following me, and whomever they may hire next doesn't know where I've gone. Of course, if it's the rule-breaking douche looking to off Raz, they know what city I'm in, but not which of my sites I'll choose to retrieve the next drive at.

If I choose one of the more tourist-filled spaces, they're less likely to try again, though the chance is never zero if someone has issued a fucking contract. People like me can slip in and out without leaving a trace, and crowds make kills even easier if you're versed in close weaponry or poisons. I prefer my signature kill method, but when the situation calls for it, I'm trained in damned near every method you can think of.

L'Academie is thorough in making certain their future members have every tool at their disposal. I can rock a lab or a fighting ring if I have to, but I'm partial to the spill of arterial blood when my blades and wires slip through skin and bone like butter.

Ruthlessness is not only expected, but rewarded in Les Invisibles.

By the time we pull up to the Mandarin Oriental Hotel, I've whittled my choices down to a few locations that might serve my needs. They're all on the tramline and close to here if I need to escape quickly. My storage unit in this city is a decent distance from these—which means I'll have to drop everything inside and hire a car to take Starla to my secret lair before I burn this identity. I'm always cautious, but now I'm almost paranoid. I may have to add an inconvenience fee to this job simply to cover the amount of disguises and paperwork I'll have to replace.

Fucking Coda—he started this bullshit.

"Vítejte v hotelu Mandarin Oriental, madame. Máte rezervaci[1]?"

The impeccably dressed porter at the door offers to load my bag on a cart, but I smile and shake my head, mimicking a normal human. *"Ano. Jmenuji se Starla Jaansen a bydlím v prezidentském apartmá[2]."* His demeanor changes immediately—like most staff. The minute I divulge my five star reservation, he knows he'll get drawn and quartered if he so much as irritates me. "I speak English, if you prefer."

I know he doesn't, but switching to my native language makes it much easier to maintain a believable accent. Since I seem incapable of choosing personas without one this job, I'd like to give my brain cells a rest so I can focus on the bigger problems. The bellman smiles broadly and nods, gesturing towards the front desk.

"I will assist you with checking in, Madame. Are you here for business or pleasure?"

Again, with the small talk. *Sigh.* But it gives me an opportunity to spread details of my legend, so I suppose I should be grateful I don't have to start the tale on my own. "Business, I'm afraid. I am here to write several pieces in your lovely city for my employers, though I suspect I'll enjoy it very much."

"A reporter? Excellent! I will have the concierge for the VIP suites send up information on tourist destinations and some local favorites for you to browse. We are at your disposal anytime, Ms. Jaansen."

I hide my smirk behind a cough. He thinks I'm a travel blogger or influencer—hence, the luxurious accommodations. That will ensure I'm given everything short of a severed leg when I ask, not to mention guaranteed privacy. They'll work to impress me, but they won't crowd me lest I report famous clients cannot trust their discretion.

"I appreciate that…" I look up at him with wide eyes, waiting for him to fill in his name as if it's important to me.

"Tomáš," he supplies as he rings the bell on the counter with a frown. He's not thrilled that the desk attendant isn't here to immediately greet me and I can tell it's going to be discussed later when a pretty girl with doe eyes and a tight uniform appears.

"Good morning! Welcome to the Mandarin Oriental Hotel. May I have your name for your reservation?"

Tomáš glares at the girl again, but I don't want to get involved in their workplace politics—it will make me memorable. So I smile back and give her my name, letting the porter seethe next to me as she fumbles through checking me in. If I were to guess, she's a relative or girlfriend of the manager and her job performance leaves a lot to be desired. That would absolutely explain why the very proper middle-aged bellman is ready to throttle her.

Incompetence is ninety percent of why I have a solid clientele, so I understand his frustration.

Once I get my room keys, I press a five hundred *koruna* bill in his palm and wink as I make my way to the elevators leading to the Baroque tower on my own. I'm sure it's not normal for someone living in this suite to take their bags up, but I'd prefer to catch the details of my route to my room without distraction. Tomáš seems ready to go on a very unprofessional yet apologetic rant about the girl and I need quiet as I map the hotel in my mind.

That's a trick Dwyn taught me; I've never met anyone as adept as him in memorizing topography and blueprints.

Wrinkling my nose, I push memories of my past aside again. I haven't thought about any of them in so long that I'd almost forgotten their faces. Now that I faced Coda in that stupid bar, all I can think about is the things we all shared and the ache of their betrayal. It's regressing me to post-escape Remy and I fucking hate it.

The elevator rings when it reaches my floor and I step off in a clean, modern looking hallway with very few doors. They have gold engraved plaques with the names of the suites, and it's easy to figure out that mine is at the far end. It's the most expensive room in the joint and by far the biggest. I don't *need* this much space, but I'll be damned if I don't pamper myself after almost being blown to bits for a flash drive that might contain nothing useful.

Waving the key in front of the sensor, I let myself in, leaving the suitcase by the door as I explore my temporary base of operations. The lower level has a bathroom, atrium, and bedroom, along with a door to the adjoining deluxe room. At the far end, they tucked the small area with the stairs to the next floor in with the kitchen. The upstairs will be where I do all my work, so I peek into the main bedroom briefly before grabbing my bag.

I enjoy the amenities of an obscenely expensive place like this because I don't have a home of my own and never have. There are crash pads littered across the globe, but they are all simple and functional hideouts for when I need to stay in place while I plan for longer jobs. None of them have luscious balconies or creature comforts—they serve their purpose when they are needed, and that makes them suitable.

The vast living area on the upper level is the open floor plan I would adore if I kept a house, and I look out at the terrace that seems made for entertaining guests. My view of the city is drool-worthy, and the decor is expertly placed to make it feel casual, yet elegant. Potted fern and plants surround the gorgeous table and loungers—the rich get pampered in ways mere humans cannot fathom in spaces like this.

Yes, I could see myself buying a suite like this if I ever retired and stayed somewhere for longer than a few days or months.

I stow the bag in a cabinet that locks and pull up the ride share app on my phone. I'd like to sleep and have a bite, but I need to head to the storage unit for an hour or two. Once I get the supplies for this part of the trip squared away and place restock orders for Berlin and Paris, I'll be able to relax. I book my ride and head downstairs, stopping by the bathroom to check my appearance. I want to marvel at the marble splendor of the master bath, but I save that for later.

Now to figure out all the ways I can get in and out of this private tower on my way to meet the driver.

An assassin leaves nothing to chance.

---

1. Welcome to the Mandarin Oriental Hotel, Madame. Do you have a reservation?
2. Yes. My name is Starla Jaansen and I'm staying in the Presidential Suite.

Forever

THE PAST IS DEAD

Paris was a clusterfuck of major proportions, and they're all pissed at me.

The ass-chewing I got from the Commandant was bush league compared to the shit the guys gave me. It's not like I *purposely* got rescued by a mystery chick they've been trailing across Europe. After I detached from Charice and head for Berlin, Mo informed me he was joining us on the hunt. Apparently, Dwynnie almost got liquified by a WMD, and now he's following a lead to Prague.

My short-spoken Italian friend refused to give me more details over the phone; instead, he demanded I meet him, Raz, and Jinx in Germany. If Dwyn confirms the chick is our girl, we'll head for the Czech Republic and if not, we can regroup in place.

Tapping my fingers on the polished seat arm, I glare at the empty private plane in disgust. I don't mind the trappings of my fame, but I despise the silence. I'd never admit it if anyone asked, but I often long for the time when I had a tight-knit crew and we formed an unbreakable circle around the one person we'd die for. When she died, she took the most vulnerable parts of us with her, and none of us have ever forgiven ourselves—it's why it's hard for us to be around one another for very long.

Remy was our heart and soul, and I'm the only one who has a marginally healthy outlet for my sorrow and regret.

I know well that my drinking, drugging, partying, fighting, and fucking anything in my path is *not* healthy, by the way. My outlet is my music and fans would be absolutely depressed to know how much of it is about our long-lost partner in crime. The other shit is simply a fucked up coping mechanism to help me make it through the fucking days without throwing myself off a bridge. Hell, I'm pretty sure the guys expect to have to peel me off the concrete one day, but I'm a stubborn bastard. Remy wouldn't have liked me even considering that shit, and as much as I run around like a prepubescent fuckwit for my public persona, I try to remember the good things she brought out in me.

Christ, I'm a sappy fuck when I'm alone; therefore, I hate it.

The scotch next to me calls my name and I toss it back with a sigh of satisfaction. Usually, my antics don't require the entirety of The Five to come running, and I'm uncertain why they're all hyped up now. Sure, some asshole set off a bomb in a German park, but with the rise of global extremists, it's likely to be written off as a terror attack. It isn't going to lead to a cub reporter digging into *Les Invisibles'* business; the internet doesn't even link it to crimes. As usual, the government is linking it to whomever they hate at the moment in the absence of evidence of someone claiming credit.

I wish I could remember more about my savior. The blonde hair and Brazilian jiu jitsu stuck in my mind, but everything else went dark not long after. I don't know why I passed out so easily—the assholes punched and kicked for a minute or two, but it wasn't prolonged. I hadn't even drank that much. The whole thing is weird as fuck, and I can't wrap my hands around the situation. My lack of recall pisses the guys off and I know they assume I was far more wasted than I was; it's not an unfair supposition, of course, but this time, it's not accurate.

Is it possible the mystery chick knocked me out?

Shit. I hadn't even *considered* that until now, but it would explain *a lot*. The world going dark, waking up in another location without coming to… if that's what happened, who the shit is this fucking girl? Maybe Dwyn is right; she *could* be an operative from some competing faction. But why didn't she kill me? She clearly had a perfect opportunity once she had me alone and unconscious. Taking out a member of The Five would no doubt help her rise in the ranks of her employers and in the underworld—all it would take is a well-timed picture on a cell phone to provide proof of her kill.

I lean back in my seat, pushing the call button for the attendant. Another drink is imperative if I'm going to go this route. Figuring out who might want me dead but is careless enough to send some silly-looking chick in a sorority outfit to do it is going to take a lot of brain power. I mean, the chances of her succeeding were only good if I was thoroughly trashed, and I didn't decide to hit that bar until the last minute. That would suggest we have a mole in my legitimate business and I'll have to call Charice.

Raz is going to have quite a few dossiers to comb through based on my staff, and the reporters Charice tipped off.

"WELCOME TO BERLIN, MR. RAMONE. WE ARE DESCENDING AT THE Berlin Brandenburg Airport. Once we're cleared to land, we will taxi to the private landing area. We have cleared your driver to meet the plane and will be ready to escort you to your destination."

My eyes pop open and I rub my face blearily. The flight wasn't long, but I caught a few winks after I brooded about my rescuer for a while. I needed it—I've been running on very little rest since the Paris incident, and the guys will expect me to jump right in.

Not that my job is physically demanding like Mo or Dwyn, but I have to focus on applying pressure in the right places, which takes brain function.

"Thank you," I mutter to the woman who clears my glasses and shit away.

She gives me a saucy wink and I groan. I am *definitely* not in the mood to play grab ass with her. It wouldn't be the first time I did, but the events of the past few days have left me suspicious of everyone who approaches me. It's not like this is the *l'Academie* plane, so I can't trust how thoroughly the staff has been vetted. Charice booked this flight and while she's careful to make certain I don't run into any psycho fans, her checks won't catch the sort of people I'm watching out for.

When we're on the ground, I pick up my messenger bag, slinging it over my shoulder as I jog down the stairs. They parked a large black SUV with the engine running, and I know one of my partners is inside, waiting to brief me. The baggage handlers move my suitcases and guitar cases into the trunk, earning themselves a glare when they slam the latter in too roughly. It doesn't matter if the case isn't housing a half million dollar instrument like the first—they don't fucking know that.

"Watch it," I growl as I yank the door open and hop in.

Jinx raises a brow at me as I shut the door harder than necessary. "Feeling temperamental, music man?"

I roll my eyes. You'd think my cover doesn't afford us a great deal of access—particularly this dick—and I'm only useful for an occasional distraction. "I'm just as pissed as you assholes about Paris and I've been on a plane alone with my thoughts for hours—what do you think?"

"I see." He tilts his head, giving me a half smirk. "Did those thoughts bear any fruit or were you too busy banging the stewardess again?"

This is why we don't work together in a group like we used to. It's not playful teasing or joking camaraderie. Without the balance of Remy in the middle, we poke at each other until someone blows up and leaves.

Usually, it's Mo.

"Fuck off, Jinxy. I was actually combing through interactions because I think if I'm being hunted, it's weird that I'm alive. So I've been working on a list of staff or press for Charice to verify so Razzie can do his thing. They're the only people who knew my last second decision to stop at that stupid tourist trap."

He hums, pulling his phone out. The SUV doesn't have a partition, so he won't call the others, but he's tapping away at his screen. "Raz thinks that's a solid possibility."

"Gee, I'm glad Professor Pokemon approves."

Jinx rolls his eyes and sighs. "I don't get why it always has to be so hard. We grew up together; we took oaths together. Why are we such a fucking mess now?"

I snort, arching my brow at him. "You know why. We were split on trusting Arnaud, and those of us who disagreed were right. We lost everything that night."

His fist slams into the seat in front of him—an unusual display of physical anger from our resident grifter. "Coda, we had to take the risk. The lower legion members told the Commandant's staff about the routing plans they found. We were going to get caught for certain without intervention."

"Instead, we blew up the only person any of us ever cared about. If they had caught her, she *might* have talked her way out of it. She was that good," I murmur, as I look out the window.

"Nonsense," Jinx snarls. "Remy was good, and the Commandant favored her, but he couldn't allow such disrespect to stand. If she'd been allowed to live, it might have been like... Rinna. Death is far preferable to what they did to that traitor. It took *years* for them to allow her to pass away, Coda. Could you have watched them do that to our girl?"

Fuck. No.

"I would have gotten us all killed trying to free her from that."

He shrugs, looking out his own window. "We all would have. Then where would the changes we've been able to push through have been? Would we have been able to stop some of the more malicious shit during training or raised age limits for full membership to protect kids? No."

My expression gets stormy and I shake my head. "I'd trade every one of those things for her to be here. Compassion isn't any of our strongest suits; we simply see the upside to creating less collateral damage to our legions."

"I didn't claim to be a humanitarian, Coda. I don't even know the names of most of the people in *l'Academie* since I graduated—only case numbers when there're issues the High Legion comes back to vote on. But I think we made sure the tactics used to break us have been… redirected in ways that are beneficial to everyone."

Turning back to him, I tilt my head. "Why is the Commandant off-campus? He *never* leaves the island."

"Mo says it's some political alliance favor. They requested him in the States for some kind of trial. You know that man doesn't share his agenda with anyone."

"How old is the bastard, anyway? Shouldn't he die soon and let us take over *Les Invisibles*?"

Jinx laughs. "Someone told me once that the Commandant had been alive longer than most nations and would continue to be alive long after we were dust. The metaphor is poetic, but I doubt it's accurate. Though, I don't know what the hell he does to stay looking not a day older than when we first saw him. Must cost the same as the GDP of a small country."

"Yeah, well, he's still an ugly son of a bitch. The eyepatch doesn't help," I grumble.

It's nice to be doing something other than bitching at one another, though I'm surprised Jinxy was as forthcoming as he was about

Remy's death. I've been writing songs about my pain for years, but I've never seen any of those dicks do anything that remotely says they're healing from the trauma of losing her.

Maybe we can finally move on as a team — together.

Forever

WTF DO I KNOW?

THE RIDE TO MY STORAGE UNIT TAKES ALMOST AN HOUR. I'M FAIRLY certain the driver is pissed—he's been muttering to himself in Croatian. Fortunately for him, it's a language I'm not fluent in. I can pick up a word or two here and there, but none of it indicates that I'd leave him alive if I turned on my translator app to hear the rest. Since I'm trying to keep a low profile until I notify my contact I've arrived in Prague, he's going to live another day.

As if it's my fault that traffic caused a thirty-minute ride to take twice as long—grow up, twatwaffle.

When we finally pull up to the gates of the facility, I exit the car without a word. I have paid him through the app, and I'll have another car come to take me back to a spot close to the hotel. I hate considering what I'll do if I can't get a ride share to drive that distance depending on when I leave, but I'm resourceful. I can find my way back without creating an angry witness who will be eager to describe his bitchy fare.

The locks at the high metal gates are biometric, and I have to slip the fingerprint belonging to Starla off to start the sequence. Once I replace it, I take one of the emerald green contacts out and scan my iris. One by one, I allow the security systems designed by my former ally to check each data point before they slide open. I know there are two security cams hidden within the design of the bomb-proof doors, but they'll catch the glare off of my sunglasses and miss their window to scan my face.

Simple tricks like that will help me keep *Les Invisibles* from realizing the rumors of my death were extremely exaggerated.

Using their own equipment and properties against them is a dangerous game, but their reach is far superior to any other organization in the world. After the explosion, it took me weeks to get from the island off Argentina to Europe without raising flags. When I first continued my chosen profession, I wasn't as flush with cash and resources as I am now. So I used all of my knowledge about their bureaucracy, infrastructure, and business practices to infiltrate their dominion in ways that would never get noticed. Hiding my shit in some of their storage areas, siphoning tiny sums, and name dropping were tricks that helped me get started.

After The Guillotine cut a bloody swath across the underworld, I didn't need to do that anymore. Well, except co-opting their buildings in a few cities where it's harder to find the space and security I require for my 'nests.' Obviously, I still do that and it amuses the piss out of me every time I update their systems to include yet another shadow identity that grants me unfettered access to places I should never be.

You'd think with the best hackers in the world at their disposal, they'd assess the weak spots in their cybersecurity, but pride goeth before a fall, I suppose.

The locks finally click open, and I step inside the spider's lair. I slide my sunglasses down, using the mirrored frames to reflect light back at the cameras as I walk confidently down the main aisle. People who scurry or look unsure are suspicious, so I strut my way towards row Omega with the air of a seasoned agent who absolutely belongs here. I house my collection of legends and tech in Omega Six—a little joke to myself—and it's the largest unit at the end of the section.

I have to repeat the biometric checks in a randomized order, then I put a series of encryption keys before my unit opens to reveal one of my bolt holes.

The space is chilly as hell because they maintain the temperature in perfect balance to keep servers and weapons in optimal condition. The locked titanium vault on the right holds an array of weapons that would make any assassin drool, though my preference is to stick with my signature kill style. On the left, a large embedded fixture holds rows of labeled garment bags with their matching accessories and IDs stowed in stacked bins. I painstakingly crafted each persona to provide an indestructible legend. Even law enforcement would be loath to find fault with the credentials I create.

I'll gather my replacement shit before I leave, but first, I want to do some research. Heading to the back end of the room, I sit my ita bag down and climb into my captain's chair. The sound of monitors and towers coming to life fills the silence, and I tug the floating keyboard rest towards me.

Looking at one screen, I open command windows to multiple layers of the web, pulling up information on Raz, the jobs people attribute to him, and the resulting chaos from those events. On the next one, I send bots to comb through the deepest corners of the dark web to find out what contractors are known for using bombs like the one in Berlin. Finally, I pull the flash drive out of my bra and push it into an air gapped tower that is completely outside of my system so I can review the info on it.

The prompt on the screen wants a key for the encryption, so I use the one I memorized from the last drive, and another audio file plays.

"Greetings again, Guillotine.

We are delighted you have accepted our rather unorthodox job. We have made all efforts to ensure that we followed your protocols to the letter, including depositing this information in all of your ascribed locations across Berlin.

The drives are all encoded with twenty-six bit encryption and without you inputting your code, the data will immediately rewrite itself over a thousand times to prevent it from falling into the wrong hands.

I must say: your fail safes are impressive, but they lend towards the dramatic, no?"

Pausing the diatribe, I sigh. One could assume my employer is French by the way he asked that question, but I have to believe that someone this shadowy and egotistical would not only use a voice modulator but also change their diction. The whole thing reeks of someone who loves Fifties spy movies, but I'm curious, so I hit 'play' to listen.

"No matter. We are eager to benefit from your services, Guillotine. La Araña has been a thorn in our side for many years, and though he never claims responsibility for his actions, we know he is the one who has ruined some of our most valuable operations. His connection to Les Invisibles has protected him for far too long, and with your help, he will be the first domino to tumble.

What happens afterward?
A new world order, of course! The uninterrupted reign of many organizations in this world who think themselves infallible is imminent.

Omnes una manet nox,[1] *Guillotine.*

We will leave another bundle of information gathered by our comrades in the city of your choosing. Use the secure link within this drive to give us coordinates of a city of your choosing and drop sites you wish us to use.

Since we have not seen La Araña in person for many years, we are aware it may take some time and continued support through our resources to track and plan your mission. The account number for your incidentals is also on this drive, and you are free to use that for expenses. We expect weekly check-

ins on your progress from whatever location you choose while you lure The Spider into your web.

Do not fail us, Guillotine. The consequences will be most dire, and the stakes could not be higher. Ridding our world of shadowy societies that control everything from places normal people cannot imagine is vital."

Just fucking great. It's some nut job crusader after Raz.

Every time I've met a charismatic weirdo trying to gather followers and 'disrupt' the status quo, it's always a rampant narcissist who plans to assume control under the flag of inclusion—right before they put their boot on everyone's neck. Humans are as much an animal as our relative species; we just have the brainpower to do our evil deeds on a global scale. It's stupidly predictable and honestly? I'll take the devil I know over the shadowy lunatic every day of the week.

The Commandant is a sadistic, capitalistic sociopath—don't mistake that. But he's also a business savant and a genius in his own right. He doesn't decide based on ideology or emotion; everything is clinically assessed and strategized to minimize the footprint of *Les Invisibles*. If he takes out a rival organization, it's with laser precision and little to no collateral damage.

I feel this lunatic thinks they're some god's gift to the world, which is naïve and deluded. Most gods range from indifferent to murderous to their own children, much less some random false prophet.

Chaos was always Dwyn's forte. I prefer plans and strategies, but that will not work with some psycho with a deity complex.

Putting my head in my hands, I let out a long, tired sigh of frustration.

On one hand, this is *not* my circus and those are no longer my monkeys. That decision was made over a decade ago and I'm not going back on it because some megalomaniac is trying his hand at the Bond villain trope. However, I'm not keen to end up in a retelling of *The Man in the High Castle*, either. And I don't actually want to murder my way through my ex-friends—not anymore, at least. The crazy asshole on the recording definitely made it sound like that could be on the table.

I should leave right now. Catch a plane to Bali and not look back. Let everyone fend for themselves while I fuck cabana boys and girls and drink alcohol out of pineapples. Even if the world might end, I'd be hanging out on the beach listening to the ocean when it went ka-boom.

It's not like a give a fuck about people, right?

Running is a bitch move, Remy.

I'm no one's bitch.

Shaking my head at my own stubborn idiocy, I turn back to the screens and start digging into the information, filling up the screens about Raz and bombers. I obviously have *no* survival instinct and should be committed to a rubber room for going along with this insanity. Something about those dumbass boys has always made me act like a fool and making this choice only solidifies it.

I, Remy Arsine Benoit, am a stupid, stupid girl and I deserve my fate.

With that decided, I set five more spiders loose within the deep darks of the 'Net: one for Dwyn, Coda, Mo, Jinx, and the last one for my arch-nemesis, The Commandant. I cannot untangle this bullshit without finding any morsel and scrap of dirt and info about all the known players. I may not be *La Araña*, but I was his pupil and I'm determined to figure out what the actual fuck is going on.

---

1. One night is awaiting us all.

Forever

I'M IN CHARGE

Coda and Jinx are somber when they arrive at our Berlin safe house. It's a tad unusual, but given that Dwyn hasn't checked in for hours, I suppose it's not unwarranted.

Wrangling this band of impulsive muppets is exhausting.

There was a time I didn't have to take control; a time when we could move seamlessly and with utmost precision. We were lethal and feared during our last few years at *l'Academie*—the High Legion was eager for us to ascend to our thrones. That smooth transition was fucked totally by a young girl with misplaced optimism, and she paid for it with her life.

I know the others have their moments of doubt and pain over the choice they forced us to make, but I have never wavered. We were selected and groomed for the positions we now hold. Our entire lives were a prequel to the moment we sat in the chamber with the High Legion, and running away to some tropical island for a childish dream was as stupid as it was naïve. We would have been on the run for the rest of our lives and even if we had the skills and resources to hide, they discovered us before we could execute the plan properly.

A plan revealed is a failure waiting to happen.

If *she* had simply *listened* to me, we could have regrouped or, better yet, abandoned the whole thing without incurring the wrath of the Commandant. Her death wouldn't have sent Coda spiraling into his cover like an addict or taken away Raz' smile. Jinx could drop the mask occasionally and Dwyn wouldn't take jobs meant to kill him with glee. And I...

Well, I wouldn't be stuck trying to manage the massive amount of untreated trauma that my team became.

She didn't deserve to die.

Intellectually, I know that. Deep inside, I recognize that she would have suffered a terrible fate if they had caught her alive. Escape wasn't possible by the time she implemented her plan, and we had to decide to trust our closest advisor to help us out of the mess. He betrayed us all, but our punishment was nothing compared to what Remy would have received if she survived.

No one will admit who killed the bastard, though his death started the legend of The Guillotine. Until more kills started piling up with the same signature, I assumed one of my team took Professor Arnaud out while he was lecturing at Oxford. But no... a new assassin killed one of the best forgers in the world like he was nothing.

Shaking my head, I put that *coglione* out of my mind. The Guillotine has undercut every single one of us on jobs in the past, and I'd like to get my hands on him to show my appreciation for his craft. Of course, he might not *survive* my show of thanks, but that's the point.

Thanks to Coda's mounting instability, our adversary slit The Cobra's throat before he could pump him for information we needed for our next job. His usual tantrum followed and now we're on a wild goose chase for the woman who saved his hide in a bar instead of regrouping for the mission we're *supposed* to be completing.

I hope the old bastard chewed his ass like a dog's toy.

I wave off the car, walking up the stairs to our penthouse apartment. *Les Invisibles* pay us handsomely for our efforts and The Five are the most highly sought after team. Our wealth has granted us the ability to invest in safe houses, crash pads, bolt holes, and hiding places throughout the world. None of them are tied to headquarters we actively use, so even the Legion has no idea where we go when we're working unless we stop at *Les Invisibles* owned properties for supplies or equipment.

When I open the door, Coda is yelling at Raz and the hacker is smirking at him as a video of him blacked out at a cafe plays on one of his dozens of monitors. I close my eyes for a moment, wishing they'd get their shit together as I have before we all get killed.

"Enough!" All eyes turn to me as I stride in and slam the door behind me. "Coda realizes he's an idiot, Raz. No need to make an unpleasant situation worse. Have we heard from Dwyn yet?"

I wish I could say it was unusual for the thief to go dark for days or weeks at a time, but it isn't. He gets distracted by a self-selected target and forgets to check in constantly. Most of the time, we end up finding him when some priceless item goes missing in a feat of impossible derring-do and the media gets wind of it. Raz has feeds set up specifically to watch for major thefts and heists to prevent this from happening.

"No. He went dark last night when he said he'd found a lead in the train station and hasn't returned any messages since. Most of the trains he *could* have caught have reached their destination by now."

Raz looks annoyed and I know that means our light-fingered friend has also ditched any equipment with tracking in it. "I know what you're thinking, R, and I still forbid you to insert a chip anywhere on his body while he sleeps."

"Christ, Mo! Every time he does this, we waste as much time finding him as we do covering up Coda's fuck-ups! One little needle would keep us in the know. He'd never notice." Raz rakes his hands through hair, agitation leaking from every pore.

"He's got a point, man. Charice had one put on me because of crazy fans. That's how you found me so quickly," Coda mumbles. "Razzie linked it to my *LI* watch app."

"You are a unique case. We're less worried about rival factions kidnapping you than crazy fans. Cops or other organizations could catch Dwyn—the chip would help them trace us. It's not the same, Coda."

Jinx rakes his hand through his hair, perching on the corner of Raz's desk. He and the hacker have a mutually beneficial relationship and his presence softens Raz's cold intellectualism. "I knew I should have tagged along."

"You came here to help me run the surveillance, J. It's not your fault." Raz finally shuts the feeds off, and Coda's posture relaxes a tad. "Dwyn does this shit; Coda's right."

"Holy fuck, say that again while I have this recording!" The rocker fumbles with his phone, grinning like a madman.

Madre de Dios, these fuckers are going to be the end of me.

"Stop fucking around. We need to figure out where Dwyn is and if he tailed this chick. It's looking more and more like she's an operative for someone, though her objective is unclear." I cross my arms over my chest, walking over to the monitors. "Did you find her on the CCTV *before* Coda made his grand entrance?"

They all look at me, and Raz turns bright red. The hacker spins in his chair, furiously clacking at the keys as he watches three or four feeds simultaneously. I'll never understand how he can do this shit—it bores me to death. I want to be up close and personal with my targets, not sitting here watching the world's most boring home videos.

"Sorry, Mo. I should have thought of this before. I get so irritated—"

I cut him off before he starts in on Coda's recklessness. "We're doing it now, Raz. No harm, no foul. It may not bear any fruit, but until we hear from Dwyn, it's the best lead we have." Turning to the others, I shift gears. "While he's scanning, talk to me about recouping our losses after The Cobra bit the dust."

"Shit, man, I didn't see a single guy anywhere *near* that fucker and I swear to Hendrix, I *wasn't* drunk!" Coda rubs a hand over his face and the shame radiates off of him like cartoon stink lines.

"I didn't say you were, man. We're all aware that the bastard slips through cracks we didn't even know were there. What I need to know now is how we're going to get the intel we expected to milk The Cobra for without his help." I look at Jinx, waiting for him to come up with a spectacular plan on the spot.

It's his fucking superpower, I goddamned swear.

"The Cobra is survived by a trophy wife, three girlfriends in various countries, and a daughter many believe he was grooming to take his place when he retired. Any or all of them could hold keys to his empire—he was paranoid as hell. He could have left fucking pieces of his books with all of them like horcruxes," Jinx muses as he stares into space. "We may have to track the women down and worm our way into their homes to find out."

Snorting, I shake my head. "That sounds like a lot of work for a whiff of a payout. Was he technophobic? Perhaps Raz can start trackers on the web to see what his grieving women are up to."

"I'd start with the daughter and the wife," Coda pipes up. "That jackass was at a label party in London once with both of them. The wife pretended to be a drunken Barbie doll, but she was watching every person in the room. Daddy's little girl was even sharper—she didn't melt under my charms for a second."

We all look at one another as Coda pouts, and for the first time in a long time, I feel the sense of brotherhood we once had. I'm miffed that Dwyn isn't here. Reconnecting will only improve our success rate, and if we can impress the High Legion, some elders will finally fucking retire so we can reign.

"Got her!" Raz yells.

Our attention goes to a very grainy still of a blonde sorority girl in AKA garb entering the bar a few minutes before Coda comes crashing in. Her face is turned away from the cameras, and she has no other identifying marks I can see in the shitty picture. Coda was right; she looks like every other blond Southern sorority girl in the States. Even her clothes are pretty stereotypical—could that be purposeful?

I'm about to ask what they think when a loud ring echoes in the quiet room. The screen we're watching flickers as Raz picks up the call and Dwyn's face pops up. That son of a bitch looks gleeful as fuck, and I'm ready to tear his lips off when he speaks.

"Aloha, fellow criminals!" He waves, showing us a background shot of the city he's in avoiding saying it over a video feed.

At least that asshole is following *one* protocol—no matter how much we trust Raz's security, we keep over-the-air communications as bland as possible. "Dwyn, where the *fuck* have you been? You missed the check-in."

His expression goes dreamy and a chorus of groans resonates behind me. "Friends, dickheads, legion members… I am in *love*."

That is not even in the realm *of what I expected him to say.*

"What?" Raz gives me an incredulous expression as he clicks the mute button. "What in the actual fuck is he talking about? He was supposed to be following a lead, not bed hopping!"

I pinch the bridge of my nose, willing the migraine forming to go away. *This* is why I don't want to be the leader; I don't want to baby-sit all these emotionally stunted asshats. Motioning for Raz to turn the sound back on, I fix Dwyn with a disapproving glare. "How is that relevant to your goddamned mission? We've been thinking you were in trouble, not getting your wick dipped!"

His pout is laced with mischief as he shrugs. "What can I say? I'm a multi-tasker."

Jesus fucking Christ.

"D, did you find the girl from the park or not? We can tell where you are and it's not Berlin," Jinx says tiredly. "Stop being an idiot and debrief us or we can't strategize."

"Fine. I can't believe my *brothers* don't want to hear about the most perfect girl in the *world,* but since you're all cranky… The chick from the park disappeared into the station. I never saw her again, but I had this hunch, and I followed another girl. *She* turned out to be the devil I've been telling you about. But I'm not sure I can find her again."

Coda scoffs disgustedly as he flops onto the couch. "Leave it to you to fuck up a perfectly good one and done."

Gritting my teeth, I try not to explode. It's not surprising, but no less infuriating, that Dwyn's been off chasing his tail while we were working. What is unusual is his intensity about this woman—he hasn't given a flying fuck about a conquest since *she* died. If we weren't in such a cluster fuck, I'd be intrigued, but we are and we don't have time for his shenanigans.

"Dwyn, do you think the mystery girl from the explosion was on the train?"

Jinx is ever the peacemaker.

"Well, Jinxy, I'm not sure. There were more people on the red-eye than I would have thought, and they sold quite a few of the private cabins out but stayed closed."

I snort. "At least as far as you know, until you locked yourself inside of one while getting pussy."

"You only *wish* you'd seen what I did," he says dreamily. "Razzie, I'll need your help to find her. She left some kind of code on my leg hip bone."

"A code?" I frown and look at the others for a moment. "D, are you *sure* it wasn't the same girl?"

"Jesus, Mo! I'm not stupid. She didn't look a fucking thing like the emo rocker that almost got spaghetti sauced. Totally different vibe, I promise. Though, I'd like to see her without the wig…"

Putting my face in my palm, I count backwards from a hundred in Italian, trying not to roar at the grinning thief.

"Dude, if she was wearing a wig, how do you know she wasn't your target?" Coda smirks from his perch, finally feeling like he's not the biggest fuck-up in the room.

Of course, all we have to do is give him a minute, I'm sure.

"Oh, fuck." Dwyn beams as he claps his hands. "That's fucking brilliant! Now you *have* to help me track her down. She might be an assassin looking to kill us!"

And our resident psycho is ass over heels in love with her.

History really does *repeat itself…*

Forever

PARANOID

I HAVEN'T GONE THROUGH ALL THE DATA I COLLECTED ON THE MASTER system yet.

While it scanned, I packed up six ID kits, placed a few more orders for supplies, and perused the weapons cabinet. What started as a simple but annoying hit feels more like a fucking Ian Fleming novel, and I'd prefer options that aren't forty minutes away. I can just store everything in all the nooks and crannies of my ridiculously enormous suite. Luckily for me, the rideshare I ordered to head back didn't balk when I refused to let him help me load the various cases and bags after I locked my bogarted unit up. If he hadn't, I would have made use of the twenty-two weapons now hidden in my person.

I don't play around when I feel threatened—it got me killed once already.

My thoughts drift back to the train and my mystery dude. I've been pretending I didn't do something that completely violates every tenet I've been clinging to since my escape—something dangerous to my profession, my freedom, and worse yet, the walls I erected inside of me to protect myself. But I *did* it, and I did it with the tiniest spark of hope that it would work.

I fucking hate being an estrogen producing human; it's really fucking inconvenient.

The scenery flies by and I lean my cheek on my hand as I stare at it blankly. There are so many question marks in my formerly organized life, and this is one time I feel my chosen isolation keenly. I don't have a team to bounce my wild ideas off, nor do I have anyone to reassure me. That's been by design and I suppose I got what I wanted, but every great once in a while, I feel the pinch. Slick was hella fucking hot, and I felt… something… for the first time in a while, but my lifestyle isn't conducive to long-term connections.

Since I escaped, the closest thing I've had to a relationship is professional camaraderie with a fellow criminal called Elysium. She doesn't know I'm The Guillotine, nor does she know my real name. We met during several jobs in London not long after I 'died.' Occasionally, we'll plan to have drinks if we're in the same city—I recognize her work well enough to use end-to-end encrypted messages to reach out if I can tell she's afoot on my turf.

But it's not like I'd call her a friend; no, she's more like a work acquaintance. I can't do proper relationships—a shrink I saw once told me I have 'unresolved emotional trauma' that prevents me from trusting people. He wanted to diagnose me with PTSD, but since I was only going to the appointments to scope out his security, he met an untimely end before he could make that official. Unfortunately for him, completing my job was a higher priority than fixing my fucked up mental health.

A shame, yes, but unavoidable.

The driver pulls up to my hotel on that gem of wisdom and I step out, placing sunglasses over my eyes. Walking to the trunk, I heft my bags out, and this time, I allow Tomáš to assist me with stacking a cart. He nods at me, but doesn't comment on why I have more luggage now than I did when I arrived. I tip him another five hundred *koruna* and enter the private elevator to the tower where the suites are alone. Tomáš didn't ask to accompany me, and I simply smiled when he waved as the doors closed.

I exit on the wrong floor purposefully, pushing the cart down the hallway to the second bank of elevators I found on my way out. Changing direction always causes confusion if someone is watching you and since I can't shake the feeling I have eyes on me, I'm still in hyper secure mode. Once I change enough times to make myself feel comfortable, I head to my actual room and press the codes to enter with my body blocking the cameras.

Of course, I brushed my fingers over the wrong keys to get prints on more than just my needed numbers—though Starla's prints are a dead end, too.

Unloading the gear one bag at a time, I stow weapons and useful items in various places at the lower level. The rest goes in the spare bedroom and by the time I close the door, I'm wiped. It's been a long time since I've had to take this many precautions to ensure my safety; usually, I'm so far below the radar that I only need my disguises and my pocket guillotine to survive.

Perhaps I've been too complacent? No, I don't think the end game is about The Guillotine. The douche on the recording made it very clear his organization—if he actually *has* one—is after The Five and *Les Invisibles*. His mention of my former shadowy employer is suspect on its own, given their penchant for eliminating anyone who breathes their name outside of booking a contract. Since I'm the only person in their storied history to escape from *l'Academie* alive, I can't pin it on a washed-out recruit.

They've got a rodent problem in their house.

I'd laugh, but since it's boomeranging back to me, it's hard to see the humor. Heading upstairs, I locate the in-room dining service menu, picking out a wide selection of foods that I can gobble down. The suite has a kitchen, so I can save anything I don't eat for later. Since I'm hungry enough to consume a fucking hippo, that might not be an issue, but it's an acceptable option. After I call, I set up my command center on the long dining table.

Tablets, phones, laptops, and various printed materials from my storage unit fill the space quickly. The first order of business is to look over my preferred drop points around the city and decide which one I'll use for the next intel drive. Whoever these whackos are, I highly doubt they will provide anything more than the voice clip and rumors, but I have to go through the motions. They don't realize I have inside knowledge of the target and I intend to keep it that way. The various web applications and code I set up at the unit will run all day and long into the night, gathering whatever bits and pieces they can. By tomorrow, I should have enough puzzle pieces to make the chessboard clearer.

That's when I'll have to develop a plan and make my final decision.

Sighing, I rub my temples. Sentimentality is not my forte and all the emotions bubbling up from this asinine situation are difficult for me to parse. I should be livid at them for doing what—as far as they know—got me killed, but I can't muster the energy to be angry anymore. I moved past that years ago and now I simply live for the thrill of the hunt. All this bullshit with The Five is fucking with my clarity, and I want it to *stop*.

The only time in the past few days where I came close to letting go of my paranoia was with Slick, and unless he solves my riddle, that's not an option. My thoughts drift back to the hard planes of his body and the wild abandon we shared in the train cabin. I rarely leave myself as vulnerable as I was with him, but *damn*. That boy was made for a rough ride, and I enjoyed every goddamn second of it. The buzzer for the door goes off and I startle, yelping when it brings me out of my sexy reverie.

Grumbling under my breath, I walk downstairs. Food is definitely a plus, but another couple of rounds with Slick's fat kielbasa wouldn't hurt, either. I grab a .45 from under the side table and tuck it into the back of my waistband as I peer at the door camera. Despite lacking my desired sausage, the room service waiter looks fairly benign. I open the door, allowing him to push the full cart in, and press one thousand *konura* into his palm.

When he's gone, I push the cart to the small interior elevator and head back to my workspace. I start with *knedliky* and *svickova na smetene*, groaning as the scent of the bread and beef fill my nostrils. I nibble as I highlight the six locations I've chosen and write their coordinates for the encrypted message I'm going to send my smug, disembodied voice client. They're all over the city; it's doubtful my enemies can cover them all if the leak is coming from their end.

Of course, I have no idea who the Latin speaking fruitcake is, nor how large their numbers are, so I could be wrong.

That's why I chose the Sex Machines Museum in the Old Town section of Prague as the real pickup point. It's always crowded and the gawkers will be an excellent cover for my lift. I can meander around, watching the snickering Europeans and embarrassed Americans until I feel it's safe to approach the drive. Plus, I get to look at all the hysterical old fashioned sex toys while I do it—win-win.

It won't help my ridiculously horny daydreams about the guy with the deep brown eyes and delicious stubble on his cheeks, but *c'est la vie*. Fucking Slick has triggered some sort of rabid tigress inside of me and either he'll find me or I'll have to scratch my itch with another hot one-nighter. It's not like I'm getting attached after a single encounter, right? Even if it *was* six hours of ache-inducing dicking, that's *not* my style.

Then why do you keep thinking about it, Remy?

I throw my hands up in the air, growling with pent-up frustration. This is unbelievable—I'm looking over my shoulder for bombs and bullets, yet I can't stop fixating on a random hookup. There's *something* about the damn fool that is burrowing into my mind and I can't put my finger on it.

"Get it together, dummy. Stop thinking with your pussy and plan this shit or you're going to get killed," I mutter to myself.

Shaking my head, I open up a Tor window and send the coordinates message to the mystery voice. Once I'm done, I tap my nails on the table, deciding if I want to eat more or go relieve some of this goddamn pressure in the shower.

The throb between my legs says shower, so I guess that's my answer.

Christ, I'm pathetic.

ONCE I MAKE USE OF THE ABSOLUTELY *ASTOUNDING* WATER PRESSURE IN the giant walk-in shower, I sample some more of the local cuisine and then head downstairs to kill Starla off. The wig, clothes, shoes, and accouterments go in separate bags to be disposed of in trash cans along the way to my surveillance. I haven't slept in almost twenty hours, but I can go thirty-six before I get fuzzy in the head. There's time left for me to take the Metro line to the museum, scope out the joint, and find the security holes.

The bevy of new personas I retrieved from my hidden unit are laid out on the bed. I pick a redheaded bob belonging to *Irina Petrovich of Moscow, Russia,* and return the others to the closet. I don't know if I'll keep her past tonight or if I can use her again tomorrow, but the high-waisted black pants, colorful shirt, and light jacket will be easy to move in while I sneak around the museum. Before I grab the boots, I apply shiny gold shadow, thick long lashes, and a bright red lip. They're badass combat boots with buckles and spikes—yet another plus to our girl Irina.

I already tucked her documents in the large hobo bag, so I run upstairs to add one of my burner phones, a tablet, and some local travel guides. Irina is here on a college trip, but she's hoping to meet fashion photographers so she can move to Europe and walk the runways.

I'm not sure I meet their requirements, but that never stopped anyone from trying.

An uneasy feeling settles in my stomach as I lock the room and scurry through the back hallways to get out of the private tower into the main part of the hotel. I walk through the main lobby with an air of confidence I don't feel, though my senses are on high alert. Everything about this week is sus; the further into this mess I sink, the worse my paranoia gets.

Tomáš doesn't even nod at me as I walk by, which tells me Irina's look is successful. That calms my nerves slightly and I exit the Mandarin Oriental into the busy street.

My entire world feels upside down and all I can do is walk on the ceiling or let gravity crash me to the ground.

THE BOYS ARE BACK IN TOWN

THAT DIPSHIT HAS BEEN RUNNING AROUND WITH THE KEY TO FINDING the mystery girl written in tattoo marker along his pelvis. I thought Mo was going to blow his stack when he found out. Coda laughed so hard he almost pissed himself, and Raz started booking a flight to Prague. It wasn't hard to find out that was where Dwyn is from the castle in the background and now we all need to get our asses there stat.

At least, that's what Mo said. I'm not so sure.

We have a primary objective we're ignoring because this situation feels hinky. The Commandant gives The Five a lot of leeway in how we tackle our operations, but he'll want a progress update soon, especially after Coda's fuck up. Having all of us key to another location to chase shadows feels like overkill, and I know I'll be the one who has to smooth it over with the Legion.

"Jinx, can you help Raz pack up his shit? He's such a fucking priss about how it's stored, and you're the only one who knows how he likes it."

That's a loaded statement if I've ever heard one.

Coda snorts and I roll my eyes at him. Mo is straight as an arrow; he'd never make that joke purposefully. The rest of us are far more circumspect about our bedmates, but neither he nor Dwyn have ever joined in. I'm not sure if that's because they aren't interested or because they're waiting for some sort of engraved invitation—knowing Coda, he might be—but they love to elbow Raz and me for our open secret. It's entirely possible that being in a group reminds them of the one time we almost told Remy how we felt and it's too hard.

We missed our chance and now she's gone forever. None of us have ever looked at anyone seriously since the night of the explosion; it's all strictly one and done, then back to work. I might be the only one who even acknowledges how broken we are. Raz is my comfort, and I know he feels the same. With him, I never have to worry that someone will get the wrong idea and get hurt. We forged our bond with fire and pain so long ago that we don't even have to speak of it.

"If you can gather all the mobile tech, I can get the rest," Raz murmurs as he brushes his fingers over mine.

I nod, knowing by the look in his eyes that his mind strayed to the past for a second as well. He's never held it against me since I sided with Mo and Coda, despite my vote being the one leading to the disaster that stole our girl from us. Dwyn would follow Remy into the gates of hell in a tutu and Raz was similarly lovesick. The rest of us were looking at strategy and statistics—but we were wrong. It was a gamble either way and we all lost.

Come to think of it, the anniversary of her death is fast approaching. Maybe that's why Dwyn is suddenly head over heels for a random chick he screwed on a train.

My heart wants to believe none of us will ever find someone who can take her place, but logically, I know it's possible he could actually be healing. Dwyn may be a cold, calculating planner when it comes to heists, but he always leads with his heart. It's why I figured he'd be the last person to ever let go of her memory. If he can find someone else, maybe the rest of us can finally move on, too?

I finish packing the glut of phones, tablets, trackers, and whatever the hell else Raz has lined up on this table. He's stocking us like we're going on a full scale mission and I'm uncertain why, but his gut is famously accurate. I can count on one hand the amount of times over the years where Raz Miranda had miscalculated the supplies we'd need for a project. He's just that good.

"Do me a favor, guys? If we have a chick serving on the plane? Help me keep her from climbing on my dick. After Paris, I'm feeling unusually monkish." Coda looks serious as he asks, but I've never known him to turn down willing pussy… ever. "I had to fend the one on my Berlin flight off with a stick."

Mo blinks, turning to him with an incredulous expression. "You did what?"

Raz snorts. "Everyone but a fucking lottery ticket or something— Coda Ramone is *not* horny. Next comes the rain of frogs, right?"

The rockstar pouts from his spot on the couch. "I'm not in the mood, Razzie. Having a potential assassin deposit me on a sidewalk after a bunch of fuckwits kicked my ass kinda took the wind out of my sails."

"*Madre Mary*, save us," Mo mutters as he shoves weapons into their cases. "It's a miracle."

Pausing as I load the last of the bags I'm in charge of on the fold out cart, I arch a brow. "Are we using one of the in theater warehouses for all the other essentials?"

"*Si*, Jinx. Omega-Six and Alpha-Nine should have everything we need outside of what we've packed. Raz sent The Commandant an encoded missive letting him know we'll be arriving in Prague within a few hours."

I frown. "Has he responded? It seems odd that he'd approve of deviating from our current assignment."

Mo gives me a feral grin. "Who says he knows why we're going? We are The Five, Jinx. The rules do not apply to us."

Yeah, that's the thinking that led to tragedy before, but I'm not going to say that out loud.

"If you say so, *Capitán*," I sigh.

There's no use fighting with him when he's got that hungry look on his face. I don't know if it's about kicking Dwyn's ass or knocking off this rival chick, but Mo is on the hunt. The last time he got like this, we ended up cleaning up a five country killing spree over a mafia boss who was beating his kids.

Hopefully, this time it's less public.

THE FLIGHT TO PRAGUE WASN'T LONG AND SINCE WE CAUGHT A GOOD tailwind, we got there earlier than expected. Raz made sure our resident psycho knew how much equipment we brought, so he was waiting on us with a non-descript passenger van. Once we're settled into a safe house, Raz will want to set the back of it up for surveillance, so I'm glad Dwyn chose wisely.

One time he showed up to get a few of us in a fucking Boxster and Mo almost lost his mind.

"You guys really think my long-haired hottie is the girl who kept Coda from losing his teeth?"

I pinch the bridge of my nose as the rocker in question dives over the seat to grab Dwyn by the throat and a scuffle starts. Thank fuck Mo insisted I drive—this is going to be a tense trip to the outskirts of the city. "Dwyn, stop baiting him and Coda. You know you fucked up. There's nothing to fight over."

"It'd be easier to get over if you asswads would stop taunting me," Coda grumbles as he falls back into the seat. "I still think that cheeky bartender spiked my drink."

"We've been over this. Charice said the hospital found nothing on the tox screen, man." Raz shrugs at him. "You just let a bunch of tourist college kids wail on your ass until a chick had to save you. Take the L."

Coda fumes for a second and snaps his fingers. "Wait a tick, asshole. If I remember Professor Shelley's shit—which I know is questionable —aren't there a bunch of poisons and shit that leave your system within an hour or two? Something like... scope... scoops... scooter..."

"You're so cute when you try to use your brain, emo boy," Dwyn says as he ruffles his hair. "Help him out, Jinxy."

Sighing, I think about it for a minute. Our training in this kind of shit is limited because none of us were assassins. Poisons, drugs, and chemicals are useful for people who want to kill or interrogate, so we received only basic classes on the subject. When we were The Six, we had an expert: Remy. She didn't like that kind of weapon; she preferred to be close up. However, she tried to teach us some of her skills just in case.

"It has a cool alternate name when herbalists use it." No surprise Raz remembers more than the rest of us.

"I think... I think it's scopolamine," I mutter. "Oh, yeah. Devil's breath. That's the other name."

Everyone quiets for a moment as we fall into the pit of our memories. There's really no avoiding it when we're all together, which is why we work like spokes on a wheel most of the time. The unavoidable subject of the past weighs more heavily on us in a group. Finally, Dwyn breaks the silence.

"Guys, you have *no idea* how hot Jazz is. Like volcanic. I can't wait to solve her riddle and go on a treasure hunt."

Mo and I exchange glances in the van's front. Dwyn isn't known for getting attached to conquests, nor does his attention stay on subjects other than thieving. His enthusiasm is even more striking in person.

"Dwyn," I start, choosing my words carefully. "Is Jazz her real name?"

He snorts. "Of fucking course not, man. I didn't give her mine, either. She didn't seem to mind."

"Jesus fuck, D! We're chasing tail you don't have an ID for? And you guys think *I'm* the screw up?!"

I watch Raz's lips quirk in the rearview mirror. Compared to the rest of us, they both are, but saying that won't help. The hacker clears his throat, turning to our thief. "What the hell is this riddle?"

"Math shit, I think." Dwyn bucks his hips up, unbuckling his belt, and Mo whips around to glare at him. "That's where it's written, Mo-Mo!"

It's possible Mauricio is going to put his fist through something while I'm driving if they don't calm down, so I step in. "Dwyn. You can show up at the safe house. No need to whip it out in the car."

His crazy laughter rings out in the small space. "Fuck, guys! It's not written on my dick. She wrote that shit along my… what do chicks call it? The Adonis belt? Right there."

I let out a sigh of relief. Mo would have lost his mind if we had to stare at D's cock while we tried to figure out what damn clue his bedmate left for him.

"Thank hell," Mo mutters. "If it was, this whole situation might seem like a clown show or something."

Sarcasm is Mo's love language.

"Jinxy, you need to turn onto this road up on your left. The alternate safe house is tucked back in this corner where no one would think to look. I know you didn't want to go to the main *LI* location in Prague, so I tapped into this abandoned warehouse before you got here."

I squint at the road Dwyn is indicating, frowning a little. "If you weren't at the main house and you just found this place, where have you been for the past day?"

A slow, maniacal grin spreads over his face. "You know me, Jinxy. I've been hunting."

Lord help us, I'm afraid to even ask what that means.

DISTRACTION

The museum was exactly as predicted, and I could locate all the cameras and blind spots with relative ease. It's not a high-value target for thefts, so it has a fairly ancient security system. Based on the model numbers of the cameras, it's also not hackable because the damn thing is recording to a DVR or possibly even DVDs. That's both a plus and a minus—while outside forces aren't tapping into the feed from a fucking VPN, neither am I.

Cell phones make scouting trips like this a breeze. Under the guise of tourism, I took photos that include entrances, exits, camera positions, model numbers, and even an excellent shot of an alarm panel. I can research the tech more thoroughly in my room and use the lovely printed map they gave me to make a camera angle diagram to memorize. No one paid the slightest bit of attention to me snapping pics and giggling to myself at the racy artifacts from kinks past.

That means I could make certain no one had changed the interior after I confirm my locations for pickup tomorrow.

True, nothing changed at the Poststadion, but it's unlikely they'll try something as noticeable as a drone delivery indoors. A new display or a blocked off hallway, however, would alert me to a potential issue—and allow me time to escape before whatever the nebulous 'they' had planned. I'm as thorough as they come and with alarm bells going off, I'm not making any assumptions.

Hustling back to the hotel on the metro, I observe the passengers. Every time someone reaches into a bag or pocket, my spine tenses. I know that's my brain on overdrive, but even the safest seat on the train can't protect me from a gunshot. Crazy people, like the shadowy client, have no problem with damage to property.

How is this bastard crazier than my former bosses? It boggles the mind.

A dark-haired teen stares at me from across the train and I give him a dirty look. He might be rude—hell, most teens are—but he could be more than a surly youth. *Les Invisibles* frequently send students from the academy out into the world for real life training missions as their version of Baker Street Selects.

Before they inducted me, the guys and I spent a year hiding in plain sight at an elite American prep school. The info we could pass on about rich families and their progeny was invaluable to a key opera-tion. That's a major part of how we became The Six and I guarantee there are junior *LI* recruits tucked away all over the world, waiting to be activated, hoping to make their bones with the High Legion.

They think you're dead, Remy. It's not like kids are being shown your mugshot.

Even if they were, between the extensive reconstructive surgery after the blast and my aptitude for concealment, they wouldn't recognize me. The assassin track has years' worth of classes in creating new looks and faces via makeup, wigs, acting, and cosmetic apparatuses —and I've always had the gift. I don't create simple disguises; I design three-dimensional people with backstories that would fool any serious professional for months before they realized the persona was fake.

By that time, I'm always gone.

I settle back in my seat, listening for the announcer to call the next stop so I can gauge how long I'm trapped here. My paranoia is out of control, and I need to have a few drinks at the hotel bar. It'd be nice if Slick would figure out my riddle, but the likelihood is low. The riddle I left would take a multi-step thinker with an IQ high enough to join MENSA. However, there aren't many guys who can fuck like that *and* keep up with my brain.

You used to know five of them…

Facepalming myself for yet again bringing up a future that *cannot* happen, I reach into my bag and pull out my tablet. I have to distract my mind; the sex on the train was good, but it's scrambled my hormones and I have to get it together. I never slept with The Five. There was an 'almost' moment before the world crashed down, but an urgent message that would ultimately destroy us interrupted it.

Professor Arnaud paid for taking my happiness with his head. However, my sorrow for what could have been will never get satisfied. Vengeance only soothed my soul for so long; the ache from what he stole from me can't be assuaged, even with blood. He didn't simply foil my plan to escape—he stole the life I should have had.

I frown at my screen, looking at the tracker on the cell phone I left Slick clues to find. I didn't intend to check on this, but the melancholy and anger flowing through me about the past is making me more emotional than usual. Everything about that encounter veered from my normal routine: the clues, the wistful thoughts, and the complete lack of protection we used.

Don't worry; Les Invisibles makes sure we can't get ourselves or anyone else pregnant once we hit puberty.

I haven't been that reckless in many years, but babies aren't the only thing I risked. It's idiotic to say, but something inside of me says I'm fine despite having no real reason to believe that. Irritation at my stupid behavior makes me swipe the tracking program away and pull up a search engine. I need to divert to a clinic instead so I can be certain. Once I find one, I access the Metro map and sigh.

This line is closest to the hotel. I'll get off early, pop in, and then go back to wait for confirmation from the Shadow Douche. I'll have to burn the Starla identity after I go, but if I ditch everything but the encrypted phone and email, it will be fine. Now I *definitely* need a drink or six—I've got enough clusterfuck on my hands.

There is nothing about this week that hasn't been ridiculous. I swear to fuck, I need to pick up a secondary job so I can kill someone. At least then I'll have a modicum of control; I carefully execute everything about my work. The world fades away when I go into a zone.

It's a good plan. *I'll get drunk and hunt up a side job to distract me while I wait for word about the drop.*

The thing about side jobs is there's always someone who wants another person dead, but it's not always conveniently located. I'm lucky to be one of the few assassins who are cross-trained in other areas. When I want to distract myself during the 'waiting phase' of a particular hit, I'll surf the dark nets for other requests. I can reasonably accept low-level hacking gigs, mid-tier heists, and selected short cons without a lot of preparation. I don't take physical shit—not because I can't, but because my instinct is to kill the fucker. You can't switch off muscle memory and mine is razor sharp.

I watch the screens set up around me carefully. The traces I have on my former employer and teammates are flickering as they gather data from places most people will never see. One is text with a blinking cursor, quiet as it awaits the response from the ubiquitous client. In front of me, there are two screens where I'm surfing the markets.

Mercatus is the largest superstore for illegal employment and procurement in the world. No one is certain who runs it, and no law enforcement agency has even heard a hint of its existence. The rumor is their servers aren't in any country and are beyond the reach of mere mortals. That's nonsense, of course, because *Mercatus* is accessed through several layers of the dark web if they have invited you. Entering the markets is a multi-step process of verifying your identity as a buyer or vendor and it's never the same; they know infinitely lax security protocols took that Silk Road and other illegal sites down.

This is where the *real* world-changing deals get made, not a stately room full of legislators or bankers. In the Sherlock Holmes stories, Moriarty wanted to be the concierge of crime—the vendors on *Mercatus* have achieved his dream. Large criminal empires like *Les Invisibles* or *The Company* mingle with smaller gangs, mobs, free-lancers, and thugs compete for every imaginable service or sale. I'm not a fan of some things available—scum like The Cobra traffic in flesh—but The Guillotine doesn't need to take requests that violate my charcoal code of ethics.

I'm running a search for posts that would fit the criteria for two of my criminal aliases—The Panther and The Duchess. Creating more identities is a pain—hell, undercover agents for shit like Mossad only have three—but reputation is *everything*. The Guillotine is terrifying because no one survives meeting them, and my side quests are less covert. I'm able to make quick cash like the other two and no one is the wiser. I met Elysium when I was posing as The Panther, in fact.

No one knows who I truly am, and it's how I stay alive.

A beep grabs my attention and I look at the black and green screen—The Duchess has a message.

After my security scans it, I open the file and read. The glitterati will be in full regalia at a diplomatic event tonight at Prague Castle. An invitation will be secured, but appropriate attire is required. It is a masquerade ball for a charity foundation and the client wants infor-mation gathered from the cell phone of one of the mega donors. Squinting, I read about the donor's proclivities, especially on trips to Eastern Europe and Asia. There's an explanation of how it will be used, but I don't give a fuck about that. I don't need the why, only the what, where, when, and who.

Besides, no one cares why you want to blackmail a pedophile—they deserve far worse.

Typing a series of messages to arrange details and payment, I smile.

Work will take my mind off the past, the creepy sensation of being watched, and the megalomaniac that hasn't confirmed our next drop. I need to go shopping for a few things to go to an event with this kind of coverage—especially as my grifter alter-ego. That woman is all flash, but I don't want to go back a second time while I'm in the city.

Picking up the burner with the number I gave the *Mercatus* client, I use a marker to write '*Duchess*' below it. After it boots up, I call the front desk of the hotel to make a reservation in another suite. It's not as nice as mine, but I need to arrive dressed as her and leave as her publicly. Since the shadowy jackass hasn't returned my last reply, I walk over and send a quick missive, stating I am unavailable for retrieval until tomorrow evening.

Whoever that dickface is, he doesn't control my schedule.

I stand and do a small pirouette, feeling the burden lift off my shoulders as I imagine tonight. Shedding Remy for a few hours to pretend to be an outgoing, wealthy minor royal at a dance sounds like the escapism I need. It's not as good as fucking a stallion like Slick, but Jinx used to say pulling off a perfect grift is like an orgasm and a chocolate chip cookie at the same time.

And I'm about to have a whole damn tray.

Forever

TROUBLE'S COMING

Dwyn wasn't exaggerating—the warehouse was perfect for an under-the-radar base of operations. Once we raided our unit for the equipment, all we had to do was stock the place he'd spent all day setting up. Everything from weapons racks to rolling boards allowed us to create a space almost as accommodating as one of our normal haunts—within a few hours, the entire HQ was ready to go.

"I'm tapped into all the feeds and I'll need a few hours to scan before we know what our next move is." I look over at Mo as he paces back and forth in front of the board containing all the meager information we have on the mystery girl.

It's not much beyond a few blurry photos, a map charting her supposed movements, and notecards with bits of intel from both Coda and Dwyn, but it's a start.

"Are we sitting around here while *The Spider* plays with his webs or what?" Coda takes a slug of the expensive scotch on the table, strumming guitar idly.

He's not *really* being a dick; the emo rocker hates staying still.

Between him and Dwyn, this part of every job is a migraine waiting to happen. Their skills are physical and mental, but they have some of the worst adult ADHD I've ever seen. The latter is in the back half of the room with a box of locks, a blindfold, and a paperclip. I'd be grateful the thief is keeping himself busy, but he occasionally turns to fling a knife at a dart board because he can't focus on only one thing unless it's a live mission.

Even then, it's a stretch.

"Coda, we have a massive amount of planning to do before we can go after this girl. It's going to take time," Jinx cajoles. I give him a smile of thanks and he winks, making my cheeks flush.

A knife flies past us, embedding in one of the inner rings of the board, and Mo whirls around to snark at Dwyn. "Why is every prep work session like baby-sitting toddlers with you two?!"

"Because watching Razzie and Jinxy flirt while you wear a hole in the floor is booooooring, Mo-Mo." Another tosser whizzes by, this time barely missing the frustrated hitter.

Mauricio isn't much for this portion, either, but the whole 'I'm the Alpha' thing is his schtick, so he has to pretend. I turn around in my chair, steepling my fingers as I consider how to prevent a fistfight in the middle of our lair. An alarm beeps behind me and I swivel back, grinning in relief. This tidbit should help immensely.

"Mo, *Le Voleur de Sang* was spotted by our facial rec program in Dresden, and *El Guapo* just arrived on a private jet at the Prague Airport." Another beep catches my attention, followed by another, and I stare at the screen. "Holy fuck. One of the suspected Horseman, *Alqatu*, and *Ape Regina* are also popping up in nearby cities according to the boards."

"Find out what the fuck is happening in Prague tonight, Raz. That's a veritable bonanza of fucking professional thieves converging all at once. Dwyn, have you been approached for a side job?"

The blindfolded psycho stops playing with toys, walking through a minefield of traps he laid himself without tripping a single one. "I had a couple of alerts, but since I was chasing my dream girl, I didn't look into them. Gotta keep my eyes on the prize."

"Jesus, D! You didn't think it was important to let us know we were coming to an Open Market?" Jinx rakes his hands through his hair, stomping over to the map with a frown. "The Five *never* come together in a place with this many…"

"Adversaries?" Coda drawls. "Let's face it; any of them would love to auction us off to the highest bidder if they caught us with our pants down."

Dwyn flops on the couch next to him, swiping the guitar to play the intro to *Desperado* while Coda gives him a dirty look. "It's a bunch of *thieves*, guys. They're not collection agents."

My screen flashes and I shake my head. "*Le Voleur de Sang* is a Swiss Army knife, Dwyn, and this alert says The Duchess has also taken a job." That's the one who's always fascinated me. Not everyone in our world keeps their identity a secret, and some of the most reclusive criminals in the world are in one spot.

Why?

"The Palace or the embassy," Jinx mutters. "Check their event schedules—those are the only places where a party would draw enough glitter to attract all of those heavy hitters."

I nod, pulling up windows and screens to hack into servers most people don't even know exist. Normal people don't realize that they closely guard the highest profile gatherings secrets; they aren't announced on public websites or in the media. The actual targets for theft or assassination are smaller and disguised as mundane closures for renovation or repairs. It keeps the paparazzi away from the true power brokers mingling with celebrities and royalty.

The evil men do oft lurks in the shadows of wealth and fame.

Not exactly Brutus' quote, but no less true. Whatever event has people rich and powerful enough to spawn over five major contracts and create an Open Market has to be a 'render unto Caesar' level soirée. I just need to…

"There!" I call as the code crawls up the screen. "Prague Castle is supposedly closed for renovations in the Summer in the East Wing. That's definitely where it's being held."

"Guest list?" Jinx asks as he grabs a dry erase for the marker board. "I assume these people aren't all here for the same specific item, so the attendees must be the reason for the OM."

"Working on it. Dwyn, quit aggravating Coda and check your goddamn messages to see what's open and what they have claimed."

Mo walks over to the two idiots grappling over the guitar and snatches it. "Coda, get over the fact that he taught himself in a week and Dwyn, stop taunting him. The Commandant will *not* be pleased if we miss a major opportunity to undercut these fools while we're here."

Pouting, Dwyn pulls out his phone and sighs. "Fine, *Senõr* Grumpy-pants." He's quiet for a moment as he looks, then sighs again. "Can't see what The Duchess took—she's triple encrypted and only left a marker. Looks like a silly necklace belonging to a diplomat's wife might be what *Alqatu* is after, because she loves shiny things. *Ape Regina* only goes after intel, so she's probably on the grift for something. The Horseman and *Le Voleur* are usually looking to eliminate, but that's a different section of *Mercatus*. *El Guapo* runs on your boards, Razzie."

"This party sounds like a helluva shindig. Maybe I should check in with Charice. It's the perfect place for Coda Ramone," the rocker says as he preens. "Jinx can mingle, too."

Mo scratches his chin. "People will look for local security. I'll check my area. This might be all hands on deck."

"Except for me," I grumble. I'll be parked in a van running the OC and tech as usual. "You'd better bring me food."

"Yeeeehaw, it's a Dead Man's Wedding!" Coda whoops as he jumps to his feet. "We haven't done one in a dog's age."

There's a reason for that, but we'll see what happens.

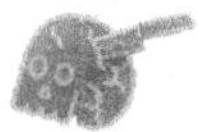

DISCOVERING THAT THIS LITTLE PARTY IS A MASQUERADE WAS A MIXED bag—it didn't matter to me, but it made Dwyn and Mo happy while Coda and Jinx damn near pouted. Another trip to our Omega unit provided us with bespoke tuxes tailored to everyone's individual needs, but I had to run out to a local artisan shop to buy the right masks. Rich folks just *love* to pretend they're in the bloody *Phantom of the Opera* and though this isn't the first shindig like this we've attended, I don't keep fancy ball crap stocked in every unit.

Tuxes are versatile, weirdly decorated face coverings are not.

That's probably a bit of gender bias, to be honest. I'd imagine the female agents in *Les Invisibles* keep an enormous variety of costumes and fancy shit in their hidey-holes simply because of expectations. The world may never move past the internalized misogyny of the past two centuries, and our recruits are trained to be prepared for nearly every eventuality. Jobs can pop up out of nowhere—like tonight—and you have to be fairly wealthy and connected to get nitpicky props at the last minute.

Like me.

I color coded the masks to match the pocket squares and bow ties of our team to help create an easy visual for the camera feeds. Dwyn's is decorated in kelly green with feline features while Jinx has a soft golden bird-like motif. Mo, as usual, insisted on a canine style with blood red and black accents. And Coda... that motherfucker demanded a rainbow color scheme with a sparkling Mardi Gras style mask full of feathers and glitter. Not stealthy in the slightest, but fitting for his persona.

I shake my head as I watch the four of them enter in various groups. From a quiet, conservative looking diplomatic envoy to a bustling entourage, my brothers have all found their way into the secret gathering of criminals, politicians, royalty, and celebrities with less than a few hours' notice. It's why we're one of the most sought after operatives in *LI* and the most dangerous members of the High Legion.

Success is a foregone conclusion for The Five.

Turning back to the plethora of monitors, I check the facial rec program as it continues to ID the guests. I tapped into the hardline at the palace earlier when I snuck in disguised as catering staff. I'm using their own security to feed images to my algorithm and as the players mingle, their files populate on a separate screen. So far, I've identified three minor royals, six movie stars, twenty diplomats, four arms dealers, two other rock stars, ten socialites, a handful of influencers, embassy staff, and various CEOs. It's a fully stocked bar of high end assholes and I'm not surprised it triggered an Open Market.

The combined money from the guests who have entered in the first hour is greater than the GDP of Central America.

"Raz, have you seen any of the players yet?"

Mo's voice is low as he pretends to be checking out a loud crowd of social media stars by the staircase. He snagged a job doing security for an oil exec from Russia and his wife, so he's keeping a low profile. The wife is at least thirty years younger than the mobbed up baron and she's been flirting with our austere hitter non-stop. Every time she pulls his low ponytail I can almost feel the tension radiate through the screen.

"Naw." I look over at the large flat screen mounted on the wall where I have the files we've assembled on our known colleagues prominently displayed. "Of course, we don't have current photos of the Horsemen and a few of the women are known to be well versed in disguises. We'll have to watch closely to mark *Regina*, *Alqatu*, or The Duchess."

"Christ, women are the devil," Mo mutters grumpily. "Even our own agents are so fucking well trained in deception that we can't always pick them out unless we see telltale behavior."

"Did you check the roster in the *Invisibles* servers to make sure we *don't* have other teams in play, Raz?" Jinx is all broad smiles as he walks confidently through the crowd, nodding at random guests as if they've met before. Our resident grifter is so gifted at his craft that he never worries for a second about being discovered. He could sell ice to a goddamn penguin, I swear to hell.

I push off the desk and slide down to another computer, doing a quick check to ensure nothing has changed. "Affirmative. It doesn't look like any of those fuckers in the Legion sent one of their own teams after The Commandant reported the market."

Of course, I would put it past Lady Volokov or The Raptor to double cross everyone by not registering their teams' missions until completed.

"You're quiet, Razzie. That means you think the Russian strumpet or the Jersey devil may be hiding a job," Dwyn says as he slips around the edges of the dance floor to the bar. "I wouldn't discount the scheming of that little triad, either."

I'm not. The High Legion comprises the upper echelon of criminals that run *LI* and *l'Academie*. There's infighting and corruption as a matter of course, but as long as we all continue bringing money into the coffers, The Commandant looks the other way. Since the incident when we became The Five and Professor Arnaud's death, factions have formed within the legion. Competition is fierce and the worst of the worst is the triad formed by the three female members. They're ruthless, unprincipled, and unconcerned with stepping on their peers to get ahead.

It's impressive, honestly. One would assume the loudest supporters of our female recruits and fair vetting processes are also the nastiest, most destructive force within the board. Led by *Trái dứa*, the group is known for operating in the shadows, even within our structure. They use misinformation, manipulation, blackmail, and threats to fill their operative teams with agents and recruits of all levels and skills. Even I have trouble rooting out what members they have their hooks in and that's saying a lot.

We should expose them for the traitors they are, but as long as they are producing even moderately successful results, the others ignore what's in front of their faces.

"Raz? Raz!"

"Fuck, sorry, Mo. I agree with D. The cackling trio of cunts probably sent some of their indentured servants the minute they heard about the event at the board meeting."

"Just fucking great," Jinx sighs. "Now we have to look for those idiots to make a mess while we're working. None of their people have any notion of craft or skill and they always cause problems. Amateurs are the bane of my existence."

"Everyone starts somewhere, Jinxy. You weren't always so silver tongued." Dwyn chuckles at his own joke and I roll my eyes. "Besides, I *enjoy* teaching the newbs a lesson in true artistry. Keeps me on my toes."

Now the crazy is excited. This is going to be a hell of a night.

PLAY WITH FIRE

THE GALA IS TASTEFULLY ELEGANT—ALL BLACK TIES AND FANCY MASKS— but the atmosphere is tense.

Liquor and good food are flowing like the nectar of the gods in every room and the chamber orchestra's light classical music echoes off the walls of the palace. It *should* feel like every other boring one percent soirée I've been to, but something in the air is setting my teeth on edge. My instincts are rarely wrong, so I sip my champagne as I watch the crowd speculatively. After a few moments of studying, reality filters in.

They filled this room with professional criminals.

You wouldn't notice if you didn't know what to look for, but when you've been trained by the best, it's so obvious that it's painful. They packed the guest list with many HVTs, but that isn't usually a recipe for a large percentage of my colleagues. We avoid 'crossing the streams' if possible because it raises the odds of someone throwing you to the wolves to divert attention from themselves.

Unless an Open Market has been declared.

My body shakes with fury. The task I accepted was not labeled part of an event like that in *Mercatus*—an obvious violation of the rules. I would never attend such an event as The Duchess and probably not even as The Guillotine unless the payment was substantially higher than I'll earn for my job tonight. Congregating with the elite and a plethora of criminals is asking to get captured or arrested. Only greedy fools accept risks like an Open Market.

I am no fool and I will hunt down the dog who led me to this mess.

Pushing off the wall, I stalk towards the bar. I need a stronger drink than champagne to cool my temper if I'm going to finish this bullshit and get the hell out of Dodge. My luck has been iffy, and I want to be long gone before one of the amateurs gets caught with their hands in a cookie jar. I nod at the bartender, ordering a martini when he approaches.

"Good choice."

I tilt my head, tamping down the urge to tell the growly Brit next to me to fuck off. Tonight, I'm *Elysia Fromme*, not Remy Benoit. Elysia is the CEO of a non-existent modeling agency specifically made to look like a front for an escort service. She would *never* piss off a potential client, so I purr my response. "I enjoy the bite of an ice cold drink as much as any man."

The platinum blonde man looks at me with sapphire eyes that feel as if they are stripping me bare, layer by layer. His grin is positively feral when he lifts his scotch to clink glasses with me. "Too bloody right, pet. Always a good time for a good nip."

"My thoughts exactly." I sip my martini and glance around the room as if I'm curious. "What brings you to this secret bacchanal?"

"Work. My boss sent me to rub elbows with the obscenely wealthy on his dime. It's a great sacrifice."

His laugh is dark and for a moment, I can see the predator in front of me, despite his mask. This man isn't one of the pansy ass CEOs or celebrities from the guest list. My drinking buddy is a professional, and he's definitely here for work—just not anything legal. I let his words settle between us for a few moments before I return his smile.

"*Alea iacta est.*[1]" I wait to see what his response is as I slow-play my suspicion.

"You've got the wrong git, I'm afraid." My companion stands, his lips curled in a bone chilling sneer. "I don't work for any of those fuckwits, nor do I associate with people who have secret bloody handshakes. My employer isn't part of your cute little band of amateurs."

I bristle at his presumptuous declaration. "*Barba non facit philoso-phum*[2]. I'm no more a pawn of those clowns than you are."

This time, his grin is wider and seems to have... some sort of fang prosthetic? I slide my hand into the hidden pocket in my ball gown, wrapping my fingers around the emergency wire I have tucked amongst the tulle.

Who the absolute fuck *is this guy?!*

"No need for your weapon, love. I've fed and I only have eyes for my target and my family."

My eyes widen as the realization hits me. *Now* I know who this motherfucker is—I'm having a martini with *Le Voleur de Sang*. If he's on a job at this cursed shindig, then I'm not only surrounded by amateurs but colleagues of my caliber. Someone with a great deal of sway set up an Open Market *and* a *deus ex machina* in the same city.

It's unheard of and extremely dangerous.

"Good to know. Your HVT isn't a CEO with a penchant for young puppies, is it?" I arch a brow as I watch what little of his face I can see beneath his demonic themed mask.

"Not today. However, I know someone who will be happy to sweep up after you... Duchess." I don't let him see my surprise at being 'identified,' as it would confirm his accusation. "I'll keep my eye on the media so I know when my mate can mete out justice."

I wink at him playfully. "You do that. It was nice to make your acquaintance, *monsieur.*" The simple phrase is my hat tip to his legend, letting him know I'm also aware of who I'm dealing with. He winks back and I move away from the bar, leaving one of the deadliest serial killers in the world alone with his scotch.

Sure, he's an assassin, but everyone knows that guy kills everything in sight—not just his target—and they're always short on blood when he's done.

As I walk through the sparkling crowd, I feel eyes on me. I don't blame them—I'm wearing an expensive gown, priceless jewelry, and a haughty demeanor. Less experienced thieves and grifters attending the market think I'm a mark; higher end professionals believe I'm competition. It's a high, thin tightrope I'm walking as I search for the object of my mission. I can't be less visible in my Duchess guise—it's how I'm able to sell my grift. But I didn't think I'd be ducking other criminals, either.

Spotting my mark on the dance floor, I wait for the song to change before tapping the CEO of the largest refugee non-profit in Europe on the shoulder. Disgustingly enough, *this* is the man open to black-mail because he regularly purchases the services of underage, traf-ficked boys. I have to force the charming smile to my lips as I hold my hand out for the next dance.

"How could I say no to such a *beautiful* woman?" The bulky man guffaws as he takes my hand in his big, meaty palm.

The less I say, the looser his lips will get, especially since he already reeks of vodka. He's repulsive in reputation and smell, so I have to breathe carefully through my mouth to get through this without gagging. "It's a pleasure to meet you, Mr. Brannigan. My name is Elysia Fromme."

"One perk of my position is that everyone always knows you before you even get to introduce yourself. Though, I suppose I am not as well known as some of the very famous movie and music stars, eh?"

Another loud laugh accompanies his lame joke and I roll my eyes internally.

He's one of those *guys. Gross.*

Laughing politely, I allow him to guide us around the dance floor. I'm not worried about wandering hands; this pig prefers his conquests to be younger and male. However, I need him to make the connection between me and my legend, so he spills his guts. The large pink diamond on my necklace has a tiny recording device behind the setting and once he admits his perversion, I can get the fuck out of this disaster zone.

"Beautiful people always steal the spotlight, I'm afraid. My models are usually the center of attention when we attend events as prestigious as this. The lack of jaded sophistication makes my stable extremely popular." I curve my lips into a flirtatious smile, hoping he can read the vicious look in my eyes.

Madams to the elite often mask their avarice with a knowing expression and a sensual affect to convey their trade without words that could entrap them. It's a bit more difficult at a masked ball, but I'd like to think I'm a solid enough grifter to use micro expressions skillfully. If it doesn't work, I'll use a bit of neuroleptics to bolster my act.

His eyes widen behind the boar mask, and I know he understands. "Such a shame you couldn't bring your lovely ladies this evening. Even scenery as luxurious as this can be improved upon."

I click my tongue and wag a finger at him playfully. "Now, now. I am an equal opportunity agency, Mr. Brannigan. My roster includes a wide variety of young, fresh faces—both male and female presenting, as well as a few non-binary options. I believe in giving my clients everything they desire and more."

When you murder people for a living and someone's tastes make your skin crawl, it's safe to say they're evil.

"How delightful!" The look of glee in his dark eyes almost makes me shiver as he twirls me and then pulls me back to him. "I would be *very* interested in booking one of your employees—maybe two—for an event at my corporate retreat. Do you have anything available in the Louis XIII range? I love the crisp, untouched flavors of special vintages."

I take a moment to realize he's using booze as a code to ask me if I have *thirteen-year-old boys* for sale. The urge to lure this motherfucker to a deserted room and pull an unscheduled Queen of Hearts floods my veins. Then I remember what my former drinking companion told me. Once I complete my mission, he'll send his mate—whatever the hell *that* means—to give this human dumpster fire what he deserves. I wait for the song to end, and give the erstwhile CEO a smile full of teeth.

"Allow me to check my inventory, Mr. Brannigan." The opposite pocket of my gown contains one of my phones and I pull it out, scrolling through screens as if I'm checking on his request. "If you would like, I may even have two thirteens for a private event tonight. I would only require a wire of the down payment to my account and the location of your event, as well as any physical preferences you may have."

Now he's downright salivating, and I'm certain he's going to give me enough rope to hang him with. My client may be a good or bad guy—I'm not sure—but they're going to get what they paid for soon. "Ms. Fromme, you are a sharp businesswoman! I would prefer two blonds, twins if you have them, and the less grass on the infield, the more satisfied I will be. This… audition… for my future event will begin at 10 PM sharp in my suite at The Ritz. Is that amenable?"

Fuck, I hope they kill this pervert. I've never been so repulsed in my life.

I pretend to click through a few more screens before holding up a QR code for him to use for the deposit. The client won't need this money and I'm not keeping it, so an appropriate and *clean* children's charity is about to receive enough money to operate for at least a year. Brannigan pulls out his phone and, like most of the über-wealthy, he doesn't even ask me what this will cost him because he can afford it. Once he scans the code and the plinking sound of a deposit hitting the account lets me know he's kept his end of the bargain, I dip my head at him.

"A pleasure doing business with you, Mr. Brannigan. Keep me in mind should you need further models for your specialized marketing." His bellowing laugh follows me as I walk across the dance floor, and I allow myself to shudder when I know he's turned around. I'm going to need a hefty drink before I feel ready to head back to my ops center at the hotel. Everything about this job has me feeling skeeved out.

This time when I approach the bar, I tell the bartender to give me tequila and leave the fucking bottle.

––––––––––

1. The die is cast.
2. A beard doesn't make one a philosopher.

Forever

WICKED ONES

DWYN IS HAVING THE TIME OF HIS LIFE. HE'S PICKING POCKETS, LIFTING jewels, and charming his way through this obscenely financially blessed gathering like it's an Olympic sport.

Our self-proclaimed leader is glaring from his position at the best vantage point in the room. He had a slight tussle with what I believe might have been a Secret Service agent, but the guy was too far away to verify without being obvious. Of course, Mo won that spat; he always wins. And now he's watching over this parade of amateurs with his lip curled as if being in the same space will somehow suck the skills right out of us.

"How many assignments have you stolen?" Raz's voice pulls me back into focus and I wait for my team to respond before I comment.

A snort echoes in my earpiece and I look over to see Coda surrounded by women of all ages as he vamps for them. Obviously, he can't answer, but my guess is he's found plenty of future work in that circle of willing pussy. His rockstar persona grants him access to more people than any of us and his charm will lead to a veritable smorgasbord of leverage.

"Haven't had many approaches since I put that idiot in his place. But I can direct the rest of you to the bigger marks," Mo says in a low voice.

"I've got a loverly bunch of coconuts!" Dwyn crows. "Plenty of loot to finance our little hunt for the perfect woman."

As if we don't have enough money to finance anything we please.

"Jinx?"

I sigh, hating when I have to share my exploits while we're still *in situ.* My skill set is more suited to solo work and I don't debrief until I'm far from my intended marks. "I was able to undercut a little mouse, set up a few cherries, did a Kansas City shuffle, and set up the beginning of a Mummy's Tiara."

Three whistles pierce my ear and I have to work not to pull the piece out of my ear. Finally, Dwyn speaks. "Jinxy, you're a one man crime spree! Is this what you do when you fuck off on your own for weeks at a time?"

"Yes, dickhead. It's what they trained me to do." Irritation colors my tone, but outside of Raz, they don't really understand what I do and how much it impacts their ability to do their jobs.

Mo clears his throat. "I think I saw *Ape Regina.* She headed out that door by the bathrooms. Dwyn, find her. That woman will be after the biggest plum."

"Aye, aye, *Signore!*"

A beeping noise interrupts us and Raz sucks in a breath. "Facial rec has ID'd *Alqatu.* Coda, you need to deal with that raven haired woman amongst your adoring fans. She's lifting a necklace from that unpleasant-looking harpy in the brocade to your left."

He coughs in answer, and I make way over to the bar. The tasteful mahogany setup is host to a myriad of people—some recognizable and some not—but what really catches my eye is a fiery redhead with a perfectly coiffed updo full of flowers and sparkling green ribbons. Her gown is a pale purple with an enormous tulle bottom covered in vines and flowers, giving her an ethereal, almost fairy-like appearance. As if she feels my gaze, she turns, bright blue eyes wide as her pink lips curve.

Spank my ass and call me Charlie… this woman is gorgeous.

I swallow hard, wending my way through the rest of the crowd as her gaze draws me like we're magnetized. There's something about the way she looks at me that is short-circuiting my brain, and I don't know if I ever felt such an intense attraction to anyone in my life. There's chatter in my ear and around me, but it doesn't compute. All I can focus on is the girl with eyes the color of sapphires.

"Well, hello," she says, looking up through her lashes flirtatiously.

The bottle of tequila on the bar is half empty and I know that's almost certainly all about her. The easy way she took control once I was hooked told me this is not a soft kitten, as her dress might suggest. No, she's full of fire and ice and everything spice. "*Enchanté.*"

A tinkling laugh escapes her lips as I take her free hand and kiss her knuckles. "Oooh. A smooth talker, I see. What brings you to this carefully concealed den of iniquity, Casanova?"

Be still my heart, she's as smart as she is beautiful.

"I am writing my life so that I may laugh at myself, and I am succeeding," I reply with a sly grin. Yes, it's a test, but I find intelligence hotter than anything else—hence Raz—and I want to see how far I can push this curvy siren.

"I see. Quite so. Well, the man who makes no mistakes usually makes nothing."

Her eyes sparkle with the challenge, and my dick hardens immediately. If she keeps this up, I may have to pull a Coda and go off grid for a few to explore. "The sweetest pleasures are those hardest to be won."

"Delightful," she murmurs as she pours herself another shot. With a wink, she crooks her fingers at the bartender. The dude moves so fast you'd think his ass was on fire to bring a second shot glass and more limes without a word from her.

"Since you've named me Casanova, and this is a masked event, shall I call you Shooter?" I gesture at the glasses and she claps her hands.

"You have *no idea* how perfect that is. I *love* it," the redhead purrs as she pours our shots. "Now, for an appropriate toast. I think… if you have not done things worthy of being written about, at least do things worthy of being read."

I'm going to devour this woman whole, and I don't give a fuck if anyone gets their dick in a knot over it.

Clinking my glass with hers, I toss the liquid back. She's picked a very expensive liquor—the tequila doesn't burn on the way down in the slightest—and before I can blink, she pours us another. "Shooter, if I didn't know better, I'd think you're trying to get me drunk."

"Hell, no, Casanova. First off, consent is sexy as hell and what I'd like to do with you requires it. Second, I'd prefer your flag not to fail at half-mast."

I almost spit my shot out.

Goddamn, this woman is hot.

My lips curve up, and I pretend to bat my lashes. "Why, ma'am, you're going to make me blush."

Shooter slams her glasses down in a fit of giggles and I beam. Making a woman this strong and confident laugh like that isn't easy, and I didn't even turn on the '*juice*', as Mo calls it. She turns towards me, arching a brow as she eyes me from top to bottom. I'm about to hold my hand out to lead her somewhere *much* more private when there's a tap on my shoulder.

Another redhead, this one tall and built like a pinup girl, gives me an amused expression. The look in her eyes is sharp, almost predatory, and she smiles through dark, lush lips as she looks at Shooter. "My husband is concerned that this gnat is bothering you. I tried to tell him you look perfectly capable of defending yourself despite your pastel attire, but once he takes a shine to people, there's no swaying him."

"Excuse me? Gnat?" I glare at the intruder, not intimidated by her glittering Jessica Rabbit-esque black ball gown and heels that put her over six feet. "Who the hell are you?"

Who the fuck has the brass ovaries to disregard a member of The Five?

"My name is unimportant. I'm not concerned with titles. My husband, however, loves to peacock around and show his off. Your companion here met him earlier." Her smile turns to a smirk, then a grin filled with four pointed fangs. "I am simply doing my mate a favor by checking on this lovely girl."

Behind her mask, Shooter's eyes widen with recognition. "Oh! You're right. I met him at the bar earlier and we exchanged business information. Please thank him for his concern, but I am in control of my faculties. Not to worry—Casanova here isn't taking advantage of me."

Mystery Amazon lets out a laugh that reminds me of smoky jazz clubs and twenty-year-old scotch. "Very well. I'll relay your reassurance, but if you should need help, all you have to do is put your lips together and blow."

I blink. Yet another smoking hot redhead with a big brain. Thank fuck this one is married, or I might actually try to convince her to join us. "Eavesdropping, were you?"

"I have *exceptional* hearing, Casanova, and enough clever men in my life to float a battleship. I recognize game when I see it." She laughs again and winks at my drinking companion. "Enjoy your reward, fellow Mata Hari. You deserve it after your performance on the dance floor."

With that, she takes the martini that appears on the bar—yet again without a word from her to the bartender—and saunters off into the crowd. I watch her, wondering just who her husband is and why she was so goddamned pleased with herself. It's almost like she could read my mind, but every good grifter can look psychic if they're well trained in micro expressions.

But I'm trained not to let them show, so she's one hell of an operative and I've never seen her before.

"I rarely witness such support from women in my profession. I'm curious who she is," Shooter mumbles to herself.

Agreed, but I will not share that tidbit with a virtual stranger even if I feel the strongest connection to a woman I've felt in years. "I suppose at a soirée like this, women have to be or someone could get hurt."

"Indeed," she replies, turning her gaze back to me. "But she's not wrong; I would like to find a place a little more private to continue our… conversation."

Yes, please.

I rise, holding out my arm. "By all means, milady. Lead the way."

Forever

SMELLS LIKE SEX

My mood at the bar was sour as fuck until Casanova rolled up. I felt his eyes in the fray and when we locked gazes, I knew I was going to break my rules yet again. Despite my well-earned paranoia of late, something about him drew me in. Maybe it was the intensity, maybe it's the fact that a masked tryst will never lead to anything and Slick hasn't figured out my clue..

I don't know and I don't care—regardless of how irrational that decision is.

Wrapping my hand around his arm, I steer us toward the back of the ballroom. If memory serves, the blueprint showed a hidden door to the outside patio along this wall. He gives me a confused look when we approach, but I reach up and grab the overly ornate sconce and pull. It opens a small crack, and I put my finger to my lips as I slip into the doorway. I can feel the heat of his body as he follows me into the short hallway lit by dim lamps that look like they survived the first World War.

I step into the moonlight with a broad smile, lifting my arms to show him the bubbling fountain, high marble obelisks, and tall hedge maze. I'm sure this area isn't meant for the public, but the structural diagrams I dug up weren't exactly legally obtained. "I thought it might be quiet out here and I was right."

Casanova's eyes light with a wicked hunger and before I know it, I'm pressed against one of the obelisks. His breath mingles with mine when he pauses with our lips shy of touching. "Such a lovely place to sully with all the deliciously nasty things I'm going to do to you, darling."

Ooh. Gimme.

Stretching my arms above my head, I hold on to the cool marble as I give him a salacious grin. "Do your worst."

"Just the words I wanted to hear," he murmurs as he steps back. His hands go to the bow tie at his neck and he whips it off with a smirk. Holding one finger up, he motions for me to turn.

I lower my arms, doing as instructed. The silk bow tie won't do much to actually hold me, so I'm not worried about allowing this little game. Honestly, danger is an aphrodisiac for an adrenaline junkie like me and I'm digging his hidden dominance. Usually, I'm the one in control. "Yes, sir."

"Put your arms behind your back," he growls in a touch, low voice.

It makes my pussy clench, so I do it without a fight, and he makes quick work of tying them at my waist. I'm surprised to feel him go through the motions of a prayer tie—a basic arm shibari knot I wouldn't have thought he had enough material for. Casanova has more than game; my uninvited savior was underestimating him. Luckily, I'm familiar so I could escape if I needed to, but it's tight enough to give me the illusion of being bound.

My instincts about men are so rarely wrong.

He spins me back around, pushing me against the obelisk as he winks through the intricate golden bird mask. "Good thing I didn't fill up on those appetizers."

When he drops to his knees and scoots under the huge fluffy tulle skirt, I swear to Mary Magdalene, my fucking thighs tremble. Strong hands pull my legs apart and he dives in without preamble. His mouth finds my clit, forcing a ragged moan from my throat and a flood of wetness from my core. Teeth tug on my piercing as his tongue flicks, and I have to struggle not to fight the bonds at my wrists. A flick of the tip of his tongue makes me whimper and I hear him rumble with satisfaction under the gown.

Casa-fucking-nova indeed. Holy fuck buckets.

Two fingers slip inside of me, curling to hit a perfect spot as he licks over the throbbing bud with a piercing I didn't realize he had. Hips bucking into him, I ride the slow thrust of his hand as my mysterious fuck buddy eats me like he's been starving for a month. All I can do is make strangled gasps and pant as an orgasm rockets towards me faster than ever before. I arch my back and push forward, rocking and squeezing his fingers until fireworks shoot behind my eyelids. My body goes taut when he bites down gently and I let out a wail of pleasure.

"Looks like you didn't have anything to worry about, Big Bad." That husky laugh follows the words from earlier and I pry my eyes open to see my redheaded friend from the bar with her arms around *Le Voleur de Sang* as she rides the most fearsome killer in the underworld *piggyback*.

My jaw drops and I can't even form words when I see the sophisticated, ruthless assassin grinning boyishly at me. "You were right, as always, my little Tailfeather. Her Royal Highness can definitely take care of herself… though it appears she allowed someone to assist this time."

"Carry on, kiddos. Far be it for us to disturb your naughty affair. We have people to eat and mates of our own to fuck at home." The woman grins at me knowingly as she adjusts the sparkling tiara that was *not* on her head previously, then squeezes her legs on *Le Voleur's* waist. "Tally ho, peacock! I'm hungry for Italians."

The killer winks at me and heads into the hedge maze without another word. Breathing heavily, I watch their exit in shock until Casanova climbs out from under my dress. He rolls to his feet like a cat and darts forward to kiss me with lips still covered in my own juices. My mind is reeling when he pulls away, pressing a lean, hard body to mine.

"You look as though you've seen a ghost, Shooter. Did their interruption cool your fire or are you ready to fly again?"

His hips grind against mine and the sensation lights my nerves on fire. I can figure out what the fuck just happened later—right now, I want to hop on this stallion and take another ride. "I said do your worst and you're definitely not done yet, Cas."

"Good girl," he murmurs. His hands slide to my waist and he spins me again, hiking my gown up. "You're a masterpiece when you come for me."

My vagina flutters at his low toned, soft praise.

Who the fuck knew I had a praise kink? Not me, because I never let anyone take charge.

The sound of his zipper and the feel of a velvety cock pressing against my ass brings me out of that thought process. His foot nudges my legs apart and within seconds, he thrusts into me with a grunt. He's not the biggest guy I've ever been with, but his dick is thick and has a nice curve, so it's rubbing me in just the right way. Cas pulls back and slams in, making me lean forward into the marble because of the knot at my wrists. The stretch of his girth and burn at my shoulder blades exquisitely combines pain and pleasure that makes me mewl like a fucking kitten.

His fingers dig into my hips as he yanks me into him as he starts to piston in and out harder and faster. "That's my girl; take it."

Annnnnd that's when I lose my goddamn mind.

"Harder, sir," I cry. He's not my dominant by any stretch, but this role-play is doing it for both of us, so I'm not going to stand on precedent. As long as he's not actually hurting me, it's not crossing a boundary. Besides, I started it and he's doing his damndest to finish it like a fucking champ.

"You *wish* you were a good little submissive, don't you?"

His hips slap loudly against my ass and I suck in a deep breath as tremors start in my thighs. Fuck if I'll admit it out loud, but if we negotiated terms, I might let him try. "I prefer being in charge."

A palm cracks on the globe of my ass and, to my surprise, it makes my walls clench around him like a vise. "Your pussy says differently."

He's got me there. My lady bits are on board even if my brain says 'hell no'.

"Then make me come so it shuts up." I look over my shoulder, giving him a saucy smirk as I meet his next thrust.

That seems to do the trick because he hammers me so hard I have to brace my legs. Sparks shoot in my veins again and the climax I was headed towards builds to a crescendo. When I can't hold on any longer, the tidal wave breaks free and I howl into the starry sky like I'm in some cheesy paranormal romance movie. His dick jerks inside of me as he joins in, baying to the moon as if we've both hopped onto the train to Crazytown. The ragged sounds die down as our bodies cool and he unties my wrists with a flick of his fingers.

"Motherfucker," I mumble as he pulls out. I stretch my arms out to the side, allowing my shoulder joints to stretch so I don't cramp. He laughs, letting go of my dress and turning me to face him. This time, when he falls to his knees, his eyes are softer. Cas lifts the voluminous tulle, pulls a golden handkerchief out of his pocket and starts cleaning me up. "Jesus, that's silk; it will be ruined!"

Tilting his head as he continues wiping up our shared mess, he gives me a look as if I'm very slow. "Aftercare is important, Shooter. I can replace handkerchiefs."

Where the hell *did this fucking dude* come *from??*

"Well, if you insist—"

"And I do."

"Then I guess I can't complain about not having come leaking out of me for the rest of the night."

A loud snort echoes in the night as he grins up at me. "You might be the most interesting woman I've met in a long time."

"Likewise, buddy." I pause, feeling an idiot. "Except for the woman part."

"Thank you for adding that. My ego was taking a real hit for a moment," Cas teases as he rises to stand.

"Uh, I doubt it after this." I gesture around us. "But it's good to know how to aim for where it hurts."

"Shooter, I'd let you hit just about anything you wanted. All you have to do is ask, darling."

I shake my head, trying to clear it of this comfortable, cutesy banter. This is a one and done situation—why am I still here? What the fuck is wrong with me lately? I'm acting like the clingy chick in a 90s movie. "Lovely as this has been, Cas. I should probably get going."

He pouts. "You aren't going to fill me in on our voyeurs from earlier? I feel cheated."

Damn that pout. It almost makes me want to—no, Remy.

My brain works hard to discourage what I do next, but I can't seem to stop myself. I reach into the pocket built into my dress and pull out my phone. "Give me your number and if you figure out who the guy was, *maybe* I'll answer your text."

"A hunt? I *like* it, Shooter. You'll find I'm very resourceful."

I'll just bet you are, dude.

Within a few seconds, I have his number programmed in and I send him a message through the encryption app I use for jobs. "There. Text me if you figure it out."

"Then you'll go on a date with me?"

"Who the hell said anything about a date? I *don't* date." I give him a stern expression as I back away towards the palace door. "I said I'd answer a text, nothing more."

"We'll see about that!"

I turn on my heel, almost running into the ball to get away from temptation. That's twice in a week and I have no idea what's going on with me.

It's almost like The Guillotine is lonely.

But that can't be.

Forever

FLIRTING WITH DISASTER

FUCKING JINX.

That feels weird to even think. It's *always* Coda going off-book, and it's always Dwyn disappearing. However, we're in the middle of a motherfucking Open Market *and* a *Deus*—unwillingly at that—and the one leveled headed asshole has stolen both their crowns.

"Raz, do you see him on the cameras?"

The exasperated sigh tells me he's frustrated as well. "No, Mo. he was at the bar and then he followed a redhead into the crowd. Then *poof!* Gone from all sight lines."

"It wasn't meeee this time!" Dwyn's sing-song makes me want to abandon my hawk-eye spot and punch him, but I refrain because he's not wrong.

Coda snorts into the mic. That's all he can do unless he works coded phrases into his conversation with all the adoring fans, so we've learned to read the emotion behind his little noises over the years.

"Coda, your last album was to *die for!*"

I smile despite my irritation with Jinx. The rocker *hated* his most recent album because he wasn't able to work in as much original material as he wanted. His label forced a bunch of pre-written garbage on him that netted a fortune but made him feel like a 'two dollar whore' being pimped.

"Yes, Cecily, it was a great success," he says.

Obviously, the sarcasm in his voice doesn't translate because he's only met with giggles. My smile turns to a smirk as I mutter, "Keep shaking that ass, buddy."

His low growl attracts more sighs and giggles, which gives Raz an opening to prod him. "Oh, Coda, I just *love* your shitty goth pop bullshit. It *speaks to my soul.*"

"This party is getting fucking lame." The women around Coda coo their sympathy, but his comment was meant for us more than them.

"Guys, I think I saw Jinxy!"

Dwyn's excited cry pauses our private torture session and I feel some tension deep from my frame. We don't always work in a group like this much—the fabled Dead Man's Wedding—but when we do, I spend a lot of my time worrying about the impulsive nature of the rest. Jinx is the least tempted by the spur-of-the-moment bullshit and his disappearance worried me.

"Where is he, D?"

There's a muffled bit and the rest of us wait until he comes back. "So I think it was him. He was headed upstairs, and he looked pretty wrinkled. I don't know what the hell happened, but I guess he's off to follow one of our targets. Coda dealt with *Alqatu*, right? *Ape Regina* was a cinch; she's hella overrated."

I frown. That means we've dealt with two of the big hitters. "Raz, is *El Guapo* handled?"

"Affirmative. I'm checking the cams for Jinx now." The hacker goes quiet for a moment as keys click and when he finally speaks, his voice is full of confusion. "Jinx took the stairs. D's right—he looks like he might have been in a tussle. He never walks around looking so rumpled. But his expression wasn't worried or irritated. I'm not sure what to make of it, Mo."

Great. We have a lovesick psycho thief, a pouty rockstar, and now a freaked out hacker at the wheel.

"If he didn't give the signal, let him be, guys. Focus on finding The Duchess, *Le Voleur*, or the Horseman. Obviously, keep your eyes peeled for the mystery chick, just in case. Hopefully Jinx will turn his earwig back on soon."

"Be nice if he explained why the hell he turned it off, too," Raz grumps. "I purposely crafted these to help us keep tabs without being interrupted by chatter. It didn't have to be shut off—he could have turned off audio, and I'd have been able to track him."

Honestly, despite his petulance, Raz has a point. Turning the tech off only impedes us if someone does something like what happened to Coda. Why *did* our gifted grifter hide his location and activity from us? It's not like him and I find myself as perturbed as our ops specialist when I consider it. Bad tradecraft gets you killed; Jinx is *never* bad at his job.

"I'm off to find a horsey, boys. Let me know if one of you notices anything I should pause my quest for, like my girl Jazz."

"Dwyn..."

But his audio is already off and so is he.

Christ, I hate being in charge.

Dwyn is a goddamn ninja when he doesn't want to be seen. He's been dark for over an hour and we still haven't located Jinx. During that time, I haven't been able to catch *Le Voleur*, but security has been quite active in short bursts. I highly doubt it's about my brothers, but given the look on one of the server's faces during the last round of quiet deployment, I'd bet my target's mission got completed.

But who was Le Voleur hunting and why didn't they clear the event if someone was murdered?

"Guys."

Raz cuts in before I can shout at the previously off-the-grid grifter. "Where the actual *fuck* have you been?!"

Maybe I'll let him handle this one.

"Calm down, man. I'm fine, but you will not *believe* what happened," Jinx says. His voice is raspy and full of… wonder?

"If you found Dwyn's gold plated pussy, I swear I'll…"

He's moved away from his crowd and though the rock star isn't usually this jealous, Jinx and Dwyn don't beat him to a conquest often, either. It's amusing, but not helpful in our current situation. "Coda, calm down. J, if you could be so kind as to explain your breach in operational security?"

"I met a girl. Not Jazz, but holy fuck. I've never… Jesus mother-fucking Christ on a pogo stick." Jinx sucks in a breath and I can tell he's struggling with words—also unusual for our smooth talking con man. "This woman was intoxicating. And I went dark, which I know was a dick move, so I'm sorry for that. I don't do this shit—ever—so it distracted you, I'm sure. But I didn't know what the fuck…"

"He's not joking." Raz's voice has gone from panicked to interested in a matter of minutes. They might be involved, but they've never been exclusive. He's clearly looking for details.

That's a conversation for later when we're not surrounded by thieves, killers, and famous people who could get us arrested.

"Since I now have three operatives with their dicks in control of their brains, I'm calling this shit. Coda, leave. Jinx, locate Dwyn and meet

Raz. I'll have to convince my employer something is unsafe before I can peel off to meet at HQ."

"See you soon, suckers," Coda grunts.

"I'll be ready." Raz waits to sign off until Jinx confirms and I cut my audio.

They don't need to know, but I'm going to probe the security first to see what kind of nonsense went on earlier.

Sweeping my eyes over the crowd, I make certain there are no immediate threats to the diplomats before I give up my position. The small rushes of guards and plainclothes security entered a door near the back wall opposite of where I was perched all night, so I quickly cut through the crowd to that section of the room. When I open it, I find a large, empty ballroom with several groups of people and local *Policie České* milling about. I can't imagine the event coordinators only involved the cops, so I eye the men and women walking around carefully.

It doesn't take long to spot possible Interpol agents—they have an air of superiority that is easily identified in a situation such as this— and a few other wildcards who could be Mossad, CIA, FBI, or even MI-6. One very stern looking blond man is watching from a corner, his bright blue eyes and sharp cheekbones a distinct contrast to all the working class LEOs in the room. I'm uncertain who he works for, but I can sense the danger emanating from him across the room. Best to stay under his radar, I think.

I slip through the door and sidle up to a studious-looking agent in a suit at the makeshift coffee bar. *"Ciao, signore. Sono la sicurezza di uno dei diplomatici presenti alla festa. Cosa sta succedendo qui dentro?"* He looks at me with wide eyes, clearly not comprehending more than 'hello, sir.' *Definitely American.* "Mi scusi. I am security for a special guest. May I inquire what is happening here?"

"Ah! Yes, sorry about that. I'm new and I haven't mastered Italian yet." The agent gives me a shamed look and I almost laugh—Americans *never* take the time to learn other languages. "We have several suspects in custody. Several thefts were reported by guests and we lined those perpetrators up in groups along that wall."

Glancing over, I see a few small-time criminals and one middle range thief. "Ah. *Va bene.* And the others?"

His Adam's apple bobs when he swallows. Whatever is coming next bothers the hell out of his green ass. "The lady in the front got nabbed while trying to break into the offices and hack into computer systems via the Czech government's hard lines. She's well known, according to my partner."

I almost snort. These clowns caught Ape Regina? How humiliating.

Of course, given this extremely dangerous Open Market and *deus ex machina*, it's likely someone dimed her out to save their own ass. That is why The Five do not take part in shit like this—until tonight. I nod, pretending to be surprised so the loose-lipped agent will continue. "*Molto buona!* The officers here must be quite skilled to pull off such a coup."

He beams, soaking in the praise as if he had anything to do with it. "Indeed! There were whispers of this event drawing many high-ranking criminals, so an inter-agency task force has been monitoring the event. That's how we caught the gentleman in the far corner. We believe he's responsible for… the mess in the upstairs bathroom."

His voice lowered when he finished that sentence and I know without a doubt, this kid puked his guts out when he saw whatever it was. "The mess? What was that? Is my client in danger?"

"Oh, no!" The agent shakes his head, looking pleased. "We definitely caught the filthy murderer. Your charge is not in any danger now."

I arch a brow, pretending to consider. "Are you sure? Who was this victim your murderer was after? Perhaps the plot is bigger, no?"

"The CEO of a record label was enjoying the company of some less than appropriately aged women in a bathroom that should have been locked." He frowns as if he's disappointed in the palace security, but I know that scenario was probably bought and paid for. "He was damn near torn to pieces and he's almost drained of blood, like a freaky vampire did it. I'm sure it was a specific message."

Fuck yes, it was. Le Voleur de Sang left his mark all the hell over that hit and the wimpy looking fuck in the chair isn't him — it's El Guapo.

"I see. Well, I am pleased to hear your security and task force were successful in their efforts. All the same, I must take my leave. I believe my employer would prefer to leave before any other unsavory issues arise. He's in a very delicate position politically and it would not be beneficial to him to be listed on crime reports. You understand, *si*?"

He swallows hard, but nods. "I do. Make haste before they decide to begin interviews with the guests. They will do their best to keep it under wraps, but no agency is without leaks."

"Grazie, signore." I shake his hand before I turn on my heel and head out the door. The press of a button on my earwig turns on the audio and as I weave my way through the crowd, I growl, "Chernobyl. I repeat, Chernobyl."

With that evacuation signal given, I make my way to the diplomat and his wife, preparing to convince them it's in their best interest to leave as soon as possible. Once I repeat what that mouthy agent told me, it shouldn't be hard.

We're going to need a hell of a debrief after this nonsense.

Forever

ENEMY

After I take the most circuitous route possible back to the Mandarin, I glide in as The Duchess. Cas did an excellent job of cleaning me up and I don't look like I've been fucked within an inch of my life, so the staff has nothing to gossip about. I'm able to take the elevators straight to my second suite and ditch the trappings of my disguise without incident. That makes my anxiety fade a bit. I needed *something* to go according to plan during this trip; it might as well be the aftermath.

I stuff the bits and bobs associated with her costume into trash bags, frowning as I relegate the gorgeous frock to a quick trip down an incinerator. Though I'm a heartless killer, I can appreciate impeccable craftsmanship and gorgeous finery as much as the next gal. Trashing this masterpiece makes my gut clench, but alas, I cannot ever reuse costumes. The risk of being photographed is too high in the age of computers in everyone's pockets.

Wending my way around the hotel and dropping my garbage bags in various chutes and cans takes a bit, but when I'm done, I head for the Presidential Suite. Once I plug in the security codes, I enter with a sigh of relief. I'm dressed in comfortable jogging clothes and a messy bun—a vestige of the actual Remy peeking through. I didn't want to spend another ID on this errand, so I tucked my bun into a ball cap and wear glasses that would obscure my features. It seemed like enough for the intended goal, and I'm hoping I wasn't wrong.

Suddenly, a loud beep emits from something upstairs and I rush to the kitchen area, taking the back steps up to the dining area where my tech is set up. One monitor is flashing and I scramble over to read the text on the screen as the alarm continues to go off. The message from my shadowy client has arrived—I'll need to listen to his latest audio to find out when he'll be dropping my newest package. Another alarm sounds, making me blink.

I whip off the cap and glasses, tossing them on the table to sit at the main terminal. There are multiple messages on the *Mercatus* boards —vendors looking for their requests. It appears quite a few of the contractors did *not* achieve their tasks, but the targets got stolen or eliminated, regardless. *Snakes on the motherfucking plane,* I think to myself. There were *Les Invisibles*, Syndicate, or Company teams snatching jobs from under the indies. I wish I'd known that, but it doesn't change what I accomplished as The Duchess. Now the clients have to figure out which operatives have what, and the prices from the Open Market will skyrocket. It's a clever plan and I'm not surprised any of the big crime organizations chose to do so.

However, that's not what is making my alarms go crazy.

My web spiders have found information on my old team and my nemesis. It's not likely to be much—there's a reason *LI* isn't whispered about—but it may help me figure out why they've become the target of a crazy megalomaniac with delusions of grandeur. I scoot my chair over to the other side of the room, scanning the snippets the bots located. There's some vague biographical stuff that's all bogus and a few news stories that suggest some of their code names were involved in specific events. *La Arana* isn't mentioned in any of them, though Jinx and Dwyn's monikers are. Even stormy-faced Mo is referenced in an article as a security man for an old mafia Don known to run his crew from a villa in Italy.

So why is Raz the target of a hit? Nothing in this round of dirt even suggests his involvement.

I can't wrap my head around why the least flamboyant, most hidden member of The Five is my client's focus. Raz never takes credit, rarely leaves his command centers, and probably still does white hat hacking on the side like he did when we were young. He's the least morally flexible of the lot, not that it's saying anything. Who could he have possibly pissed off so badly?

Shaking my head, I push away from that screen and go back to the main computer. Perhaps if I keep pulling the thread on the shadowy asshole, I'll be able to figure out why he's coming after *Les Invisibles.* I don't care if he takes down The Commandant and his merry band of High Legion cunts. However, something about his focus on The Five makes me nervous. I've been so careful for so long. Is it possible someone knows I survived the explosion? Will he come after me next? I can't take the chance.

Sure, Remy. That's the only reason you're trying to solve this riddle instead of just taking your ex-friend's head like you normally would.

The voice in my head is as unwelcome as it is accurate. I haven't seen or heard from the boys I loved so dearly for a decade, but being immersed in their sphere again is making my head spin. Getting my rocks off with Slick and Cas only made it worse—the appeal of having someone around who might keep up with me is making me soft and I fucking *hate* it. I can't maintain my reputation or my lifestyle if I'm dragging dick around with me. It would never work.

A low growl escapes my throat and I click on the file, hoping to distract myself with a nut job.

"Greetings once more, Guillotine.

Your missive was received, and I am delighted to confirm the details of our next drop in this lovely city.

In two days hence, we shall place the items in the locations you have indicated. It will take us that time to make certain we have everything set up in the manner you requested. Your requests are quite specific and we must prepare our materials to comply.

Once you receive them, you will follow all instructions for maintaining contact and updating us on your progress. Failure to comply will terminate your contract.
That is not a step we wish for you to take, Guillotine, as it will designate you as a loose end—something we cannot tolerate.

Your artistry is world renown and it would be a waste to eliminate someone as skilled as yourself for something so trivial.

Take care to read all documents and files carefully now that you have accepted our contract, Guillotine.

We will be watching.

Kindest Regards and caveat emptor."

My eyes roll into the back of my head as the audio cuts off.

Buyer beware? Is this dude for real?

I cannot stress enough how much I *hate* crazy motherfuckers. Usually, I turn down jobs from whack-a-doos, but fucking *Raz Miranda* is why I didn't tell this asshole to get bent. The men from my past have me knee deep in the shit yet again, and I have *no idea* where this bus to Loco-ville is going to stop.

The party tonight was proof of that—I met *Le Voleur de Sang* and his wife, apparently, and they *liked me.* How fucking bizarre is this whole situation? I've been on my own, keeping my head down, and doing my thing for over ten years. In four days, I've been closer to more dangerous people than in all of that time put together. All of this exposure is making my skin crawl and the inability to plan my moves five steps ahead is even worse.

What am I going to do?

Tapping my fingernail against my teeth, I consider all the players.

Coda is probably with one or more of The Five by now. His news feeds are quiet and it's a good bet they're looking for his 'savior'. That means one, maybe two, of them are working on that. If I'm lucky, it's not Mo. I doubt his rabid dog hunting style has changed much since his youth, and I don't want to go up against him with all of this uncertainty.

My client—I'm going to call him Shadow Douche—obviously has money and backers, though how many, I can't be certain. Ego driven narcissists typically gather their flying monkeys in the darkness so they can maintain an unimpeachable image in public. His grandiose plans are likely revenge for a perceived slight, and that makes him dangerous. I've known people to turn their backs on family and friends for as little as money, but for revenge? People with this sort of mentality will burn the entire *world* down simply to embarrass one solitary person who didn't agree with them. If Shadow Douche has minions, it will be a thousand times worse.

This is a war that will never end if I'm right.

I'm so fucking glad I ended up in the middle of this fucking nonsense.

So far, I don't think any of those high-end bitches and jackasses working the Open Market are a part of this. There might have been teams from the big players and a bunch of indie contractors from *Mercatus*, but the only person I'm concerned about from that debacle is whoever pulled the strings.

An Open Market and a *deus ex machina* in the same location at the same time is unheard of and the power it had to have taken to arrange it is scary. Many, many favors got traded or called in to risk so many criminals being caught or eliminated at the same time. Our services have value and take training and skill—especially those in the deeper end of the talent pool, like myself. It could have damaged the field for years if it went sideways.

That wouldn't make *any* of our clients happy and it sure as fuck wouldn't make anyone's wallet happy.

No, I don't think the vendors were the issue; it was the power broker behind the scenes.

I don't believe The Commandant is part of this—yet. The Five are probably acting of their own accord and they have more latitude before they'll have to make him aware. As long as they don't fuck up any assigned jobs while they dick around with my cold trails, they can stay on Naomi as long as they want. *Les Invisibles* is the least of my worries currently.

Raking my hand through my hair, I study the small drawing I've been sketching with the players in their various bubbles. It's obvious the intersection includes my ex-best friends, but I haven't connected the dots fully enough. I know Coda didn't recognize me and I'm certain my face isn't being splashed anywhere. So why does it feel like I have eyes on me 24/7? Is it them or my douchebag client?

Okay. I'm not getting answers on this tonight.

I check all the screens one more time and roll out of the chair. It's late and though I sleep little, I think a shower and a nap will help me recenter my thoughts. Food will follow and once I'm properly fueled, I can think about the other two issues I didn't even touch on.

Slick and Cas, both of whom I left bread crumbs for after I 'wham bammed' them—something I never do, and can't figure out why I did this time, either. If I didn't know me, I'd think a fucking amateur was using my skin as a fake Remy suit. I'm a goddamn mess.

Trudging down the stairs to the luxurious bathroom, I turn on the faucets and look at the two phones I brought with me, just in case.

Houston, we might have a problem.

The simple truth is I'm waiting for one or both of them to figure out my little puzzles and if they do, I don't even know what the plan is. It's not like I can invite them to join me in my life of derring-do and intrigue—that's ridiculous. The only way I could possibly have had any sort of permanent partner in my life died in an explosion a decade ago. There's no 'happy ending' for assassins beyond living to retire and partying for the rest of your days.

Better you remember that now, Remy, or you're going to get hurt—again.

DAREDEVIL

CHERNOBYL*?!*

Mo never calls the nuclear code—he's far too cocky to think we need to beat a hasty retreat—but here I am skedaddling out an upstairs window and shimmying up a drainpipe like I'm in a *Pink Panther* movie. We set that word after the disaster where we lost Remy; we'd never considered needing a protocol to invoke for when all hell broke loose.

We were that *young and full of dumbass bravado.*

Once the line dropped, each of us knew we had to find a covert way out of the building before scattering for the next couple of hours. No one is to come within a ten-mile radius of each other or our current safe house until the sun comes up. Our comms will stay dark and we deactivate all tracking to prevent someone capturing one to find the entire cell. This kind of result is why The Five don't take part in bull-shit events like Open Markets or the equivalents for the other specialties. Open Markets are 'county fairs' for grifters and thieves, *deus ex machina* are challenges for hitters and assassins, Zero Days are hacker bonanzas, and *Commedia dell'Arte* is a fucking free-for-all. I can't say it has not tempted me a time or two, but not with my own skill's parties.

I'd much prefer to crash the other's big criminal Olympics to see if I can work my magic while my colleagues are focused on completely different targets. Mo says it makes me a crazy son of a bitch and he's probably right. There are so few people at my level to challenge me, though, and stealing my way through a crowd of potential assassins feels like a right fine shot of adrenaline I don't get as often as I'd like. Alas, he put his foot down and if I went around him, he'd squeal to the Commandant to spite me.

The last thing I need is that crusty old bastard to put a leash on me because I couldn't hold my wad.

By the time I finish my inner grumbling, I've reached the top of the pipe and I swing myself onto the roof. I pause for a moment, envisioning the schematics of the rooftops of the palace and the surrounding buildings. Everything is uneven and I'm suddenly grateful that our ridiculously over-prepared hacker insisted on each of us being equipped with our own version of a safety net. For me, that's built-in mods to my clothing and a fancy ass gadget.

I tap the smartwatch, hitting the app with a cheeky 'Q' on it. Fucker thinks he's part of the Bond crowd and I can't wait to rub in his face that dear old misogynistic James didn't spend most of his time in a van. A few more clicks have the soles of my shoes spouting spikes for climbing and once I take my suit coat off, the vest flaps slide loose in the back. It's already made of lightweight, wearable Kevlar, but the flaps reveal hooks I can tug if I need them.

Taking my replacement glasses out of the coat, I drop it and head towards the south end to begin my journey across rooftops until I reach the location mapped on the device. If I get there without deviation, I'll head for the ground. Transportation options vary there and it will depend on the level of LEO response I see which one I take to the next point.

This is my favorite part.

My arms pump at my side as I run towards the edge of the building, taking a flying leap across the divide as I aim for a flagpole. Luckily, the wrought iron holds my weight as I flip over it twice from the momentum and my palms burn with friction. No fucking gloves—that's on me. I didn't think I need them and that's what I get for being so goddamn overconfident. I grunt, kicking my legs out until I get going again, and when I hit the perfect arc, I let go of the bar.

Fuck yeah!

The metal of the penthouse balcony rail hits the backs of my knees hard and I groan audibly. I'm in fucking *amazing* shape, but this gymnast shit with no warm up is for the fucking birds. Thieves definitely practice all this crap for when we *might* need it, but in reality, we usually don't. Ego, carelessness, and plain cheap assholes are our most direct routes into whatever we need. All this cat burglar, *Entrapment* crap is never the answer—except for today. I catch my breath and slide off the rail, walking over to the closed doors to see if I hear anyone inside. An empty suite means I can knock the fucking climbing off, but once I hear the faint sound of a TV, I know I'm not that lucky.

Rolling my eyes, I climb back onto the rail and start up the side of the building, using the decorated exterior as hand and footholds as I make my way to the roof of this place so I can map the next waypoint in my journey.

Fucking Mo. I'm going to throttle that motherfucker.

AFTER FIVE MORE FEATS OF DARING AND ONE PULLED RIP CORD, I FINALLY touchdown past the bridge near one of the main hotel areas. I cut the chute with the knife clipped at my lower back and touch the buttons on my watch to make my shoes normal again. The ease with which I do all of this without attracting attention is because, though I've never had to make use of Raz's favorite failsafe, I've wasted quite a few of them practicing. I *never* use tech I'm unfamiliar with in the field and *definitely* not as my nuclear option escape route. The hacker cursed me out more than a few times when he had to replace them over and over, but my dedication paid off tonight. I could activate, use, and ditch the damned thing in less than ten minutes and they have not made me.

That's tradecraft for you; it's a dying art.

I stop, pretending to consider my options as I exit the alleyway and look around the busy street. There are lots of hotels with bars I can slip into and drink until the predetermined meet-up time. Because I wasn't on an *actual* mission, I wasn't forced to leave any of my loot behind—all the money, jewels, and collectibles are tucked neatly into my hidden pockets and holsters. I'm just lucky I calculated my weight plus a decent amount of extra loot heft when I had Raz design the damn chute. Otherwise, I could have hit the ground in a *much* less elegant way.

Ducking into the Mandarin, I stride into their lobby and nod at the employees like they should know me. The attitude and suit—though rumpled—keep them from questioning me as I walk into the bar/lounge. Once I tuck myself in the corner, I order a bourbon on the rocks. My phone and earwigs are silent, so I grab a napkin. When the drink arrives, I charm a pen from the flirty server. I might as well keep my brain busy while I'm stuck here.

Christ, I hate sitting still like this, but whoever designed that royally buggered event at the palace is the one who needs to be peeled like a grape, not Mo.

The bourbon is excellent and while I sip, I open the pictures on my phone so I can see the one I took of the code on my hipbone. I'd be lying if I said I knew what it meant right away and that bothers the *fuck* out of me. The damned thing is just four strings of numbers that don't seem to mean a damned thing.

512431.6728-04316.572

59.337018.0618

34.6876135.1929

38.89795738.897957

I don't know if they are in order or if they are part of an equation… they're simply written in groups, one after the other, and at the end, there's a small sketch of a lipstick print. Jazz is a cheeky monkey for this and if I hadn't been so frustrated to wake up alone, I might not have even seen them before they washed off in a shower.

No wonder I'm obsessed—she's fucking perfect for me.

Raz would be *amazing* at this. Even without the tech surrounding him, numbers make as much sense to him as schematics do to me. Code, equations, math, science… it's all his motherloving *jam*, and he'd sit awake for the next week if it would mean solving this without having to use an algorithm. He's always trying to beat the tech to the answer, and it makes Jinx and Coda laugh their asses off. Nothing much makes Mo laugh anymore, but maybe that morose motherfucker will take his head out of his ass if we find my girl.

I think she could make sunshine fly out of his ass if she tried hard enough.

Scribbling on the napkin, I turn it around and around trying to figure out what she was trying to tell me. It has to be both simple and complex; the elegance of a true intellect is their ability to think on multiple levels and in multiple dimensions. Jazz and I didn't have a long conversation because I was busy giving her something else long —*heh*—but I know what my gut says. It says she's the real deal, and I'd be stupid to underestimate her. So nothing too outrageous on the fly, but nothing a random average Joe would get, either. It doesn't fit any of the cipher variations I can remember off the top of my head from *l'Academie* and I can't use the internet for another couple hours.

"What the hell are you doing *here*, you absolute twatwaffle?"

The affronted hiss is familiar, and I look up to see Coda standing in front of my table. He's got on a black hoodie pulled up to hide his famous face and hair and dark black jeans. He got rid of his fancy duds on the way and I can tell he expected to plop down in this ritzy lounge and drink until our meeting. Discovering me in his chosen haunt means one of us should leave and since he arrived last, it should be him.

I shouldn't be gleeful about it, but I am.

"As if I can control what direction the wind blows a goddamned chute at that height. My routes are never fixed since they depend on ever changing variables that none of you other fuckers have to contend with. I'm not just cutting through a traffic jam or picking a lock, you know." I arch my brow at him, waiting for him to understand that the mere physical constraints of my escapes are far more intense than anyone else's.

Huffing, he drops into the chair across from me and scrubs a hand over his face. "Fine, but don't tell General Assface we stayed in the same location. I'm exhausted from entertaining a bunch of vapid bints all night while the rest of you played and got laid."

"Awww. Poor sad emo rock star… *write me a song about your pain, Coda,*" I coo as I smirk at him. He rolls his eyes and gestures for the server, nodding at me until I order an entire bottle.

His eyes skate over the napkin, squinting as he studies it. "Is that the infamous code?"

"Yep," I say, spinning the napkin again as if it will change my perspective. "We need Raz, man."

"The girl fucked your brains out, scrawled a math code on your hip, and skittered off before you woke up? How much *did* you drink?" His grin is knowing, and I shrug carelessly.

"Only split a bottle of tequila. Watched it being opened; no drugs. Just wore me the *fuck* out. This girl is the Holy Grail of women."

When the bottle comes, he pours us two fingers and looks at his watch. "I hope so, man. The last time we all chased a chick this hard, she blew herself to smithereens and took our hearts with her. Our judgment has to be better now, right?"

"You're asking me?" I give him my best psycho smirk and he laughs loud enough to draw attention.

"Good point, man, good point."

Forever

GIVE 'EM HELL

According to the news feeds, I left that clusterfuck at the perfect time last night. I was halfway to the hotel when law enforcement descended on the ballroom like a swarm of scarabs and I couldn't be more pleased. Some unlucky staff members discovered the signature mess left by *Le Voleur* and the event planners could no longer hide the swath of criminal activity occurring under their noses.

He and his wife were the clear victors of the deus ex machina—which should surprise no one.

Truthfully, I'm more surprised by the amount of upper echelon operatives attending either event—it led to several high-level apprehensions. It's likely pricey lawyers will free those people or they'll escape before trial, but the outrage on all the areas of *Mercatus* from various organizations was vehement. No one seems to know who activated either large scale free-for-all, and many clients got left scrambling as their jobs seem unfulfilled.

Of course, The Duchess is arranging her transfers because I'm a goddamned professional, but the ensuing chaos is making the underworld panic. Kills, bribes, thefts, and other missions may have gotten completed, but no one has emerged to take credit for swiping the spoils—yet. That kind of uncertainty has our already skittish clientele scrambling for information and that will definitely drive up prices.

Perhaps that was the goal?

It's no matter. Despite my reckless abandon with Cas, I was able to complete my task and respond to my employer for the night. I also put a face to a villain I want to ensure I never cross, and that's a handy tidbit to keep my ass safe in the future. I'm not sure why he took a shine to me or why his wife felt so familiar, but it doesn't hurt to have nodding acquaintances with that much power. We can trade favors amongst our brethren, and I don't have any stored up. With Shadow Douche looming, I suppose a somewhat friendly face in the dark can't hurt.

I slept like a rock for the second time in two weeks. The nightmares became less frequent as the years passed, but I've never regained a healthy sleep pattern after my escape. Finding two one-off guys who got me to actually rest is disconcerting, but the stress of all this para-noia has to play into that. I'm operating almost at the level I did when I first started out on my own—watching every crack and crevice for someone who wants me dead.

I thought I'd left that shit behind once I became The Guillotine, but here I am.

Unfortunately for me, there's no time to suss out the whys at the moment. The Douche drop is tonight and I have to pick my alter ego carefully. I don't want anything close to the Duchess disguise or any of the ones I've used in Prague recently, so I have to sort through the selection downstairs. Weapons and various back-ups plans need to be combed over and I have to ready everything else in the suite for a quick exit once I retrieve the drive. I didn't intend to linger this long in one city, particularly in these conditions, but after last night, it's imperative that I hustle to my next stop.

Time to get serious, Remy. Quit thinking with your pussy and get down to business.

MY INTERNAL PEP TALK DID THE TRICK.

Afterwards, I ordered another spread of local delicacies and munched while I decided which city I want to hole up in next. Feeling nostalgic, I picked Istanbul so I can amuse myself humming under my breath the whole time—something *has* to be funny or I'll blow my top soon—and it's close enough to the continent that I can choose land, sea, or air routes out if need be. Plus, the ability to hide under a scarf without drawing attention is another bonus.

Since I want to be extremely mobile and very memorable, I picked a flashy identity for this trip: *Stella Buonotti of Venice, Italy.* The layered, electric blue wig paired with the magenta two piece leathers and a decorative crop top will create a peacocking effect I believe suits the occasion. People will look at me constantly, but all they will remember is the hair and the outfit, not what I was doing as I made my way around the museum. The visual misdirection will give me time to scope out all the fail safes, scoop up the drive, and get out while people are still tittering about my unique appearance.

Sadly, it appears both of my gentleman callers weren't up to snuff quickly enough to locate me before the endgame. Que sera...

Thank fuck I brought a few modified weapons because Stella's kit is *not* made to hide any bulk. I have my Guillotine wires hidden in a full service rocker jewelry set, so I'll be armed with no less than six unobtrusive ways to kill anyone who gets close. I can wedge a few of my knives in various locations as well, especially since I chose asskicking blue combat boots for this disguise. It's possible I might add a few other surprises I thought to grab despite not being my usual preferred methods.

A girl can never be too cautious when she's ducking a sociopath with delusions of grandeur and several major criminal syndicates who think she's dead.

Before I head to the bathroom, I pack up all the tech, disappointingly quiet burners, and the rest of my shit. It takes a bit to move it piece by piece down to the Duchess' room, but once the suite is empty but for the bare minimum, I'm ready.

A ping on the phone in my pocket reveals my private charter to Istanbul was confirmed. If everything goes well, The Duchess' luggage will get transported to the airport while I'm working and when I get the files, I can head straight to my flight. It's only about two hours by plane and weather permitting, this disastrous stay will be in my rearview by tomorrow morning.

THE STREETS ARE CROWDED TONIGHT. I EXITED THE METRO EARLY, preferring to take an entirely different route to and from the Sex Machine Museum than I did on my recon trip. Winding my way through the locals and tourists, I have to conceal my smile as people stare exactly as intended. The striking blue and pink combo garners whispers and surreptitiously pointing at me in either awe or disdain. The only thing anyone will recall is the disguise—my face, though beautifully made-up—will be blank in comparison.

Sometimes plain sight is the best place to hide, especially if you make certain something skews your biometrics in front of the cameras.

I'm more concerned about the capabilities of tech than a lot of my contemporaries because of the shit Raz taught me, even if it was a long time ago. That thought makes me frown as I hurry toward the museum a little more quickly. I need to sort this shit out before the hacker's hit gets picked up by another operative—if Shadow Douche didn't already contract it to multiple people hoping to catch the elusive *La Araña* more easily with a spray of bullets rather than a precision shot.

When I get to the entrance, I switch from sunglasses to spy frames and start scanning the minute I join the group of people awaiting the next tour. I keep my eyes on my phone like any annoying Zoomer, knowing the combination of that and my appearance will deter nosy busybodies. They'd much rather scoff at a 'young person on their phone' than snoop at what I'm doing or ask inane questions. Plus, the app that has their cam feeds is allowing me to check for any changes in topography from a few days ago.

Shuffling along with the odd mix of people who find old sex toys interesting, I pretend to study a few exhibits, always keeping careful watch. Pervy Euro trash men, blushing Americans, and giggling teens make up much of my group. Normally, the interaction would fascinate me, but I'm at last focused on getting to the planter at the corner of a four-way split in the hallway. It's an open space with plenty of exits and exactly where I need to be to retrieve my plunder before I slip out.

The guide stops in the middle, giving the same speech as before, encouraging guests to wander this part freely to 'discover the history of kink' on their own. That's my cue to saunter over to the wall and lean against it, fingers tapping at my keys while the bulk of the crowd disperses to the different sections. I sigh in pretend boredom, then hold my phone up to my ear like I'm making a call.

The rudeness will hasten their scattering; everyone hates people having loud conversations on their phone in public.

"I don't know, Bizzy. It's a little sketch and boring. Your mom is so old school." Pause. "Well, I'm in a hallway next to some kind of enormous plant… what kind? I don't know, let me use my app.."

Leaning down, I pretend to snap a picture for the fake app and while I'm there, I find the drive stuck inside of the leafy giant. Relief floods my veins as I palm it and rise, jabbering into the cell like a complete moron. I turn to head down the East hall when a throat clears behind me.

Son of a bitch. How the fuck did anyone know I would come to this *drop point?*

Three large dudes are looking at me with dark smirks as they crack their knuckles. I'm not sure where the hell they came from or who they are, but this means trouble. Either Shadow Douche is actually after *me* or I just confirmed that he hired other contractors for *my* mission.

No matter which is correct, I'm going to find that motherfucker and mount his head on my non-existent mantle.

Luckily, I've already tucked my prize away, so I give the goons a bored look while I calculate the success rate of the plans for escape. Given the space and limitations of the old ass building… I'm going to have to fight my way out. Time to use what the gods gave me.

I curl my lip up when they don't speak, dropping into a loose fighting stance. One of them has the nerve to laugh and I tilt my head, letting my mind settle into what Mo used to call the 'ice zone.' No genuine emotions, no distractions… only precise, clinical movements chosen to maximize their damage and create a window for withdrawal.

"*Buenna notte*, gentleman. I don't believe we've met. Stella Buonotti, at your service. And you are…?"

The leader smirks. "Going to take that drive off of you, little girl. I'd advise being smart—we outnumber and outsize you. Hand it over and you won't get hurt."

I pretend to consider that while I scope out the possible weak points on his partners, then shrug. "Thanks for the offer, but I'll settle for kicking your asses instead. Appreciate the thought, though."

They all laugh, and the tallest one steps out of formation. "This will only take a second, Boss."

Crooking my finger, I give the monster a flirty wink. "That's exactly what all the girls think when they see you, buddy. Good to know I was right."

I should admit killing people before they know I'm there prevents my smart mouth from doing shit like this all the time.

"Go for it, Nachte. I want to see this bitch bleed."

Yup. My big, fat mouth for the win.

BALLROOM BLITZ

Coda and Dwyn didn't show up at the base after the predetermined 'dark time.'

I left Jinx with Raz, waxing poetic over the woman he nailed while he was supposed to be working. The level of unpredictability in my team is why I work alone so often—I can't abide their 'fly by the seat of their pants' attitude. While the hacker is marginally better, he's easily influenced by his other half. I'd love to put them through the paces to get our machine running the way it should be, but if I can't get them to observe basic protocols, forcing a more regimented routine will only encourage them to rebel.

It's infuriating. I don't know how she did it and I'll never be able to replicate it.

The thought makes me angry, and I stride into the lobby of the Mandarin Oriental with renewed vigor.

When I get my hands on those idiots, I'm going to strangle them until the twisted fuckers stop getting off on it. My lips curve up over sharp incisors. I hate them, but they've been part of my fearsome visage since *l'Academie*. Induction transformation is a long, arduous process, especially for the young teens involved, but at least The Five have culled the more barbaric parts of it when we took our positions. Now the recruits have some say in what modifications they receive and how often they refresh them—unlike when The Commandant insisted on giving me wolf's fangs to terrify my targets.

They look scary and otherworldly, but I don't need fake dog teeth to strike fear in the hearts of my marks. Years of martial arts, weapons handling, and the time I spent in the underground rings gave life to the whispers about *The Fist of Salamanca*. It's not a name I accept or respond to anymore, but I certainly earned it in the pits through blood, sweat, and tears. Once I'd exorcized my demons about our former girl, I crawled out of those wretched hellholes and rejoined the team. My fighting was akin to Coda's partying, Dwyn's crazy heists, Raz's insistence on do-gooder hacks, or Jinx's stint under-cover in Mossad. All of our silly criminal nicknames come from that time and none of us have any love for them.

So that's what I'll use to piss these assholes off.

I spot them in the lounge's corner, surrounded by bottles and napkins. The scene is surreal, but I don't care what they're doing—leaving all of us hanging for hours is unacceptable, especially in our current tenuous situation. "Well, well. If it isn't *The Chameleon* and *Emo Cowboy*. Having fun, boys?"

Their heads turn, and two matching glares pin me down as I approach. I'm not worried about how drunk or pissy they are; they've compromised our escape during our most urgent call sign. Not only did they miss check-in, they've clearly been here *together* the entire time. No one is supposed to have contact until the 'dark zone' expires. Everything about this is completely against our agreed protocols.

"Mo!" Dwyn's face breaks into a grin as he gestures at the mess on their table. "We figured it out... *without Razzie!*"

Blinking, I frown at the clowns. "You did what?"

Coda gives me that lazy grin that drives his fans wild. "We cracked the code on his crotch. Took a lot of work and some serious internet searching, man. But we did it. And it's *here*."

"What's here?" My annoyance slips past my confusion. I have no idea what the hell he's on about, but adding internet usage on their devices makes this goddamn farce even worse.

The thief waves a napkin full of scribbles at me. "Her message took us here... at the Mandarin. I mean, we were already here. I was, then Coda showed. *But...* train girl... Jazz. She *wanted* me to come here. But we can't get any further."

Is he fucking serious?! They've been here deciphering a stupid code on his ass from a random girl instead of following our assigned roles after that clusterfuck at the castle?

They nod and look so proud I almost let it go, but I can't. Everything about the past week has been one giant mistake after another and they've all occurred because each of my team members has done whatever the fuck they please over and over. We're not even functioning like a team right now—it's like being back in school with four horny teenagers who have no idea what discipline is.

Raking my hand through my hair, I shake my head. I can't do this. For years, I've been grappling with keeping all of us sane and functioning like the most sought after crew in the criminal underworld. All it took for that to regress was two people getting laid and one to get knocked out—all by pretty girls. That means I've taught them nothing and all my hard work has failed.

"You know what? Never mind," I mutter. Turning on my heel, I walk right out of the bar without another word. As I walk towards the lobby, I hear them yelling, but I don't respond. This has been coming for a long time and I was a fool to believe I could ever fix the giant, gaping hole left by the girl we lost a decade ago.

When she died, so did our team and I should have accepted it years ago.

I'm going to get my shit together and go back to the tasks I need to do for the assignment we've all abandoned in favor of chasing their 'white whale' women. Italy is not my favorite place, but I prefer working on my own to this nonsense every day of the week.

"Arrivederci, signore!"

That voice…

Stopping in my tracks, I watch a blue-haired woman wave at the porter, beaming as she steps out onto the street. Her look is flawless, and she commanded the attention of everyone around her with a single kind word to the bellhop. The way she moves is fluid, and the carriage in her spine is confident as she walks down the street. There's something about it that trips my wires and I don't know why.

Idiot teammates forgotten, I stalk out into the crowd, following her as my instincts scream at me to pay attention. Since the island, I rarely ignore them and this girl has the hairs on my neck standing straight up.

I have to see where this leads.

SHE WENT INTO THE SEX MACHINE MUSEUM—WHATEVER THE HELL *THAT* is—and I watched. I'm not a dickhead like the other two, so I texted Jinx and Raz with my location, but not my reason for staying on the prowl. Making sure they knew the *cogliones* were at the Mandarin getting drunk and drawing sketches wasn't a priority, but again, I'm not irresponsible. They danced carefully around my temper when I relayed the information, so they probably think I'm out blowing off steam about the reckless behavior of our teammates.

Perhaps a bit, but something about the woman I followed has my hackles raised and I'm not ready to theorize why yet.

Movement catches my eyes in the alley just off the entrance and I frown when I see three large, square goons in black slip in through the employee door. If those are employees of this museum, I'll suck my own dick. Men built like that choose a small subset of careers and usually I'm dealing with their ilk in my assignments. That's either a group of thugs or a professional team headed into a building full of normal people—never a good sign.

Concern for the crowd isn't really my style, but keeping attention off of my presence is. I push off the wall, striding over to follow their ingress. The latch on the heavy door is broken and I roll my eyes at the inartful handling. These guys are low level and whether they're a hit or retrieval team, I know from this one detail they are not even in the same ballpark as The Five. This is small time loser craft—I don't have to worry about any surprise tech or skills.

Creeping along the back rooms, I trace their path by listening for tell-tale sounds—namely silence. Surprise is the best weapon for guys as poorly trained as this, and they're probably betting on their numbers to make up for their lack of ability.

I fucking hate amateurs.

"Go for it, Nachte. I want to see this bitch bleed."

Madre Mary, his name is… night? Where is Dwyn to laugh like a hyena at this shit?

There's a brief pause and my lips curve when I hear the crack of a well landed punch on bone. The howl of the recipient is distinctly male and I grin even bigger. Their target isn't taking the gang-up lying down; I like that. A seed of excitement blooms in my chest, hoping I'm right about my theory that it's the spicy looking girl in pink leathers. Watching a chick fight like a warrior is an immense turn on and I almost never get to see it because the goombahs I contract to are such old world misogynists.

"Aw! Did the big, bad bearded douche get an owie?" The smirk in her voice is clear, but an accent is not. I can't place her origin at all, so

I can't fathom who she works for. "I suppose that will teach you to gang up on a defenseless little girl like me."

A volley of fight sounds and grunts punctuates her taunt, only a few of which sound female. Punk Rock Barbie is beating the absolute *shit* out of the tall bearded Slavic guy in the group. I inch closer, peering into the mirror angled at corners to keep people from running into one another. My breath catches when she flips back onto her feet with ease and launches herself at him in a flurry of *Krav Maga* that would make one of the fight teachers at *l'Academie* drool into their gym clothes. Her form is perfect and her speed is astounding—I cannot *believe* I've never seen this woman before.

Unfortunately, the leader of this band of fools doesn't play fair, and he turns to the stockier man with the weasley mustache. With a nod, the roided out toad jumps into the fight from behind the azure haired fighter. She laughs, executing a spin kick that smacks into his jaw and makes him stumble back before winking at her other opponent. The muscled barbarian growls like an animal, lowering his head to come barreling at her as she dances along the edge of the open space in the hallway intersection. Her shriek of fury when she bounces off a corner hard tells me they found a weak spot— and that's like signing a death warrant in an unmatched fight like this.

Time to step in.

I have no idea why I do it, but I walk around the corner with an arched brow, holding my arms out at my sides. "*Ciao*, gentleman. It seems you're hassling this lovely young lady. May I ask why?"

All three of them whip their heads around to look at me and it gives the mystery chick long enough to slump against the wall for a moment and catch her breath. By the way she slammed back into it, I believe she may have an injured shoulder and she just popped it back into socket without so much as a whimper. *That* makes my cock throb like it's going to jump out of my pants. A woman who can fight *and* take pain like a champ? Where in the devil's name did she fall out of the sky from?

"Get lost, asshole. We have business here and you don't want to get involved," the wiry leader says in a heavy Russian accent.

Blinking, I give him a smile. "Oh, but I want to! Three on one seems a bit of overkill, no?"

His eyes narrow as he looks over at the bearded 'night' guy sporting a bloody nose, busted lip, and various bruises as he tries to hide his hand on what may be a broken rib, then at the short man who already has blood on him. "No one asked for your opinion. If you don't beat it, you're next."

Ooh. How erudite and terrifying.

"I'm fine. Get lost. I don't need a white knight, dude," the girl rasps from where she's eyeing the crowd. Her gaze is sharp and I'm sure she's assessing what wounds she gave the goons while trying to decide how much danger I present. The look she's sporting is that of a predator examining the herd, and yet again, I find my body straining to get closer to her.

"You heard the bitch."

"Tsk. How rude of you. I admit I don't know this woman, but so far, I've only seen her defend herself against your aggression. Calling her a bitch for it is rude." I walk forward carefully, keeping to the outside of the ring we're all trapped in as I make my way towards the injured warrior that's captured my attention so thoroughly.

"Who the fuck is this guy, the manners police? Let's take them both out, boss."

Before I can respond, the three of them advance on Pinky and she pushes off the wall to meet them. Using the momentum from the hard surface, she does a perfect kick-flip that floors the big guy. They crash to the ground and she pummels him as if her life depends on it. The other two move to come at her from behind and I slam my fist into the jaw of the short guy. While he reels, I pivot and yank the leader back by his shirt. A leg sweep and a stomp on his kneecap have him howling quickly.

None of these guys were even in the same zip code as either of us, much less the same league.

"Not to intrude, but do you think he's had enough?" I ask as I throw an elbow into the face of the staggering, stocky goon. He's determined, I'll give him that, but he doesn't have the technique or endurance to keep this up for long. His boss is still on the ground and the girl I stalked here is turning their companion's face into hamburger.

The blue-haired girl finally stops pounding on the guy and looks up at me in annoyance. "If I want your opinion, I'll beat it out of you, too, asshole."

I blink in shock. Not that I did it for kudos, but I *did* just save her cute little ass. Besides, she's well trained, but nothing I saw her do screams competition. She has a brass set, though. I can respect that.

"Now you're wondering if I could—the answer is a resounding 'yes', by the way—because you think you were my white knight or some bullshit." I don't respond, but her smirk deepens. "I let you help because my fucking shoulder hurts and that's the end. I could have saved my damn self if I had to. Only a guy would work harder than he has to in order to soothe his ego."

Ouch. Her mouth hits as hard as her fists.

"I'm afraid I have to protest. Lumping me in with the whole of the species seems premature, Smurfette."

Her eyes narrow at the joking nickname, and she walks the room, kicking the downed idiots. I arch a brow and she shrugs. "Gotta see if they're breathing. Everyone knows that."

No, they don't. Only professionals do a breather sweep after a fight.

"I see. You couldn't tell by the rise of their chests?" I tilt my head, hoping her answer will confirm my suspicion.

All I get is a snort, which is answer enough. Chests don't always rattle, dying people hang on the grab weapons, and operatives know you intend to leave witnesses. The sweep is to verify whether you have decisions to make. Her fingers move to the choker around her neck for a moment as she studies the knocked out thugs thoughtfully.

"Yes, and no." Her gaze cuts back to me suspiciously. "Where did you come from?"

"Side entrance, like them."

"Why?"

"Good Samaritan?" I say as I paste on an innocent expression. She won't buy it, but maybe I can buy some time while I try to figure out why this girl is under my skin. Something is just out of the reach of my fucking brain and I can't grasp it.

"A unicorn would have been more believable." Shaking her head, she walks over and picks up a small bag, slinging it over the arm she didn't have to reset. "Doesn't matter. For your own good, forget you saw me, forget this happened, and go on about your life."

I frown. Does shit like that actually work for normal people? I sure as fuck wouldn't expect it to, but the look on her face makes me think she's being serious. "Why would I do that? Shouldn't we call the police? They attacked you."

"Come now, Ironman. You don't believe I'm stupid, do you?" She backs away towards the hallway as she flips the bird at me. "I know you're some flavor of security or contractor—it's in the way you move. We both know you won't call the cops and if you're smart, you'll let me leave without interfering. After all, you have no idea what I'm armed with."

This time, I scoff as I look at the skintight outfit. "Not much, Bluey. That's obvious."

Her lips curve as she continues moving away. "Maybe *I am* the weapon."

Before I can answer, she blows me a kiss and then takes off into the crowd near the exhibits.

Who the fuck was that girl?

HISTORY WILL NOT REPEAT

THERE ARE TWO THINGS I KNOW FOR CERTAIN AFTER THAT FUCKING debacle: one, the sexy guy who jumped in to save me was undoubtedly a professional and two, the idiots who attacked me were low rent minions. I might have considered a bit of 'after fight' stress release, but that any of them found me in the middle of a job despite my usual thorough pre-drop precautions is insane. I vetted the hell out of that location before listing it as a possibility, and I did a careful walkthrough after it got confirmed. Either I have hackers trailing my system—doubtful, but never impossible—or I'm right about the Shadow Douche setting me up to get iced.

Neither option is appealing.

Shaking my head as I drop pieces of the Stella disguise in random garbage cans, I follow a twisty route around the city to avoid a tail. I'm not using public transportation until I do a nuts and bolts review of my tech to make sure I'm not being traced by someone like Raz. It's going to take a lot longer to get back to the hotel and I'm definitely going to need the emergency pack with a staff uniform I hid by the service entrance. I don't want to walk through that lobby until I'm checking out for good.

I cannot *believe* that for the second time in two weeks I'm running around a city stripped bare of any disguise. The amount of times I've had to do that over the years is negligible—I specifically avoid it so I don't somehow get uploaded into some idiotic facial rec program. Even shots from social media are fodder for agencies like the NSA or Mossad, so the last thing I want is to be caught in the background of some tourist photo and outed. That's not completely unfixable, but bone shaving hurts like hell and I hate recovering from surgery. My goal is to be smart enough to not need a reconstruction as often as *Les Invisibles* operatives get it.

My eyes dart around, taking in my surroundings cautiously as I stand and wait for a light to turn so I can cross the street. A group of laughing twenty-something guys rock up next to me and I have to hold back my growl as their eyes rove over me. Without the wig and pink leather jacket, I had to put a knit cap over my hair to distract people from its unique coloring. I'm left in the black bra and low slung leather pants, so I know why they're all staring. Sighing, I flick the snowy white and black streaked braid over my shoulder. The beanie has worked out until now, but since this is the longest light in the known universe, I've got droolers.

If men only realized how incredibly uncomfortable it makes women for them to do this in public...

"Hey, cutie. You look like you're down to party. We're headed to—"

Without looking, I hold up my hand in the universal stop gesture. "Not interested."

"Aw, don't be like that! We're good guys. You'll have a great time partying with us," another one jumps in.

I keep my eyes on the light I'm waiting for. "Get lost."

Annoying laughter and snorts follow my response. I think I've made my point until the next dipshit throws his hat in the ring. "No need to be a frigid bitch. We're only offering to show you a good time, goth girl."

It takes a lot of restraint, but I lower the hand and slip it behind my back. Women everywhere face this kind of bullshit—in bars, clubs, gyms, classrooms, on the street—and it never ends. You don't have to be dressed sexy or even take part, but here are men acting like baboons presenting their ass to a mate. Boys learn it as young as elementary school and carry on through with that entitlement because, in most places, no one ever addresses their creepy bullshit. But I'm not normal and neither was my upbringing.

"I don't think you're ready for my idea of a good time." I turn my head slowly, giving them the dead eyes of a girl who was raised to be a killer. The knife from the small of my back spins on my palm like a bartender's mixing tin and I bat my lashes as the tiny nicks from the blade bleed on my palm.

All seven dipshits in the group look at me in horror and back away. It only takes a moment to flick my knife closed, and I lick my palm with a smirk. That has them turning tail and moving away as they whine and grumble to one another about psychos. It isn't the first time someone has used that label to describe The Guillotine and it won't be the last time, either. Refocusing my attention, I note the 'walk' sign is lit up and I make my way across the busy street at a leisurely pace.

I'm not above giving guys a lesson about approaching random women on the street like they're slabs of meat.

BY THE TIME I SMUGGLE MYSELF INTO THE HOTEL, IT'S AFTER DARK. I DID a lot of doubling back and taking roundabout twists and turns, but my paranoia is at an all-time high. All the 'coincidences' of the past few weeks have me questioning every dipshit I see, and to be honest, I don't want to end up fighting a crew of morons twice in a day. My shoulder hurts like hell and if I have to pop it back in place more than twice in a day, I guarantee I'll develop a long-term issue. I definitely don't have time for months of physical therapy or surgery.

The minute I unlock the door to my suite, I walk to the buffet table by the door and pull the sniffer out of the fake flower arrangement. Before I scan my equipment and packing up, I have to make certain no one has accessed my space to plant mics or cameras while I was out. That gang of tools at the drop may have been a distraction rather than a threat and it would explain someone hiring guys so far out of my league. Unskilled fighters weren't likely to actually take me out, but they kept me busy long enough to send a tech crew to break in.

I turn it on while I work the ties on my boots, silently removing them so my feet are bare on the sparkling tile. The screen lights up and I watch the numbers on the scanner flicker as it runs through various frequencies. Once it comes up blank in the five-foot range of the door, I stroll to the right, beginning a sweep of the first floor. I stalk the entire sitting room, bathrooms, kitchen, spare bedroom, and halls one by one until it's clear. Breathing a soft sigh of relief, I climb the back stairs carefully, hoping there's not a creak I'm unaware of. The entire second floor and balcony will have to be scanned and then I'll be able to start on my tech. If I have pitch things I will, but I'd prefer not right before exiting stage right to my next location.

Fucking Coda. Saving his dumbass in Paris started this shit and now, once again, I'm waist deep in someone trying to kill me.

The irritation at the same boys who damned near succeeded in offing me because the cause of my current troubles makes me grumble internally as I do the slow walk through the upper floor with the big detector. My fury froths while I work and by the time I feel comfortable that my temporary HQ is spy-free, I let out a howl of anger. After the explosion on the island, I spent *years* building my new persona and covering my tracks so I could operate in the shadows.

I endured dozens of surgeries on the burns, physical therapy, and retrained in skills without taking chemical pain medication. I did all of that shit so I could work on my own without fear of *Les Invisibles* tracking me down to finish the job. The amount of tears I shed over the first three years would fill the Grand goddamn Canyon and despite the gargantuan effort I made to separate myself from my past… here they are again, destroying everything I've built.

The universe enjoys fucking with me; that's the only explanation.

Stomping over to the main computers, I slam my body into the chair and boot up the system. I don't leave it on while I'm out because I want it to stay air-gapped from outside signals. Hotel Wi-Fi here is quite insistent about 'helping me' by trying to pick up my devices—something I *never* do. Publicly accessible networks are a treasure trove for hackers far less skilled than myself or Raz, but people jump on them with phones, tablets, Kindles, and more like good little automatons. That gives even the mildly trained criminals the ability to get information, access, and deposit any number of nasties onto the device that most users would never notice.

My screens light up around the table in front of me and at the makeshift station I created behind me. I access the commands necessary to send ghost spiders through all of their rootkits and partitions. If someone has tracked me via the internet, I'll know within a couple of hours. Once I'm diagnosed Trojan-free, I'm going to load this flash drive, get the info, and hightail it out of Dodge before any other imbeciles locate me.

I'm sad I won't get to meet up with Slick or Cas again, but maybe… maybe once I get to a new spot, I can use their dump phones to see where in Europe they are. It's possible they travel for work; lots of people do, right?

I don't even know who I am right now; mooning over two hookups, no matter how hot they were, is completely unlike me. Over the years, I've hooked up with a legendary number of men and women and never *once* started plotting to find them again for round two. Models, criminals, movie stars, normal people, geniuses—hell, I got laid in a fucking hot-air balloon once and never went looking for those three guys. What the fuck is it about these two guys that has me acting like a horny teenager?

Take a shower and get your shit together, Remy.

It's good advice, and since my shoulder hurts like a motherfucker, I'm going to take it. Washing away the fight from the museum will make me feel better and honestly, these leather pants are chafing.

I'm gonna wash those men right out of my hair—just watch me.

THE STEADY BLINK OF THE SCREENS AS CODE WHIZZES BY IN THE windows scanning my drives and peripherals is hypnotizing, but it's almost done. My shoulder is aching less after the long, hot shower and I feel a hell of a lot more prepared to deal with the task at hand. Once this is complete, I have to load the cursed flash drive from the museum and see what Shadow Douche left for me.

I can't imagine this client has a useful cache of info on Raz, even if the organization they represent is larger than I realize. *La Araña* hasn't stayed off the radar for all these years by being sloppy. The voice recording was surprising, but in the age of signal scanners, catching a small snippet of conversation held in a public place takes more luck than skill. Even the bits of code aren't impressive—they don't definitively link to him. I only know they're authentic because of our history. Anyone else wouldn't have that information.

What has he foiled that set these freaks on his trail?

Jobs assumed to be his work have never gotten verified and anything he does for *LI* would put the rest of The Five in their sights as well. None of the other guys were mentioned yet, so either this is something Raz did on the side or the Douche is targeting them one by one. That thought is disturbing—The Five are heirs apparent to the Council and set to help run *Les Invisibles* when the next group retires. If this group wants to knock them off the board, taking out the guys would be a good first step.

A chorus of alarms on my main computer interrupts my musings and I slide the chair over to view the results. The lack of tracking or spy malware on my system makes me heave a sigh of relief—I can ditch all the equipment and start fresh, but it's a pain in the ass I don't need right now. Also, it highlights the fact that two separate groups located me while I've been moving with more caution than usual and they *aren't* getting their information from my tech. Either Shadow Douche is setting me up or I have serious security problems with my cache of identities.

But none of them have ever gotten used before and they were shelved years ago. It can't be the IDs; no one has even called me by any name.

I rub a hand over my face in frustration. The amount of precautions I've taken since Paris is triple my normal level; the team of dipshits *has* to be the Shadow Douche. But why? If he wants me to kill Raz, taking me out before I find him is counter-productive. And the hot dude who tried to play 'savior' was leagues beyond them in training. I don't know who he's attached to, but he's an Olympian compared to their back alley brawlers. He didn't chase me, either, so I don't know if he was actually there for me or I lucked out.

The threads wrapped around my life are strangling me, so I push out of the chair in annoyance. Stalking over to the bag I took to the museum, I grab the flash drive and insert it into the computer I had air gapped from the rest of the system. I used double protection because right now, I don't trust anyone, least of all this mysterious employer who wants to imitate Dr. Claw.

"Greetings again, Guillotine!

It impressed us that you could retrieve this missive. Your reputation is not exaggerated—accessing this drive means you either dispensed our teams at the locations or avoided them entirely.

I am most pleased to inform you that your first deposit will show up in the provided bitcoin account as soon as this video ends. You have proved yourself every bit as ruthless, cunning, and resourceful as your previous clients claim. This is the beginning of a beautiful partnership, I believe, because like us, you are not enamored with the current leadership in the underworld.

The reign of terror the few have over the many will end, and you will help us begin that process.

Included on this drive are folders with photos attributed to La Araña, missions and codes believed to be created by him, and various rumors that we have been gathering for some time. The information is accurate and recent, so we hope it will lead you to the next step in locating him.

Be cautious when you review it, as we have placed an encryption code within that will overwrite the files much more securely than any program on the planet. You will need to memorize it all, as leaving clues, even a digital one, is sloppy tradecraft.

Our numbers are many—do not consider double crossing us or escaping with your payment without completing your job. There is nowhere to hide; we are embedded in every corner of every place you might believe you have an ally.

We are waiting for your next contact with bated breath, Guillotine."

Crazy as a fucking loon. Just great.

Taking a deep breath, I click on files and start working through them so I know where I'm headed next.

HEATHENS

"WHAT IN THE *FUCK* HAPPENED TO YOU?" I BLINK WHEN MO STALKS into our makeshift HQ like a dark cloud.. His hair is half out of his 'work' ponytail, his suit is rumpled, and he's got a bruise forming on his jaw.

"You," he points at me and the whirls on Coda, *"and you didn't follow protocol."*

Coda smirks at him, raising a glass of bourbon in a mock salute. "Yet neither of us looks like someone tried to steal our wallet."

A muffled snort from the bank of computers tells me Raz is paying attention again. He and Jinx have been cataloging the items we all snatched at the bullshit ball so we can drop them and get paid. Outside of the mark *Le Voleur* got to before Mo, we made a tidy sum at the fucked up festival of thieves, so we've been getting settled while we waited on our pissy leader.

"There was a girl," Mo starts, but Jinx cuts him off.

"Yeah, at least three of us know *that* story, dude. Surprising that the monk of the group is the next to fall prey, but I would have expected you to be in a *much* better mood."

The hitter slams his palm on the table and snarls. *"Enough!* Unlike you twits, I didn't get my wick dipped while I was supposed to be working. When I found out Coda and Jinx were *together* in Mandarin, *not following protocol,* I left. There was a girl leaving at the same time and something about her tipped me off, so I followed her."

"Blonde hair, cute, Southern?" Coda asks as he scratches his head.

"No."

"Hot as fuck, long dark ponytail, sexy office clothes?" I offer.

"No."

Jinx beams and waggles his brows. "Curvy redhead in a gorgeous ball gown?"

"Fuck no." Mo shakes his head as he looks at us, his expression frustrated. "Blue hair, pink leathers and amazing tits."

We all look at one another, shrugging, until I hold up a finger. "Amazing tits fits. She had steel, lots of it, and UV tats I could feel but not see in the dark."

"Are we trying to decide if this is all the same girl or measuring for the contest?" Coda frowns. "Because I don't remember shit and I definitely didn't get to fuck her."

Mo stomps over to the bar, pouring himself a scotch before looking at Raz. "Did you see any of these women in any of the cities?"

The hacker finally looks up from his computer, sighing at us as if we're useless. "You know we couldn't get a glimpse of the blonde in Paris and I didn't see Dwyn's train chick. No cams in the right spots. I caught a few redheads at that clusterfuck Open Market, but none that I could run for facial rec. Both of the two I followed were excellent at keeping their features off video. I'll check the footage from outside the Mandarin for your blue girl."

"It's unlikely we met the same girl. They seem to vary in body type and appearance enough that it's simply a coincidence," Jinx says as he studies his phone with a frown. "I'm fairly certain the redhead I know as Shooter is a pro. She was definitely working at the Market and she seemed to know another couple."

I tilt my head as I think about that. Jazzy was very polished and now that I think back, her room wasn't full of the usual female trappings. In fact, I'm not sure I saw any luggage or personal effects. It might have been a secondary location. "Jazzy was extremely witty. The rest of the code has Coda, and I stumped and we came at it from every angle."

That gets Raz's attention. He swivels around, ignoring the flashing screens he was watching. "Give it to me."

"Jesus, here he goes," Coda grumbles. "I *knew* this asshole was going to horn in to prove he's smarter than us."

"Just give it to him." Mo snatches the paper out of my hand and gives it to our resident geek. "I don't know if we're being played by one woman or a group of pros, but I'm not wasting time on pride. We have tasks we need to finish for our *actual* jobs and the manhunt for your Mata Hari is distracting."

"I *like* that name!" I grin and clap my hands in glee. "That's what we call her until we find out more info."

Jinx rolls his eyes as finally tears his eyes away from his phone. "Whatever, D. I didn't get a code from my lady. She told me I had to figure out who the couple who interrupted us were and text her. I'll be damned if I know who they were, though. I accounted for all the couple teams for at other heists according to the forums."

"What did they look like? I had the best view in the room." Raz snorts again and Mo amends his words. "Outside of van boy here, but he's busy with feeds and codes."

"Van boy," Coda laughs, pouring himself another glass. "That one is gonna stick."

"Get fucked, Coda."

"Man, I wish." He runs his hand through the colorful strands of his hair, pushing it out of his eyes, and arches a brow at me. "You're awfully quiet, psycho. Cat got your tongue?"

"Nope. I'm amused that you and Mo got the short end of the stick in every way. Neither of you got laid, didn't get to parachute out of the building, no loot… Jinx and I are ballers."

"There was a fight in the Sex Machines Museum. That's where I was." Mo smirks at me, clearly having withheld this so he could lord it over me. "They followed the blue girl in and when I found her, she was fighting off three huge goons by herself—with an injured shoulder."

"What?!"

Talk about unfair! I love watching chick fights, especially when the chick is a good fighter.

"Pause for a minute. There's a *Sex Machines Museum?*" Coda throws his hands up and makes an irritated sound. "How did I not know this and how the *fuck* did Mo the Monk end up there instead of me?"

"Maybe if you hadn't stayed at the Mandarin to jack around with Dwyn, you might have seen the blue-haired girl. That's what happens when you don't follow the fucking rules, Coda." Our leader looks pleased with himself for a moment, finally taking a seat. It's obvious he took a few hits in the fight when he groans and leans his head back on the chair. "But since you got knocked out like a little bitch at the last brawl, I'm not sure trading places with me would have been good for your image."

Coda pouts when the rest of us laugh and I look at the men I've called brothers since we were small. There hasn't been this much banter and snark in our group projects in a long, long time. When our girl died, she took pieces of us with her we've never gotten back. Losing her made everything seem less fun, and it's taken a toll on our friendship.

I don't care if this is one girl or a new fucking crew; we need to find them and nail that shit down.

"Was she a good fighter?" They look at me in surprise—I'm not usually one to ask pertinent questions. "I mean, you said she was holding her own, so…"

"Fuck, *yes*, she was," Mo sighs. "Someone has obviously trained her in multiple disciplines, but her moves were like poetry. The whole time we were fighting, she shot her mouth off, too."

That's his kryptonite—mouthy women who are strong enough to challenge him—and he hasn't found it in a long time.

"You had a stiffy the entire time… no question," Coda guffaws. "Monk or not, women who give you lip float your boat."

Mo glares at him. "I appreciate a sharp wit."

"Hell, man, don't be defensive. The only one of us who's typically too fucked to notice is Coda," Jinx says as he walks over and plops onto the couch next to me. "Perks of being a *rock star*, I suppose."

"It gets old sometimes, even for me. I'm as much an object to the groupies as they are to me, dude. Bragging rights on the clock app or Insta—that's what they're looking for. Charice has to wand people before they come into suites anymore to keep phones out."

I blink. I've never heard him complain about lack of substance in his sex life before. Usually our emo friend is happy to jump into whatever amount of bodies are willing and lose himself.

This week has been the weirdest shit I've seen in years.

"Someone write that shit down because he'll never admit to saying it later," Raz calls over his shoulder. "Also, I think I've found a couple of things while you fuckers are over there braiding each other's hair."

Jumping to my feet, I bound over, twirling the knife from my pocket between my fingers. "You realize I'd happily carve pieces off of you just to teach you a lesson?"

He rolls his eyes and Jinx glares at me. "Stop, D. He's kidding."

"Defending his honor, how sweet," Coda mutters as he and Mo join us at the desk.

"What did you find, Raz?" Mo asks as he crosses his arms over his chest. "Ignore the idiot. He's not allowed to carve anything unless instructed."

The screen on the left blinks and a feed appears. It's a shitty old camera, probably one of the street cams from a nearby business. A blue-haired girl rushes by, looking like every scene kid's wet dream, and mere seconds later, Mo walks by as he stalks her. Another screen flashes and we watch their progress down the street until they hit the museum. The chick goes in and Mo stays back, but not once is her face even slightly in the frame. It's like she knows where every single camera in the area is and how to avoid them.

Jinx whistles low. "She's *good*."

"Agreed," I murmur. "You'd never know by the way she carries herself that every step is intentional. Her presentation is fluid and loose, even with the injury Mo mentioned."

"So is this some new all-woman crew, you think?" Coda leans against the far side of the desk, chewing on his lip ring. "The only one of those left is that bitch from the Council. Her minions are all girls, but they're usually busy doing her dirty work or managing her skin trade. Not like them to be running about hitting dead drops."

"You think that's why Blue here was at the museum? Maybe she's just kinky," I shrug and they roll their eyes at me. "Okay, so it's probably a suitable spot for a pickup; you're right. Tourists don't notice shit even when it's picking their pockets. The dudes trying to beat her down were competing for the contract, maybe?"

Mo stays silent for a moment, then shakes his head. "They didn't seem intent on taking anything from her. I doubt they knew she had anything of value. Their goal looked to be kicking her ass—or worse."

"Hot Smurf girl has enemies. Nice." Scratching my chin, I watch as Raz pulls up another set of screens. These are maps and coordinates. "What the hell is this, man?"

"Your code, bro. They're *coordinates*."

His grin is smug and I almost stab him, anyway. *Damn Mo and his rules.* "Coordinates to what? How does that help?"

"The first set leads to the real life house they used in the boy wizard films. Took me a bit to figure out maybe I had to make a few leaps, but I *think* I have it. Potter is the seeker, and she wants you to *seek*."

"Oh, come on!" Coda throws his hands in the air. "How the fuck does any normal person get that out of the human house from the movie? Jesus."

"I used to do Geocaching, you dipshit. That's what the clues for that are like. Sue me."

Mo sucks in a breath and finally grits out, "Tell us the rest, Raz."

"Got it. So after I figured that out, the next set led to a city in China, then a hotel in Japan, and then to the big white monstrosity in D.C. When I put it together, I got this: seek mandarin hotel president." Stacking his hands behind his head, our computer whiz gives us all a very satisfied smirk. "All three of you dickheads were at the Mandarin Hotel, just not in the Presidential Suite."

Son. Of. A. Bitch.

"Damn." Jinx whispers. "Your dream girl was in the same building alright, but you missed the actual location, D."

Irritation flares through me and I fling the knife, watching it embed in the wall as I growl. "Jesus Christ. I should have shown the damn thing to the keyboard warrior earlier. She's probably gone!"

"Does that mean we need to focus on the hot little number I met at the party? We cracked your train girl and Mo's blue hair—at least, as far as we can until Raz figures out where she went after the fight."

"Fine," I sigh as I look at Jinx, then nod at Raz. "Can you get footage around the palace to see if we can track her when she leaves?"

"Will do."

Once he turns back to his little wonderland of codes, I stalk over and grab a bottle of tequila. Once I yank the lid out, I take a swig from the bottle. "Who's got cards? I'm in the mood to take someone's money."

Jinx saves the day when he holds his hand up to keep Mo from snarking at me. "I do. We have time for a bit of Hold 'Em while the software is scanning."

Damn right we do.

SMILE

I'M NOT A FAN OF BEING TRAPPED IN A METAL BOX HURLING THROUGH the skies for long periods of time.

If I inspect it, my unease ties back to one of the more unorthodox training units during my time at *l'Academie*. Not only did we take what military folks refer to as SEER training, but *Les Invisibles* operatives are required to complete a three-month captivity course once a year. Future agents are put through progressively more grueling situations from kindergarten age through their final year and initiated operatives receive refresher courses periodically.

Hell on earth exists, and it's on the smaller island they use for this course in South America.

A shiver runs through me as I remember clawing my way out of graves, plane crashes, and various life-threatening scenarios while being hunted by armed agents. The gate above the grounds reads '*Mors infirmos recipit*'[1]—a sentiment they take literally. Operatives routinely die during captivity resistance and the Council rewards the killers with bounties. Before my escape, I took out dozens of the hunters during my stays there. It's brutal, unforgiving, and sharpens every student into the emotionless weapons *Les Invisibles* needs to fill their roster.

My hand shoots out, pushing the call button for the flight attendant. She arrives with a bright white smile and scurries off to procure the bourbon I ordered. Thinking about CapRes has my mind wandering to the boys I left behind and it's making my empty rib cage ache where my heart should be.

Dramatic, I know, but I've grown used to the void and since I got into this mess in Paris, it's shrinking.

Once I have the double hit of smoky flavor, I close my eyes and breathe slowly. For the past decade, my life has been a precision arrow of determination: escape, move on, establish my business, and happily kill people all over the globe. Until last week, I believed I was satisfied with my success; in fact, I thought I was living my dream.

But my old dream is haunting me and it's put everything in jeopardy. Saving Coda started this chain of ridiculous events and now I'm trapped in first class as I head to London to ferret out my target. I don't actually want to kill Raz, and I don't trust the douche who hired me to do so. Everything is upside down and to top it off, I got a text from Slick before I boarded.

I have no idea what to do with that shit.

The Remy who knew how to relate to people for longer than one night hasn't been around since I faked my death. I don't know if I even remember how to chit chat or flirt without the intent of getting laid. My playfulness with Cas was a means to an end and that I know how to do. But truly connecting with anyone is simply not in my toolkit anymore.

Maybe I'm a fool for giving either of them the opportunity to find me. I'm being followed by multiple groups of criminals and I live out of storage spaces around the globe. I don't have a home, friends, or even a plant. What kind of relationship could I possibly offer anyone?

I click the screen off and take another drink of the Maker's. I'd prefer a better label, but beggars can't be choosers. The whiskey helps soothe my frayed nerves, but it doesn't change the reality of my situation. Ignoring Slick is probably for the best, even if my pussy throbs just *thinking* about meeting up with him again. Pinching the bridge of my nose, I continue musing until the buzz of my phone on the tray in front of me scares the hell out of me.

Who in the fuck is trying to contact me when I'm at cruising altitude?

Hefting a sigh as I flip it and look down to see which of many burner lines I have forwarding while I travel is pinging me. My eyes widen when I realize the message is yet another omen about my personal life.

Unknown: How did you make friends with Le Voleur de Sang and his consort?

Casanova solved his riddle, and now he's making a play. Between him, Slick, and the specter of my past, my focus is split. There are too many variables at play and the chessboard in my mind is crowded. I have to remove pieces from the game or I'm going to get killed.

The pilot's voice crackles over the intercom to announce our descent into Heathrow, and I toss the rest of my drink back before it gets snatched. It's time to put up or shut up so I can handle my business. Once I hole up in my new base of operations, I'll text both of them and see what happens. They may be nowhere near London and all the knots in my gut are for nothing.

The Guillotine doesn't cower in the face of a challenge, and these boys are just a blip on my radar.

THE FLAT I BOOKED IS IN SOUTH KENSINGTON. THE DISTINCTIVE RED brick and stucco fronted homes and converted apartments are pricey because of location, but there's also a decent amount of foot traffic. I decided I'd forego hotels for the start of my stay here specifically to avoid dealing with staff members who might notice when I come and go. I'd like to slow down the burning of IDs per city or I'll have to take a long break to create replacements. There's far too much at stake right now to do that and I have no idea how long it will take to suss out the Shadow Douche's game plan.

Waste not, want not.

My current facade is *Callista Roman of Chicago, IL.* Her legend is a liquor distributor here for a conference, which meant I could dress in semi-casual jeans and a blouse on the plane. Comfort is luxury with disguises and even her wispy honey blond wig is less onerous than others I've worn this week. My eyes are a brilliant green with the contacts in and I airbrushed enough color on my pale skin to make me look sun-kissed. American women, particularly professionals at this level, seem to equate that look with success, so I made sure I'd fit in if I got cornered by any other expats.

"We're here," the rideshare driver says as we pull to a stop. He's been quiet, leaving a football match on the radio and occasionally muttering under his breath. Compared to bothering me or trying to pick me up, I'll take an obsessed Man U dude every time. "Do you need help?"

"No, thank you." I flash him a smile as I open the car door. "If you'll pop the trunk, I'll be fine."

The outside of my rental is sparkling white brick and surrounded by other converted properties. I chose it for location and space, but looking at my surroundings, I may have gone a wee bit overboard. When the trunk pops open, I grab the small cases and wave at the driver before heading up the short steps to the black front door. A quick check on my phone gives me the code to the keypad from the rental agent and I'm inside within seconds, stowing my cases near the stairs until I decide where I'm unpacking.

"Jesus. The pictures didn't do this place justice," I mutter as I walk through the first floor. There's a dining room *and* a 'reception' room before the massive kitchen. When I take the stairs to the lower level, I find a bedroom and a home gym, as well as a small office. "No wonder I'm paying so damn much."

I know the upstairs has two bedrooms and a library according to the website, so I leave that until later. Pulling my cases into the reception room, I set up my tech piece by piece. It's an excellent distraction because I texted both guys once I landed and I have yet to hear from them. My head and my heart—not to mention my libido—are torn if that's a good thing. But I can't sit and pine over their lack of response; no, I have work to do if I'm going to keep Raz alive.

Once everything is up and running, I review the parts of the dossier that suggest Raz may have a semi-permanent base in London. Intel like this is super sketchy, especially when referencing someone as skilled at hiding as him, but there are blurry pictures, Wi-Fi back-traces, and a few other artifacts I believe mean he at least visits the city often. It's as good a place to start as any and since the trail on my old friend is sparse, I'll take what I can get.

If he has an HQ here, is it his alone or does The Five have one of their mini-compounds in London?

Scratching my chin, I ponder that question. They always planned to have joint escape hatches around the globe—much like mine—but who knows what changed when they went from boys to men? They may work together and not see each other at all now. Coda seemed fairly unhappy at the bar, though his demeanor was crafted to make him seem like the life of the party. He's not okay and either the others can't or won't help.

His music should have told them that, but men are never so dense as when they're trying to see what's right in front of them.

My fingers fly over the keys as I start tracers doing deep dives into various real estate records over the past thirteen years. I assume they'd be thrifty and want to be off the beaten path or in a commercial space if it's a true safe house. Coda's face would definitely draw too much attention to their spot if they bought anything in the public eye. They would purchase the property through a trail of never ending shelf corps they used to create shell companies, and they'd likely use dollars versus pounds or Euros.

If I can find their nest, I can keep the bird from falling out of the tree… or something like that. I reserve the right to change my mind. Just because I'm feeling sentimental about the past doesn't mean I won't find out Raz has become a monster and choose to take him *and* the douche out. That will put me out of commission for longer than I'd like, but fuck it. I've got enough money to retire for seven life-times. Someone else is always there to step up and take our place in my world.

I scoot down the table, deciding to check *Mercatus* to see what the fallout from the fuckfest in Prague looks like. The forums are lit up with angry posts from both clients and contractors claiming they were deceived about jobs. Moderators are trying to quell the concern that an Open Market and *deus ex machina* got jammed into one event by offering discounted service fees. The more threads I read, the stronger the feeling in my gut gets; *Mercatus* convened neither of those large events. We have caught them with their pants down as much as the rest of us and can't admit it.

Why, though? Who did it serve to put that many people in one place? What did it get them?

Clicking on the menu, I head to profiles and find that quite a few of my colleagues got detained by a wide variety of security and intelli-gence agencies afterward. The list is fairly extensive, but many of them will bribe, lie, or coerce their way out of those charges, eventu-ally. It took out numerous independent contractors—ones like me who aren't allied to the vast organizations. Maybe that was the goal —removing wildcards from the deck before deciding how to play their hand.

That means Douche could have orchestrated the entire thing.

He wouldn't have known I'd be there, though. That asshole is far too smug not to make a point of knowing I have two alter egos, so I think The Duchess is safe from being associated with The Guillotine for the moment. With his vendetta against at least one member of The Five, I have no idea why he'd want to take out people who don't work for the extensive empires like The Company or *Il Noche* instead. I wonder if they approached any of my peers who were at the stupid ball with the hit on Raz before me. Was this his version of revenge on people who refused to join his cause?

I rub my temples as I try to visualize the links and people I recognized working at the palace. They were all assassins, thieves, and grifters. Hackers, hitters, and fixers weren't lured there, so Shadow Douche must have plans that involve the skill sets he targeted. How that figures into his 'grand future' or the hit on Raz, I'm not sure. Typically, I'm great at seeing the whole chessboard in three dimensions and using game theory to predict the moves before they happen, but this is so nebulous.

My eyes pop open when a random thought occurs, and I rearrange the pieces in my head. I can't work the puzzle because I'm missing pieces. There are signs or clues I haven't been given or flat out didn't pay attention to because they didn't relate to me. Something like this has to be months in the planning at a minimum, so it stands to reason he would have been making moves one by one for a while.

I work alone, so I rarely keep abreast of the gossip on *Mercatus* or even in the community. Unless a big event hits the news, I'm unlikely to have seen or heard about it. There's a gap in my viewfinder, so I need someone to help me fill in the spots so I can extrapolate my next move. Unfortunately, I'm one of the least social criminals in the world unless I'm trotting out the Duchess persona. Even then, I only have one person I can call that I'm fairly certain won't knife me in the back: Elysium.

Selecting a new burner phone from my charging dock, I make a label for it before I turn it on. While it's loading all of my necessary information and updating, I slide into an encrypted area of *Mercatus* and click on the icon of the sorceress duck. Elysium loves cartoons, particularly from the 80s and 90s. She had to explain this to me once and though I don't think she's a bumbling fool, she definitely has the bearing of the Morticia-esque water fowl.

HeavyIsTheCrown: Looking to meet for collaboration.
Morgana: Carmen Sandiego?
HeavyIsTheCrown: Dickens.
Morgana: Yahtzee. Two hours wheels down.
HeavyIsTheCrown: Tower?
Morgana: Five by five.

With that, she signs off and I breathe a sigh of relief. Elysium prefers all communication not done in person to be in coded phrases, but unlike old timey spy movies, she expects me to translate everything into pop culture. I have spent little time with the thief, but she's skilled and highly sought after, so her quirks are accepted. Much like mine, until this dickbag started sending me files I don't normally accept.

I look at my watch. If she'll be in the country in two hours, I have time to track down a few locations from the fuzzy pictures.

Time to go to work, Remy, even if you're mooning over boys that didn't text back.

---

1. Death welcomes the weak.

Forever

MONTERO

"CHECK AGAIN, JINXY!"

Looking up from my laptop, I catch Mo's eye. He grimaces back at me and I know he's concerned about this shit, too. Dwyn gets so obsessed with things sometimes that he loses all perspective and we have to pull him back from the ledge of totally off his rocker. He's always close, but when he hyper fixates, it's much, *much* worse. This Jazz chick has him spinning on all cylinders and since he decided she's the same woman, Jinx's Shooter and Mo's blue-haired fighter, it's like he ate a bag full of sugar followed by a case of Monster.

"D, I looked thirty seconds ago. Watch your own phone." Jinx stretches his legs out in front of him, slouching on the couch with a petulant look.

I know that look—he's frustrated that despite our team think tank figuring out her riddle; it took hours for the girl to respond and now she's got him on read again.

"Guys, watched pots never boil or some shit. Stop focusing on your phones and play cards. Better yet, Mo-Mo would die of shock if you did any work." Coda yawns as he reclines in his seat across from the couch with studio headphones on his ears. He's been using them to drown out Dwyn's ramblings and I wish like hell I'd put mine in the carry-on, not the cases in the hold.

Mo doesn't answer. He simply snorts and goes back to reviewing files. The dude is so laser focused on running everything that he rarely takes a second to sleep, much less relax. The insomnia started after the explosion on the island and it's gotten worse over the years. I have no idea how he survives without rest, but he never appears to be affected by it anymore. I asked if the docs helped once and he shrugged, telling me to fuck off and mother someone else.

It's been a concern for a while, but I haven't been able to get into the medical unit's files without leaving crumbs. Oddly, the security on the medical wing is even tighter than anywhere else in the compound. The Commandant is definitely hiding some serious shit if bumps and bruises are locked up tighter than the ledger and bank books, but I have to go slowly. We've spent years making that remnant from World War 2 believe we're going to run *LI* the way he sees fit and that would get wasted if I got caught hacking the database to find out what sleep aid Mo uses.

"Yeah, well, *you* didn't meet this girl, Coda. She just hauled your ass to a cafe and left you. You can't possibly understand," Dwyn says. He throws a pillow across the plane at the rockstar and pouts when Coda deflects it.

"I'm still not sold on it being one girl, you know." I close my laptop when I see Jinx frowning at his phone again while we're all distracted. "This meeting in London she proposed will let us confirm or deny it."

"Maybe," Mo says as he looks at them. "What then? What if she is the same person?"

Dwyn beams as he clutches his hands to his heart. "Then she has to meet Razzie and not-drunk Coda."

That suggestion hits a little close to home for me and I push out of my seat. "Yeah, well, we'll see. You idiots should get some rest. I doubt Mo has us scheduled for a vacation while we're in London tracking this mystery chick down. I'm gonna take the bed."

I can feel their eyes on me as I walk into the small bedroom they equip all the private planes *Les Invisibles* owns with. Once I shut the door, I flop on the bed and bury my face in the soft pillows, hoping it will muffle the growl. We haven't dated the same woman since Remy died and I'm not sure we can have a relationship like that again.

Hell, I'm not sure I can have one at all outside of Jinx—I'm too fucked up.

"Raz?" The soft voice follows the sound of the door opening and closing again. Jinx always knows when I'm struggling with shit; we've been together for far too long for him to miss my distress.

"What?" I mutter into the satin pillowcase.

His sigh is frustrated, and I suppose that's fair. When I'm feeling vulnerable, I withdraw and he has to pull every thought and feeling out of me like he's an expert torturer. I don't *mean* to be that way, but I also have no control over how my trauma manifests. All I can do is try not to be a fuckhead and apologize if I am on accident—that's all anyone can do.

"You know what? Clearly, the thought of this girl being a single person and getting involved with several of us has you twisted." The bed dips as he sits on the edge and rests a hand on the back of my knee. "Because of her, right?"

I flip over and throw my arm over my head as I sprawl out. "Of *course*, because of her! *None* of us have actually healed, J. We're all *'lost boys, broken toys, making noise'*… like Coda's stupid song says. It would be unfair to bring some poor woman into our mess, even if she is part of our world."

Jinx arches a brow. "If you keep quoting his shit, we won't be able to fit Coda's ego on the plane with us anymore."

The laugh escapes before I can stop it, and I wrap my arms around myself. "Fuck, I needed that. You're not wrong, but it's funny as shit."

Crawling up beside me, he wiggles into my side, sitting his chin on my shoulder. His presence is calming, and I tilt my head a bit to give him a grateful look before lacing my fingers with his. "Between the five of us, the length of our relationships since the island *combined* isn't even as long as we knew her."

"Jesus Christ, Raz. We can't all stay married to a ghost forever." His lips curve and he narrows his eyes at me. "And I take exception to that statement."

I huff, knowing he means us as a couple, but we've never been good at defining that. "I didn't say we should, J. I'm saying if this *is* one girl and we want to share her, we need to be honest about our issues. Mo is so closed off that he barely registers a human sometimes. Coda and D have been way off the rails for a long time. You put up a good show, but you don't connect with anyone who isn't me or a mark. I'm…"

"Stubborn. Damaged. Afraid. Introverted," Jinx offers as I scowl.

'Yes, but also I have so much resentment and anger. We all do. Putting someone else in the slot she left without warning them isn't fair. We won't mean to compare them, but it will happen. It will lead to problems. Maybe we need to exorcise our own demons before we add someone to the fire."

He nods, looking into the space just beyond me as he considers. "Maybe. But losing Remy taught me you have to live life for now, babe. The woman I met enchanted me in a way I haven't felt since then. Dwyn is so lovesick over his girl that Mo hasn't even had to tell him not to throw knives in the plane."

I blink. *Holy shit, he's right.*

"This opportunity may never come around again. I mean, the likelihood of finding someone in our line of work who can fight well enough to impress Mo is daring enough to capture D's attention, and knows classical lit well enough to go against me? And we don't know if she was the chick strong enough to heft conked out Coda, but if so, it's like kismet. Most people don't even get that once, much less twice in a lifetime."

Squeezing his hand tightly, I nod. "She's smart enough to make me work to solve a code, too."

"And somehow, friendly with the most ruthless assassin The Company offers. She charmed the woman he called his 'mate' first, though. But our intel on *Le Voleur* didn't have any interpersonal connections, so that's another thing she's given us." His grin is teasing as he pauses. "Do you think that's enough to *consider* auditioning her?"

"Shut up," I mutter as I give his shoulder a shove. "We're not taking fucking resumes. Don't be a twat."

Jinx sits up, tugging his shirt off with one hand as he smirks at me. He pulled me out of the funk I was sinking into and he knows it. *Bastard.* "Since you're done moping, we have this tiny little room to ourselves and enough time to renew our membership, don't you think?"

"Mile high or proudly bi?" I ask. My lips twitch as he undoes his pants. "They're never sending us a toaster oven; I keep telling you that."

"You definitely need something better to do with your mouth." Moving to kneel, he slides his hand into my hair, tugging me forward roughly. "Luckily, I have the solution to that problem."

I open my mouth to snark back, but his cock pushes between my lips before I get the chance. Inhaling his scent as I take all of his length in until he hits the back of my throat, I hum softly. That earns me a groan of approval, so I do it again as I run my tongue along the vein on the underside of his cock. Jinx is always in charge and I crave our time together because I can let go of the tightly harnessed control I normally have on myself. My teeth scrape lightly as I move up and down his curved shaft slowly, waiting for him to urge me to pick up the rhythm. When I reach the tip, I suckle on him, flicking the tip of my tongue over the spot under the head that makes me crazy.

"Christ, Raz. We wait too long in between. Your fucking mouth…"

Swallowing him down in one quick motion, I reach up to roll his balls in my hand. He's not wrong, but our group was fractured and it keeps us all apart. His hips rock when I brush my fingers over the back of his sack, and I know it's time to speed up. I meet the thrusts as he fucks my mouth, breathing through my nose and holding onto his thigh with my other hand. My own dick is weeping; I can feel it.

"Just like that. Take it all the way. Keep going; I'm close."

His low muttering is hot as fuck and I work to keep up with the pace he's setting without choking. Increasing the suction a little, I tug on his balls a little harder and he lets out a snarl. His hand grips my hair tight and I can feel the shudder run through him before his cock jerks and he comes, spilling in my mouth in hot, salty jets. When his hips stop moving, I pull back, swallowing with a wink as I lie back.

"Fuck, I love when you do that," he says as he flops down beside me. "And you goddamn well know it."

I stroke my dick slowly as I look at his flushed face and messy hair. "I might."

"Give me a minute to catch my breath and I'll show you how much I like it."

"Deal."

FRIENDS IN LOW PLACES

THE BAR IS A DIVE, BUT IT'S A PERFECT SPOT FOR A MEETING LIKE MINE. The smell of stale pints, sweaty football fans, and whiskey isn't as enjoyable as sipping martinis at the Rosewood, but it will do in a pinch. I have a bottle of tequila in front of me and two glasses for when my occasional comrade in crime arrives. Until then, I'm pretending to watch the match on the TV and avoiding the occasional punter who tries his luck. I'd hoped I could fly under the male gaze by being low key, but that didn't work. Even dressed down in jeans, a Nirvana tee, and a leather jacket, my Callista disguise is drawing attention.

I literally cannot with the audacity men shove up their ass and walk around carrying every day.

"How many of these fools have almost gotten their fingers broken so far?"

I look up and see Elysium in her full glory. The world renown thief has two modes: peacock and invisible girl. Today, she's chosen the former because the wild purple braids compliment her rich copper skin and she's rocking skin tight black jeans with a hot pink corset and neon yellow Doc Martens that lace to her knees. Everything about her screams 'look at me!' while I'm practically fading into the background. I can't help but tease her since we'd agreed to keep this on the down low. "This is subtle? Elton John might have drawn fewer eyeballs."

"Oh, Duchess. You're so inflexible with rules. You need to live a little." She laughs, flashing bright white teeth against her matching pink lipstick. The action makes her face scrunch and the diamond snakebites in each cheek sparkle at me in the lowlight.

She's getting ready to find out how much I've been breaking my own rules in a second.

Pouring the tequila in the shot glasses, I push one at her and she sits down on the stool next to mine. "You won't be saying that after you hear what I've been up to. I'm not one for collaboration and this situation feels dire enough to cross that line as well."

"I'm all ears," she says, holding up her glass to clink with mine before we toss back our shots.

"About two weeks ago, I was leaving a job location when I received a new bid. They sent the request through my normal channels, but followed none of my client protocols. The prospect was aware they were out of line, but they sent the contract and information, regardless."

Her brows furrow. "Did you tell them to get fucked?"

"No." I pause for a moment and weigh my words. "I set up a drop for more information because the specific target was… known to me and I was very curious how this job came to be."

"Oh, *that* is always a mistake." She pours another shot as I nod, and we drink again.

"Yes." I slam the glass on the bar as I think of how easily I allowed myself to be manipulated because I was swimming in sentiment after saving Coda. Amateur-hour, indeed. "So, I had the feeling I might have been followed on an unrelated matter, which meant extra tight security as I approached the drop in the next location. It felt like there were eyes on me on the way, in the location, and even when I picked up my intel early. I was certain it was about my previous client until I came back at the arranged time and someone tried to blow me the hell up."

Elysium's eyes bug out. "No fucking way! Was that *you* in Germany? I knew the media was full of shit. I've dated boom boom dudes, so I knew the explosion was *not* a gas line. By the way, if you ever think about doing one—don't. Most paranoid assholes on the planet and they *never* sleep."

I don't sleep much, either. Assassins and explosive experts have a lot more to fear than thieves.

"Well, I escaped mostly unscathed and made my way to another city to get away from the blast radius while I decrypted the shit." I pour us another shot, hoping to prepare her for this info. "It's some creepy douche hiding behind filters and voice changers who want to take down the big orgs. Like, my job is supposedly step one to reforming the criminal underworld. His shit definitely has 'paging Dr. Evil' vibes."

"Fuck, not another one. I mean, it feels like some fucker is trying to oust the leaders in most of the big corporations every week." She shakes her head, glancing around us. "We all know none of the big five are perfect—that's why I'm freelance. But we don't have any complete nutters running the show at the moment, so why tip the apple cart?"

I shrug. "I have no love for any of them, either, and you know I'm freelance. Which is what brings me to my next part: the party in Prague where half the notorious independent contractors got nabbed? I'm uncertain this dickhead didn't arrange for the Open Market and *Deus* to get them all cleared away. I was there, but I left before the real shit went down. The entire night seemed planned— including all the arrests."

"To do that... to have that kind of pull... Your Shadow man must have enormous pull in the underworld. And money—-an absolute fuck ton of money," she muses. "Perhaps that's why he's hiding behind the mask, so to speak. Might be recognizable."

Why the fuck didn't I think of that?

"It's possible," I agree. "But have you heard of any newcomers with the money or access to even start something like this? I realized on my way to London that the recent events cannot be the first ones that he set into motion. Taking over the major organizations would require many wheels to be set in motion over a long period. The job they contracted me for is a *big* leap forward in terms of statements. It's not his first move."

The thief pulls out her phone, tapping a fingernail on her teeth as she scrolls through something for a minute. "We may have to request access to the *Mercatus* archives to find the trail. Have you tried searching the dark web and upper layers of the 'Net for things that might fit your theory?"

"I've got some programs running." I keep my response vague because as The Duchess, I have to remind myself that Elysium thinks I belong in her class of criminal. She has no idea my primary jobs are those of The Guillotine and I can't reveal what other skills I have that most thieves wouldn't. "A hacker I know designed them for casing my marks, but they'll work for this as well."

The hacker is me, of course.

"Good, because that means the simple stuff is taken care of. The harder part will be getting access to *Mercatus* logs." Her expression turns serious as she looks at me. "The only way to get an audience with Caesar is to render unto him a service."

"Of fucking course," I mutter. "The creator of the online criminal hub demands a tribute before he'll even speak to you. I'd bet my favorite pick set that he's a pasty old asshole who lives in a basement filled with Mountain Dew and Dorito dust." Elysium snorts, then collapses in a fit of laughter as I shrug. "I mean, it fits the whole Casar thing, right?"

"That was poetry, woman. Absolute poetry." She wipes her eyes and grins. "If we're going to do a job together to get this bastard's attention, I'm gonna need to call you something other than 'Duchess,' you know. I feel like I'm talking to some white girl's purse dog when I say it."

"Okay. But then you have to give me your name," I counter. "You can call me Callista."

Yeah, I'm giving her an alias when she's agreeing to help me. I'm too fucking on edge to give out a real name.

"Elysium *is* my name. But if you can call me Lys for short—all my friends do."

I blink at her like she's spoken a dead language. "Friends?"

"Yeah. Like the people you hang out with? People you trust to let your hair down in front of? Maybe even bang occasionally, like me?" Her brows furrow as she looks at me. "Are you telling me you don't have friends?"

My face turns bright red, and I pour another shot, tossing it back. "No time. Never anywhere long enough. I'm a solo act."

"Uh-huh. That explains why you had to call me to bounce this crazy shit off. You don't have anyone else," Lys says as she studies me. "Except your body language says that might not be exactly true."

Groaning, I shake my head. "It was until two weeks ago when all this shit started. Now… I don't know what the hell is going on."

"Then sit here and help me finish this bottle while we talk it out, Callista. I have the feeling we're talking about some spicy tea and I'm here for it."

Never in my life have I had a girl talk gossip session, and it looks like I'm not getting out of this one.

"It all started with seeing this guy I dated once in a bar fight…"

MEMORIES

It's really fucking weird to feel like the odd man out.

Being a famous face, I'm usually in the thick of any public shenanigans. Somehow, I've been relegated to the metaphorical van with Raz and I *hate* it. Jinx, Dwyn, and Mo have all met the mystery girl when they were conscious—leaving me to founder one between humiliation that those popped collar dicks got the drop on me and jealousy that the two of them got to fuck her.

Green-eyed monster, that's me to tee at the moment.

"Coda, are you paying attention? Jesus Christ, man." Raz's grumble makes me sit up straighter and Dwyn smirks as he spins a knife on his palm. They've caught me.

"I was. I lost the thread when Mo started droning on about tech shit. You know I can't focus on that and neither can D." Crossing my arms over my chest, I glare at the thief because I know they checked him out, too.

Dwyn shrugs. "I do when it's about keeping my sexy ass alive, friend. Knowing where the cameras are and how Razzie is timing his blackouts is necessary for my part of this mission. I want to stay out of jail so I can meet up with Jazz."

Mo snorts and shakes his head. "I can't believe you're still this hung up on a woman."

My eyes narrow and I grin at the fighter knowingly. "Tell us again about her Krav Maga, Mo-Mo. Describe the fight without getting a hard on and you can tease Dwyn."

"Guys..." Jinx jumps in, ever the peacemaker. "Let's get back to the mission specs. The sooner we get this shit for our original assignment completed, the sooner we can focus on identifying our girl."

"*Et tu, Brute?*" Raz mutters. Jinx winks at him and he chuckles low.

The two of them are such an odd combination together and it's fascinating. Our group has been working together since we arrived on the island as children and despite the distance since she died, we fall into old routines easily. The history between us was forged in blood and tears—even Remy had trouble working her way into her eventual spot in the middle of us.

For a second, I flash back to the day I met the white-haired girl with bright violet eyes. We were only eight, but you grow up quickly when you live at l'Academie. It was during our yearly captivity resistance training, and I'd been in the jungle for at least a week. The rest of the guys were handling other tasks because the sun was up and the rules were very clear that each person has to survive on their own. We only met up at night to avoid being caught on camera, so I was alone while I hunted for game.

You don't get weapons—only the opponents do—so I had a sharp spear Mo carved with a knife that he took off the first person he killed on day one. The big ass cat must have creeped through the brush like a fucking ninja because it was on me before I even knew it was there. I struggled with it, taking a few good swipes with enormous claws as I scrabbled to get the spear back.

Suddenly, a high-pitched war cry echoed off the hills, startling both of us, and a flash of white descended from a higher tree. The thing landed on top of us both, screaming like a banshee as it jerked the head of the jaguar back and damn near cut its head off. Blood spurted from its jugular, coating my face until it dropped on top of me. When I finally wiped my face clean, I couldn't believe what I saw.

A small girl with long, tangled white hair stood with a piece of wire she must have somehow cut from the fences that surround the training area wrapped around her hands. Her face and body were covered in a makeshift ghillie suit and dirt, but the brilliance of her eyes captivated me immediately.

Snorting, she unwraps the wire, rubbing her bloody palms on her legs. "Are you hard of hearing or is it because you have your head up your ass so far you can't hear anything?"

I had no idea what to make of that, so I just stared.

"Damn. Maybe you are deaf and dumb. Shit, I'm sorry, but that fucker was trailing you for like thirty minutes."

Vulgar language starts pretty early on here, so it did not surprise me at what she said as much as the tone she took with me. My brothers and I ruled our class—people gave us a wide berth because of it. And this chick was familiar, but I don't think I'd ever seen her say anything to anyone unless a teacher called on her. She ate alone and never participated in any activities outside of training.

Yet here she was, acting like I was an idiot.

It was fascinating.

I finally found my brain and pushed myself up off the ground. Once I had my spear again, I backed up, making sure I had enough space to run if she decided to take me out. Everyone knew eliminating other competitors earned you bonus points on your score and she might have killed the cat so she could claim her victory.

"I'm not deaf. I didn't hear it. What, do you have bat ears?" I challenged her because I had to—reputation and all.

She shrugs. "It's easier to hear things when your mouth isn't always running."

"So you know who I am. And you know I'm neither deaf nor dumb," I countered as a grin crept over my face. The spunk she showed was so completely different from the way she presented herself in class that I couldn't help but play along. Most of the girls here fawned over me and the guys because we were popular. "I suppose it is; you've got me, feral girl."

That made her mad, and she glared at me. "I know how to survive this nightmare. It's not pretty, but neither is being eaten by a jaguar."

I look at the dead animal and nod, conceding her point. "Fair enough. Should we split the meat? I'll help with the gross parts."

"Gross parts?" She gave me an odd look. "You mean skinning and shit? I can do it faster and better than you, guaranteed. But take the beast—I've got plenty of stores in my nest. You probably need the help."

"I—"

Before I can get my retort out, she grins at me, salutes, and takes off into the brush.

I didn't see her again until they picked us up at the end of the exercise, but every morning, I found a package of animal meat wrapped in leaves and perfectly prepped for eating outside of my makeshift shelter. None of the guys ever saw her do it, no matter who was on watch. It drove Mo crazy that she consistently slipped in and out of our perimeter without leaving a trace.

After that, I started seeking her out when we weren't in class. She wouldn't even tell me her name for the first few months, so I just called her 'feral girl.'

That was the first step Remy Arsine Benoit took towards being one of The Six—saving my life.

"Coda, goddamnit!"

I blink, coming out of my reverie to see all four of my brothers looking at me with angry glares. "Uh..."

"Fuck, he was totally spaced—*again*," Jinx moans as he rubs his hand over his face.

Dwyn flings his knife at me, hitting the couch just shy of my ear. "Now we all have to listen to Mo drone on for a *third time*, you asshole!"

Pulling the blade out, I roll my eyes. "I'm the same asshole I've always been. You know I'd stay engaged better if I had my guitar, but our fearless leader insisted I put it away."

The dick in question huffs, but he walks over and picks up my acoustic, shoving it at me. "Fine. But if you space out this time, I'm kicking your ass."

"Aye, aye, Captain Asshat!"

With a long-suffering sigh, he pinches the bridge of his nose and starts outlining the parts of our missions again.

MY PART, AS USUAL, IS NOWHERE NEAR AS COMPLEX AS SOME OTHERS. Jinx and I are attending yet another snooty party, though this time, we're more distraction than function. The estate where it's being held is Mo's target, and he's posing as part of my security team. Raz is running ops from the van nearby, so he'll be close enough to come if we need an extraction.

Dwyn is on his own and given that he's breaking into the country home of a government minister attending this shindig, I worry more about him going off the rails. Our thief has a penchant for taking unnecessary risks when it comes to his heists and stealing a hard drive is boring to him. He'll be dancing through the fucking place, looking for more alluring things to swipe while he's there.

That's the shit that gets you caught—unless you're Dwyn Shanahan.

"Coda?"

I roll my eyes and listen in on the ever-present earwig. Since I'm exiting the town car and there are cameras, I can't respond, but I lift my hand in a signal that the hacker watching the cameras can see.

"Jinx is *en route* with his socialite. If you could suspend the contest for the evening so I'm able to monitor D, it would be most helpful. When you all compete during jobs, I have to split my focus in case one of you does something stupid," Raz says drily.

I consider it for a moment, but Jinx cuts in. "I'm not playing tonight. Have at it, music man."

The retort on the tip of my tongue dies before I can mutter it. First Dwyn is smitten and now Jinx is refusing to bag easy prey? *This girl's pussy must be made of magic and fairy dust.* I don't bother asking the monk—he never plays our games in public. My eyes skate over to him and he chuckles, shrugging his shoulders slightly.

"Raz, if you don't find out who this chick is tonight, I'm crashing their dates so I can see. This is bullshit."

That gets a laugh out of all of them, and I have to physically force myself to smile as I wave at the people who rush up when I walk in. Groupies are usually fun—even the rich ones—but I know the guys I grew up with. Any woman that's piqued their interest so intensely will be a hell of a lot better than anything these girls can offer.

I think I'll wait until I meet her.

I take the arm of the gushing hostess, patting her hand as she walks me into the party. She's giving me the look and normally, I'd be all over some cougar fun, but tonight, I'm all business.

Coda Ramone, playboy rockstar, is off the market for a bit.

Forever

OH SHIT

I'M NOT USED TO WORKING WITH OTHER PEOPLE, BUT WHILE ELYSIUM HAD her sources put out feelers about my mystery employer, she convinced me to work a job with her. I suspect she could do it herself, but I'm in knots about the planned meetings with Slick and Casanova. After a *lot* of drinks, that entire tale came out, and it surprised me to find I enjoyed having her weigh in on my experience.

Decisions have been all my responsibility since I arose from my watery grave like a phoenix, but she made good points.

Slick might not be in our line of work, but Cas almost certainly is. Attendance at that clusterfuck was split between marks and professionals—he was *definitely* not a mark. So one or both of my rendezvous could be worth checking out. Fifty-fifty odds are worth a shot, especially since it's the first time in a very long time I've cared to seek another round.

That was her take, anyway, and maybe I needed someone to convince me that my instincts were right. My faith in my intuition is pretty tenuous after recent events. Her support got me to text them both back and set up separate meetings in the next few days.

However, all that girl bonding led to where I am now: dressed as a waiter at some fancy party so I can case the joint. Elysium is elegant as hell in her Josephine Baker-esque attire—she's doing the charming society maven part while I find the gaps in security. Once I locate the entrance to the supposed underground vault, I'll give her the info over our comms and she'll meet me there.

It took a lot of convincing to get me to take part because this is a last-minute job with little to no intel and even as The Duchess, I don't fly by the seat of my pants the way she does. She took this client right before I asked for our meeting and hasn't had time to do very much prep. I would have simply told her no if the client wasn't so sympathetic.

I know, not my usual oeuvre, but stealing a necklace pilfered by the Nazis and returning it to its original owner before they die is probably the most good karma I'll earn all year.

"Callista? Do you read?"

Holding my tray of champagne flutes high, I turn my head so I can shift my hair in front of my face before I reply. "Over and out, Snowman."

The laugh that trills over our line is delighted. "*Smokey & The Bandit*... classic. Give me the nod when you have the location."

I don't respond; I continue on through the cocktail hour, letting people snatch glasses of bubbly until I'm out. We're in a reception room, so the guests will be allowed into the main dining room, eventually. While we're in the open, I need to do recon, so I pick a corner to work my way along the walls first. Once I'm satisfied nothing in this area is what we're looking for, I put my tray under my arm and walk brusquely toward the kitchen. There's a myriad of places down this way, and if I can slip past the beefy guards, I might even make it upstairs.

Who knows if this crusty old German has some Batman elevator to his illegal artifact vault?

Making my way through the bustling kitchen, I veer off towards what our head catering staffer called 'servants' quarters'. We were told this was the only place we could eat, use the bathroom, or clean up any spills, so I assume it's where the day-to-day household staff are housed. I watch carefully to ensure none of them are lurking about, then make my way to the back staircase at the end of the hall. It has steps going up and down, which leaves me wondering if my whimsical Batcave musings were correct or if the Baron Whatever was dumb enough to design his house so obviously.

"Taking the down staircase in back. I hope he's this arrogant," I mutter into my mic.

Silence is my answer, so I know Elysium is otherwise engaged. She's probably picking pockets and stealing shit as she goes—true thieves can *never* resist the challenge. I have to pray she doesn't get caught doing bullshit like that while I'm scouting the house. Shaking my head, I creep down the stairs to find an enormous oak door with a keypad. My fingers slip into the belt of tools I'm wearing under the ugly catering pants, fishing out my current phone. A few clicks have me into the home Wi-Fi network and I open my RNG app to sync it to the keypad. The numbers flash over the screen, but I'm not leaving anything to chance because I have no idea if the guards do rounds down here.

I open another compartment on the belt while my program is trying to brute force the code, pulling out a small bag of fingerprint powder. Blowing gently, I coat the keys, looking for where the smudges are darkest. It's six digits and the zero key is *heavily* smudged. That leads me to believe it's probably a date. This is where prep and research would be extremely helpful. Profiling a mark is a science and an art—I don't know enough about this fucker to do the sort of deductive leaps I'd normally do. Also, I know fuck all about safeguards in the alarms in this joint, so I have no idea if it will sound a klaxon if I enter the wrong code.

"Lys. Have you met the hosts?"

"Affirmative."

"Summary of the Baron?"

"Old. Pervy. Handsy. Eyes like a hawk. Regimented. Ex-military," Lys murmurs. "High rank."

Hmmm. "How old?"

"Late seventies. Good shape. Lots of plastic work, though. Seems to take joy in poking fun at his wife in front of her. She's quiet as a mouse."

That actually helps. Old world asshole with military training in his seventies—or older—means the owner of this vault was old enough to be indoctrinated at the time the necklace we seek was stolen. Taking pleasure in being cruel to his wife speaks to his nature, and finding it funny oozes superiority complex. I'd wager this date is something he finds immensely satisfying and has to do with his secret stash of gross memorabilia. The app is still running combinations, so I close my eyes and try to think back to all the military history drilled into our minds during classes at *l'Academie.* The Allied dates are easiest to remember as they're still celebrated, but this would have to be significant to the enemy. I'm fairly certain Ol' Klaus up there is still a believer since he had no compunction about buying something with a provenance like this.

It comes to me in a flash of brilliance—the day the Germans bombed London. His smug arrogance would find that especially humorous for a house in London, especially since it's in the area that took heavy damage back then. I pause with my fingers over the keys, trying to decide if I should try it or wait out the hacking tool. It's been at least ten minutes and while I haven't seen or heard anyone, I'll get trapped in this atrium with nowhere to hide if they do come in.

Trust your gut, Remy. It's all you have.

I take a deep breath and punch in zero-nine-zero-seven-four-zero. The lights flash on the pad and my heart leaps into my chest, but finally, a loud click and the swing of the door tell me I extrapolated correctly. A sigh escapes as I pull out another item from my belt, spraying the hairspray into the room before I take a step past the door frame. "No lasers, thank fuck."

"Lasers are cool, though." Lys pauses for a second then adds, "You're missing some shit up here. Two hotties and a rockstar."

"It's a hard-knock life."

She snorts and cuts her mic, leaving me in silence as I enter the wine cellar. They carved its walls into the rock, making it truly appear to be a cave. Sturdy oak shelves full of bottles fill the room... some more dusty than others. I assume the less touched bottles are older, but most collectors have a special display they keep the jewels of their collection in. Walking the aisles slowly, I notice a set of shelves tucked at the end of a cobwebby row that seems clean and shiny.

That's odd. Time to investigate.

Honestly, this kind of stuff is the *only* reason I came up with The Duchess' alter ego. Killing people in different methods requires planning, wit, and skill, but not like grifting or thieving. Those two are constantly challenging my brain to spin the chessboard and find creative ways to overcome problems. When I plan assassinations, I'm so methodical that rarely do I have complications and it gets a bit... old hat. Though, I haven't killed anyone for over a week. That's feeling a bit off, too.

Don't judge me for having layers.

"Houston, we might have a problem." Lys' voice is low, but I hear the concern over the line.

"Target in sight, Goose," I reply as I walk down the aisle and start inspecting the odd shelf.

"Great. But the group of hot guys are acting sus. One of them is pretending he doesn't know the other two, but I guarantee they're all wearing earwigs," she breathes into the mic. "I'm being careful so they don't see me talking; I'm certain they're pros."

Elysium is good at what she does—I know she's never gotten caught and there are some high-profile jobs attributed to her, so if she says we have a problem, she's probably right. I checked *Mercatus* before we came to make sure we weren't walking into a mess like Prague, but nothing came up. Who are these dudes then? My eyes widen when I realize she said one word that I should have paid attention to: rock star.

Oh, fuck.

"Lys, is the rock star Coda Ramone?"

"Affirmative, Maverick."

My hands shake as I keep feeling the shelves for a hidden lever or latch. If Coda is here, it's possible the two other guys are the other members of The Five. I haven't seen any of them besides him because they stay out of the media and wipe all traces when they leave missions. I have no idea what any of them look like—not just because they have grown from boys to men, but because of *Les Invisibles* penchant for altering appearances surgically. It could be a coincidence—they could just be Coda's security team—but I don't want to chance it. I need to find this fucking vault and get the hell out of here!

It's not like they'd recognize me, I know.. Between getting older, the Callista disguise, and thinking I'm dead, I should be safe.

"What are they doing that you are concerned about?" I ask as I click into a signal scanning app on my phone. There isn't a button anywhere, so I assume either RF or Bluetooth activates this damn entrance.

She sucks in a breath before she replies. "I've overheard two of them asking about a woman. I'm circulating as I meet and greet. I know the eagle-eyed one pretending to be security made me for a pro, but I don't know him. The other two are casually tossing in questions referring to someone they hope will be here, but get this: the descriptions of her vary."

Son of a bitch!

"Stay away from them if you can, Lys. I'm working on what I believe is the door we need. When I get it open, slip into the staff hallway, go down the corridor, and head downstairs. *Do not come until I give you the signal.* I have to make sure I didn't stumble on this old perv's sex dungeon."

"Ten-four, little buddy."

My hands tremble more as I run the scanner over the wine rack, praying I've located our target rather than my other guess. Elysium and I need to get the fuck out of here before Coda and the other guys decide to follow her. Best case, they'll grill her about her client and it will put her on their radar; worst case, they'll start surveilling her if they think she's connected to whoever they're looking for. My role as The Duchess could end if the latter is their aim.

Did I outdo them at the party from hell? I didn't think anyone else would bid on that job after I took it.

A loud click pulls me out of my thoughts and I pump my fist in the air as the shelf swings out, revealing a dark stairway. I turn the flashlight on my phone on and see old stone steps that head down into my blackness. Whatever is down here must have been converted from some war era hiding spot. This house is at least a century old, if not more, so it's possible this was some kind of escape route. I'll have to suck it up and go down with no clue what I'll run into.

Just. Great.

I descend the slippery stone stairs carefully, shining my light around to make certain I will not fall and break my neck. It's creepy as fuck, but I've been in spaces like this before, European castles and mansions that pre-date the turn of the century are *full* of hidden shit like this. It's how I knew to look. There are torches on the wall, but fuck if I'm going to pull out a lighter and start some *National Treasure*-type row of fire. That would eliminate all hope of being stealthy for sure. At the bottom of the twisting steps, there's a giant vault door with a tech panel on the side.

Jackpot.

Of course, I have no idea if I've got enough firepower in the shit I strapped under my clothes to get through the layers of security a panel that large could hold. But I'll be damned if I didn't at least *locate* the Nazi horde. I walk over to the panel, pressing the button on the side and waiting as it slides open. My eyes close when I see what looks to be scanners for fingerprints and retinas, plus a keyboard for typing codes.

Fuck, fuck, double fuckitty fuck. This is going to be a problem.

"Found it. Eyes needed to breach. I can handle the prints and codes."

Lys groans softly. "Got it. Keep working and I'll see if I can finagle an eyeball."

Grinning to myself, I tap one of the keys to what sequence the pieces need to be entered. The fingerprint scanner flashes, so I pull the powder out of my belt again, along with a small jar of liquid latex. I dip my index finger into it and look at the time on my phone. It'll take about five minutes to dry, so I set about dusting the hell out of the keypad until I find a solid print to mimic. Once that's done, I use my non-latexed hand to open the app to scan for the code. I'm already on the network because of the shelves, so this should move much more quickly than the first keypad.

"Target acquired. I'll see if I can get him to mug up for selfies and use the optical to grab his eyes. Hopefully, he doesn't grab my ass."

The life of a female operative is full of moments where you have to decide if allowing some dope to grope you is worth obtaining the shit they hired you for.

Now all I have to do is wait.

Forever

DANGEROUS

"THIS IS BULLSHIT; I'M BORED."

Fucking Coda. He's usually in his element, flirting with everything that moves.

"At least you're not in the van, idiot," I mutter.

Mo lets out of his aggravated sighs. "Stop it, children. Jinx, how are you doing with the Baron's wife? Did you get anything out of her?"

"Well, she's not getting what she wants out of me, and it's making things difficult. But if I keep supplying the champagne, I'll get it out of her."

The shudder in his tone makes me laugh. He doesn't mind using his sexy ass in grifts unless the mark is old or filled with way too much plastic. I'm guessing the Baroness is fifty-fifty on that account. It's hard to tell from the ancient cameras in their security system. I would have expected better surveillance at a house filled with expensive art and sculptures, but it's beyond archaic. It makes me wonder what the rich asshole who lives here spent all of his money on instead.

"Did you see the chick I was talking about?" Coda cuts in. "I'm sure I've seen her before."

"She looks familiar and the way she works the room says pro." Jinx pauses and addresses me. "Raz, can you find the woman in the flapper looking dress and run her through recognition?"

"Will do. Should I be worried we haven't heard from Dwyn yet?"

The line goes silent as everyone thinks about my question. The thief is so unpredictable and unhinged when he's working that silence could be a good or bad thing. Theoretically, he would activate the distress signal on his watch if someone nabbed him. Dwyn is far from predictable, though, so he might decide escaping custody is the ultimate game. In that case, we wouldn't know a thing about what he was doing until he either got out or needed help.

"Christ, I don't know," Mo says. "He's like spit in the wind. We won't know dick until he turns his comms on."

Which is a goddamned nightmare because the rest of us are easily a half hour away from his target. Immediate extraction is not *an option.*

The line crackles as the sound of automatic weapon fire rings out. Screams and shouts echo in the background of the guys' comms, so I slide over to the camera bank, flicking through the feeds to see what area of the house the noise is coming from. The main room is full of terrified looking guests and it takes a few minutes until I find an angle that lets me see what the hell is going on in that house. There are at least six masked people carrying Beretta 9mm semi-autos surrounding the crowd of wealthy guests, including the guys. Their silence lets me know they are too close to a bogie to speak or they're in a direct sight line.

We've all had years of captivity resistance training at *l'Academie,* so I know we can handle a hostage situation without getting killed—*if* the rest of the assholes in there don't piss the strike team off.

"I see them. I'll start running the guest list to see if it's loot or a snatch and grab." My words sound confident, but we all know how easily this situation can go sideways, especially when there are scared civilians involved.

We're trained to disengage from our humanity and allow whatever happens to happen, as long as our mission is protected—which means if people die, they die.

I slide over to the Linux based machines and type as fast as possible, using my exploit in the Baron's network to break into the files on the devices in the old mansion. After a few moments, I find an 'official' invite list and a second file labeled 'non-official guest list'. Rolling my eyes at fucking rich morons, I feed the names into my web spiders and bots, sending them trawling through every layer of the internet to find dirt that could lead to this kind of bullshit. None of them seem important outside of having enormous fortunes; that could be enough, but this appears to be a trained team.

Leaving the searches running, I go back to the cameras to look for the Baron's security team. Every single one I find is down, but not from obvious fatal injuries. They could be knocked out and there could be more I don't have on camera—the gaps in the coverage of both the inside and outside of this monstrosity are big enough to drive Mack trucks through. That's why I'm not discounting a group of amateurs; the members of The Five could have infiltrated this estate and gotten away scot-free by the time we were ten. It's not a giant leap to assume some local knobheads heard about a fancy party and found the firepower to make it happen.

I'm so focused on figuring out how the armed people got in that the low, measured tone of our leaders startles me. Mo almost never panics—it's just not in his nature. "Ten visible hostiles. Unclear if count is final. All armed. Leader unclear. Demands unclear."

That is not a good sign. Taking that many hostages without immediately announcing their demands is a bad sign.

"Do any of them seem like Section Eight?"

"Negative."

Mo's assurance that none of the hostiles he can see are insane helps, but it doesn't take much to piss off some guys on amateur teams. They're poster children for anger management classes or total psychos—and not in the lovable way Dwyn is. It occurs to me again that we haven't heard from our knife-wielding thief all night. This evening is as fucked up as the damn party in Prague and I'm wondering if there's a reason for that. We *never* have ops go as poorly as they have since Coda's minor issue in Paris; we wouldn't have survived as long as we have if so.

When one of my searches beeps, I scoot back over and squint at the results. The name didn't throw up a flag; no, the image search has netted the girl Mo suspected was a pro. She's known as Elysium and she's a thief easily as accomplished as Dwyn. I doubt she has anything to do with the morons in black who entered by shooting semi-automatic weapons into a crowded space, but she's definitely a potential ally if things go sideways.

"The girl is a thief. Possible friendly if needed, Jinx."

"Why are you telling him? I'm charming!" Coda grumbles. "Plus, I have to piss like a racehorse, and these fuckers haven't said a goddamned word yet."

Jesus, he's such a whiner. "Because you're a fucking rock star and maybe it's not the time to break cover with some chick we don't know?"

"Oh… yeah, okay."

"Shut up unless it's relevant—all of you. We don't need these people to notice us talking to ourselves and figure out we should be bound," Mo hisses. "We need an exit strategy, Raz. Now."

He's got a point.

"On it."

Abandoning the cameras, I keep the searches running while I dig into blueprints and records. If I can figure out a way to slip them out before this shit pops off, it would be better for everyone. We can always place an untraceable call to the authorities after we're out of range. The house is old as hell and there could be a thousand unmarked passages or tunnels; I'll have to go into historical archives to see if I can find out the real schematic.

"We are the Collective. The proliferation of obscene wealth across the globe has led to economic, environmental, and social disasters of unimaginable proportions. Greed and avarice control every aspect of our lives and threaten the existence of humanity." The voice doesn't appear to be coming from any of the gun wielding minions, but they're masked, so it's hard to tell. It could be a recording blasting out of one of their phones.

This is a group of nutters determined to make a very public statement.

"Worst-case scenario," I say over the line. "Armageddon."

I watch my brothers as they inch towards one another as carefully as possible. Mo isn't far from Coda, so he gets by his side without drawing attention to himself. Jinx is far away, but he's been in tight situations before. Even if he gets caught moving, he's likely to talk his way out of it—that's his gift and I have faith in him.

Doesn't mean there isn't a knot the size of a fist in my gut, though.

Mo clears his throat quietly before speaking. "They dressed hostiles to prevent identifying gender or features. They are taking care not to be seen; that bodes well for an outcome that isn't a room full of dead people."

He's right. If the bad guys stay disguised, they don't intend to eliminate witnesses because they aren't worried about someone finding out who they are. When they reveal themselves, your chances of getting out alive drop by sixty percent. "Jinx, stop heading for them and contact the Elysium chick. If she's here to steal something, it's likely she will have studied the floor plans even more thoroughly than we did. She might have even run a trial op."

His nod is visible on screen and I scoot away from the feeds showing the room they trapped the guys in so I don't pointlessly obsess over

Jinx's safety. I haven't found anything on recent blueprints that would help, but rich people don't always get permits to do shit in their homes. They assume they're above 'regular people' laws and try to hide their panic rooms or escape hatches, so people like us can't exploit public documents. It's very possible there are multiple hidey-holes in this place and I won't find any of them in schematics.

I hate old fucking structures like this.

Something catches my eye on the feed from the other rooms in the house, and I frown. It's gone before I can focus on it and this idiot doesn't have a system that records online. He might have a DVR in the house, but for all I know, the feed is being recorded on goddamned VHS tapes. That would explain why I can get into the cameras but can't back up and watch when these jackasses got in the building.

Maybe they have more operatives in other parts of the house. The 'We are the Collective' shit could be an elaborate smokescreen for a heist. I frown, pushing off the desk and sliding my chair down to the master computer running the scans. No names on the guest list have popped a flag, but I start up another search for the Baron's name. If this Elysium is world class and she's here, there must be more than the minor works of famous artists here. She wouldn't be here to steal low rent art like that, which means this team could be there to liberate the valuables as well.

"Running a check on the Baron's holdings. Between the master thief and this bunch of merc looking fuckers, I think he might have more stashed in this faux schloss than we know about. We came here for intelligence; Elysium came to steal. Nothing on the walls is valuable enough to get her out of bed." Coda snorts softly; he knows I'm an art snob, and this is the moment it finally pays off.

Usually Dwyn beats me to it.

"Affirmative. Jinx, are you close?" Mo can't see the room as well as he'd prefer, I know. He likes to find a spot like he did in Prague, where he can be Zeus looking down from Olympus. This vantage point has to be making him insane.

"He probably won't reply, but he's getting close. It's slow going because she's close to the hostile," I reply.

The line goes quiet again and I go back to watching the scans and cameras as I wait.

I haven't been this nervous on a job since the night she died—and look how that turned out.

CHAOS

I'M IN THE MIDDLE OF REMOVING THE OSTENTATIOUS DIAMOND AND RUBY necklace from its perch inside of the state-of-the-art case when the gunshots echo in my ear.

Luckily, I don't drop the motherfucking thing—there's a pressure plate, temp gauge, and a goddamned net of optics around the inside of this innocent-looking box. It took me almost twenty minutes to use the basic tools in my belt to rig all of them at once, and I was cursing Lys the whole time. I should have been the foil upstairs and *she* should have been down here tangling with the stupid ass thief bullshit.

Now there's semi-auto fire upstairs and I'm stuck down here trying not to set off a bazillion alarms.

"Situation FUBAR, Maverick. Asshole count unknown. Might be a heist, might be a pickup. Focus on our mission."

The voice on the other end is strained, and I sigh silently. They trained Elysium in all methods pertaining to stealing, but she didn't attend *l'Academie* and she didn't befriend guys in other disciplines. She doesn't have the slightest fucking clue what will need to be done to get us out of here before this whole thing goes to hell on a Harley. Telling me to stay put is the stupidest possible solution anyone could come up with because this *is* my forte.

Of course, she doesn't know that. She thinks I'm The Duchess, grifter extraordinaire.

That's why I cut her some slack while I finish closing this ridiculous case. Once I get the gum and the weights settled so it fools the pressure sensor, I slowly close the lid and back away. My improvised solution holds and when no alarms sound, I let out the breath I was holding. Looking at the necklace, I shake my head—blood money has bought this so many times and likely bought it originally. No one who has the funds for this kind of bling is ever *truly* innocent. But I'm not here to judge, just to nick the damn thing and get the fuck out.

Unfortunately, that feat is considerably harder since some fuckwads are holding the party hostage upstairs.

I swear, saving Coda in Paris was a harbinger of doom—nothing has gone right since I did it.

Another volley of bullets rings out and I close my eyes when a flashback from the past slams into me unbidden.

The machine gun fire came from the hill.

I knew better than to come out in the open during the daytime, but a curious monkey knocked my water supply over during the night. It was my fault for not securing it well enough, but the heat demanded I search for more or I'd dehydrate. So I crept out carefully, staying under the canopy of trees as much as possible. This is my fourth year of cap res training and I refuse to let the assholes win by getting killed.

I was always alone; it's the rules, but not everyone followed them—like him.

The boy with the sad eyes and slicked back blue undercut I saved last year must be somewhere on the island with his posse. When we got back to the school, he eventually told me his name was Coda, but his friends have never warmed up to me. They stayed closed off, so he visited me occasionally without them. He had a pretty voice and it would have been a shame if he died in the jungle.

But I didn't know what part of this hellhole they were hiding in, so I couldn't leave him my extra rations.

The sun was bright as I tried to find the glint of a muzzle. If I located the sniper perch, I'd be able to circumvent it and get to the clean water. Otherwise, I'd die of thirst or lead before an animal found me.

I've almost got it worked out when a handsome boy carrying homemade rope and a piece of metal walks by. He's counting on his fingers as if trying to work something out and I see the figure on the hill raise out of the brush slightly as they adjust their barrel.

Without thinking, I rush out of my hiding spot, tackling the oblivious moron to the ground as the bullet zips past us. It misses by a hair and once I hear the telltale sound of a reload, I wrap myself around the idiot I saved and alligator death roll us towards the underbrush. He's too dumbfounded to speak, so I keep us going until we're in the shadows I burst out of. Bullets are still flying, but the sniper's visibility is significantly reduced.

Big brown eyes look at me in terror when I put a finger to my lips and pull the cape of my ghillie suit over us to obscure my hair.

"Stay quiet. Don't move. I'll tell you when."

He nodded, and we stayed there for hours as we waited for the l'Academie thug to relinquish his position and leave for the day. By the time they did, we were hungry and tired. Neither of us spoke as I guided him to the best source of water and food.

When we finished, I didn't wait for thanks; I just disappeared into the brush.

"CALLISTA!"

The hiss of Lys' voice brings me back from the day I saved Raz Miranda's life. "What?"

"Did you get it?"

"Fucking hell, woman. Yes, I got it, but don't risk talking unless it's *absolutely necessary.* We know nothing about the people holding you all hostage except they have serious guns. Anything could set them off and people will end up dead. I'm not super concerned about the sheep, but I enjoy your banter."

"Awww.... You *like* me. You want to be my *friend.* You don't want me *dead,*" she taunts in a sing-song voice.

"Shhhhhh!!!!"

This dealing with other people thing is as annoying as it is satisfying. As funny as she is, Lys isn't really aware of the danger she's in. She's used to wiggling out of every situation, as most thieves do. I've been in a variety of tight spots in countries full of roving drug cartels and gangs and mercenaries who do shit like this... every minute they don't make demands, the fate of the hostages gets dimmer.

I have to transform. I can't be The Duchess right now—we need The Guillotine.

Stalking out of the vault, I backtrack until I'm in the fancy wine cellar and collect myself. I close my eyes, letting the calm, detached feeling wash over me when I tug my favorite weapon out of my pocket. Even as The Duchess, I carry it—sometimes for reassurance and sometimes out of necessity. Today, necessity knocked and I'm ready to answer. I take a few more centering breaths while I slide the wire hidden in the lipstick container open and closed meditatively.

When I find my center, I open my eyes and it's like the world has changed.

I palm the lipstick and slip out into the staff hallway. The area is quiet, and I don't see anyone lurking about. Making my way to the kitchen, I stay out of the camera angles like I did earlier; it's impossible to know if this crew of jagoffs has someone in the security office. When I get to the walk-in freezers, I damn near trip over the dead body of a house security guard. One to the back of the head says they mean business, but they're probably not true pros.

I would have used a silent method, so it didn't alert....

The mess I find in the kitchen corresponds with using a gun. They must have used handguns with silencers to cut through the staff here. Everything is a mess of blood, guts, bodies, and brain matter, including the food they were preparing. The shots I heard over the earwig were higher firepower than the casings in here, so there are more of them in other parts of the house, or they're strapped to the gills. Neither option is appealing, but I continue stepping over bodies until I reach the two sets of sliding doors.

One leads into the main room where the hostages are being kept and the other will take me down a hallway to the front stairs. I have to quickly decide whether I want to clear the rest of the house before attempting to get to Elysium or if I should try to sneak her out immediately. Clenching my hand around the case, I consider the logistics. I have two weapons: surprise and my skills. What I lack is information, and going in blind could get everyone killed, including me.

Upstairs it is. I need to get into their goddamned security room.

I don't even peek into the main room for fear of some sentimentality for Lys or even my asshole exes, causing me to change my mind. Obviously, I don't have confirmation which of them is here, but I've had a long time to forgive their youthful idiocy. They don't need to die anymore than Lys does. With that decided, I head for the stairs, but I pause when I step over the body of a chef who tried to run.

She's dressed in all black, unlike me, and she even has a cap on her head.

Time to rob the corpses—again.

Stripping off the white tux shirt of my waiter's uniform, I toss it aside. I wrestle the black chef coat off the rapidly stiffening body of the woman on the floor with a grunt. The temperature from the ovens is speeding up decomp—it's going to stink to hell and back after a while. I fucking hope to Christ I'm out of this place by that time. Nothing sticks to your hair like rotting corpse stench; it's worse than skunk. I pull the cap off and sniff it quickly, making sure it's not already unsalvageable. It passes, so I take it off, grabbing the hair band as well. Shoving Callista's blonde curls under the cap, I twist the rest of the wig into a knot at the base of my neck.

Now that I've muted my appearance, I feel more comfortable as I slink up the stairs slowly. I listen for voices every few steps, but the silence is heavy. My feet hit the landing and I drop to a crouch before peeking around the corner to see if there are operatives in the hall-way. Again, not a soul to be found, so I make my way along the wall. I stop at each door, listening for signs of life, but there's nothing.

That is, until I reach the security room at the end of the hall.

It's another bloodbath, but they did not shoot these guys. Whoever was in here is fond of knives and had time. Guts hang out of bellies, an eyeball is on the floor, one guy might be missing his tongue… Their psycho must have been the advance man; his job was to take out security cameras and keep the guards downstairs unaware. I frown, shaking my head. This wasn't necessary, though.

I'm not concerned about the guards, mind. What bothers me is that the level of brutality here is inefficient and sloppy. It's clear the knife-wielder had the element of surprise, so they could have slit the throats of the guards without a lot of trouble. All of them were seated and were probably facing the bank of screens.

Why take the time to create this house of horrors shit? Who is it a message for?

Sighing, I pick my way to the cleanest spot near the screens and start watching. I have to study every single inch of that room and the people in it before I attempt a rescue. I refuse to risk my ass for anyone unless I know I'll be able to get out—that's a lesson I learned a *long* time ago.

And someone trapped three of the people who taught it to me in that goddamned mess.

OUT OF CONTROL

THE SHEER INSANITY OF BEING TRAPPED IN THIS ROOM BY A BUNCH OF low rent motherfuckers is humiliating. If we didn't have Coda along, I would pick them off one by one, regardless of how many bystanders I took with me. But the Commandant would lose his fucking if we destroyed the cover we spent a decade cultivating and I can't leave him in the hands of a crew who are unknowns.

"Jinx is within range of the girl now. I still haven't heard from D."

Fucking Dwyn.

Raz is concerned and with good reason. It's clear these people are putting on a show; they made a broad announcement but haven't said a word since. There must be a bigger plan at work because they haven't collected any valuables, nor have they selected anyone to snatch. A kidnapping or retrieval would have been over once they had their mitts on the target. None of them are moving from the perimeter, so they aren't trying to locate anyone.

I speak carefully, turning my head like I'm speaking to Coda. "If anyone in *LI* finds out about this, we'll never live it down."

"Agreed," the rocker adds. "Dwyn's going to be a nightmare."

"That's assuming I don't wring his goddamn neck for staying no contact for hours." I turn back to the crowd, eyeing the silent goons with their guns trained on the crowd.

A crackle on the line announces Jinx turning on his mic and we all shut up as we listen.

"I thought nobody put Baby in a corner," he says and we all groan.

Some smooth talker he is.

"Nice try, handsome. I made you from across the room."

Raz snorts and even I grin. This Elysium woman might be okay after all. If she knocks Coda down a peg as well, I'll enjoy our brief collaboration. It's quiet for a moment and I don't know if that's because Jinx is huffing or if the eyes of our masked captors are on them.

"Good. That will make the rest of this conversation *infinitely* easier," he replies. "Whoever these people are, they are *not* here to make a political statement, despite what they claim."

Elysium snorts softly. "Duh. They would have singled one of the seven-figure ninnies out by now. They haven't touched anyone to record a message, so it's theater. I assume it's to grab something or someone in the house. Which one is a toss up at the moment, though, because the ones guarding us aren't exactly Hans Grubers."

I whistle low. *This girl is good.* "Ask her for help, Jinx. She obviously knows what she's doing. Since she hasn't mentioned intervention, we know she won't insist we play the hero. That's aligned with our goal to get out before this turns ugly."

"My associates and I need to be gone before this turns into a free-for-all or worse, law enforcement show up. Since you are likely here for reasons other than mingling, I propose we form a short-term alliance," Jinx tells her.

The girl laughs again, though this time she dissolves into quiet giggles. I look at Coda, who shrugs, and Raz sighs over the line.

We're all thinking the same thing: thieves are fucking crazy and she's no exception.

"Oh, you sweet, adorable boys! We don't need to do anything to get out of here. Our John McClain is done raiding my bounty, so I expect something rather astounding to come along at any moment."

Pinching the bridge of my nose, I sidle closer to the rock star. "I don't know what's with all the movie references, but she's as infuriating as our absent brother."

"Agreed," Coda rumbles low. "Though I'm intrigued by whomever she's got roaming free in the house. The *Die Hard* references make me think it's a player."

"Ask her who the hell it is!" Raz interjects on the earpieces.

A heavy sigh is the response, but our silver tongued compatriot complies. "Elysium—yes, we know your name—who are you working with? Your dossier doesn't list a partner."

"I don't normally have one. This was an even exchange of favors from my new bestie." She makes a noise as if she's just figured something out. "With that kind of information, you *have* to be *Les Invisibles*! Fuck, your people *always* have the most attractive, conceited motherfuckers on the planet."

Jinx stays quiet, neither confirming nor denying her words.

"Yeah, yeah—I know. The whole '*invisibilia sunt, umbrae tantum relictae*' deal." Jinx must look shocked when she recites our motto because I sure as fuck do. "Don't look at me like I'm a ghost. I dated a guy a couple of years ago that belonged to your lot. He talked in his sleep—a lot. I didn't want to end up dead, so I kept my mouth shut. The crazy old bastard who runs your people is ruthless."

Truer words… the Commandant would have ordered the elimination of both the operative and her. Hell, it probably would have gotten assigned to me. Before she spills more, I clear my throat. Jinx waits and I speak, "Don't let her tell you who it was. You know what will happen."

"Never repeat that again, doll, and definitely don't say the name of your ex out loud. You're lucky this won't ever make it to the right ears. Consider that a *mitzvah* for working with us tonight," he says roughly. "Now, who do you have crawling through vents or whatever?"

"I'm not at liberty to reveal that, man. Shame on you for even asking —it's against the code." There's a pause, and she adds, "But you probably didn't know that. You're not a thief, so I'll let it slide. Just know that her reputation precedes her and I trust she'll help get this bullshit sorted."

"You! The two of you chattering! What do you think you're doing?"

Every muscle in my body freezes as I hear the booming voice approaching over the comms. The asshole must have seen them talking, and now my fears have come to pass. If they're volatile, this might push their entire team over the edge and cause a massacre. Jinx will have to use every ounce of charm he possesses to keep the situation calm. Elysium's partner may be working on neutralizing the problem, but she's going to have to hurry the fuck up.

"She's frightened, man. I was just trying to keep her calm for you. No harm, no foul," Jinx says in a measured tone.

"We said to shut the hell up. Are you deaf or stupid?"

The voice is closer now, and though I can't see them from my vantage point, I can tell there's some sort of modulator under the mask. It makes their voices deeper and scarier—that's a tactic strike teams use for snatch and grabs in nighttime raids. Hell, I've used one before, but it's not my preference. I prefer calm precision and a commanding presence to resorting to fear as a method of control. Scared people act irrationally and that fucks up missions.

Jinx is quiet for a moment, but then he speaks again. "Neither, man. I'm sorry to break the rules. I figured you'll get whatever it is you want faster if people aren't in hysterics. We'll stay quiet."

"Fuck that. We will not tolerate disrespect." The ominous click of a handgun makes my blood pump faster and a loud boom echoes through our comms. *"Everyone behold the example of those who do not heed the words of the Collective."*

"Jinx! Jinx! Say something. Croak. Fuck, man, anything..." Raz sounds panicked as hell and, though I want to know what's going on, I have to stop him from getting our brother killed.

"Say nothing, J. If you whimper in pain, we'll know you're alive. That's all we need," I growl.

I have to hold it together. We've been close to losing someone once or twice since our time at *l'Academie*, but nothing like this. It's much easier to judge a stab or bullet wound when you can see it and we're all blind in our current positions. It's not worth risking another person to move, but I can feel the tension coming from Coda next to me. He's silent, but I know he's having the same flashback we're all having... the night she died in the explosion.

None of us is healed enough from that wound to deal with losing Jinx—it would be devastating.

"Wait! Wait!" Elysium's soft plea makes me listen. "I have medical training. I was a nurse. Let me help him so the shoulder wound doesn't become a dead body."

A clever way of letting anyone listening know the state of the person with her. I'm not sure if she did it for *her* partner or if she assumed we were wired, but I'd kiss her if I was close enough. Jinx isn't likely to die from a shoulder wound—Dwyn holed up for four days in an abandoned bank vault with one in Russia once. Her words help me refocus my internal panic and I murmur into the earwig, "Everyone, stay calm. The thief has him for now."

"Fine. Stupid women and their fragile hearts." The sound of the slide on the handgun is too close for my comfort as the would-be terrorist snorts. "Care for the idiot who almost got you killed if you like. Just shut up."

Another crackle on the line distracts me and suddenly the voice we'd been waiting to hear yells, "The thief *does not* have him… but he will!"

Fucking Dwyn. Always making his entrance at the worst fucking moment.

"Dwyn, you can't…"

"Mo-Mo, you don't get to decide this. I'm out of pocket and on my way. Razzie, you better have the fucking schematics of that place on my phone before I hit the goddamned driveway, or so help me…"

Coda groans low, scrubbing his face with his hand. "There's no stopping him now, guys."

"Hell no, there's no stopping me! I'm coming, Jinxy!"

The crazed battle cry makes me want to bang my head against the wall. Raz won't say a damn word because he's worried about J and Coda all but gave him permission. I'm out voted and even if I weren't, Dwyn is always the wildcard. The idiot has zero regard for his safety and his loyalty is unmatched—he's coming for Jinx no matter what I say.

"Fine. Raz, get him what he needs. Everyone stays pitch black unless completely necessary. We have no idea who Elysium has roaming this place working on an escape hatch—we only know that it's a female. Keep your eyes peeled for a friendly, D."

"Sir, yes, sir!"

I turn to Coda, giving him a pleading look, but he shrugs. "You know I believe in chaos theory, man. Another card up our sleeve can only help. And D is the best creeper in the biz; he'll get in without setting off a single alarm. Then these fuckers should be worried; you know how he gets when someone puts his people in danger."

"Yes, I do."

Unhinged is the word that comes to mind. I've never met a thief who enjoyed carving people into pieces before, but that was Remy's influence on him.

"Blueprints and links coming to you now, D." Raz is barely whispering and I imagine his fingers are flying over the keys like he's on fast forward.

Taking a deep breath, I force myself to shove all of my feelings inside so I can be the asshole who takes charge. "Raz, we need you on cams. Find the friendly. Coda, smile at scared women and make them forget the shooter. Jinx lay there and let the chick deal with the bullethole. We're going silent now."

The line stays dead, and I turn my head to eyeball the cameras in the room. I think I just saw one move out of the corner of my eye and I didn't think the tech here was good enough to do that. It makes me wonder if something in this room specifically got upgraded on purpose. Nothing about this house, this party, or this mission feels right. I knew it was off when we walked in, but I frequently feel that way when I don't have weeks to plan an incursion.

A communique from the Commandant ordered us to get the information from the Baroness and use it to find an object we needed to trade a low level mobster. That exchange would lead to another with a drug cartel, and after that, a liaison in Italy. It's a winding path to the same old gangster I would have been watching if I hadn't had to leave to fetch Coda, so I couldn't refuse his command. The long way is a direct consequence of having to rescue my brother and trail the mystery girl—if I didn't comply, we all would have been recalled to the island. We would have lost the trail of the operative, possibly forever.

Even The Five have to bend the knee sometimes.

Forever

BODIES

Of all the motherfucking shit to happen while I'm on a 'seat of my pants' mission, a fake hostage situation was not even on the list.

I found a joystick in the cabinet when I took over the surveillance room and I've been trying to find angles that will help me get in with the least collateral damage. I don't give a shit about the guests—I find myself strangely attached to Lys now, and I'd be upset if she got hurt. It's a weird feeling and I'm not fond of it, so I shake it off.

The asshole who got himself shot didn't help, either.

His dumbass isn't visible yet, but I heard Lys trying to convince one of these clowns to let her do first aid. I don't doubt she's skilled in field medics, but a nurse is a stretch. Except... she's a thief and they're a step away from grifters most of the time. Her ability to lie helps get her into places she shouldn't be; it's not surprising she can pretend to be a medical professional. I just hope she actually knows enough to convince the idiots holding them hostage while I formulate a plan.

Moving the only two cameras that seem to actually respond to the stick, I try to see around the clumps of the elite huddling in small groups. When I finally get an angle that allows me to see Lys, I gasp and drop the damn thing. Blinking slowly, I lean in as if getting closer to the screen will change what I see.

My lovely Casanova is the impulsive moron who got himself shot.

I knew he had to be a pro because he was at the Open Market, but… I sure as hell didn't expect him to be one of the 'hot guys' Lys was talking about, nor did I imagine he'd get himself *shot*. I close my eyes again, knowing I have to turn this off or I'll never be able to do the things I need to do in order to save them. And yes, now my goal is to save him *and* Lys, so I'm doubly fucked.

"The Guillotine works alone. She creeps from the shadows and completes her mission before anyone even knows she's there," I mutter under my breath.

It's a stupid mantra, but emotion is clouding my judgement at the moment and I can't let that happen. Reaching into the pocket of the stolen chef's jacket, I pull out the lipstick sized weapon and click it open and closed rhythmically until the cold washes over me. My mind clears as I go completely numb from head to toe and when I open my eyes again, all I see is the wire when it opens. The zen of singular purpose settles in my gut and I look at the other screens.

There are guards ringing the ballroom and though they are skillfully trying to avoid the stationary security cams, at least five other targets are moving around the house. They aren't sweeping for leftover people; their movements are too precise. They know far too much about how the house and its shitty alarms are set up. This is the *real* reason for the incursion—they're looking for something.

"Do *not* speak, Elysium. There are five more operatives roaming the estate. I believe they are here to find something, which means your situation was a farce until one of the inexperienced douches in the ballroom shot the guy. That puts them in a terrible position because the extra hostels are *much* more skilled. They will definitely abandon the crew with the crowd once they locate their target. We both know that will leave all the hostages in a lot of danger. I'm going to make my way to you. Nod a little if you understand."

The thief nods, and I sigh in relief. She moves slightly under the guise of checking something and I can see that Cas looks pale, but stable. I don't know how she knew I'd want to see that, but I'm glad she showed me. Spinning around in the chair, I take a deep breath before I rise and go to the dead guards. I don't need much to get this done, but anything extra won't hurt.

Ignoring the guns, I swipe a knife from the small of one's back and a small canister of pepper spray. I prefer close combat and though I'm good with a variety of guns because of Mo; I don't want to increase the number of bullets in that room. I head over to the closet, finding their outer wear and exchange the stupid chef's hat for a black stocking cap. When I find a jar of black shoe polish, I grin to myself —this will do nicely.

Now I just need to get out there and make these fuckers wish they'd never set foot in the same zip code as The Guillotine.

The hallway outside of the security office is dark. From what I saw on the cameras, there's a staircase at the other end as well and it will take me to the second floor. They built this place like a Mad Hatter designed it and I have no idea if it has more secret rooms than the one in the wine cellar, but that has to be the reason the thieves are still wandering around. They might even look for the room I stole the necklace from—but if so, they're never going to find it. Tossing bedrooms and offices will not help you locate a stash of illegitimate artifacts; the people who buy and sell this kind of shit are far more paranoid than that.

I slip down the stairs, keeping flush to the wall as I move towards the sound of someone grumbling under their breath. The corridor is clear, so I stop just short of the doorframe to listen to what's going on inside. Holding my phone up, I switch to selfie mode and use it to see around the corner. There's a medium-sized person in all black and the same mask, rooting through drawers and tossing shit everywhere. Their voice is a low mutter, but the masks must have those voice changers built in, because that's what it sounds like. I have no idea if it's a woman or a man—bad news because that changes how I approach targets to neutralize them.

It sounds anti-feminist but physicality plays a huge role in how you sneak up on someone. Anatomy is anatomy and there's no getting around that.

Watching for a few more seconds, I give up and tuck my phone away. Looks like I'm going in blind and I'll have to adjust as I go. This entire job has been nothing but irritating discoveries paired with plain bad luck. Someone must have my goddamned voodoo doll and if they do, I wish they'd quit playing with it. I grip the knife as I quietly step into the room and make my way through the mess. Once I'm behind the target, I wrap my free arm around their neck in a bulldog choke, yanking their head back. The masked robber gasps for air as I wait for them to get lightheaded.

It only takes twenty-five pounds of pressure—equivalent to a strong handshake—and seven seconds to do damage that will be fatal, so I have to hurry.

"Who are you? Why are you here?" I hiss in a low, gravelly voice. Loosening my arm a bit, I wait.

"Fuck you," the modulated voice spits.

With a sigh of irritation, I give them one more chance, pressing the blade of my knife to their jugular.. "Tell me or die."

"Never. Our allegiance is for life."

I tried. It's more than I usually do.

The knife slides across the skin of the thief's throat like butter and blood spurts everywhere. This is why I prefer rear choke holds to front—less dry cleaning. Tightening my grip until the body in my arms stops struggling, I wait for telltale signs of death. Once it's limp, I drop the dead hostile and walk over to the place they were rummaging for clues. I can't see anything that tells me what the group's goal is, so I bend over and pull off the mask. It's a ratty-looking guy I don't recognize from either of my identities and I kick the still body in frustration. No clues there, either.

Wiping the blade on the borrowed pants, I leave the way I came, checking the hallway once more. It's still empty, so I mutter into the mic, "One down, four to go. Out."

Silence is my answer, which is for the best. Keeping Lys updated is important, but I don't want to get her killed while I eliminate these morons along the way. She's busy tending to Cas and I have no ability to worry about that situation while I'm hunting. I wonder briefly how he knows Coda, since she seemed to think her three hot dudes were pretending not to be together when it hits me—*Cas is one of them.*

Holy. Fucking. Shitballs.

That realization smacks me so hard I stop, holding onto the wall as my world rocks. My Casanova is one of The Five—one of the guys whose betrayal destroyed me so completely that I had to fake my own death and rise from the ashes of an explosion like a wounded phoenix.

And I fucked the living shit out of him at a party in public.

My hands shake and I have to put the hand holding the knife to my mouth to keep from making any sound. Panicking, I open the next door, rushing inside and closing it. Back against the wood, I let the shock ripple through my frame and tears well in my eyes. Not once in a decade did I consider I'd run into one of them and *not* recognize them. I should have known it was possible because of the way we're trained and the steps *Les Invisibles* takes to keep their agents from being entered into any databases, but I just didn't put the pieces together. Even as I knew my own image was secure, I didn't make the leap to consider theirs would be as well.

But which one is he?

My mind goes back to the islands without permission and a memory flashes behind my lids…

The moon was bright that night.

It meant I had to be extremely careful about exposing myself, even with the camouflage of my new ghillie suit. Every year I have to escape the second they free us in this wretched place so I can make a new one. I got better with every training—my third one made the first suit look like a child did it—which, of course, was exactly the case.

We didn't celebrate birthdays at l'Academie because no one knew when the orphans they bought were born, but I knew I was eleven. The classes I took at the school told me I'd eventually have to worry about female bullshit, but luckily, it hadn't happened yet. My nightmare was having to go through captivity training while bleeding profusely for a week every month of the three we were required to spend surviving their bullshit. Animals could scent the blood and it would make everything a thousand times harder.

That might be why the upper classes seem to take a lot of losses in their months in this hellhole.
Or maybe the older we get, the less humanity we have left and killing anyone who crosses your path gets easier with each passing year.

I didn't discount that possibility in the slightest.
Being able to hide in the trees and brush is part of what keeps me alive—that and my lack of connections to anyone else in my class. I didn't have any emotional attachment to the people I might have to dispatch if they challenged me.

Except the two boys I saved in prior exercises—Coda and Raz.

Their group still refused to accept me, but the two of them would seek me out to hang occasionally and I found I didn't mind having them around after we were picked up from CR. In fact, it was comforting to have people to talk to, even if they couldn't admit it in public. Coda played songs for me, and Raz taught me how to work computers; two things I never would have bothered with if they hadn't shown me their passion for them.

So I left them gifts when I could this round. It's almost over, though, and the Academie thugs are getting more aggressive during the day. They get bonuses when they take one of us out, I heard, and I suppose that sum gets bigger when the agents age up because the assholes I'd killed so far were worse than past training. They'd even leered at me in a way that makes my stomach turn and I knew as I got older, those expressions mean they have permission for far worse things than murder.

At no time in history have men not used rape as a weapon against women —whether combatants or civilians. Captivity Resistance training would be no different, I learned.

A sound made me stop in my tracks as I made my way to the small oasis I discovered last week. It had more foliage coverage than any water source I'd ever found before, and I'd been using it to keep myself hidden from night predators. I shimmed up a tree quickly and looked out over the water, only to see a large Academie operative watching a boy approach the edge of the water with homemade canteens strapped to his chest with vines.

We were told the opponents didn't stay here at night in years past, so I knew the boy would only listen for nocturnal animals.

The agent smiled evilly, his white teeth gleaming against the dark face paint he'd used to conceal himself. His glee told me they had purposefully lied to us—a lesson in not believing anything your captors tell you. As the boy kneeled to fill the water jugs, he moved and I finally remembered who the kid in danger was.

He was one of my boys' group members.

They'd be devastated, so I grabbed a thick vine, and without thinking, launched myself across the small pond with a snarling war cry.

The boy looked up, startled, and that's when he saw the agent barrel towards him with a huge bowie knife.

It would not happen on my watch. I let go of the vine, using my momentum to propel myself into the gaping kid and knock him to the ground. The nasty-looking agent in black growled at us like a fucking animal and I rolled to my feet, getting into a defensive position. When he came at me, I ducked under his legs, using his size and speed difference to throw him off balance.

We fought for what seemed like forever until I could get on his back and like usual, wrap my wire around his neck until it cut deeply into his skin. My palms burned with the reopening of the scars from previous years, but I pulled and pulled until I hit the bone. His body went limp, and we fell to the ground hard, smashing me into the dirt.

The boy walked over with big chocolate brown eyes and stared at me in shock. "You saved me. Just like they said—you're a killer."

I shrugged and pushed the heavy asshole off of me. "You're welcome. The rules have changed; tell them."

That's when I took off into the night, leaving him to watch me escape.

After they picked us up that year, I found out his name was Jinx.

When the memory fades, I know exactly who got shot in the ballroom.

Casanova is Jinx Monroe, grifter extraordinaire.

Forever

PSYCHO

FUCKING JINX!

I spent the past few hours completely focused on my task—getting the HD from an impossible location—and that's why I had my ears off. My brain needed to focus and their chatter would have distracted me—it always does. The tech in that place was insane, and we hit it very last minute, which normally is my fucking jam. However, this time, I wanted to make certain I didn't get injured or caught so I could make my date with Jazz, so I disconnected. It worked and when I finally tapped into the comms, I stayed quiet while I listened to one of my best friends get shot.

Then Mo pulled his typical fuckhead shit and tried to keep me away —not happening. I packed my shit, secured the drive, and flew through the streets like my ass was on fire to get to the house where my team was trapped. I didn't even bother to climb in the van and check the shit out with Raz. I'm capable of much more dangerous, last-minute bullshit than sneaking into this rich fucker's house to rescue people.

I had to take the earwig out after Mo bitched me out, so I have no clue what's been going on since.

Right now, I'm lurking behind a tree on the front lawn. I'm still dressed in thief gear, so I'm hidden enough by shadows to watch without being seen on exterior cams. My walk around the house told me I'd be best served by coming up the front and into a window on the third floor. The alarms have to be off for their team to get in, so I'm not worried about a screaming announcement if I pry or break a pane to get in. I didn't find dogs or outdoor security guards to thwart me—the only people out here are the dead bodies from when the crew of dick whistles entered earlier.

My eyes narrow as I fish the earpiece out of my pocket and put it in.

"How many?" I hear Mo mutter.

The woman they've been calling Elysium whispers, "She says two down, two to go on the second floor."

I frown at the silence that follows. The Five *never* have others do our dirty work, but the guys—even control freak Mo—are allowing this lower tier thief's friend to navigate their rescue. Something about all of this is both surreal and off at the same time. Her assurance that her partner is top-notch trips a wire in me; the partner has to be extremely well known in our world for Elysium to refuse to give even her code name on the line.

Who runs in my circles that is so skilled that saying their name would be verboten?

They nailed *El Guapo* and *Ape Regina* at the Open Market. Word is, they're still working out their releases. Most of the other big names at the party were hitters or assassins. They call me *The Ghost*, which I hate with the passion of a thousand red suns, so I know that moniker was present but not caught. There are only a few other elite thieves who might be well known enough to hide their presence: *An Taibhse, Umbra Vulpes, Dmitriy Laska,* and…

Fuck me.

The Duchess is the only other female at our level. No wonder Elysium doesn't want to name her—her reputation is built on being half grifter, half thief, and all solitary. She never joins crews, nor does she follow any of the 'gentleman's rules' of our trade. She was at the Open Market according to *Mercatus* and her job, plus quite a few I didn't snake, got completed. The chick got in and out without ever revealing herself or getting nailed, plus she abandoned every other colleague in the building without a second glance.

Ice water runs in that thief's veins, but here she is helping a lower tier pro complete a job. WTF is that about?

Pushing off the tree, I creep along the edges of the lush foliage until I'm close to the house again. The Duchess is also known for not incurring collateral damage to get missions done, but the conversation on the comms suggests she's working her way through thugs one by one. I can only assume they're dead and that's not something they train my people for. Obviously, I am, because the guys and our former girl cross-trained one another, but that's uncommon.

Yet here The Duchess is, knocking off people like it's her calling.

I shake my head, feeling like I'm trying to put together puzzle pieces the others can't see because they're too emotionally involved in the situation inside. Solving riddles isn't usually my thing, but Razzie is probably totally useless because of Jinxy. He's been silent as a church mouse and that's not like him at all. I can't go help him, though. I have to use my gifts to either assist or finish what the mysterious Duchess is doing inside.

Even if it kills me.

ONCE I UNLATCH THE WINDOW THROUGH THE BROKEN PANE, I CLIMB IN and tug the rope from my grappler inside. I don't have time to bother with retracting it, so Razzie is going to have to buy me another miniature after we ditch this nonsense. My primary goal is to get down to the second level and figure out how I can get The Duchess to partner with me so we don't clash and fuck up this rescue mission. Slipping out the door, I walk carefully down the hall and take the stairs at the end. Based on my observation of the house, I *think* these are the back 'staff' steps, so I shouldn't emerge in a blind hallway where some idiot will see me. The second floor is as dark as the third floor, so I know she's still here. Turning the lights on would only make any approach harder and thieves frequently train their eyes to see better in the darkness.

A light thump in a room halfway down the corridor gives me the clue I'm looking for, so I sprint lightly towards it until I'm lurking outside of it.

"Such absolute bullshit. None of these douches will tell me who they work for or what they want. There's no indication left behind to help me. All three have been willing to give their lives for the cause —whatever it is—and if I can't figure it out, I'll have to kill every one of them to save Cas and Lys. This is a goddamn nightmare."

My lips quirk as I listen to her grumble and kick things as she tries to sort through the wreckage I can see from the crack in the doorway. The outline of someone dressed in a beanie, oversized chef's garb, and holding a large knife is kind of hot. I have to shake my head to clear it so I can focus. I'm not immune to the charms of talented pros who handle their business by any stretch. Watching her rifle through the shit scattered everywhere and occasionally give the corpse a frustrated kick makes my dick twitch, if I'm honest.

"Who are you? Show yourself." The Duchess spins around, glaring at the crack in the doorway as she drops into a fighting pose. It's hard to make much of her face out with the shoe polish camouflage she's smeared all over it, but her eyes are a brilliant blue.

Hot damn, someone trained her in knife fighting. This woman gets better and better, I swear.

"Whoa, whoa. I think we have friends in common," I say as I speak into the crack. "Downstairs. In danger."

Staying in position, she asks, "What friends?"

She's sure as hell not dumb. I push the door open and slip inside before closing it again. Her eyes fly open wide when I enter and I tilt my head. I have my hands up to show her I'm not brandishing a weapon, but she's staring at me like she's seen a ghost. And she sure as fuck doesn't *know* I'm The Ghost, so I have no idea why. "Ones being held hostage—one of which has been shot—and who could hear us if we turned on the tech."

"Holy. Fucking. Shit. What are the *odds*?!" she whispers to herself.

I frown. "What the hell are you talking about?"

"Nothing. Forget it," The Duchess says as she sheathes her blade. "There's one more bogie on this floor, and I know everyone in the kitchen is dead. We can start there after we take care of the last one and neutralize everything until we hit the ballroom. I know the layout, so with two of us, we should be able to use a version of the Edward Albee to pick the crew in the ballroom off one by one."

"You want to use a grift to take the armed guards out?" I squint at her, feeling the sensation of something being just outside of my consciousness again. The way she dropped into the fighting pose, the lack of emotion when discussing business, the knowledge of famous cons… all of it so familiar.

I've probably met her somewhere and didn't know it was her. That has to be it. We crossed paths on a job.

Her sigh is frustrated. "Yes. We do the Albee in range of a single guard. When they come out to check-which they *always* do—I'll take out the guard and you head towards the next location. The footage showed them spread out around the crowd to form a ring of firepower. There are enough guests in there to make it hard for the masked fools to see one another."

"Okay. What about comms? If we have them, they should, too."

"Duh. But from what I can tell, the fuckwads up here are in charge and we know they're not telling the people downstairs anything, even before I started killing them. The ballroom is their Trojan horse, dude. Everyone down there was expendable to this team up here once they found their prize. And we're wasting time because the one left may be the leader."

The Duchess lifts her chin and brushes past me, clearly done discussing the plan. I'd argue, but she's hotter than hell taking charge like this, even dressed like a coal mining hobo. I'll be lucky if I don't grab her ass when we start the Albee.

If I do, she'll probably stab me.

I can live with that.

Glaring at me when I follow her into the hallway, the thief in question asks, "What are you grinning about?"

"Nothing. I'm a sucker for tough women who order me around."

"Jesus Christ on a pogo stick," she mutters as she walks away.

That's not a 'no'.

"Maybe after we save the day, we could burn a little energy off. I haven't consorted with the enemy in a while and I think—" I whisper.

"Shut. Up."

"Don't say 'no' right away! I'm game for many dangerous and illegal activities. I *live* for getting off while we... get off."

Whirling around, she pokes my chest. "I said shut up. I hear the last hostile, you horny moron."

Oh. That's fair, I suppose. I'm still not letting her get away without sampling that fiery mouth.

"And stop looking at my ass. You can't even see it in these stupid pants," she grumbles.

How the fuck did she know?!

Holding her hand up, The Duchess pauses at the last door on the right side of the hallway. There's someone rattling around as they search for whatever elusive goal this team has. I watch her do the old 'phone as a mirror' bit, smiling as I see the literal *beast* of a man rifling through shit. There's no way this normal sized chick is going after that monster, so I'll get to save the day. It'll make me look very attractive for a post-rescue romp and I'm here for it.

"Stay put. I'll deal with him and you can help me search after."

"Uhhhh…"

"Just be quiet!"

Those are the last words she says before I watch her glide into the dark room via the shadows. I position myself so I can rush in when she needs help, but I'm not going to stop her. Sometimes a little humble pie is good for you and she's getting ready to chomp some down.

But that's not what happens.

My jaw damn near hits the floor when I see the world renown thief and grifter sweep the giant bastard's legs out from under him, straddle his chest, and hold her knife to his jugular before he can register she's in the room.

"Who do you work for? Why are you here?" she growls.

"Our allegiance is for life."

Her free hand makes a fist, and she clocks the guys hard. "Not that shit again. You have to be the leader. The morons downstairs are pawns. I'll spare you if you tell me why you're targeting this event. Who or what are you after?"

"I'm already dead." The flattened giant moans. "Go fuck yourself."

"Fine!"

I don't have time to respond before the sexy and crazy as *fuck* chick punches him one more time before using the knife to slit his throat from ear to ear. "Whoa."

"Oh, grow up," The Duchess says in irritation. "We'll have to do this the hard way, but just in case this bullshit has to do with your people or me, I'm going to leave a little message behind. Hopefully, their leader gets it."

I've never in my life found a Columbian necktie as hot as when I watch her do it so quickly that it's like she was tying her shoes.

For the second time this month, I think I'm in love.

Forever

KILLER IN THE MIRROR

I CANNOT *BELIEVE THE GUY* I *SCREWED ON THE TRAIN — MY SLICK — IS THE adult version of Dwyn O' Shanahan.*

He doesn't realize who I am yet—not as Remy, Jazz, *or* The Guillotine. I know that's a testament to both aging and my ability to be a chameleon. Jinx is partially responsible for that skill and I'm sure somewhere deep in my psyche, it's why I'm so eager to save his bacon instead of running for the hills. Elysium would get out eventually, I know, and she'd forgive me if I yeeted myself into the night. The Duchess has never been known for sympathy for her colleagues. But I can't—not when the second man I connected with in over a decade is bleeding all over the floor in the ballroom.

Knowing that it's Jinx complicates the situation even more. If Coda and Jinx are out there, the hot security guy *must* be Mo and Raz has to be somewhere nearby in a mobile command center. The boys who broke my heart and started me on my journey to make a name for myself are *all* in danger now. If I stopped to save Coda in Paris and I'm working to save Raz from Shadow Douche, how can I refuse to help Dwyn save them when a bunch of loose cannons with machine guns are threatening them? It would be a waste of my time and energy up to now and a waste of five incredibly talented colleagues to let them get shot full of holes by cut-rate guns for hire.

Way to rationalize your actions, Remy.

"You're awfully quiet," Dwyn says as he follows me down to the kitchen. "I get it. Sometimes, when our kind have to do messy shit like this, it takes a minute to reconcile it."

I turn and give him a look that shows how stupid that statement is. "This isn't my first rodeo, cowboy. As always, it was them or me and I'm *always* going to choose me. I learned that lesson a long time ago."

His brow furrows. "Then why are you helping your girl get my guys out of here?"

"Even sociopathic serial killers love their mothers... mostly," I mutter as I push past him to frisk the rest of the guards and kitchen staff for more weapons. I don't want to use my trademark in front of anyone if I can avoid it; there are far too many secrets about my identity I'm trying to balance at the same time.

Dwyn pauses, pulling a pair of knives out of his pockets and twirling them on his palms. "Fair point, dirty girl. You win this round, but I'll keep trying."

Those words throw me back to a memory and I swallow hard as I push the past back into the box where it belongs. I don't have time to indulge in another montage of my time at *l'Academie* right now. I have to dispense with the rest of the assholes ruining my day, free the others, and get the *hell* away from The Five in a setting that might compromise my true identities.

I'm not scheduling my meet-ups with the guys I knew as Cas or Slick yet because I can't bring myself to make that decision. I can cross that bridge once I see if it gets burned.

"Good to know you're not shy about doing what needs to be done," I say as I nod at the spinning knives. "I can't carry your weight from across the room." His shocked expression tells me I hit his pride and I have to fight to keep a smile from spreading over my features.

"Listen up, dirty girl," he says as he walks closer. "I'm letting you be in charge because I like it and even covered in that mess, you're still sexy as fuck. Don't mistake that for weakness on my part. Watching you kill might make my dick jump, but you're not my supervisor."

I pause before I speak. My eyes drift downward to the tight black tactical pants he's wearing, noting he's not lying about the cock twitching. Since I'm very familiar with how much I enjoy that appendage, I don't have a good retort to push out of my dry mouth. I snort, arching a brow at him, and turn to search the last useful corpse. His laugh is husky and I make a face he can't see—he knows he influenced me.

Good job, Remy. You let him get the upper hand.

"Since you're busy telling tragic lies to yourself about how much you liked what I said, I'm going to take a peek in the hallway. I want to identify the first victim of our Albee con."

Wiping my hands on my legs as I straighten, I shake my head. "Nope. I'm done here, and I already marked the best approaches on the map in my head from the feeds I watched before you butted in. We're going to start with the fool on the east side of the ballroom."

"Mmmm. Why would that be?" Dwyn eyes me as he stops the knife on his right hand to point it in my direction. "Not that I'm unimpressed with your ability to create a visual map in your mind. Few of us can do that."

I ignore the map comment because it's far too close to hinting at who I really am. "The masked person on the east side was fidgeting constantly. Either they have a condition—like ADHD or what have you—or that idiot has to piss. We won't have to make a lot of noise to get them to ask for permission to check it out. Since we eliminated the leaders, they'll go anyway hoping to relieve whatever itch they have. Chip shot."

Tapping the blade against his teeth, he nods. "Solid idea. I can get behind that. Let's go."

It takes everything in me not to roll my eyes as I start down the hallway to the ballroom doors on the east side. "Good thing I wasn't looking for permission."

"You're going to get us killed so you can text your tramp!"

Dwyn hides his grin behind my head. The Albee is harder to pull off because I'm dressed for subterfuge, not glitz and glamor, so we have to make sure my face is not facing the gun-toting marks. "Since I knocked you up, you don't even dress up for formal affairs. How can you blame me?"

Ouch. What a typical rich douche canoe thing to say.

I stab my finger into his chest, letting the blonde curls I freed from the hat bounce as I move. "Maybe if you were packing anything but a fat wallet in those pants, I would!"

He winces, making a hurt face at me, and I have to stave off a laugh. Between seeing him as Slick and the fun-loving psycho from my youth, I'm having trouble holding on to the faux anger. I close my eyes and channel the fury I felt when they betrayed me—something I've moved past, but it will help me put on the show we need to for the hostage takers.

"Oh, nice. Insulting the manhood you're bitching about me sharing with someone else. How *typical*! As if you didn't marry me for that fat wallet in the first place!"

My lips quirk and I smirk, raising my voice higher this time. "Fine! Abandon me for your two-timing whore—enjoy having conversations at third grade level for the rest of your life. Or... at least until she finds the next sucker to elevate her status with."

The sound of thumping footsteps makes my pulse pick up, but I know we have to keep going until I see the look in his eyes that tells me the first hostile is behind me.

"Jules *loves* me—clearly more than you ever did." Dwyn cuts his eyes to the side briefly and yells, "And she's much smarter than third grade! She graduated high school!"

This motherfucker is determined to make me snort and fuck this shit up.

"Of course she did, dear. *Last year.*" I pull the hand with my special ring back and act as if I'm going to slap the living shit out of him. Dwyn doesn't flinch when my palm meets his face with enough impetus to rattle his molars.

Okay, maybe I harbor a little *anger at them still—sue me.*

"HEY!"

Stepping aside as he pretends to just notice the armed asshole coming towards us, the smooth talking thief plasters a big grin on his face. "Oh, hello. I'm sorry about the noise. I came out to answer texts on my phone and my hormonal wife made a scene—*again.*"

I don't turn around; I'm waiting for the idiot to grab me when I refuse to move.

"You ain't supposed to be out here. All the piggies stay in the pen," the weird modified voice intones. "Get back inside before I turn you over to the boss for a lesson in doing what you're told."

They set the pitch on his modulator high, and he sounds like a crazy ass cartoon character, but the words he used give me a big clue—the muscle is very local and very low end. Whoever the speech maker was in the ballroom, they're several rungs higher on the ladder than the rest of the crew, even if they're below the former thieves upstairs. This fucking incursion was planned by someone *much* more intelligent and experienced than anyone they sent into this house.

Sigh. Which means we either stumbled into some big crew's heist or this has to do with Shadow Douche or my stalkers.

Fuck. Me. With. A. Jell-O. Pop.

My erstwhile partner holds his hands up and moves to go in. "Sorry, man. I thought stepping out so I wouldn't be distracting was the mark of a professional."

"Get in the ballroom!"

Waiting for the moron to figure out I'm not moving, I place one hand over the other. I have a plethora of weapons hidden on me at the moment, but something about bringing up the feelings of the past has me itching for control. I need to remind myself of who I am— what the phoenix who rose out of literal ashes became all on her own.

A rough hand clamps on my shoulder, letting me know it's time. Before he can bark another order, I turn my chin into my shoulder, throw my hip forward, and raise my elbow. Stepping backwards, I twist my arms out of his and knee the jackass in the face hard. He howls with pain, stumbling backwards as he cradles his nose. His eyes widen when he realizes I covered my face in shoe polish and I'm not wearing maternity clothes. I wink at him before launching a volley of punches, ducking his feeble attempts to counterattack without trouble. One hard kick to his chest puts him on the ground and I drop to my knees, yanking him up.

"Tell me who you work for," I hiss. I band my arms across his throat, but he can get enough air to breathe. When he doesn't answer, I twist the jewel on my ring, releasing my emergency wire, tugging it out to slice through his carotid with ease. The gurgling sound he makes is gross, so I let the body flop to ground as I roll back to my feet.

Luckily, I've pushed the button to retract my secret weapon when Dwyn peeks back around the corner to check in.

"No joy again?" He walks over and kicks the body with a sigh of irritation.

I grimace. "Not a word this time. I have no idea what their boss has on these fuckers. Even the cannon fodder down here won't give anything up."

"Cheer up, killer. We have at least ten more to go before we get to the head honcho. You can offer them all the same reprieve." He rakes his hand through his hair as he looks down. "Or not. Either way works for me."

Snorting, I point toward our next target. "As if you have any say in the matter—cute."

His grin is sexy as hell and I have to look away when he rumbles, "Like I said before, I'm happy to follow your orders now and later when we hit the sheets, dirty girl. Just help me save our friends and I'll show you just how happy it makes me."

How am I supposed to focus after that?

Forever

HOSTAGE

I CANNOT BELIEVE THAT ASSHOLE GOT HIMSELF SHOT!

They all bitch about *me* going off-book, but here's Jinx trying to con a dipshit holding a fucking Mac 10 and now Dwyn is completely off the ranch. He hasn't said a word since he declared he was coming—whether Mo liked it or not—a fact that our grumpy ass leader hasn't missed. He's standing next to me in a pose so tense he might shatter to pieces if someone hit him hard enough.

Comms went damn near silent after he got a tiny bit of information out of Elysium about her friend. Raz is probably trying to monitor every camera at once while he bites his nails. Jinx has been trying to help him break the nasty habit for years, but after the explosion, it became one of his major coping mechanisms. That and all his goofy anonymous white hat do-gooder bullshit keep him sane like my music does for me, I suppose.

It still doesn't excuse the only two free members of our elite crew not keeping the rest of us in the loop. I assume D is going to run into Elysium's friend. That could be a good thing or bad thing depending on how ornery the friend is. Dwyn is contrary under normal circumstances, but under stress, he's an immovable force once he sets his mind to shit. Hence Mo letting his disobedience go; he knew he'd never be able to convince the mercurial psycho of anything when he's emotionally hyper focused.

"I had a brief burst over my line," the voice of the thief holding the tourniquet on our brother drifts over our comms. "I heard grunting, fighting, and then my partner questioning someone before saying something about 'downstairs'. She must have eliminated the threats on the second floor."

Keeping my mouth shut, I wait and hope either Dwyn or Raz say something. It doesn't happen and Mo carefully murmurs a response. "Your partner is a female?"

The snort makes me grin. "Who run the world, asshole? Notice you have twice as many people as me and you're all trapped while my gal is cutting through these cock waffles like a hot knife through butter."

Mo gives me a frustrated look and I shrug. Beggars can't be choosers and Elysium isn't wrong. "Fine. Keep us updated." He turns the mic off and leans in to murmur to me, "A badass chick killing people is who Dwyn is going to meet up with? We'll be lucky if we don't rot here while he nails her."

"I mean… smoke 'em if you got 'em, buddy. Can't say I wouldn't be tempted and if you even think about saying you wouldn't, I'm going to punch you in the dick." Mo glares and I sigh. "Come on, man. We're trapped like rats and D won't let us get killed. I think."

"Breaker, breaker!" The voice of our missing thief interrupts my snarking and Mo lets out a breath of relief. "Found the partner and *hol-eeee shit*. You idiots will not *believe* how smoking hot she is! It doesn't even matter that she's covered in shoe polish and wearing some big dude's baggy chef clothes. Her *Krav* is like poetry."

"Mossad?" Mo mouths at me.

I shake my head. Even ex-agents and rogues wouldn't be embedded in our world deeply enough to befriend a top tier thief like Elysium.

Doesn't mean one of them didn't train this girl, though. "Who does she work for?"

"No one! It's The Duchess, man. I wouldn't have pegged her for a killer, but… hell, all I want now is for her to peg *me*."

You can practically hear *him swooning. That's twice this month and I might hate him.*

"Focus, D. Where is she? I assume you aren't waxing poetic in front of her," Mo asks.

"Oh! She's finishing this asswad that we pulled an Albee on. I could do it, but watching her bleed people is making my cock throb."

My eyes narrow as I think about what he's saying. Besides his braggy sex shit, there's something important in his words. The Duchess, if this is really her, has never been known for collateral damage, nor have we have considered her a strong grifter. Not only that, but Dwyn said she knew *Krav Maga,* and absolutely none of those things fit together.

There aren't many independent contractors who are 'Swiss Army knives'—it's better to specialize and rise in the ranks of your skill set if you're not attached to one of the major organizations. But this woman seems to have enough experience in all those things to impress Dwyn and even though he wants to fuck her, he wouldn't exaggerate her skills.

Who is The Duchess really? Where did she come from?

"D, keep it in your pants long enough to resolve this bullshit. We need to get Jinx patched up by a real doc, not a thief who seems to know field medic procedures. He may not bleed out, but sepsis and a host of other crap are possible given our surroundings. You know Coda and I can't break his cover or the old man will recall the lot of us," Mo finally replies.

I can tell by the look on his face he's running through the same thought process as I am, so I nod. Telling Dwyn our suspicions will only make the rogue thief he's working with feel more dangerous and therefore kick his crazy up a notch. That idiot *thrives* on risking his life and we need him to fucking focus. "Mo's right, though it hurts my soul to say it."

"Affirmative, jackholes. I'll loop you in when I can. Turning the mics off now."

Scrubbing a hand over my face, I shift positions to see if I can get a better view of Jinx and Elysium. It's rotten luck we were out-of-pocket mingling when this all went down. I'm too recognizable to sneak our way closer; it would raise questions about how we know the guy on the floor. I don't have the foggiest how many people in this room are known journalists, much less covert amateurs who bribed someone to get in. Since the masked people didn't confiscate devices, I assume they've thrown a net over the house, so that's why my phone hasn't blown up with calls from Charice or a chorus of social media pings.

Luckily for us, Raz built our comms on spy satellite networks that aren't affected by trivial things like 300 GHz blockers—we could damn near get a signal in outer space.

Of course, if any of this shit gets out eventually, it'll be a great promo. Hopefully grumpy pants over here kept out of any shots. He hates when the paps catch him out around me because he says it lowers his standing in the hitter community. It's fine to guard heads of state and crooked CEOs, but not silly rock stars and celebs. His kind are weird on the best days and downright anti-social on their worst.

Hanging with The Five has kept Mo from becoming a weapon hoarding recluse for sure.

"Our girl says they've dispatched two more goons. That leaves seven, including the speechmaker."

I frown when Elysium updates us because it occurs to me we haven't heard from the grandstanding dipshit in a while. Jerking my head at Mo, I shift slightly, trying to move a bit to see if the so-called leader comes into view. That one had on one of those ridiculous TikTok masks that glow with X's for eyes—something that damn near screamed amateur. I can't pick out the lights, so I don't know if the fool switched it off or if they've gone incognito.

I wouldn't blame them since Dwyn and The Duchess took out their bosses.

"Do you think the mini-boss took a powder?" I murmur to Mo.

He shakes his head, waiting for Raz to chime in from the ops van. When he doesn't, grumbled curses are his only response. We move again, only inching toward a better vantage point so no one notices. The small change allows me to step up a level onto the railing at the bottom of the bar. That change in height, small as it is, helps me see over the heads of shorter hostages.

"There are only five people in black now. I don't know if that's our rescuers' doing or if some of their crew has figured out they're being picked off."

"Yet the one in front of Jinx remains," our leader growls softly. "Either that's the leader without the first mask or the fucker is enjoying watching him suffer too much to take off."

We can only hope it's the first, despite the challenge that might present. A sadist with a prone victim and a room full of targets left alone is never a good option.

"Three to go."

This time it's Dwyn and I'm itching to ask him more questions about his companion. She must be close because he didn't elaborate like before. Curiosity is killing me, though, and my focus is slipping because of the tension and lack of shit to do.

Honestly, I'm surprised I haven't gotten fidgety yet.

"Coda, you have to control it. This is like when we were kids and you had to get through the pit exercise. Every time they put you in an enclosed space for a long time during CR training, you had to find a way to stay sane."

It's like the dick read my mind and I wonder if I was actually doing the things without even realizing it. "I know; I know. Scales. Fingering. Music helps me focus."

"Right," he replies. "Just keep your hands out of sight and do what you need to until D and the girl get to Jinx."

Nodding, I tap my fingertips on my legs, running through the scales. I hate being a weak link, but it helps that Dwyn is just as unpredictable. His ups and downs make mine look like nothing and I'm pretty sure his crazy ass behavior got worse by the time we ascended to our place as The Five. Years of grueling physical and psychological torture in the guise of training made his already fragile sanity snap, and it's never recovered.

Accepting our myriad of trauma and grief induced mental illnesses is part of what bonds us.

"I'm perfectly normal, you know."

I glare at the most stubborn, closed off motherfucker I know while I recite the C chords in my head. "Sure you are, Mo-Mo. You keep tragically lying to yourself and the rest of us will keep being broken toys without an Andy to play with us. Enjoy your denial."

Turning away from me in a huff, Mo doesn't reply. I knew he wouldn't because he absolutely *hates* talking about the night we lost everything and how it's affected us. But my volley hit its mark, and he leaves me alone to manage my hyperactivity in peace.

That's all I wanted, anyway.

WHISKEY FEVER

Every second I'm not running for the hills, I'm risking my ass.

What's more troubling is that I know that and I'm not changing course.

Dwyn and I have taken out all but two of the crew in the ballroom. I realize one is the hair-triggered dick in front of Jinx and Lys, but what I can't suss out is whether either of them was in charge. My happily psychotic ex-friend watched me eliminate the true fuckwits in charge upstairs, but there was some sort of spokesperson in the ballroom. That person has either yeeted themselves out of danger or they're one of the two remaining jackholes.

"Trying to suss out who's the big cheese, dirty girl?"

I roll my eyes at the nickname. It's close to Coda's old 'Feral Girl' moniker and, besides, I'm not dirty. I used what was on-hand to create the best camouflage for the dark hallways. It's not like I smell bad or anything. "Yes. Something about this situation doesn't sit right with me. Two teams operating independently who have separate goals is unusual; it's even weirder that they have such disparate skill sets. Obviously, the hostage takers are a distraction for the douches upstairs, but no one will talk. Usually, that kind of allegiance is reserved for the big orgs like yours."

He pauses, scratching his chin for a minute. "That's true. None of the big cabals would send idiots like this, even as cannon fodder. It leaves too much room for a rookie mistake that would reveal their true intent. Besides, the reason for my crew being here wasn't in response to a cattle call on *Mercatus*. They gave us an order from the top to achieve several goals at several locations tonight. Those goals tie into a bigger operation, so this isn't a set-up."

Unless it is and your precious Commandant was too egotistical to realize he's got enemies smart enough to play on his massive god complex.

"Even the best strategizers in the highest positions have blind spots. They cannot see dissension within their ranks or enemies who seem beneath their notice," I say as we walk down the corridor. "The fall from the throne is often farther than the distance appears."

"How poetic! You remind me of my brother—the one your friend is trying to keep stable in the ballroom. He always has the best words; it's his gift."

I blink as a memory that contradicts him assaults me, pushing me to stop and put my head against the wall.

"They accepted the pleasures of morning, the bright sun, the whelming sea and sweet air, as a time when play was good and life so full that hope was unnecessary and therefore forgotten."

I frowned as I watched the handsome boy walk back and forth in the clearing. He seemed upset, though I couldn't understand why. He'd killed a large wild pig and the meat would surely help sustain him and the rest of their popular group for days if they butchered it correctly. They could even use the scraps for bait for other animals and fishing. There was absolutely nothing to look so sad about.

He stopped and looked up into the sky before he murmured, "Fancy thinking the Beast was something you could hunt and kill![1]*"*

His name escaped me. I knew he was part of the gang Coda, Raz, and Jinx ran with. They did not invite me to hang out with them when they were all together—the three boys I saved during this training in previous years visited me separately.

Coda tried to explain their unit and why I couldn't join, but I waved him off. I was fine on my own and always would be. It was a pleasant change to have occasional visitors, but I knew better than to trust any human.

After all, they were the ones who shipped us off to this makeshift 'Most Dangerous Game' wonderland once a year to weed out the weak. I knew allowing the those guys to have access to me was a gamble, and I didn't care if their buddies didn't accept me.

Remy Arsine Benoit had plans and other people would only make those harder to execute.

"He knelt among the shadows and felt his isolation bitterly. They were savages, it was true; but they were human.[2]"

The lines he kept reciting were very familiar. Besides extra training, I spent a lot of time in the library learning everything I could absorb. Despite my eleventh birthday being last month—so they said—I was leaps and bounds ahead of most of the students my age. Professors at proper schools would have sped up my studies once they realized it, but at l'Academie, no one skipped grades. Your classmates were expected to either rise to your level or fall behind until they got bested or killed.

I knew the book; it spoke to me in a way I doubt many adults could have understood because they hadn't lived the situation. Every year, captivity and resistance training is a live action simulation of stories like Lord of the Flies and the reality of accepting humanity's capability for savagery is diffi-cult. They forced us to come to terms with that realization as children and the shock of it branded us for the rest of our lives.

Trust no one. Depend on yourself. Eliminate all threats without hesitation. Remain a ghost.

That is the way of Les Invisibles.

"The world, that understandable and lawful world, was slipping away. Once there was this and that; and now-and the ship had gone.[3]*"*

The last quote was almost whispered as he stared at the dead animal. Peeking out from the foliage, anxiety coursed through my veins. While I was hidden, he was damn near on display in an unprotected space with what seemed to be no regard for his safety. Unlike the three I'd saved in past years, this boy was clearly the alpha.

The term didn't apply exactly to a human eleven-year-old boy, but even the way he moved as he circled his catch spoke volumes. This boy was a predator, like me, and his bare torso was covered in blood and gore from slitting the pig's throat. His long hair had slipped out of some fastener because it was littered with leaves, sticks, and mud in a very Tarzan of the Jungle way.

He was beautiful and fierce, with a mind like a chess master. I wouldn't find that out until later, though.
I watched him as he mourned the animal and we lost all of our innocence in this place, unwilling to leave him exposed while he worked through the emotions he clearly did not want to share with the others. It felt invasive, but also a bit re-affirming that someone else saw our life similarly to me.

When a cadre of l'Academie killers burst into the clearing with very hungry-looking wolves flanking them, I wasn't shocked. Each year, the challenges presented by the environment or the academy staff were more difficult—this was the first time the human hunters brought animal predators along for the ride.

I squinted at the enormous dire wolves as they snapped their jaws in anticipation and I realized they'd probably been starved and beaten before they were led out on leashes to cull the herd of students who couldn't survive on their own.

It's possible they've killed children my age already tonight before scenting the bloody hog and finding the philosophical boy I was watching.

"What are we? Humans? Or animals? Or savages?[4]"

I had no choice but to reveal myself when I realized he might be ready to sacrifice himself to these gun-wielding dillweeds. Covered in ghillie suit number four, I charged out into the moonlight with a roar I hoped mimicked some sort of swamp monster. If I threw them off enough, perhaps the boy would regain his senses and make quick work of the wolves. He stared at me as I continued making insane sounds and then at the two l'Academie dicks who took off at the sight. Still, he didn't move, and I had to throw off the heavy part of the camo to drop into the fighting position.

The difference in size between me and the roided out guards was becoming less significant as the years went by, but it was not completely unnoticeable. Smelly asshole number one let go of his canine and rushed me, but that was a mistake. My speed and size allowed me to duck his grasp and use his momentum to shove him into a tree. The sound of bones cracking echoed in the air and I pulled my wire out, yanking his throat up to slice through it quickly.

He opened his mouth to say something as I turned back and I practically screamed, "Get off your ass and fight, Plato! You can ponder your belly button if we survive."

That woke him up, and he rolled to his feet like a jungle cat. In the next few minutes, our bodies moved in an almost coordinated, deadly dance as we worked together to kill every single being in that hollow except one another. Harsh pants filled the air when the last body fell and we finally faced one another. He didn't speak, so I huffed over to my suit, draping myself in the life saving disguise again.

"Maybe recite classic lit in your camp, not in the middle of a goddamned jungle like a tool," I muttered. It was obvious he wasn't even going to thank me.

White teeth showed against his dirty face as he smiled for the first time since I saw him. "You kill like they made you for death and destruction. It's haunting and beautiful."

I snorted, stomping over to the pig. "You philosophize like a leader who wants to die before his men."

"Don't they all?"

"Fair point. That's why I don't have any men."

With that, I took off into the brush, leaving him with the prize and the consequences of his inaction. We had three more weeks of training—I thought—and I didn't have the luxury of debating our existence with the boy who fought like a vicious dancer in motion.

I had to survive on my own.

"Yo! Hey, dirty girl! Woo-hoo! Come back to me. Are you having a stroke?"

Dwyn's voice brings me back to reality in a blink and I lift my head from the wall. My expression is irritable as I swat his hands away. "No, I'm not having a stroke. Get away from me."

"Woman, you Checked. The Fuck. Out. What was I supposed to think?" His brow creases adorably, and I have to fight the urge to smooth it out.

Pushing off the wall, I cross my arms over my chest. "Perhaps that everyone in our trade has unresolved issues and likely a touch of PTSD that could flare at any moment?"

Wincing, he rubs the back of his neck. "Ouch, you got me. Criminals all have their stories about cheating death no matter what their specialty is. At least you came back within a few minutes. I've seen people killed because they stayed under for too long."

"Right. So let me catch my fucking breath while we head to this last fool and then I'll have a clear head for the boss at the end of the level."

"Video games references. Fuck, you sure know how to get a thief's motor running. I'm thinking you'd make a sexy ass Princess Peach and I could raid your—"

"Shut. Up." I growl as I shove him, then walk away. I don't mean it, of course, but after the memory of Mo and the island stripped my soul bare in this hallway, I can't deal with his cutesy innuendo.

"Ooh, feisty! Maybe you should be a villain. Can Bowser be sexy? I'm sure some Halloween costume shop has a get-up like that. You could light my ass on fire anytime, dirty girl. This plumber will let you unclog his pipes if that's your bag."

Jesus Christ. What in the hell am I going to do about this idiot?

---

1. Lord of the Flies, William Golding
2. Lord of the Flies, William Golding
3. Lord of the Flies, William Golding
4. Lord of the Flies, William Golding

Forester

WALLS COULD TALK

"Status. Anyone," I ask as Coda and I look out over the crowd. Silence greets me, and I squeeze my hands into fists at my side in frustration.

I hate being this out of control. I want to hit something.

The feel of splitting cartilage or breaking bones has been my comfort zone since we were kids. Once it was clear my path was veering towards being what *l'Academie* called a 'hitter', I embraced my natural talents immediately. Using fighting as my pressure valve for stress led to competing in the underground fight club, which earned me the dumbass 'Fist of Salamanca' moniker.

Criminals are a narcissistic lot—naming themselves shit and accepting titles as if they're in some campy spy novel. But The Five are so elite that we can't help but get noticed even when we're not trying. Hence, the other guys being tagged with similarly stupid names as well.

The Fist, The Ghost, Alharba', La Araña, and The Cowboy are ridiculous, but we can't get rid of them.

Though, I will admit there are those who didn't name themselves but have extremely badass code names despite my feelings about using them. *Le Voleur* and The Guillotine didn't select their own, but they strike fear into every other assassin and skill group, even in whispers. I suppose I wouldn't protest as much as I do if they had given me their names.

"Mo? Mo?"

Coda's tone is low but urgent and I shake my head, pulling myself out of my mental meanderings. "What, man?"

"I don't see any of the guards except the one near Jinx. I think they actually thinned the herd to one. Luckily, the other guests haven't noticed it yet. The dipshit in the middle with his automatic pointed at Elysium and J is what's keeping everyone from stampeding. They're all too scared and self-involved to notice most of their captors are MIA."

Squinting, I verify what my brother said as I glance over the crowd. Most of the guests are pretending they are talking in small groups or playing with their phones—a vain attempt to see if they can get a signal to post on social media or call for help, no doubt. What they *aren't* doing is looking at their surroundings, so Coda is right—they don't know the threat has almost passed.

Normal humans are as clueless as they are boring.

The comms crackle and Dwyn cuts in. "Last hostile down. Paused for a moment to deal with something—no, not my dick, Mo. Putting together the plan for the incursion for the ultimate target. Be ready."

I scratch my chin when he cuts his mic again. His statement about taking care of something that wasn't humping is curious. It couldn't have been another guard or stray guest; he would have simply said that. *Did he and Elysium's partner have a disagreement?* They better not have because if they aren't on the same page when they try to get inside this mess, they could get both of our friends killed. Masked moron number ten is not stable at all, and whoever it is won't bat a lash before spraying the crowd with bullets.

"What do you think went on?"

"I don't know, Coda. D only elaborates when he feels like it and he's chosen this incredibly inappropriate moment to keep secrets. Whatever it is, they need to get over it because if people get shot, I'm going to beat his ass bloody."

Coda clicks his tongue and wags a finger at me. "You need anger management, dude. The answer to everything is not kicking someone's ass until they cry uncle. We keep telling you that."

Snorting, I turn on my mic. "Raz, you're gonna need to snap out of it and get control of these goddamn cameras. The feed from the entire event needs to be wiped—we can't have anyone seeing any of this. Wipe anything connected to the Wi-Fi here with some virus or whatever the hell you do. The guests are just as much a problem as the bogies."

"What the fuck do you guys think I've been doing?" Raz finally speaks, his voice full of strain and irritation. "I'm the one who threw the net over the building to keep the transmission from getting out. I've been hacking every device in the building one by one to trigger a failsafe if certain words appear in their videos, posts, or texts. It will wipe their device completely, which should distract whoever it is long enough to make them forget about it. This kind of shit takes focus and I haven't been sitting around biting my fingernails."

Feisty Raz only shows up when he's worried about someone and Jinx bleeding on the floor has set that off.

"Got it. Good job. That will help immensely if we make it out of this clusterfuck intact," I reply.

Coda blinks and whistles softly. "Mo gave you a compliment, dude. Bask, because it only happens once a decade."

They both laugh, and I glare at the rocker. I'm always willing to give praise for a job well done, but I have to withhold it more often than not because they've done something crazy and something good. "Shut it, Coda. Raz, keep working."

Nudging my partner, I jerk my head towards the section of the ballroom where Jinx is being held. "I'm splitting off so I can get a better vantage point. If I'm not with you, it will be less noticeable and there aren't any others to stop me from getting in strike distance."

He rolls his eyes and sighs. "You can't possibly let anyone else have the glory, can you?"

"Fuck off. You steal the stage everywhere you go. All I want to do is get close enough to help if they need it. We have no idea what this woman's skills are; she may have just gotten lucky upstairs. D is pretty starry eyed, so forgive me if I'm not willing to risk our brother when his dick is doing the thinking."

"Fair," he says. "I'll stay put."

It takes an irritatingly long time to move through the crowd without drawing attention to myself. I'm good at subterfuge by trade, but slipping around pockets of grumpy or trembling snobs without them speaking to me was harder than I predicted. Women grabbed me and pretended to swoon like a Southern belle; men huffed and puffed as if they were protecting the women by not flexing their muscles at the hostage takers. Both approaches made me want to run for the hills of Italy and hide from the public for at least six months.

My years of training on the island have made me completely unable to put up with the day-to-day guiles of normal people. Their lack of intelligence and skill bore me; I have no patience for their machinations. When I'm on jobs, I can play the role of an aloof bodyguard or mercenary that makes it believable that I don't talk much. But when I'm caught in public like this, it stretches my capacity to the limit.

The only people I can stand being around are my brothers—and at one time, her.

Now is not the time to relive the past, even if I'm at the mercy of my most unpredictable team member and a woman I've never met.

I pause for a second, flexing my fists at my side as the lack of control makes my entire body tense. This situation is so beyond fucked up and I haven't had the chance to process how it's affecting me. Between a surprise attack, Jinx going off-book, and D disobeying orders, the structure I depend on to balance my rage has been systematically dismantled piece by piece. Coda might have been right; I'm aching for revenge. Not for the reason he thought, but because these motherfuckers have completely thrown my perfectly planned mission into a clown show.

That alone is justification for ripping them limb from limb.

Once I get myself settled, I wind my way through the crowd again, approaching the ring of people who are surrounding the gunman and our friends. I stay out of the sight line of the masked thug so I don't draw their attention, but I know Jinx sees me. He nods his head ever so slightly and whispers something to the pretty thief holding pressure on his wound. She looks up at me, fluttering her lashes in a calculated signal that lets me know she knows I'm on their side.

"In position."

My brief transmission lets Coda and Raz know I'm ready, but I don't know if Dwyn even has the comms open to hear me. He's been so cagey about what's going on in the background that I'm uncertain what he and the mystery partner have planned.

My answer comes when Coda mutters, "Holy shit."

I look up to see a couple entering the room with loud, drunken giggles that catch the attention of every head in the room.

Apparently, their idea of subterfuge and mine differ.

"Who the hell do you think you are?" The last masked thug's voice is still weird and high-pitched, but the volume on his electronics must be turned way up. They raise their semi-auto, swinging it at the

crowd until the guests standing between them and the two loud drunks disperse. *"How did you get out of the ballroom?"*

Dwyn looks up, playing the role of a drunken fool who'd snuck out to get laid perfectly. "Oh, I didn't get out, my good man! Now, getting off is another story entirely."

The woman with him giggles and slaps his chest playfully as they stumble towards the scene with the confidence of sexed up fools. "Bad, bad Marcus! You're telling everyone what we've been up to! The scandal!"

"I said, who the hell are you and what are you doing?"

The gun swings up again, pointing at them as the crazy fucker loses control.

Fuck, I hope this isn't the only part of their plan.

Forever

HIT & RUN

WHEN THE GUY WITH THE BOAR'S HEAD MASK AIMS AT JINX AND LYS, MY breath catches in my throat. Our plan was risky; we knew when we agreed on it. But this twist on our Albee con was the best chance we had of getting close to our friends without setting off the final hostage taker.

Dwyn kindly allowed me time to gather myself after my trip down memory lane without pushing any further, but when I told him we'd have to detour to the staff bathroom, he balked. I had to explain my 'bug out' bag stashed in there when I first arrived and why I hadn't used it yet. The damn thing really was for an emergency and nothing that has happened so far necessitated impersonating a guest. In fact, until now, doing so probably would have made it harder to free our friends.

But he didn't fight me and within a few minutes, I was stripping the bulky clothes off and scrubbing my skin free of the blood tint that soaked through. Once my body and face were clean, I did a full check of my hair, ignoring the way Dwyn eyed my body when I asked him to make sure the back didn't have any brains or fluids in it. I did a few swipes of basic makeup and shimmied my ass into the black satin sheath dress and strappy heels.

The real disbelief came as he watched me strap on the weapons in the bag, including the icepick like chopsticks that held my hair up in a messy twist. His comments were snarky but laden with innuendo and I had to dismiss them so I could ask the one thing that might actually derail our mission: I had to ask him to kiss me and muss me up like we'd been getting naughty in some private hidey-hole while the bullshit in the ballroom went on.

Trust me, he did a thorough job and I'm still feeling the scrape of his stubble as a pleasant sting on my lips.

"We're soooo sorry, sir," I coo at the crazy fucker waving his weapon. I fix a pout on my lips and press myself against Dwyn, holding onto his lapels. "I couldn't make it through this silly party without a little… encouragement. Champagne does awful things to me."

Arms wrap around my waist and I grip the material in my hands hard when the man I've been thinking about since our romp on the train grabs my ass and squeezes. "My poor dove is a mess of want when those bubbles get to her. Lucky for me, that's what the servers were handing out!"

"If you two drunken morons don't get back in line and away from me, I will kill this asshole and his bitch!"

I frown, pretending to look puzzled as I let go of Dwyn and hobble towards them slowly. It takes all of my focus to make it seem like I'm wobbling in the tall heels without looking too exaggerated. I don't actually want to fall, but I need to seem like I'm non-threatening. "Is that a gun? Oh my, how sexy is that? Marcus, you didn't tell me this was one of those murder parties!"

That accomplishes my goal. Our would-be killer stalks over to me, pressing the muzzle of the gun against my stomach as he growls into my face. *"Are you stupid, bitch? I will kill you and everyone in here!"*

This is the moment. The guy is going to figure out who I am—whether it's Remy, The Guillotine, or The Duchess, it won't matter.

I lock eyes with Lys and then Jinx before I reach down, putting my short side hand on the gun and pushing it away from my stomach. My body blades away from the line of fire on the long side, and I wrap my other hand over the weapon to keep it from redirecting. A few rounds shoot off into the air and screams echo through the room as the people hit the floor.

Actually, that's much better. I would have thought of it if I'd cared about collateral damage before.

The snarl of the pigman makes me grin and I use my heel to stomp his instep, then knee him in the crotch as hard as possible. He doubles over and I know I have him—I'll have to make this quick or Dwyn is going to jump in. It's risky, but I let go of the gun and click the button on the side of my faux cocktail ring. When the gem pops free, I grasp it and pull the wire from the hidden compartment with a feral grin. One swift twist and a yank have my old friend cutting through his skin like it's a soft cheese.

A choking sound and the feel of hot blood spilling onto my feet brings me out of the haze of the kill. Raising my eyes, I see the face of the boy who lamented killing a hog so long ago. He's a man now—a dangerously sexy man with sharp cheekbones and flashing eyes— but he's watching me with the same expression he did when we were kids and I killed the agents.

Respect, awe, and sadness are radiating from him as he eyes me from a spot in the crowd.

We don't have time for this.

I plead with him with my eyes as I let the last body of the night drop. He nods slightly, so slightly that I might have been the only person to see it. Taking that as my cue, I rush over to Lys, grabbing her hand and yanking her away from the members of The Five.

"Run! Follow me," I hiss as we head out the back and through the kitchen to the staff exit.

She follows me, but I don't miss her grumbled complaint. "Only you would save the day and refuse to claim the rewards."

Being face-to face with the men who betrayed me and have wormed their way back into my life in the middle of a disaster is not a reward.

Elysium simply doesn't understand that yet.

LYS DROVE LIKE A MANIAC TO GET US OUT OF THERE AND BY THE TIME WE arrived at the drop location, I was calmer than when we left. She didn't force me to tell her why I didn't want to talk to the men we'd partnered with before we left, which only solidified my decision to work with her. My heart was pounding like a bass drum and I had to clasp my hands together to keep them from shaking. The combination of seeing those boys—my boys—and having to execute a last-minute rescue to save people was too much.

I thought I'd resolved all this a shit a long time ago and the more I allow emotions to creep into my psyche, the more I find out I'd been lying to myself.

We stop at the deserted sanatorium and Lys switches the car off, staring into the night before she turns to me. "Thank you for saving me and the guy, but you have a lot of explaining to do."

I sigh, looking out the window into the darkness. "I do. Clearly, my skill set is greater than what I allow people to see as The Duchess."

"Uh, yeah, but that's not what I meant," Elysium snarks. "Lots of people hide the breadth of their abilities to keep themselves alive. I'm much more interested in what in the fuck happened with those guys."

Yikes. This is a far longer conversation than we can have here.

"I don't know if I'm ready to share all of that information and definitely not out in the open like this."

She snorts and pulls the keys out. "So sum up what you can before we go inside. I'd like to focus."

"I've met them before. It was a surprise to see them, especially since the one who got shot is Casanova from Prague and my partner from upstairs is Slick." I turn to look at her, my face full of the confusion I can't seem to wrap my mind around.

"Holy fuckballs, Callista! How did you fuck two separate dudes you've met before and none of you know about it?"

Scratching my head, I make another pained face. "Also, my name isn't Callista, but that's a very long story. To answer your question, I knew them as kids. I'd never seen them as adults and I've figured out who they are, but I don't think they've made me. All the disguises, you know."

Her jaw drops. "But… those guys are definitely members of Les Invisibles, Callista. That means you…"

Damnit. How did she figure that out? Are the rules flexible now or something?

"Don't say that shit out loud, Lys. It could get you killed." I sigh and shake my head. "Yes, at one time, I was one of them. No, I can't go into that here and now."

"The only way out of *LI* is death; everyone knows that," she whispers. "Did you die?"

"Yes." I shrug and tug the skirt of the cocktail dress up, revealing the thief's belt I'd strapped over my hips underneath. Opening a pocket, I pull out the necklace we were recovering and hold it in my hand. "Which is another reason they don't recognize me—they were there when I died. You don't expect to see someone who can't possibly exist."

"Jesus fucking Christ in an Oreo, Calli. This is the most exciting night I've had in forever and I am not a boring girl." Her eyes find mine and she tilts her head. "If those guys are Cas and Slick, what are you going to do about the dates? They have to know you're not some plain Jane normie from a train by now."

"Uh, yeah. That notion is dispelled for certain. I'm pretty sure the one watching us from the crowd might make one of my real identities and it won't take them long to put most of the picture together. They're all geniuses, but together, they're an unstoppable force." My smile is wistful, but I know tonight changes everything. I won't be able to go back to the life I created after the explosion.

I could, however, cut and run with one of my 'retirement' plans and force them to hunt me down.

"Listen up, mystery woman," Lys says. Her forceful tone makes me pull myself out of the wallowing I was starting internally, and I wait for her to finish. "Here's what's going to happen. We're going to drop this shit off, jet back to London, and hole up wherever your place is. You're going to contact those boys and tell them you need to meet. Dates are canceled, but they should bring their damn friends. Don't give them anything; just see what they say."

Pondering it for a second, I nod slowly. "That could work. If they asked why the dates are cancelled, it might be a hint that they haven't put the pieces together."

"Doubtful. If they were trained by the psychos you say they were, their acting skills will be on point no matter what profession they chose. However, it will give you enough time to sit down with many bottles of tequila and tell me all about this fiasco you're embroiled in." Her smile is broad and though every single brain cell in my head screams against it, I nod in agreement.

The truth is, I've been carrying all this shit alone for so long that I don't know how to put it down and I have to.

"Okay. I'm in."

Elysium pumps her fist in the air and I laugh softly. "Now that's what I want to see, girl. You gotta let loose a little. You're wound so tight I thought you were going to shoot into space at the bar. I don't know what these dudes are going to be for you, but my role from now on is to be your wacky BFF."

I arch a brow at her. "What if I don't agree with that?"

Her long nail looks like a claw as she points at me. "You don't get a choice. Get over it and get on board."

"You know, normally, I kill people who dare tell me what to do. This is very odd," I murmur.

"Callista, you ain't seen nothin' yet."

That said, she opens her car door and jumps out, motioning for me to follow her to the abandoned building to complete the drop.

My life will never be the same. Maybe that's a good thing?

SPIDER IN THE ROSES

"So we agree? The chick last night who called herself The Duchess is the woman you and I met on the train and in Prague?" Dwyn is pacing the recovery room at the London clinic Les Invisibles provides for its operatives. The knives in his hands are spinning like pinwheels and though the nurses keep glaring at him, he has yet to pause them.

"Yes," I reply tiredly.

The bullet wound was red and swollen, a fact Raz did not miss the minute we left amongst the panicked sheep from the ballroom. Coda and Mo had to take his original transport to maintain his cover, but when the girls beat a hasty retreat, we followed suit. Dwyn took the wheel, driving like a maniac while Raz started tending to the wound fussily. His concern was appreciated, but the hovering made me crazy, so I accepted D's offer to hit up the *LI* clinic to make sure everything got taken care of correctly.

That calmed Raz down enough to make the bumpy ass ride bearable, and I could have kissed the nutty thief for suggesting it. Now we're all here and they have hooked me up to enough painkillers and antibiotics to float a battleship. It's making my mind groggy, but we can't wait to have this conversation.

"But is she actually The Duchess?" Mo muses. "I watched her disarm the idiot, and it looked very similar to tactics I've taught over the years at *l'Academie*. She doesn't appear familiar, though I felt the same about the woman I saw at the museum in Prague."

"They're all the same woman!" Coda shouts. "Look over here."

I blink, surprised that he's not floating in space after having to harness his ADHD for so long at the event. "Look at what, Coda?"

He holds up a laptop he must have swiped from the van when he went out to smoke earlier. "Razzie wiped the cams and devices as best he could, but he didn't tell you he also sets everything his worm thing eats to upload to this program on here. I've been splicing this shit while you all argued. It's not my bag, so don't make fun of how rough it is, assholes."

Raz looks the most shocked, but he takes the proffered device and holds it up where we can all see. The video plays, showing clips we'd already seen of the woman in question from Paris, train stations, and the ill-fated party. However, he also added the street cams of Mo's fighter chick and every scrap of video Raz collected this evening. As it plays, I lift my hands up and peer through them like a kid. It helps me focus on smaller details and when a few more frames flash by, I gasp.

The woman all of us have met in different places over the past two weeks is definitely the same woman in a bunch of very well done disguises.

"He's right. They're all her. If you break her down into symmetry and watch how she moves, even in the little details… it is one woman with multiple identities." Lying back on the pillows, I let that knowledge rush over me.

"What do we do now? She's not stupid. She won't keep those dates you made with her." Mo folds his arms over his chest, looking contemplative.

I don't blame him. We haven't even considered going after the same woman since Remy and it feels a bit like we're dishonoring her memory by thinking about it now. The looks on my brothers' faces confirm they're feeling similar, but Dwyn is the one who speaks up first.

"Who cares? I mean, obviously I care about the date thing. What I don't care about is if she's the same chick in different fonts. That girl is made for me—you didn't see her cut through those useless morons upstairs. It was hot as fuck and so was the take-down in the ballroom." He pauses and flings one of his knives, embedding it in the wall above the bed I'm in. "And I also don't care if the rest of you want her, too."

Coda blinks and looks at him in surprise. "You want to replace her?"

"No, you idiot," he sneers in response. "We could never replace her. But she's dead and we are not. It's time we stopped acting like we blew up that night as well."

I flinch when Raz yanks his knife out of the wall and sends it flying back at the thief. As usual, his hands are so fast it defies belief, because Dwyn reaches up to snatch it out of the air with ease. My lover is the only one who hasn't actually met The Duchess, and he also took the longest to even talk about her death. It's no surprise he's having trouble with the idea of bringing another woman into our group.

"She's dead because of us," Raz snarls. "We don't get to be happy after we got her killed."

"Bullshit."

We all look at Mo. He never weighs in on this subject; he avoids talking about Remy at all costs. But he hasn't put his hair back into the ponytail and he didn't run for the bathroom to clean up the second we got here like usual. His desperate need for control hasn't been sated since we arrived, and that alone is odd. This interjection is even weirder, so I stay quiet to see what he has to say.

"For a decade we've all struggled and scraped by, holding onto each other and whatever unhealthy coping mechanisms we developed. I agree with Dwyn; it's time we stop punishing ourselves and start living. I don't know if this woman is the one, but we all know we function better as a unit and individuals when we share rather than push each other away."

Of all the things I expected him to say, that was not even in the same vicinity as what I thought was coming.

"I agree," Coda says. "If I don't get my shit together, I'm going to fuck up my cover one day and the Commandant will shove my ass in a hole so deep Hobbits won't be able to find me. Forgiving myself might chase away the demons that make them do stupid shit—sort of."

My gaze flicks to Raz as he stands by the door, looking furious. "I think we all have to unanimously decide for this to work."

"Well, Razzie? Are you going to fuck this up for all of us because you want to keep paying homage to a ghost?" Dwyn glares at him, his hands still occupied with the blades. I can only hope he doesn't throw another one.

"I'm not agreeing to shit when it comes to someone I've never met who spent the past two weeks lying to us separately and now as a group. Set a meeting with her—with all of us. Then I'll tell you what I think."

I let out the breath I was holding slowly. "Okay. I'm in if Raz is." They all look at me in confusion and I shrug, then wince when it pulls the bullet wound in my shoulder. "Shit. Stop looking at me like that. I enjoyed the hell out of my time with Shooter, but I won't do anything to force Raz into something he isn't comfortable with."

Dwyn rolls his eyes and huffs. "If I suck your dick, will you side with me, too?"

"Mmm. Depends on how good a job you do." That gets a laugh out of him, followed by Mo, and eventually we're all cutting up. The nurses give us all dirty looks and after a few minutes, we calm down. "I think if we wait until morning, she might text us. I don't know why I think that, but something in the look she gave before they took off tells me she will."

"Then we wait until tomorrow," Mo says as he drops into the chair. "And you hit the button again and rest. We're not leaving until the docs clear you. I can't have you cause permanent injury because you were being stubborn."

"Sir, yes, sir," I reply before saluting and pushing the button for the meds. "See you all on the other side."

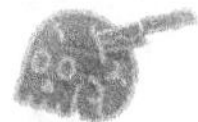

WHEN I WAKE UP LATER, THE ONLY ONE IN THE ROOM IS DWYN. I SQUINT at the unusually still thief in the dim light of the early morning, wondering what happened.

"D, where is everyone?"

He stretches his legs out, cracking his neck as he moves it from side to side. "Fetching. Raz is replacing equipment and moving our base to another safe house. Mo and Coda are getting us food and clothes."

"And you stayed rather than run around London?"

"I stayed for a very specific reason," he says as he rolls to his feet. "One only you and I can know for the moment."

I frown. "What in the hell are you going to say that we can't tell the others, D?"

"She's not The Duchess—or not just The Duchess." My eyes widen and he holds his hand up. "I don't care and I know by the way you talked about her after the party, you don't, either. You're hoping Razzie will fall in line when he meets her; I get that."

"I... Well, I won't hurt him; you're right. But I..."

Rolling his eyes, he waves me off again. "Don't lie to me, Jinxy. Thieves are almost as good at reading people as grifters. That's how I figured this out when no one else did."

"Dwyn, spit it out, man. What are you trying to say?"

"Our girl isn't only The Duchess... She's someone far more well known and sought after. I caught it when I sat here and started going over everything that happened once I arrived at the estate."

"Damnit, who is she, D?" I slam my palm on the tray next to my bed in frustration.

"She's The Guillotine."

I blink, my mouth hanging open as I watch him pace back and forth at the end of the bed. "What?"

He snorts, shaking one of his knives at me. "Don't write me off without hearing what I know. It's not one thing, but a couple of little things that clicked into place."

"Dwyn, no one has a clue who The Guillotine is, but a woman couldn't achieve some of the shit he's done. Certainly not one the size of the girl we're talking about."

"I watched her heave two deadweight bodies that were more than twice her size. She's strong, fast, and deadly. And most telling, she killed every single one of those fuckers by slitting their throats. I didn't see a wire, but it's not far off her normal kill method. She's so fast, I couldn't even tell how she took out the pig mask. All I saw was blood."

Blinking, I try to take in what he's telling me. This whole situation is completely FUBAR, and no one is acting like themselves. Raz isn't angry, Mo isn't logical, Coda isn't focused, and I'll be damned if I can remember Dwyn being able to piece together tiny details like this. We're all behaving the opposite of our normal selves and the only thing different is the addition of this woman.

"Why is this a secret?"

"Because they might pull out of our agreement if they find out before we agree to it, and I can't let that happen." He runs his free hand through his hair and gives me a pleading look. "I don't know why I know she's perfect for us, but I do. And I haven't felt this way since… you know. So I'm not letting it go."

"Fine," I sigh. "I'll keep your secret until we meet up with her and discuss all of this shit. But if it seems like it's going to be a problem, I'll rat you out in a second. Got it?"

His grin is full of mischief. "Agreed, Jinxy. We've all got to learn to compromise if we're going to take care of our girl. She won't put up with our silly bickering; even Mo's going to learn to take a firm spanking now and again."

"Oh?"

"You didn't see her face when I said she could peg me," he winks and turns on his heel, heading into the hallway.

Son. Of. A. Bitch.

Forever

NOT DEAD YET

WHO LET THE FUCKING BAND OF GREMLINS AND THEIR BRASS BAND IN?

I groan low, rolling over and squinting around the room blearily for the noise that is intent on splitting my skull. It's coming from the bank of equipment on the other side of the room and I moan. Moving feels like an impossible task at the moment, but the noise is killing me.

"Unnnnghhhhhh…"

No shit, babe.

A brief montage of the shenanigans we got into last night flashes in front of my eyes, and I realize why I feel like my mouth is made of dust bunnies. We took down three bottles of Don Julio 1042 while I told her as much of my life story as I felt comfortable with. She was okay with me admitting I couldn't give her every single detail yet and, by the end, I actually felt better.

Having someone listen without trying to fix my broken pieces was more helpful than any therapy session I've ever had.

But we might have overdone it on the booze.

I haven't woken up with a hangover like this since I was a fucking teenager. Taking a deep, fortifying breath, I roll over and reach for the edge of the couch. I grip it tightly as I drag myself up until I'm kneeling. Dizziness slams into me and I curse under my breath, but I don't stop. When I'm finally on my feet, the world rocks around me, making my stomach pitch.

Damnit, Remy. You had to open the third bottle, didn't you?

The memory of yelling 'YOLO' as we passed it back and forth during a raucous round of karaoke makes me cringe. I let my hair down more than I have since I died and I'm definitely paying the price now.

Waiting until everything comes into focus, I take the first tentative steps toward the loud alarms going off at my workstation. Now that I can see, I realize it's coming from the Shadow Douche set-up. I push the roiling waves in my gut down and move faster, eager to find out what has that asshole contacting me well before our agreed upon date.

Whatever it is, it can't be good.

I sink into the chair gratefully when I get to the table, leaning back and closing my eyes until everything is stable again. "I hope to hell I don't have to do anything today or we're all dead," I mutter.

"Mmmm. Me, too," Elysium chimes in from the nest we made on the floor.

She's still comfy in the blankets; she has no reason to complain.

The grumpy internal snark makes me smile slightly and I'm surprised to find even that hurts. I pry my lids open and settle in, clicking the mouse to activate my security protocols and VPN. Even fighting off this monster headache won't make me neglect the shit that keeps me alive, and this is no different. Once it's all running, I open the cloud storage where Shadow Douche leaves his rants with a sigh. This will be the first time Lys gets to hear his grandstanding bullshit, and I'm actually looking forward to what she has to say about it. Maybe she'll catch a clue I didn't know to look for.

"Salutations, Guillotine!

I come to you with a heart full of disappointment.
You committed to a task for my organization and after last night, I am left wondering whether we can trust you to fulfill that contract.

Last night, you attended a social event filled with pathos and excitement. You had a stellar opportunity to execute your part of this bargain while the obstacles in your way were distracted. Instead of completing your mission in good faith, you assisted fellow criminals in stopping another team from achieving their goals.

I must admit it astonished me when the news reached me.

You were chosen because you have a certain lack of conscience when it comes to collateral damage. That single-minded focus on eliminating the targets you acquire was a powerful selling point when we selected you for our job. Based on previous behavior, we believed you would strive to achieve your aim with little to no concern over the environment or people within it.

The incident last night proved that assumption incorrect. You worked with several operatives to free the hostages instead of locating La Araña's hiding spot.

Tsk tsk.

As punishment for your betrayal, we believe it is only fitting to tack additional objectives onto your job if you are to be paid in full.

You will eliminate Raz Miranda at the next chance and, in order to receive payment, you will also eliminate his lover, Jinx Monroe.

That is just ironic enough to show you the seriousness with which we take our order, Guillotine.

Saving his life at the party will now lead to his swift demise at your own hands.

Do not refuse us this boon or it will force us to send operatives of our own to remove the other obstacles to your success.

Tell Elysium hello for us. We will contact her in the future, I'm certain."

"What a pompous asshole," Lys grumbles from the floor. "He can lick my dirty dishes."

Laughter bursts from my lips and I groan as it makes my head throb more. "Fuck, woman. Don't make me laugh. Every inch of my body is aching from last night. Thank hell I didn't let you talk me into the absinthe as well."

She giggles, then groans, flopping onto her back. "Yeah, the Green Fairy would have been a big mistake. I'll save that journey into oblivion for a later girls' night."

"I'd like to request that trip be put off for… ever, maybe." I open the bottle of water on the table and take a long draw on it despite not knowing how long it was sitting there. My body needs the moisture and I have to get my sense about me before I deal with the madness we listened to a moment ago. "In fact, I may swear off alcohol for a while."

"Sure you are," she says, chuckling softly. "I can't believe that the son of a whore is trying to force you to kill a second person for free. *Who does that?* I've known plenty of assassins in my day and none of them are your caliber, but they wouldn't give a client a freebie because he disagreed with their choice of venue."

I snort. "He doesn't follow any of my rules like every other client, either. I'm only humoring him until I can figure out what the endgame is. Being told to kill Jinx as well tells me he's familiar with their crew on a level that shows he has a mole in *Les Invisibles*. Those guys are too fucking good to let details of their private lives get out in the wild like that."

Sitting up, she leans on her hands as she looks at me. "Do you think this fucker knows you have a connection with them?"

"I don't know. It seems like he'd lord it over me if he did. He must not know my real name or history with them, just that they are attached to one another."

"Why, though? Most teams aren't together as long as those guys have been. Shit happens and teams break up. Why have your men been a crew for as long as they have and not fallen out?"

Shit. I didn't tell her my real identity, and I definitely didn't tell her the name our community calls my guys, but I'm going to have to now.

"Because they're The Five, Lys."

"Holy forking shirtballs, Calli! You grew up with heirs apparent to the entire *Les Invisibles* organization? Are you shitting me right now?" Elysium looks at me as if I've grown a second head and I let my head drop. "Those fuckers are some of the most dangerous assholes on the planet."

My head drops and I stay quiet while I decide what I'm going to do. I obviously have no intention of killing Raz or Jinx, but I can't move forward with researching the Shadow Douche if they're tripping over themselves to find me. After last night, there's no way in hell they won't devote all of their resources to locating The Duchess, even if it's just to find out why I helped them. I know how their minds work and they will not let this go.

"I have to contact one of them. There's no other option. I have to text one of the two I have info for and arrange a meeting. Otherwise, they're going to be in our way and it might get us all killed."

She pounds one of her hands on the ground in frustration. "Why are men always in the *goddamned way*? I wake up every damn day wondering why the universe didn't make me a lesbian. It can't be harder than dealing with dumb shits who think with an organ that spends most of its time dangling limply."

"I don't know, Lys. I ask myself the same thing all the time."

"Fine. Get your phone and let's figure out what you're going to tell these fools so we can get it over with. I'm in the mood for some seriously greasy food and we can't go anywhere until you set a time."

How did I live all these years without someone like her? Three days of being friends and I swear to fuck, I'd marry this girl if we both swung in that direction.

A FEW HOURS LATER, WE'RE FINALLY OUT AND ABOUT, BUT NEITHER OF the guys has returned my text yet. I'm more than mildly irritated at being left on 'read', but I'm trying not to let it make my mood worse. Lys and I have been stuffing our faces full of hangover food at the pub down the street from my rental and chatting about our favorite jobs.

She's a far more accomplished thief than I realized—some of her work is damn near legendary.

"So I broke in and switched all the fucking mummies, just to teach that assface a lesson!"

I grin. "Did he figure it out?"

"Not until they photographed one of his exhibits for a major publication and some amateur archeologist pointed it out in a scathing YouTube video that went viral. That was one of the most satisfying acts of petty revenge I've ever pulled, to be honest. Serves him right for making me party to his cheating ass without my consent."

She shivers, her purple braids shaking on her shoulder, and I smile. "I think you made your point nicely, and you didn't even take any of his fingernails. I might have peeled him from head to toe. That is… if I'm being honest, too."

"Peeled him? Fuck, Calli." She picks up her Bloody Mary and chugs it, then wipes her mouth. "I keep forgetting that killers solve everything through blood and gore."

"Does it bother you?" I ask quietly.

"Hell, no. I don't give a single fuck about random assholes, but it's a change in perspective." Elysium motions for the waitress to bring her another. She was adamant about the 'hair of the dog', but I'm waiting for this stupid text and I have to stay sharp.

"Good. I would hate to—" We both freeze when my phone goes off, buzzing its way across the wooden table. "Shit."

"Check it! See what they have to say!"

I pick up the phone, unlocking the screen and looking at the encrypted messaging app.

Unknown: Meet in Battersea tonight at 10 pm. Bring the thief.

"Well, that was anticlimactic," I grumble. "Not even a 'hello' or 'thanks for saving my bacon' to be seen."

Sipping her drink, Lys shrugs. "Maybe that's better. If you don't give anything away, you're at a distinct advantage. Let's finish up our food and take a little spin around that park, so we have the layout down."

"Sounds like a plan."

Hopefully, we don't run into any other bullshit along the way.

Forever

THIEF

I don't turn around from the workstation in our new base of operations when Jinx asks, but the muscles in my back tense. My frustration doesn't stem from being jealous about his minor obsession with this girl, and I don't want any of them to assume so. The anger consuming me is about a girl who saved my life in the woods many years ago who died too soon because of our poor decisions. To me, there is no one who could measure up, and even trying is an exercise in futility. I can't believe the rest of them are even considering it.

Yes, our memories are idealized, but the pain of losing her has never stopped haunting any of us—and we deserve that torture.

"You betcha, Jinxy. I had to wait a bit to make sure I didn't seem too eager, though. I told her to meet us in Battersea at 10 pm, just like we agreed." Dwyn is all over the place with his excitement and it's making it hard for me to focus. He's lobbing knives and axes like it's his job and constantly ducking a bladed weapon wasn't on my bingo card today.

"Cut it out, O' Shanahan. If you hit the equipment, I'm going to kick your ass myself," I snarl over my shoulder. "Some of us are working."

"On what?" he snarks back. "We're not doing anything until after we meet with Jazzy Duchess, whoever she is. Mo said so."

Closing my eyes, I count down from twenty in my head. Dwyn can't help his hyperactive shit anymore than I can help my introverted need to recharge occasionally. The only person who could ever help him get control of it is the one I'm pissed about.

Ironic, isn't it?

Remy could soothe the energy in him or ramp it up to a million, but she always handled the fallout with grace. I can understand why he'd miss having someone like that around, but it doesn't mean we should start accepting applications.

No one could fill her shoes—not in a million years.

"I have to break down everything that's happened in the past two days and transmit reports to the Council. You know I have to do this and every time we finish something, you act like it's a new piece of info, D. Go practice picking locks or something, so I can finish this."

I can sense the vibe in the room change, and I'm sure Jinx just led him away before he shot his mouth off. He's doing okay now that he's doped and stitched up correctly, so he's back to taking care of me. I'd complain, but honestly, I like it. And I'm not in the mood to get in a pissing match with Dwyn about this mystery girl that everyone has their boxers in a knot over. I don't care how amazing she is; I'm not signing on this shit.

"He's gone now. You'll have quiet," Mo says as he walks up to me.

I nod. "Thanks."

"Don't thank me; Jinx hauled him off. But I doubt your irritability is about D's itchy hands."

Save me from the armchair analysis.

"Probably not, but that's my business and no one else's."

He makes a thoughtful sound but doesn't push away from my desk. "Perhaps it feels that way, but have you considered that your decision affects all of us? I'm not saying you have to change how you feel —fuck knows I don't when people push me. But I also know none of us can go on living with a ghost in our beds. You have Jinx and it's real, even if you agree to see others amicably. The rest of us have to accept no-strings attached encounters because we know our group would be in danger if we had people coming in and out of our lives constantly. It's why we'd all decided on her all those years ago."

Spinning my chair around, I glare at him. "Don't you think I *know* that? Of course I realize I'm affecting everyone! What I don't know is why suddenly you're all gung-ho to replace someone we simply cannot replace."

"Replace?" Mo shakes his head. "Never. None of us would ever do that; we know it's not possible. But it is possible to find someone we can all care about differently. I'm not fully on board, either, but when all three of them seemed to pay attention to someone for the first time in a decade, I realized it was time to take a chance. Knowing she's part of our lifestyle makes that decision even easier, Raz. We won't have to lie to her constantly."

I think about that for a moment. *He's not wrong—about any of it.* It helps to hear Mo's on the fence about the whole thing as well, but I also needed to hear the other stuff. I was far too mired in my own stubborn emotions to consider what the consequences would be for the others. Talk about a mirror moment—my reflection was selfish and unfair because I wouldn't listen to my brothers trying to explain their side. Holding onto her when she's gone forever is only preventing them from moving on healthily—and probably me, too.

I don't want to be the person who only thinks of themself and uses my traumas to control everyone else.

"Okay, man. I see your point. I'll think about it." He grins a little and I flip him off. "Now go away while I finish this or the Commandant will have all of our asses. I'll come find you guys before we have to go to the meet."

"Don't forget to print up all the docs for the briefing beforehand."

"Yeah, yeah. Fuck off."

As if I don't know how to do my job.

"THERE'S A BUILDING WITH CLASSROOMS TOWARDS THE BACK. WE should be able to get in and once we do, we'll send a text to her with instructions on where to go," I finish.

Mo scratches his chin as he looks at the map. "That's very specific. Did you choose this space for a reason?"

"Yes." I look at all of them seriously. "I am trying to be open to this idea, but the last time this woman met someone in an open-air space, she and D almost got blown to smithereens. The last two times she tried to complete jobs in enclosed yet public spaces, there were hit squads who had to be dealt with and Jinx got shot. I don't know if someone is after her or if she has the world's most rotten luck, but I want us to have a controlled space where we don't have to worry about collateral damage or death from above."

Dwyn snorts. "Razzie, you can't control everything. Ask Mo-Mo. He's been trying to figure that shit out for years and never worked it out."

Rolling my eyes, I sigh. "Look, it's tucked away in the damn chil-dren's zoo and it's not a place most people would think to look. We can leave early and scope it out, then let her know where to meet us so she can watch for people following her tonight. Is that more acceptable?"

"Are we gonna stay there? I doubt that will go over well with the punters touring the zoo," Jinx says. "We'll have to check it out, leave, and come back."

"Obviously. But I'll leave my little friends so we know if it's been compromised somehow." I hold up a handful of micro cams and sensors. "That should keep our space safe."

"Okay," Mo nods as he stands. "Let's get our asses in gear and set up the space, then all we have to do is wait."

I don't miss the grateful look he gives me, nor the bounce in my brothers' steps as they leave to grab their shit.

This girl had better be something awfully fucking special…

"Where is she?" I ask as I look at my watch in the darkness again. "She's ten minutes late."

"Calm down, Razzie. She's coming. We'd think she was unprofessional if she didn't scope the place out before she entered, right?" Dwyn is leaning against the dry erase board on the wall as he twirls a new set of blades.

Jinx comes up to me and sits his chin on my shoulder. "We would, and you know it."

"Fine. You're both right. I'm just not a fan of being out in the open after that fiasco yesterday. Something about it still isn't sitting right with me. I've watched the tapes over and over, but I can't put my finger on what is bothering me."

"Walk us through it while we wait," Coda offers as he hops up on a table. "Let us help you unwind whatever it is."

I ponder that for a moment and sigh. "Okay. So Dwyn hit that building—it had secure info and a fuck ton more, but he had zero problems getting in and out."

"That's because I'm the shizz, baby!"

"D, knock it off. We're being serious," Mo chastises. "Go on."

"If something were to go wrong, it should have been there. But it didn't. A bunch of rejects invaded a country estate owned by an old German Nazi collector that had mildly valuable art and possibly some black market shit locked up… but nothing that would warrant two teams holding a ballroom hostage. The jackass who owns the place is in and out of the country all the time. There's no way a heist had to occur with that many variables," I explain. "Nothing about it fits."

"Huh," Coda says as swings his legs. "That's true. And if it was a snatch mission, they didn't even look at the guests most of the time. So no one went missing that I saw, and I'd bet you didn't see anyone being hustled out with a black bag, right?"

"Right. Overkill for a theft and no victims being ushered out, nor reported in the news cycle. So why the *hell* were they *there*?"

Dwyn flings a knife and it lands in the wall just outside of the board I'm leaning on. "Well, The Duchess tried to get information out of every single one of those fuckwads and all they would say is 'our allegiance is for life' and some choice curse words."

I arch a brow. "How did she try to get it out of them?"

"The fun way, Razzie. They should have responded, but they let her kill them instead. It was both annoying and exhilarating at the same time."

"He's right. They should have folded like a house of cards."

All five of us look up to see a hooded figure silhouetted in the doorway. She steps inside, closing the door before walking into the middle of our group without hesitation. A shrug has the hood of her sweatshirt falling from her head and a woman with long red hair wearing tactical pants and combat boots stands before us. A smirk plays on her lips as we all look at her in silence.

"Boys, I agreed to meet you here, but if you're going to gape at me all night, we will not get very far."

My eyes narrow. I'm in no mood for sarcasm or cutesy bullshit. "You're late."

"Yes. Spank me later, because I have bigger concerns at the moment."

Wait, what?

Dwyn beams at her words, throwing his other knife directly at her face, and he claps like a child when she catches it without hesitation. Blood pours from her palm and she drops the weapon to lift her palm to her mouth and lick it clean.

"Was that all you have to say? If so, *sayonara*, suckers."

"No way, Jazzy. You lived up to your bad girl persona by tricking Jinx, me, and Mo-Mo, but you're not getting away that easily now." Dwyn turns to the rest of us and stage whispers, "Did you see what she just did? My cock is going to bust through my pants."

Her laugh is like velvet, but I'm still tripping on her words. Despite the sarcasm, there's something… something I can't quite grasp about them. I ignore Dwyn having his childish glee moment while I try to nail down what's bothering me.

"Point of fact: I didn't set out to trick anyone. I happen to be good at my job and you were all casualties of tradecraft."

Jinx lets go of me and walks over to her. "Excellent tradecraft, I'd say. I might have suspected you of being The Duchess at the Open Market—at least after the dust settled. I would never have made you for The Guillotine."

Her expression doesn't even flicker. Not one micro expression crosses her face, so I have no idea if she expected us to know that or not.

"Very good, gentlemen." She tilts her head and plasters a mischievous smile on her face. "I'd expect no less from The Five."

"Holy fuck," Coda whispers.

The girl laughs again, wrapping her arms around herself. "Oh, Coda Ramone. You are exactly how I would have imagined you to be."

"Huh?" The rocker frowns and looks at the rest of us. Mo shrugs and I can feel the weird sensation pulling at me again.

The sound. The words. The attitude. The knowledge. The skills.

Suddenly, I know what I need to do. Tapping the earbud hidden in my ear, I activate the listening feature and pull out my phone. I scroll until I find what I'm looking for: a very old voicemail that I haven't listened to in years, but couldn't bring myself to delete. A few seconds in, I have it. I know exactly why all of this feels wrong and what's bothering me.

I don't say anything. Whipping my gun out of the holster under my arm, I stride over to her and put the barrel against her temple. My entire body is vibrating with fury as I look into the emerald eyes of the woman in front of me with unbridled fury.

"Tell them. Tell them *now* or I'll finish the job."

VILLAINS (PT 1)

THE BARREL ON MY FOREHEAD DOESN'T BOTHER ME. IT'S NOT THE FIRST gun pointed at me, nor is it the first time I've had one to my forehead like this.

But the man in front of me is well aware of that.

I should have known Raz would put the pieces together. He's always been the most brilliant and best multi-step thinker in the group. His IQ trumps mine, and that's nothing to shake your finger at. Now he's looking at me as if he'd truly love to finish the job that Professor Arnaud and the fuckwits at *l'Academie* started all those years ago. It's a wee bit sad, but I can understand why.

As much as I mourned them—and myself—they had to mourn me and their part in my death.

"If it was going to be anyone, I should have known it would be you," I mumble. Slowly, I reach up and pull the wig off of my head. Next, I unzip the hoodie to reveal the tiny, backless crop top that will allow them to search for the marks they will need to confirm Raz's theory. Then I remove the wig caps one by one and let the waterfall of white hair fall to my waist. Last, I put my finger in each eye and pop out the contacts masking my unique eye color. When I'm done, I look up at them, tossing the UV light I crammed in my pants pocket at Coda. "Go on, then. Do what you must."

He fumbles for a second, but I assume that has to be because he can't process what he's seeing. When it takes too long, Mo strides over and grabs the device from him, clicking it on and pointing it at me. The light crawls over my body and I turn slowly so they can see the tattoos running over me until they get to what they're looking for.

Just below my right breast on my ribcage, the brand of *Les Invisibles* is still raised. I've had UV ink swirled around it to distract from the symbol, but in the middle, shining like a beacon, is the mark of The Six. I never had it removed, just augmented my work around it so it didn't appear to be the mark of an organization.

"Mother. Fucker," Dwyn breathes as his eyes widen. "It's… It's…"

"The rumors of my death were greatly exaggerated," I snark as I look at Jinx. The curve of his lips gives me hope and I turn my gaze to the man holding the light on me.

"I'll say," Coda mutters. "This is some Elvis level bullshit right here."

"Thank you very much." I do my best impression of The King, but it doesn't get the laughs I wanted. "Look…"

"We carried a casket," Raz snarls as he yanks the gun away and turns on his heel. "We had to bargain with that old bastard to get them to call it an accident. Do you know what price we paid for your bullshit?!"

That sends me over the edge. *How fucking dare he talk about the price they paid?* Nothing that happened to them could remotely compare to the ordeal I went through escaping that hellhole, reinventing myself, and starting out on my own for the first time in my entire life.

"Look, you sanctimonious twat. I didn't come here to rehash the past, but since you opened that steaming pile of shit; take a big, nutty bite." I look at each of them one by one before I continue. "You may have hurt and you may have gotten punished for whatever you did after I was gone. But none of that compares with what I had to do to get away from there without anyone knowing."

Raz opens his mouth, but I hold up my hand. "No, sir. You don't get to snark at me about your poor wittle feelings. I had to do things I never imagined, even growing up in *LI*. Once I'd swum the thirty miles to shore while injured, dehydrated and ducking fucking sharks, I had to do things I will never speak of again. Once I had enough money, I got out of the country. It took months to make my way to Europe and the entire time, I took on the jobs almost no one will take. I had nightmares for the first five years; I still sleep less than most humans."

Mo frowns, and even Coda rubs the back of his neck, but they stay quiet.

"When I finally got to Europe, it was almost a year after the explosion. Things had healed wrong. I had no identity, and Remy was dead. I'd never in my life been on my own with no support before, but I knew what to do to establish myself. So I did more horrible things to fund that. And little by little, I built a reputation as a bloodthirsty, ruthless villain they began to call 'The Guillotine'. It suited me and I let it ride, even though no one seemed to realize I was a female. After a while, I purposely allowed the legend to be devoid of any identifying information—it helped me work in the shadows."

"I tracked Arnaud down in my second year. He'd left the safety of *l'Academie*—something I'm sure you all had a part in—and I made him pay for swaying you all to betray me. That didn't fix me and I went on a famous bender they called '*La Revolution de Guillotine*'. I never liked the stupid naming thing, but man, did that blood and gore fest get me clients. *Et voila*, I was established."

Jinx clears his throat and looks around before asking, "Why didn't you come for us? I mean, even for revenge if you hated us so much."

My smile is bitter as I pull the pocket wire out and fiddle with it to quell my anxiety. "Because I never healed from your bullshit. I thought about sneaking into rooms and slicing every one of your heads off repeatedly… But I couldn't even plan your deaths without plunging myself into the darkness. When I let the darkness in, I ceased to exist. So, eventually, I pretended you all died instead of me."

"Your solution was to play 'if you can't see me, I can't see you' like when we were kids?" Dwyn gives me a tiny smirk and I feel one knot in my chest loosen.

"Sort of?" I shrug my shoulders. "I got the UV ink over time to cover the mark. I covered all the scars from training. I created my network, all on my own, and by the time I finished that, revenge didn't seem important anymore. The life I had with you in it ended when that bomb went off on the boat and I didn't look back."

"We grieved for you. We mourned. Hell, none of us has had a serious relationship with anyone outside of this group for over a decade, Remy." The quiet statement comes from Coda, and he lifts his beautiful sapphire eyes to mine. "The number of times one of us has bailed another out of some semi-suicidal mission or bender is more than I'd prefer to admit."

"Especially him," Mo grumbles as he crosses his arms over his chest.

I sigh, sliding the garrote open and closed, letting the familiar motion soothe me. "Would it help to say that I haven't helped myself to round two with a person since the boat? The first time I even considered it was…"

"With us." Dwyn's face lights up when he realizes what it took me far longer to figure out.

I nod silently, not looking any of them in the eyes. "Yes."

"Why?" Raz whirls around and glares at me. "Why did you leave them bullshit clues and take off?"

Letting my weapon snap back into place, I wrap my arms around myself. "Hell if I know. I did it with Dwyn before I slipped out to my real compartment to hide. I was shocked at myself all day afterward.

Then that fucking party happened, and I was trying to leave, and Jinx stopped me. I did it again, and I had no idea why."

"You know why," Mo growls. "Just admit it."

Tears prick behind my eyes and I refuse to let anyone see that. "Look, asshole. I'm broken; I'm so fucking broken that the three therapists I saw all couldn't even figure out where to begin before I killed them. I quit trying after that. I've lived like an unattached vagabond ever since. I don't have an actual home—only crashpads and storage units—and Lys is the first almost-friend I've ever had. And I kind of only did that three days ago. Don't ask me to tell you why in the hell I do anything right now, because I do. not. know."

Before anyone else can interrogate me, a loud alarm sounds from what seems to be Raz's pocket. His eyes widen and he pulls the device out, looking at the screen with a perturbed expression.

"Fuck. Fuck, fuck, fuck… How in the goddamn hell is this possible?" he yells.

"Raz!" Jinx walks over and puts his hand on his arm. "Slow down and tell us what's wrong."

He whirls on me and snarls, "Did you do this? Is this your ultimate revenge?"

"Is what my ultimate revenge, you twatwaffle? I have no idea what you're even talking about!" I scream back.

This kind of shit is why I stayed alone and unencumbered all of those years. All men do is cause fucking problems and then blame them on you simply because you don't have a dick to swing back at them. Newsflash for these motherfuckers: I *will not* let them treat me like shit again.

"I set up cams and shit earlier. Because I remember what it looked like in Berlin, I also set up sensors and a few other things. Nothing— not one thing—has tripped any of it all afternoon or I would not have let us walk in here. But…"

Mo sucks in a deep breath and lets it out slowly. "But what, Raz?"

"The alarms are going off. Not for now, while we're here, but they're alerting me from the fucking past." He glares at me again, and I throw my hands up.

"I didn't even know we were coming here until, like, an hour beforehand! You fuckers hid it from me!"

"Plenty of time to—"

"Raz, what timestamps do those messages have on them?" Jinx tilts his head as he asks, looking hopeful.

He frowns and scrolls for a moment, then sighs. "Earlier than when we told her. Fuck."

"Unless I'm a goddamned psychic, it wasn't me!" I point at him, my expression mutinous. "Why would I do something to this place and walk into it? That's fucking bad tradecraft and you know it!"

"I wasn't really thinking about—"

Another loud sound interrupts his retort, this time a computerized voice that booms through the room. "Execute. Three, two, one…"

"Out, out, out!" Mo shouts as his eyes widen. "Go!"

They drop all pretense as we drop our bullshit and run for the door like the hounds of Hades are on our heels. Cramming our way through the doorway, we burst into the hall leading to the classroom and every one of us sprints towards the entrance we came in through. I look over my shoulder, seeing the boys I loved in the men I'm running with, and in that moment, the world explodes.

I knew saving that dick in Paris was going to get me killed.

Then everything goes black.

Preorder Ruthless now!

GET A SECRET BONUS SCENE!

For a secret bonus scene that follows this book, *click the link below, sign up for my newsletter, and get your freebie.*

Get your bonus scene here!

REVIEWS, PRINT, AND MERCHANDISE

If you have enjoyed this story, please review it.
It helps other readers find my work,
which helps me as an indie author.

Thank you!

Reviews are appreciated on the following platforms

TikTok
Instagram
Facebook
Bookbub
StoryGraph
Threads
Goodreads
Amazon

To purchase print copies or merchandise, go to The Worlds of Cassandra Featherstone

STALK CASSANDRA FEATHERSTONE IN THE DARK CORNERS OF THE WEB

JOIN MY FACEBOOK GROUP AND FOLLOW ME EVERYWHERE!

WANT MORE?

SIGN UP FOR MY BI-WEEKLY MANIFESTO FOR A FREE SERIES SAMPLER:

Join my Ream as a FREE follower or exclusive subscriber to get access to cover reveals, WIPs, Serial Stories, and personal chats from me!

CASSANDRA FEATHERSTONE

SNEAK PEEK: VEILED FLAME

LOSER

Kat

The little blue icon on my app has been glaring at me all day, but I'm too damn nervous to open it. Everyone at Woodlawn High has been buzzing all day with their notifications and the squeals of joy and moans of despair were too much for me to take. My anxiety is through the roof—this is the moment I've been waiting for since middle school, but I can't seem to force myself to bite the billet and check.

Maybe it's because I don't have the support system most of my classmates have?

That's probably true, given I've always been a loner and I don't fit into any specific 'caste' here. It's hard to make friends when you get shuffled from foster home to foster home over the years. I've rarely stayed anywhere long enough to make a friend, much less a group of them.

I'm not delinquent or anything—the families I've been placed with just return me like a pair of pants that doesn't fit after a year or so. The caseworkers click their tongues sympathetically and hunt down a new placement, but I've never been given a reason *why* people don't want me around. One lady said I must be born under a bad sign and hell if I knew what that meant other than I'm not good enough to keep around.

It would be different, almost understandable, if I misbehaved or got bad grades. But I don't—I'm always in the top five percent of my class and I do everything I'm asked. I don't even lord my smarts over the other kids or adults. Being presentable and unassuming was something I adapted long ago to improve my probability of staying in a home long term.

Unfortunately, it never worked and though I should be a shoo-in for scholarships and acceptances galore, I can't bring myself to be rejected yet again.

So I wait for the last bell of the day, slinging my bag over my shoulder and trudging home to the latest in my temporary housing. I can't even contemplate looking at the possible heartache waiting for me in the college application system WHS insisted we use. The fear is too great and despite knowing I'll be on my own for good at the end of this year, I'm unable to risk the pain.

I hate being this way.

My court mandated therapist says it's some sort of attachment disorder that's common in foster kids, but I think that's bullshit. The problem isn't *me* not forming attachments; it's asshole adults not forming one to me. Being left at a safe haven in a fucking basket as a baby wasn't because *I* did anything wrong—again, fucking adults couldn't handle their commitments.

As usual, I arrive home to an empty house. There are two other kids who live here—Bryce and Blake—but they're at football practice. Of course, the Jamesons *love* them; they get to strut around at games because their strays are the stars of the team. I'm not mistreated, but I'm definitely an afterthought. Both of my 'parents' are still at work, so I drop my bag on the couch and head for the kitchen to get a snack.

Don't get me wrong. I *could* have been placed in far worse homes than any of the seven I've been in since elementary school. None of the ex-fosters starved, beat, molested, or abused me. They were all decent folks with jobs and houses that weren't hellholes, but they never liked me.

I have no idea why. I tried to be everything they wanted.

But when the end of each school year came, I was handed in like a textbook and off I went to some group home until the next contestant stepped up. It baffled everyone, not just me, but that's what happened every single time.

Sighing, I pull some fruit out of the fridge and grab a soda. I have homework to do and if I want to have time to work on my stories, I'll need to get it done before the house is full of people at dinner time. Bryce and Blake will have gotten messages about their applications, too, and I'd bet my pinkie toe those idiots got into some big sports school. Brett and Allison will be oozing happiness for them and I don't know if I'll be able to keep food down if I have to admit my failure when they ask.

Being eighteen sucks ass.

After I grab my books and tablet, I head down to the den. I have to give my current parents credit; they set up a very nice workspace for us to study in the converted basement. By the time they took me in, the Jamesons created a cozy room down here where the three of us could relax and do our work for school without being interrupted. It might have been more for the boys than me, but I appreciated it all the same. Desks, a couch, big chairs, and bookshelves fill the space, making it almost seem like our mini-library. They even put a small fridge for drinks and snacks in case we had to be up late to cram.

It's my favorite place in the entire house and I spend most of my time here.

I sink into the huge armchair, putting my drink and snack on the side table. It only takes a few minutes to arrange myself in the soft cushions and I pause to tug my headphones out of my pocket. Music always soothes my jagged edges and I need it to stay focused on the bullshit AP Calculus I need to keep my average up in. My course load is heavy, but I applied to tough colleges. I wouldn't have a chance to get in, especially on a scholarship, if I wasn't taking equally challenging classes in comparison to all the prep school kids.

As always, the sounds of Vivaldi carry me away as I scrawl equations on my screen and before long, thoughts of the blue notification completely fade away.

"Kat!"

The shouts barely register as I continue working on the problem set, gnawing on my lower lip in concentration.

"Jesus fuck, where is she? I could eat a hippo!"

"Kat!"

Thumping followed by what could pass for a stampede of elephants jerks me out of my math filled trance when Bryce and Blake come down the stairs. They smell as bad as the aforementioned pachyderm's cage, so they must have rushed home right after practice. The blond twins glare at me as if I'm the offending element despite being sweaty and covered in dirt and grass stains.

This doesn't bode well.

Usually, they're tired and hungry after practices so I'm used to cranky ass boys, but tonight, there's a light to their faces. That had to mean they've gotten their letters and dinner will be a gush fest in honor of their perfection. I'm going to need all of my strength to fake smile and nod as Brett and Allison fawn over them.

I don't begrudge them their success—not really. They work hard and play even harder on the field. It's not their fault they're the American dream teens and I'm the nerdy basement troll no one wants. But it's awfully hard living in the shadow of their bright light, especially when I'm no less intelligent or talented.

"I'm finishing the AP Calc, guys. What do you want?"

They roll their eyes at me before Blake scoffs. "It's not due until Monday. You're so hyper."

Duh. I take anxiety meds, douchebag; of course I'm 'hyper.'

"I can only be who I am, Blake." That earns me a snort from Bryce and I know it's because he thinks that's the problem. "Is dinner ready?"

"Almost. Get upstairs and set the table so we can shower—Brett's orders." Blake grins smugly.

The two of them seem to always arrange it so chores get passed to me for some half-assed reason and this is no exception. Sighing, I put my stuff aside, fully intending to hide down here after the dinner mess is cleaned up. Likely by me, but like I said, I could definitely live in worse foster homes so I let it go. Doing some chores isn't worth risking the group home for the last few months of my high school career.

They take off running up the stairs and I wait for them to disappear before I follow suit. My phone is tucked in my pocket and I feel like it's a stone of shame I have to bear. I know once the adults make over the twins' success, they will remember me, and I'll be forced to find out what disappointment lies in wait for me. The dread weighs on me, but I head into the sunny kitchen and pick up the pre-prepared pile of plates, silverware, and napkins on the counter.

Allison looks up from the stove and gives me a half-smile, nodding as I take the dishes into the dining room. Like I said, no one is mean or horrid, they just seem…obligated. After a while, it makes it hard to waste time trying to be bright and sunny. Being reserved makes it a hell of a lot easier not to feel rebuffed when they don't pay attention to you regardless.

"Make sure you include champagne glasses for your dad and I!" she calls from the other room.

The twins definitely got acceptance somewhere big. Brett must have gotten the bubbly on the way home.

Once I set the table, I return to help Allison bring out the roast and sides. I'm a little amazed at her efficiency when it comes to getting the housework done while working full time, but I suppose it's something people with real parents get taught as they grow up. My home life has been so fractured that I haven't learned how to cook more than very basic shit from YouTube videos. That may be a problem after graduation, but I've never felt comfortable enough to ask Allison if she'd teach me. I'm sure she would try, but it doesn't feel right.

"How was school, Kat?"

I look over my shoulder, seeing Brett in the entry to the dining room. He's already changed from work and smiling, but I see the distraction in his eyes. He's waiting for the boys to come down. "It was fine. I've got a Calc test at the end of the week. I'll be studying a lot to get ready."

"Good, good. No matter what happens with applications, keeping your grades up will ensure no one pulls any offers," he says.

Those words aren't for me. They are for the two wet haired boys who just appeared behind him.

"Kat's too much of a geek to ever let her grades slip, Dad," Blake says as he pushes past his brother and drops into his usual chair at the table. "Grab me a Powerade since you're in the kitchen, mouse!"

Both Brett and Bryce stare at me and I turn around, heading to the fridge despite the fact that I was *not* closer than the other twin. Out of habit, I take two of the drinks and a soda for myself. I've been here long enough to know Bryce will send me back to get him one as well. It would feel like typical sibling stuff, but for some reason, I just *know* they do it to fuck with me. I have no idea why I feel that way, but trusting my gut has been the one thing that helped me get through all the upheaval in my life over the years. It's a good gauge for knowing when I'll get booted or if people are being earnest in their reactions.

The therapist says that's some sort of trauma induced early trigger warning shit, by the way.

After I hand out the drinks, I sit down on my side of the table and we wait for Allison to come out. Brett is at his seat at the far end of the table and the twins are punching each other as they look at something on their phones. I know where this is all going but I drop my gaze to the table, swallowing the coppery taste of fear as it courses through my body.

I'm going to be exposed and there's nothing I can do to stop it.

Read the first three episodes free on Kindle Vella: https://www.ama zon.com/kindle-vella/story/B0BSTMB1X3

SNEAK PEEK: FAILED STATE

EVERY DAY IS MONDAY

Sydney

"Jesus fucking Christ," I mutter as I slog through the streets of Tempest Seven. "Just because they locked us up like animals doesn't mean we have to live like them."

Pausing in my walk to the education center, I look around myself in abject disgust. The inhabitants of this end of Tempest Seven aren't the bottom of the proverbial barrel, but outside of the 'lockdown losers', people stuck here never seem to get out of the cycle of poverty and despair. I don't think it means we have to throw garbage everywhere and give the drones nice shots to prove to the humans that we're as unworthy as the leaders of this stupid country say we are.

What would it hurt to tidy up, even if we don't have much?

Honestly, I believe it's only a third rooted in laziness. I think the other parts are exhaustion and hopelessness. Since the First Infected Being Sweep of 2020, supernaturals all over this country were tracked, catalogued, reassigned, and declared property of the government. By the time they ran the second through fourth sweeps, the population of some supernatural species dropped by fifty percent. The rules on how to track us down and receive your bounty were infuriatingly vague, which gave the most violent psychopaths in the world a free license to kill, maim, rape, and disappear anyone caught on the 'Non-Human Watchlist'.

I was a baby when my mother left, but my father taught me everything I needed to know about being a shifter. Unfortunately, he was one of the people who ended up on that list and was killed in the Second Infected Being Sweep of 2020. That sweep was brutal, and since I was a 'half-breed' orphan, I was placed in the orphanage in Tempest Seven. From the moment every child and teen arrived, they were forced to attend the Federal Enrichment Assimilation & Re-Education Center.

Our human professors taught us that being born this way is a punishment from their God, especially if you were a mixed type. At first, we tried to tell them about our various species, but it became clear very quickly what would happen if we didn't fall in line. You either learned to smile and nod, providing the rote answers and scripts they gave you when tested or interrogated, or you died.

Now, in 2024, there are no rebellions against the Federated Human States of America, nor are there any aid workers from other countries left to help or try to get us out. The world has given up on the former United States—it's been ruled a failed state by the United Nations and cordoned off at every border on land and sea.

We're on our own in the former land of the free and home of the brave.

"As if anyone would want to come here anyway. Shit went downhill fast after that baboon was elected," I mutter to myself. I realize I've spoken louder than I thought and I look around carefully, making certain I'm not near a Confession Enforcement zone or any other beings. My breath releases slowly when I confirm that I'm totally alone and not in a hot zone.

No one watches out for others now; the temptation to gain things your family or group needs is too high. A random person would dime me out for a week's supply of crackers and I can't blame them. Food and drink are rationed, our clothes are drab and provided, and the world is dimmer since the Sweeps. They force us to stay small so they're in control, and we have to live with it because of the fucking Markers.

My hand flies to the back of my neck, grunting in irritation as I scratch at the tattoo that covers the skin where the implant is located. These were the second step on the path to the current tyranny of our 'benevolent' government. That spray tanned fuck won the election because the humans here were that goddamn stupid, and then the virus hit. COVID brought America to its knees and like all good con artists, President Taterman used the distraction to funnel money into secret programs under DARPA.

Men who stare at goats my skinny ass.

They released a widely contested study that blamed the virus on the 'infected'. Unfortunately, they defined that as beings living in our country that had paranormal capabilities. The rest of the world laughed at the senile old fuck until the media hype was so huge that the various species around the world convened a leadership meeting. With so many cameras and videos everywhere, it was only a matter of time until a random human caught one of us doing something and bam! A viral TikTok would expose all of us whether we were ready or not. The vote was close, but the supernatural community decided to come out of hiding to protest their innocence.

'The Unveiling' was the most watched TV event in decades, and the consensus was our leaders had done the right thing. At least, until the next study was released. This one made Taterman damn near salivate as he screamed into the TV cameras about the 'unclean' liars and thieves who have been hiding in plain sight, taking our jobs, and stealing the lives humans should have. It quickly devolved into a mass panic and our kind were left scrambling.

We'd told them who and where we were, like a bunch of fools.

Thus, the evil assholes at the top started their mission to protect the humans from us and reclaim their country. Supernaturals in other nations were fine, but the atmosphere here became dangerous within the blink of an eye. Taterman stacked his own deck in the courts and the legislature by fear-mongering, especially since the world was still reeling from a pandemic. Eventually, he was able to get the support he needed for the first Sweep.

Secret Supernatural Enforcement Agents used databases, social media, DNA websites, immigration records, and everything they could to gather the biggest dragnet of personal information ever assembled. Civil rights advocates and other world leaders were vocally opposed to such violations, but nothing could stop the juggernaut of hatred. Once they identified every supe in the nation—to the best of their ability— that's when they stripped our citizenship, robbed us blind, and re-assigned every single one to the sectors they'd been building in secret.

Let's be honest—they're supe prison camps.

But the humans felt safe once more because while we were all being shuffled all over like cattle, the rest of the scientific community worldwide started to get COVID under control. Taterman crowed about the United States' involvement, taking credit for slowing the spread by locking up the infected beings. No one but his nutty followers believed him, but at that point, it didn't matter.

So when they came to implant the Markers, no one spoke up.

We all have them, and depending on what you are and how powerful you are, they are different. But resting above the spot where they cut us open to shove in the controller, there's a matching tattoo of the logo that is now on the flag of the Federated Human States of America… but that came much, much later.

Democracy dies in the dark, the old slogan said… and here lies her rotted corpse.

"Hey, Syd. It's a beautiful day in the neighborhood, huh?"

My brooding gets interrupted by the arrival of Thad, my friend since we got placed here four years ago. He's a bear shifter and the size of a small SUV, but it doesn't bother me. I survived the sector version of high school partially because we stuck together. My brains and his bulk were a good match and it kept us from getting cornered by the gangs and cliques.

Okay, fine, it kept me from getting cornered. Obviously, Thad held his own without me.

"That sentiment hasn't been applicable for half a decade, man." I toss my braid over my shoulder and wait for him to catch up. It's our second week at the F.E.A.R. Academy's college level program and being late is more than frowned upon. I have to give us extra time every morning because Thad lumbers out of bed like his animal— slow and grumpy. "We gotta get moving."

The dark haired shifter looks at me, scratching the piratical scruff he's usually sporting. "You're ridiculously concerned about rules for someone with such a rebel spirit."

"Rebels die, Thad. I'm very aware of that." Turning on my heel, I head toward the huge building at the end of the main drag with a heavy heart. Losing Dad was hard and I'll never forgive him for assuming humans are anything but ignorant beasts that barely rise above their simian relatives.

We continue walking in silence until we reach the steps. The line is stretched down them as the guards run the wand over each student to check for weapons. After that, we put our bags on the conveyor belt for the magical detection while the security mages in government issued loyalty collars scan us for anything the wands wouldn't catch. It's not quick, but it keeps fights in the schools non-lethal most of the time.

That's the official reason, but the real purpose is to allow the staff to abuse students if they step out of line. The Markers not only brand and track us, but they siphon energy and power in small bits to keep us all weak enough to be controlled. Weapons would even the score and the humans who run these stupid ass brainwashing cults would be at risk.

"Look who's last at the trough again." The wry voice of the only demon in Tempest Seven gets my attention. Huck Monroe saunters up, tilting his worn black cowboy hat back as he smirks at me. "Y'all are just cruisin' for a bruisin'. I swear, you don't have the sense that the Devil gave a goose."

My eyes narrow at him briefly, then I turn forward and shuffle along as the line moves. "You don't have to hang out with us, Huck. In fact, it'd be great if you fucked off and stayed there."

Thad laughs, bumping his shoulder against the annoying fear demon's and I sigh. Huck was sent here during the First Sweep, like us, and he's been a Southern bramble in my side ever since. It's my bad luck that Thad enjoys his folksy charm and it means he sticks to us like glue during school hours.

"Sometimes you're meaner than a wet panther shifter, Sydney Jolie. I should take you at your word and mosey off, but I like your boy."

Huck's pitch black eyes are hidden by his Ray-Bans, but I know they're sparkling with amusement. He finds my dislike funny, and I don't get why. But then, I don't get a fucking thing about men, especially supes, nor do I want to. Life in our sector is hard enough without having to consider birth control or babies or even finding privacy. I'll save that for the day when I get the fuck out of here.

"I heard they're bringing in a new group of students today." Thad changes the subject quickly, knowing I'll continue to needle Huck and vice versa until one of us loses their temper. "The rumors say the shipment has vamps, losers, and traitors. I'm worried this sector is turning into a dumping ground for psychos."

It wouldn't surprise me if the humans started segregating the camps by species, value, or even criminality. Even after they corralled us into the sectors, the leaders have continued to exert their influence and power over us. The Markers were first, then the lockdowns for the ones they deemed dangerous, and now they're shuffling people weekly at random. I've often wondered if all of this is covering up something like what went on in the 1940s among the humans, but I haven't seen any proof.

Our media is monitored and curated, so unless you know someone with a highly illegal device, you have no idea what's happening outside of the FHSA.

"Next! Keep it moving, you little shits," the yell from the front of the line brings me back to reality again.

"Wicker is the fucking worst," Thad mumbles as we ascend the steps to stand behind the person being inspected. "Watch his hands, Syd."

"I'm aware." Despite thinking we're the scum of the earth, some of the human staff and enforcement in the sectors are fucking creeps. Some supes are willing to trade sex for perks, but that doesn't stop the predators from being creeps to those who don't. "I'll let you go first so Bishop gets me."

"Got it," he says as he muscles in front of me. "Huck, stay behind her."

"Why, I'd be delighted, Thaddeus."

I guess he's useful sometimes, but he'd better not let it go to his head.

Get it now!

SNEAK PEEK: HELL ON WHEELS

BAD BLOOD

Rogue

"I don't need you anymore," Mina scoffs.

Holding my face in a disinterested mask, I arch a single brow at the witch, who has been my best friend for three years. We've struggled for months to connect in the same way we did when we first met, but so many things have conspired against us: life, outside influences, time—even our own team members. I met Mina because of our love for the derby, and now it might be the only thing left we share.

Blue hair shakes as she packs her gear, clearly done with our conversation as well. I don't have the words to respond to her, and I'm not sure if she actually wants me to. The divide between us has grown so large that I stopped imagining a world where I would ever get my friend back. I've been expecting this for a month or two; Mina's been distant and there were rumblings she might switch teams to climb the ranks in the Silver City Sickos.

Turning on my heel, I open my locker and dump my things into the duffle silently. Skates, socks, pants, shirts… I shove it all in and grab my leather jacket. I can feel her eyes on me as I sling it over my shoulder and head for the door. She probably expects me to fight her or have some sort of emotional breakdown, but after the things Mina has done lately, I refuse to give her the satisfaction.

You did your best, Rogue. You accepted every cut, scrape, and bruise with quiet grace.

"No outburst? I'm surprised, R. I thought you'd at least try to get me to keep propping you up."

My eyes narrow and I count to ten in my head, letting out a deep breath. I avoided letting this festering wound affect the team for so long, and now it's all going to come out. The shame of what I allowed to happen when others couldn't see floods me and I have to dig my nails into my palms to keep from screaming. Mina wants to taste my pain, and if I give it to her, I can't ever get it back.

Only losers let their enemies see the damage they've done.

If only I could turn back the clock and figure out what started this mess, I'd change it and Mina would laugh with me as we head out for a drink after the match. But that's not possible and there's far too much blood in the water to go back, especially if she's defecting to the Sickos. Those bitches are the nastiest, pettiest team in the league, and they're known for playing dirty to win.

When we first joined the Babe City Bombers, we swore we'd never turn into those psychos, but here we are. It's amazing what some press coverage and a viral video of her doing a twirl will do to someone. Mina has bought into her fifteen minutes and she's been slowly turning into a person I don't know. Out of two practices and one match a week, it's amazing if I don't go home to cry myself to sleep at least once.

Just take your stuff and go outside. Rebel will wait for you.

My stepbrother is the closest person to me in the Universe and if I go out there crying, he might just disarticulate Mina piece by piece in the parking lot. The amount of rage he has for how she's made me feel over the past few months has grown to a level that scares me a little. Only fear of violating our oaths as Guardians has kept him from serving up much deserved revenge on her.

*Of course, her magic is **much** weaker than ours, and the High Council would take that into account.*

Our adoptive parents aren't perfect, but they'd lose the plot if we got exiled, so turn the other cheek it is.

I ignore the continued prodding from behind me as I walk over to the back door of the rink and head outside. As predicted, Rebel is waiting for me, his ass propped against the hood of his black Shelby GT500. His brow creases as he takes me in, and before I can open my mouth, he's stalking to the door with murder in his eyes.

"Reb, stop! It won't solve anything!" I call, running my hand over my face.

He wheels around, the iridescent flecks in his eyes giving away the Fae in him. "I'm tired of watching you suffer because your ex-friend decided she's an influencer. She's a one hit wonder with her head shoved up her ass so far she's kissing it. What she needs is a fucking reality check, Skates."

I pinch the bridge of my nose. He's not wrong, and that makes it hard to hold him back. I can't say I'd hate seeing him bring her to knees and if anyone could do it, Reb's best suited to do so. There's absolutely nothing Mina can say that would bother him—her powers are useless against his. No coercion or manipulation she could conjure would even touch him.

I've been avoiding taking care of it myself because of the impact it would have on the team, but now that's she's fucking off...

Reb smirks as he tiles his head. "Are you finally considering telling her to get fucked, little sis?"

"Do not call me that. I'm not little, nor am I your sister. Reck was my brother and since they sent him away, I'm stuck with you," I grouse as I kick rocks across the pavement.

He laughs, winking at me as he walks back to the sweet ass vehicle he plans to race tonight. "If you stop being such a pain in the ass, I *might* let you drive tonight. Think you can handle that?"

Uh, yes, please, asshole.

The stink of this evening is wearing off as I speed around the curves of the winding hills. Tonight's race is a longer one, but I don't mind because when I stepped out into the crowd wearing Rebel's cheeky grin, a roar of excitement filled the air. We'd both be in the fucking thick of it if the jug-eared bitch whose family runs the club knew it was me behind the wheel, but since she rarely descends from her throne, it's unlikely she'll ever catch the scent.

Roadrunner Racing is a front for laundering cash for the Stuhll Mob, and they're known for being vicious thieves and thugs. The matron of the family is the second wife of the dumbest rhino shifter I've ever met, but she more than makes up for his lack of brains with her sociopathic whims. Merra is a tiny fennec Fox shifter, but her thirst for money and power is unrivaled. Rumor has it she swindled her family into the poorhouse before she fell in with Thad, but since no one can actually *locate* any of them, it stays a whispered threat.

Together, they own half the slums in the city, and the club is just another way for them to clean their extorted protection money. Crossing them isn't the brightest plan Reb and I have ever come up with, but it may be one of the most dangerous.

Gotta get your kicks somehow, though, right?

Scenery flies by as I shift around the curvy roads, occasionally checking to see if any of the losers have gotten any closer. All I see is an empty road, so I press the button on the dash that connects me to Reb's open line. He's staying concealed in the pit area, but when I get closer to the finish, I'll want to know what the crowd looks like. The last thing I need is some asshole with powers that will automatically see through the Fae glamor if I get out of the car for the peacocking.

"How's it looking? Any worries?"

A snort echoes in the car as my stepbrother comes online. "No snitches at the moment. I'm eyeing the gates."

We're talking in our own code—it's not like we're on an encrypted line. Gamblers are a tricky breed no matter what species they are; techno-warlocks have blended science and magic to influence everything from supe races to human sporting events, so caution is prudent. Even if we didn't get dimed out to the Queen Bitch, neither of us wants to end up being blackmailed. Guardians are only beholden to the Society, and if we get compromised in our private lives, it could spill into our professional pursuits.

That's the shit that starts wars, and I'd prefer not to go down in history as some fucked up Helen of Troy.

"Good. I'm almost there. Have the champers ready because we're gonna party tonight."

His laugh is dark and I can picture him pushing his green hair out of his eyes as he replies. "I'm not pulling a bunch of revved up asswads off your tipsy ass again. You suck at controlling the pheromones when you drink."

I roll my eyes briefly, trying not to snark back at him. Reb is a full-blooded Unseelie and I'm a half-breed; the other half of my unknown bio parents was a succubus and I have zero frame of reference for learning to control my powers now that I'm an adult. If my actual brother Reck was around, I'd at least have someone to commiserate with, but since the only one around when I emerged was Reb, I'm stuck with his snark.

Being discarded orphans blows goat shifters and no one will ever convince me of anything different.

"You're being morose again, Rogue. My parents ditched me, too, because they were afraid I'd come out a hybrid. You don't have a copyright on being left behind," he grumbles.

I guess that's true, but his full blood status sure makes our adoptive 'family' favor him.

"Reb, until they trade your twin as currency because he's not worth the effort to feed and clothe, you don't get to play the 'poor me' game with me. Back off."

There's a lengthy pause before he answers and when he does, his voice is full of bitterness. "We've said too much on an open line. I'll see you at the checkers."

Great. I didn't mean to piss off my only ally. He'll get plastered at the after party and despite his grand pronouncements, it will be me prying hungry bitches off him before he becomes a baby daddy at 21.

Just fucking fabulous.

Throwing the Shelby into a higher gear, I put the pedal to the floor and fly down the back half of the track. My night is now a thousand times more stressful, and I wanted to lose myself in the heat of the engine to forget my earlier spat with my ex-best friend. I swear to hell, men are the biggest babies on the planet.

My mood continues to darken as I crest the last hill, thoughts of murder and mayhem fogging my brain. By the time I'm cruising down the strip, I've worked myself into a lather that can only be contained by copious amounts of alcohol and sex. It's not the healthiest coping mechanism mentally, sure, but half of my power stems from sexual energy, so I don't examine it too closely.

Never dwell on shit you can't control, Rogue.

Reck used to tell me that before they sent him away, and he was always right. Unfortunately, I didn't listen then, and it's highly doubtful I will now.

I foresee a bar fight in my future and I can't say I'm not looking forward to it.

After all, it's not against the rules to play dirty there.

Get it now!

ABOUT CASSANDRA FEATHERSTONE

Cassandra Featherstone has channeled her lifelong passion for writing into a flourishing career, a journey that started when she first grasped a pencil as a gifted child with ADHD.

Her debut novel, born during the solitude of COVID lockdown in March 2020, draws on a tapestry of personal encounters and insights that resonate deeply with her readers.

An international bestseller, Cassandra has topped Amazon charts in categories such as LGBT Anthologies, LGBTQ+ Mystery, and Bisexual Romance, among others. Her works navigate the complexities of bullying, PTSD, body dysmorphia, mental health struggles, personal reinvention, and the empowerment of claiming one's own space. Importantly, Cassandra offers a thoughtful and respectful portrayal of LGBTQIA+ relationships, subtly reflecting her own connection with the community through her narratives.

Her literary repertoire spans sci-fi fantasy, urban fantasy, paranormal, and comedic genres in academy whychoose settings, with a strong commitment to portraying consensual, safe, and accurately depicted BDSM and kink lifestyles. Her books are an invitation to explore transformative stories that are both inclusive and engaging.

Often affectionately called 'The Muppet' for her wacky theater kid personality, she resides in the Midwest with her tech-savvy husband, their creatively inclined college student, a literary-minded dog, and four scheming cats.

READ MORE AT CASSANDRA'S WEBSITE OR HER FACEBOOK PAGE. SIGN UP FOR EXCLUSIVE CONTENT AND UPDATES HERE.

FIND HER ON ANY OF THE SOCIAL MEDIA BELOW AS SHE *LOVES* TO CHAT AND *NEVER* SLEEPS!

ALSO BY CASSANDRA FEATHERSTONE

THE MISFIT PROTECTION PROGRAM SERIES

Road to the Hollow

Return to the Hollow

Home to the Hollow

Rejected in the Hollow

Revealed in the Hollow

Healing in the Hollow

Revenge in the Hollow

AUDIO OF THE MISFIT PROTECTION PROGRAM SERIES

Road to the Hollow

APEX ACADEMY CAPERS

Come Out and Prey

Let Us Prey

In Prey We Trust

Oh Holy Spite (3.5 novella)

Eat. Prey. Love.

Prey It Ain't So (4.5 novel)

Prey It By Ear

AUDIO OF THE APEX ACADEMY CAPERS SERIES

Come Out & Prey

Let Us Prey

In Prey We Trust

TRANSLATIONS OF THE APEX ACADEMY CAPERS SERIES

Come Out & Prey (German)

Let Us Prey (German)

In Prey Trust (German)

DISCORDIA UNIVERSITY

Veiled Flame (Book One)

Quiet Burn (Book Two)

Zero Spark (Book Three)

AUDIO OF THE DISCORDIA UNIVERSITY SERIES

Veiled Flame (Book One)

Quiet Burn (Book Two)

SECRETS OF STATE U

Blood on the Ice (Book One)

Suspicions on the Stage (Book Two)

TBA TITLE (BOOK THREE)

FAETAL ATTRACTION

Hell on Wheels (Book One)

Jammer in the Box (Book Two)

F.E.A.R. ACADEMY

Failed State (Book One)

Trigger Protocol (Book Two)

VILLAINS & VIXENS

Bloodthirsty (Book One)

Ruthless (Book Two)

Wicked (Book Three)

AUDIO OF THE VILLAINS & VIXENS SERIES

Bloodthirsty

Ruthless

TRIANGLES & TRIBULATIONS

Hoist the Flag (PQ)

Yo-Ho Holes (Book One)

**CHILDREN OF THE MOON-
WITH SERENITY RAYNE**

New Moon Rising (Book One)

Waxing Crescent (Book Two)

Waxing Gibbous (Book Three)

Samhain Secrets (Novella 3.5)

Full Moon (Book Four)

Waning Gibbous (Book Five)

Waning Crescent (Book Six)

RISE OF THE RESISTANCE

Ream Exclusive Prequels

Hooked on a Feline (Book One)

Peacock Me Like A Hurricane

Love The Way You Lion (Book Three)

TBA Title (Book Four)

REAM SERIALS

Secrets of State U

Discordia University

Denizens of the Dark

Faetal Attraction

Agents of the Ouroboros

Rise of the Resistance

F.E.A.R. Academy

ANTHOLOGIES

Unwritten

Shifters Unleashed

Jingle My Balls

Love is in the Air

Silent Night

Snowed In

All Hallows Eve